THE PENDRAGON PROTOCOL

PHILIP PURSER-HALLARD

Proudly Published by Snowbooks in 2014

Snowbooks Ltd.
email: info@snowbooks.com
www.snowbooks.com

British Library Cataloguing in Publication Data
A catalogue record for this book is available from the
British Library.

ISBN 9781909679177

THE PENDRAGON PROTOCOL

BOOK ONE OF THE DEVICES TRILOGY

To my son [SPOILER], whose name started the whole thing off.

'What haunting?' asked Camilla.

'How something we may call Britain is always haunted by something we may call Logres. Haven't you noticed that we are two countries? After every Arthur, a Mordred; behind every Milton, a Cromwell: a nation of poets, a nation of shopkeepers; the home of Sidney – and of Cecil Rhodes. Is it any wonder they call us hypocrites? But what they mistake for hypocrisy is really the struggle between Logres and Britain.'

CS Lewis, *That Hideous Strength*

I
THE FASTNESS

1. THE CLOAK

Jory stands on the tarmac pavement between two ranks of privet-hedged, pebble-dashed houses, wearing the armour of a Knight of the Circle. Ahead of him along the road, one of these innocuous suburban semis is harbouring a monster.

Jory's sword and helm are urban grey like his armour – as inconspicuous against the road and pavement as one might reasonably expect, which isn't very. His shield's a vibrant red with tracery of gold.

The house is double-glazed, three bedrooms, probably ideal for a small family or a young professional couple. Instead it's being used as an ogre's lair, which is why Jory is here.

...*No*, the Knight reflects, distractedly drumming his fingers on his sword-hilt, *not an ogre*. Not just that, anyway. It would be easy to dismiss James Ribbens as a brutish, savage monster, lost to humanity – it's certainly what Ribbens himself wants to be – but ultimately he's as human as Jory himself.

'So, is he in there?' he asks his squire, keeping his eyes on Ribbens' stronghold for the moment.

'We can't be totally sure, actually,' Paul Parsons admits. He's been conferring with a laptop-tapping man-at-arms while Jory makes his informal survey of the target. He nods at a blue Volvo in Ribbens' driveway. 'The car's still there. But you know, he could have nipped out through a neighbour's garden at the back.'

The street is drenched with early-morning sunlight. All along the road, birds are singing in the trees, staking out their territory with fortunately untranslatable invective. A baking-bread smell drifts from the row of shops around the corner from the surveillance van's parking-space. The van's the same unobtrusive grey as Jory's and Paul's armour, marked with a nondescript logo commissioned, from the least adventurous design agency the Circle could find, specifically for its undercover work.

Jory asks, 'Any clue how he's armed?'

'No record of a firearm certificate, sir,' the man-at-arms replies. Jory's been too distracted to learn his name, but to save us all from tedious awkwardness, I'll tell you now that it's Bob Thackett. The man-at-arms in the front of the van is Johnny Clark.

'Doesn't mean he hasn't got a gun,' says Paul, once again pointing out the obvious in case it's escaped everybody else here.

Jory pauses to take stock. As I've said, he and Paul are armed with swords: high-carbon steel blades, polymer-coated, made at a Sheffield steelworks which the Circle's custom keeps in business. Their armour's custom-made in Birmingham, from boron-carbide ceramic and an obscure counterpart of Kevlar. Paul's is the off-the-peg model, but Jory's is tailored to his measurements and movements, and its familiar pressure on his limbs and torso is the nearest he comes these days to an intimate relationship. Their shields are curves of polyester film, tough enough to withstand the blast of a nearby nailbomb, or to deflect the bullets from the gun that Ribbens may or may not have once they get in there to arrest him.

Paul's shield, like those of all the Circle's squires, is grey, its top third sensibly transparent for vision purposes. Jory's serves a ceremonial function as well as a tactical one, hence its emblazoning. The lower two-thirds of his are painted in a bright heraldic scarlet, against which gold lines trace a five-pointed star. (No, not a circle.)

They'd be much better off packing guns of their own, of course – semi-automatic weapons, like the ones the men-at-arms have in holsters under their flak-jackets. (Those are SIG P226 pistols, if you're a fan of meaningless chains of alphanumerics.) But that would be a breach of the Circle's code of honour, which is strict not only about rules of engagement, but also about its employees' social status. A Knight or squire does not wield a projectile weapon, or at least not without risking shame, disgrace and ignominy.

Bob Thackett agrees placidly with Paul. 'No, sir. But from what you hear his lot ain't much for guns. They like their knives more.' A glib judgement it may be, but it's true enough that so far, and despite the diversity of his methods, none of Ribbens' victims has been shot.

It's a worry, nonetheless. The Circle's defensive kit may be state-of-the-art, but nothing's invulnerable. If Ribbens is toting a gun when Jory and Paul go in there, a lucky shot could easily incapacitate one of them. If they're really unlucky he might get them both, and then they'll end up dead.

Jory knows he's doing God's work, but in his years with the Circle he's learned the devil's in the detail.

At six in the morning Snowdon Street is quiet, but not deserted. The houses' occupants are stirring: a couple of cars have left already for sadistically early shiftwork. The corner shop's taking in a newspaper delivery, while up on a trailer crane a boiler-suited council worker's changing a streetlamp bulb.

Jory peers up at the sky. He'd prefer to be doing this at solar noon, but that's not his decision. Even so, he has a duty of care to Paul. He'd best go in alone.

'You've gone through the briefing, presumably?' he asks. The notes Malory gave them include police and newspaper reports, a sheaf of crime-scene photos, Ribbens' full employment record, a three-page psych profile built from stacks of nested bullet points, and a paragraph of twelfth-century Latin pseudohistory.

Paul nods. 'Retho of Arvaius, yeah?' he says. 'It's a new one on me.'

'You should read more,' Jory tells him absently.

In the long view, he knows, history is circular – British history particularly. This, at least, is what the Circle teaches its agents, and given the length of time the organisation's survived, they if anyone ought to know.

A distant siren joins in the birdsong, followed by another. The men-at-arms are authorised to deal with the police, but it's better avoided if possible.

'No sense in waiting,' Jory says, and they bow their heads in prayer.

* * *

You'll have gathered we're doing this in modern English, without the pritheeing and forsoothage. We're also in the prose rather than the poetry section at the library, which is the other big choice you make when telling this kind of story.

Not that I can't manage a certain something when it comes to archaisms and rhyme-schemes. But this story's different. It's the world we live in, and the way it works, and it doesn't get more prosaic than that.

Of course, the fact that it's about twenty-first-century Britain means it's a story about history too, and the way the past can wield the present as a weapon. That's why I'm using the present tense, in fact – the story's all about immediate impressions, the balancing-point between cause and effect. I'm not some celestial eye-witness hovering above it all – like Ribbens, I'm just a bloke, though thankfully with more wholesome hobbies. I know this stuff because I know Jory and the others. I've talked to him, and I've talked to Bob Thackett, and to Malory, and Kinsey and Cantrell and the rest of them. I talk to everyone.

That's what I do: I go to places, I talk to people, I splice their separate threads of narrative into one big rope of story. I don't have a story of my own, and even if I did, this wouldn't be it. (Well, all right, I may turn up a couple of times. What can I say? I was there.)

There's no big mystery about me: my name's Dale. Dale the Tale, if you want to get all bardic about it. But honestly, I'd rather you just pretended I wasn't here. Never mind my voice, my accent, my mannerisms. Watch the trick, not the magician.

The past… well, like they say, the past is another country, and that means we're all immigrants. The past and future are the superpowers; the present, our tiny island nation, is forever caught between the majestic authority of the one and the seductive propaganda of the other.

…OK, perhaps that last bit is a touch poetic. I can't guarantee that won't happen sometimes.

Again, it's what I do.

* * *

As Paul and Jory jog down Snowdon Street, Jory feels the early-morning sunshine seeping through his armour. The day will be scorching later, but as yet it's providing little warmth. The cold doesn't bother Jory overmuch, but it could affect his performance. It's lucky, really, that he has his strength, training, skill, armour and weaponry to fall back on.

Jory's fought the bad guys often enough now that qualms about his own safety have all but deserted him. Even his surprise that he can do this sort of thing without them has nearly vanished. He's calm and brisk as he details Paul to stand guard on the trim front lawn and watch the exits from the property while Jory goes in alone.

His shield-charge makes short work of the front door. It buckles and splinters, finally splitting to send frosted-glass shards spattering across the tiled floor of the hallway, as Jory clatters in on metalled boots. He glances round, taking in magnolia banisters, a full-length mirror, coathooks. He quickly checks the inner doors, discovering a gleaming kitchen-diner, a living-room arranged around a giant wall-mounted TV, a cupboardful of plastic storage boxes.

He moves quickly through the downstairs, confirming that it's empty. More than that, it feels meaningless, lacking the overlaid significance that is the sure sign that a person treats it as a home. Ribbens hasn't been living here long, but it should have been long enough. Instead this is a well-fitted show home, a film-set, a simulacrum. Jory knows the effect – he's felt it in some of the other residences he's visited on Circle business. He sometimes wonders whether his Knightsbridge flat feels this way to Malory.

He mounts the stairs fast, throwing open the first door he reaches. Duck-egg blue walls, polished chrome and porcelain, a smell of cleaning-products… perhaps a whiff of something more. The bathroom's as physically empty as the rooms downstairs, but in that other sense, perhaps not quite so vacant. The first bedroom is both: bed bare, empty wardrobe, a landscape photo on the wall so generic that even Jory's well-honed skills of observation tell him nothing about it. Second bedroom likewise, though that one hasn't even got a bed.

The master bedroom, though… that's like a transplant from a different house. Cluttered and chaotic, strewn with mugs and plates, clothes and bedclothes hunched in Himalayan piles around a bed which (judging by look and smell) hasn't been changed in months. Pages of handwriting snowdrift the room, along with dismembered printed books. Jory recognises the torn cover of one Penguin Classic, and any residual doubt he had about Ribbens evaporates.

What's missing is the master bedroom's master. Cursing, Jory descends the stairs at a run. An instant's glance through the front door-frame yields an afterimage of Paul watching guardedly, Clark and Thacker remonstrating, a posse of angry police. Jory casts around for potential hiding places.

The walk-in larder has no hidden depths. It's unlikely that Ribbens has excavated a concealed cellar under the stairs. That only leaves the back garden.

Jory leaves marks in the kitchen-diner's wood laminate which will never polish out as he stomps across to stare through patio doors at the house's rear garden. A prow of wooden decking overlooks a grassy harbour where rosebushes float like buoys. Either Ribbens, a junior manager with an unsuccessful firm of pet food suppliers, has plenty of time on his hands and no imagination, or he gets a jobbing gardener in.

Either way, there's a toolshed.

It's in the far corner of the lawn, a ramshackle shipwreck creosoted greyish-black. The door's fitted with a sturdy mortise lock. The dawn sunlight climbing the adjacent houses has only reached the furthest corner of the garden, but there are withered rosebushes in its permanent shade.

Jory doesn't let the glass doors impede him. Another shield-charge bursts them into fragments, skittering across the decking, showering the lawn, crunching beneath his boots as he approaches the shed at a run. He slides his sword smoothly from its scabbard and shouts:

'James Ribbens! I'm a Knight of the Circle. I'm here to take you into custody, in the name of the Circle and its Head. Open the door!'

A leftover corner of glass drops and shatters, as if his yell's dislodged it.

On the sunward side of the shed, there's a window, plastered on the inside with newspaper. This one's clear plastic rather than glass, and Jory bashes it in easily with his sword-hilt.

This is where the question of Ribbens' gun ownership could become lethally relevant. Jory's been shot before and knows what to expect, but that doesn't mean he welcomes the prospect. As it turns out, though, there's no sudden violent shove, no dull ringing noise portending temporary deafness, no all-encompassing urge to faint. Instead he pulls the hanging newspaper away with his left gauntlet, then flinches as a face appears in the gap, inches from his own. He recognises it immediately.

It isn't Ribbens. Rather unexpectedly, it's the Bishop of Winchester.

The bishop's eyes are wide with terror, his mouth sealed shut with duct tape. Someone else's hands hold his full, grey beard away from his neck and a kitchen-knife to his exposed throat.

Ribbens' face, grimy and also bearded, bobs into view behind the cleric, grimacing humourlessly.

'Back off, eh?' Ribbens hisses. 'Back right off back up to the house, Knight, right now, eh? Unless you want a faceful of His Grace's throat-blood.'

Technically the bishop's only a Right Reverend, but Jory isn't going to quibble.

* * *

What does it feel like to be James Ribbens, do you imagine? To have lost yourself so completely that all thoughts of respect for human life or compassion for human suffering mean nothing to you, compared with the need to crush and bleed the life out of a person, then carve them up to make yourself a memento?

You might think it feels like power, like freedom, like victory over the petty limitations of humanity's nature. If so, I'm afraid you're a fucking psychopath.

(Excuse my French. Had to be said.)

What it feels like is despair. The despair of knowing yourself helpless, pathetic, cringing, battered down; degraded beyond contempt, your own and others'. Feeling yourself used, manipulated, a tool for a dirty job that's never washed afterwards, and certainly won't be kept when the job's over, because what would be the point? The crushing grip of anciency upon your soul, twisting you this way and that like a knife in an animal gut. The terrifying incomprehension of these motives, savage and alien, which have somehow become your own. The horror, and the night-sweats, and the sickening gut-terror which has you rushing from a meeting to puke your innards up in the disabled loo.

The pleasure's there, of course: the contentment of the tool which does its master's bidding well, the satisfaction of being useful, needed even. But the joy, the exultation, the savage jubilation of the kill – all those belong to someone else entirely.

And underneath it all, the everlasting, never-fading wish that somehow circumstances had been different, that something, anything whatsoever had happened to get in the way, so that you never even saw that bloody book.

...I'm only speculating, you understand. Extrapolating, I might say on my worse days. James Ribbens is one of the ones I won't get the chance to speak to.

* * *

'Mr Ribbens,' Jory says, thrusting his sword into the ground and raising his hands. 'You should think carefully before doing anything sudden. You're in enough trouble as it is.'

The bishop whimpers into his gag. His name is Leonard Crown and Jory knows him vaguely. He's one of the senior clergy who act as unofficial chaplains to the

Circle, taking the Knights' confessions and presiding at the occasional communion. For Ribbens to choose him as a victim – or, as he's now become, a hostage – could be a huge coincidence, but it's more likely that it shows a degree of mythopolitical awareness that's worrying in a murderer.

Ribbens silences his captive with a vicious beard-tug. 'I said get back!' he repeats.

Jory shrugs, lowers the hands. 'I'm afraid not,' he says. He needs to play this carefully and for time, but that's no excuse for being dishonest. 'Either you'll try to escape, which won't be easy dragging a hostage and will probably end up with the police having to shoot you, or you'll kill the bishop and I'll have no reason to hold back. Neither of those is an outcome I'd be happy with, frankly. Would you?'

Ribbens swears loudly. He drags the bishop back into the shed's gloom, and Jory hears some frantic agitated muttering. Crown is gagged, so unless there's anyone else in there, Ribbens would appear to be having an argument with himself.

Jory knows better, of course. Quietly he retrieves his sword and sheathes it, taking a swift glance around the garden. Beyond it, a cat on a windowsill is watching him with interest; the birds are still throwing their vocal weight about; a neighbour is chattering excitedly into his mobile phone. The creeping sunlight's reached the shed roof now.

If Clark and Thacker keep the police busy for a few more minutes, and he can keep Ribbens talking for that long, then – assuming the killer can't talk and slaughter clerics at the same time – Jory can still pull this off without a hitch.

'Who are you talking to in there, Ribbens?' Jory demands. 'What stories is he telling you?'

The muttering stops. A moment later, both men's faces reappear. The bishop is still gagged. His eyes are closed, whether in prayer or a faint; Ribbens' are, if anything, wilder than before. 'What the hell does that mean, eh?' he snaps, his voice a good half-octave higher.

'Does this really feel like your choice, Ribbens?' Jory asks. 'Do you want this to be the story of your life? Did you really want to be a serial killer when you grew up?'

'*Serial* killer?' Ribbens sounds genuinely indignant.

'You've murdered at least eight men and collected trophies from their bodies,' Jory points out reasonably. Bishop Len whimpers.

'Oh, so I'm mad now, am I, Knight?' Ribbens grunts. 'Eh? You're standing there in your armour with your big sword like it's the Dark Ages and telling me *I'm* mad?'

It's not a bad point, by any means. Technically that is what Jory's saying, or part of it at least: he knows Ribbens' affliction is rather more than merely psychiatric. 'For some of us it's still the Dark Ages,' he suggests, aware still of the encroaching sunlight.

* * *

Last year, a man named Roger King, a middle manager with an unsuccessful chain of pet food suppliers, failed to come home from the pub one Friday evening. King was a dangerous bruiser, a rugby prop forward with a reputation as a workplace bully, so even after his disappearance was reported the police took the view that he could probably take care of himself.

Their working theory, such as it was, was that King had left his wife for another woman and neglected to mention the fact to anybody, notably Mrs King. Some cursory inquiries at his workplace revealed that he'd been sleeping with one of his junior colleagues: she hadn't seen him since that Friday either, but the police theorised that a man with one mistress could well have kept a stable of them. It took the discovery of King's body on a piece of urban wasteland to convince them that they'd be better advised to investigate further.

King had been buried in an unused, overgrown strip of land between a builders' merchants and a railway line. He was naked, and his beard – a curly, spadelike affair which had been quite a liability on the rugby field – had been crudely hacked off, leaving only straggly stubble behind.

The police interviewed his colleagues again, with a lot more rigour this time, but their only real conclusion was that none of them had liked him very much. Even the woman he'd been having the affair with had lost interest by then.

It was a young uniformed constable with ambitions of detectivehood who first annoyed his superiors by making connections. Noel Law, a retired headteacher, had been found a few weeks after King's disappearance, bludgeoned to death at his home. He'd always been eccentric, and since retirement he'd been cultivating a long white beard in the style of an Old Testament patriarch (or 'Gandalf', as the local children had it). Like King's, it had been crudely pruned post mortem.

PC Barry Jenkins kept his suspicions private until his search of the national police database turned up three more recent deaths: Eli Gold, an orthodox Jewish town councillor; Raj Singh, a bank manager and observant Sikh, and Jonathan Masters, an elderly magistrate and cricketing enthusiast with a WG Grace fetish. The deaths themselves had nothing in common – a beating, a strangulation, a stabbing – and the bodies had been found in locations ranging from a dark alley to a lake. Nonetheless, all three men had had their beards raggedly removed.

These murders had been local tragedies in their various towns and cities, but had been given little nationwide publicity. Law seemed to be the victim of a failed robbery, while Gold, Singh and Masters had backgrounds allowing for a range of political, financial and racial motives. The sole common factor would only have presented itself to somebody who, like PC Jenkins, was actively looking for it.

Since the connection was made, though, murder with beard theft has become a hot topic across the tabloid press and in the more prurient corners of the internet. The wilder speculations have included voodoo-style cults and organised crime syndicates, but the most popular explanation is the obvious and – and it happens – correct one: a serial killer, immediately and unimaginatively dubbed the Beard Collector. Enterprising members of the public have helpfully identified other possible victims from across the British Isles, and as far afield as Tel Aviv and Philadelphia.

The Circle's made its own connections. Malory Wendiman in particular noted almost at once that not only were all the victims men with experience of authority, but that they all had names implying high status: King, Gold, Law, Raj, Masters. (Crown is another, of course.) Malory has tentatively singled out three more cases across the UK, including a Glasgow police inspector whose parents burdened him with the name Stuart Prince.

Roger King remains the first victim, though. And the number of people who'd have seen him as an authority figure is distinctly limited.

Cross-referencing between police records and various sources of civic data, Malory has pinpointed the origin and vector of the devicial outbreak: a library copy of Geoffrey of Monmouth's *Historia Regum Britanniae*, translated by Lewis Thorpe, published by Penguin and browsed at random – then borrowed and perused with growing interest – by James Ribbens during a wet lunch-hour spent seething about his obnoxious boss getting it on with one of their younger, prettier colleagues.

The book was never returned. From what Jory saw just now in the bedroom, they'll have to add vandalising library property to the charge-sheet.

* * *

From inside Ribbens' house, Jory hears voices raised in anger: Paul's, Bob Thackett's, a woman's. The police must have gained access to the building.

'At least mine *have* beards,' Ribbens says abruptly. 'My *men*. The kings I conquer. Where's yours then, Knight, eh? Someone taken it already?' He starts to laugh. 'Is your boss as well-groomed as you? A shaven Head, is he?'

The laughter's becoming shriller. Time's running short.

'Never mind my boss,' Jory says. 'What about yours? Not Roger King – the one you replaced him with. Why did you decide you fancied killing other powerful men and stealing their beards? How does a man come up with an idea like that? Not on his own I'll bet.'

Ribbens is still laughing.

'It was Retho, wasn't it?' Jory suggests, and the laughter cuts off like a clown under the guillotine.

'What do you know about Retho?' Ribbens asks – his voice now sombre, even reverent.

'The giant Retho,' Jory says. 'An ogre who lived on Mount Arvaius.' He imagines Ribbens buying this house, drawn like a homing pigeon to this street, any street anywhere with this name. 'It's an old name for Mount Snowdon.'

He goes on. 'Retho owned a fur coat, made from all the beards of the kings he'd slain. It's an old Welsh story – originally Retho was Rhudda Gawr, the Red Giant. In later versions he becomes King Rience of North Wales. The myth evolves, but the central device is always the same.'

For all Jory's seen of Ribbens – his face and hands, through the narrow shed window – the Beard Collector could be naked in there. He's certain, though, that he can name one item the murderer's wearing.

'A cloak of beards,' he says. 'Retho killed many kings, and with every regicide he added a new beard to his cloak. He needed King Arthur's beard to complete the set, but Arthur was the High King of all Britain. Retho wanted to humiliate him, or perhaps he was more afraid of him than the others. So he pretended mercy. He sent a message ordering Arthur to pluck out his own beard, and send it to Retho. Arthur refused, of course, and challenged the giant to single combat.'

Ribbens is silent, gazing enthralled at Jory, like a small child hearing all this for the first time. The bishop hangs limply in his arms.

The sound of a commotion comes from the house, and Jory glances back to see four uniformed police officers burst through the ruined patio doors like Keystone Kops. Behind them comes Thacker, followed a moment later by Paul.

Further along the terrace, the sun finally breasts the rooftops, and Jory sees the angular shadow of his helm falling onto the shed in front of him. He straightens slightly as the morning rays infuse him with their warmth.

'Arthur called him the strongest foe he'd ever faced,' he says.

He steps forward, watching his shadow grow across the darkened wood. 'Still, he killed him. King Arthur slew the giant Retho. He took his beard *and* his cloak.'

With arms whose strength waxes with the rising sun, he reaches out and pulls off the side of the shed.

2. THE HEAD

Young Jimmy Ribbens may never have meant to become a notorious mass-murderer, but just ten years ago a life of dressing in armour and fighting monsters with a great big sword would have been Jordan Taylor's most deeply cherished fantasy. On the whole, of course, seventeen-year-old Jory would have preferred to be rescuing a beautiful maiden in distress rather than a beardy cleric, but the general principle would still have been important to him.

Jory was a child shaped by stories – his relentless appetite for reading them matched only by a strenuous urge to act them out. Unlike most book-obsessed children, who content themselves with a wistful yearning to take part in the stories they read, Jory spent much of his time out in the countryside near his parents' estate, running, climbing, swimming and building with a succession of loyal, but basically interchangeable, bosom friends. Ghost stories, fairy stories, sea stories; stories about cowboys and soldiers and detectives; stories of witchcraft and spycraft and spacecraft: he read, loved and recreated them all. Most of his adult personality was formed during this early course of reading and muscular re-enactment.

When I say 'his parent's estate', you shouldn't misunderstand me. In the Circle's terms Jory qualifies as nobility, but they don't measure social class the way you or I might. His mum and dad lived in a two-up-two-down terraced redbrick on a housing estate, on the outskirts of an undistinguished southern English town. There was nothing grotty about it, no inner-city squalor, but it wasn't exactly landscaped lakes with gazebos and pergolas.

This is important, because in all respects other than his actual background the teenage Jory was a scion of the British establishment. A scholarship to a fee-paying school of the kind we Brits perversely call 'public' had seen to that, and the three years he spent at one of the country's top universities (studying literature, of course) would seal the deal.

As I've suggested, young Jory was catholic in his reading-matter, and university would ensure he continued that way. Still, despite his acquaintance with literary heroes from Frodo Baggins to Biggles, James Bond to Bertie Wooster, since he was very young one story had obsessed him above all others. That was, of course, the story of King Arthur and the Knights of the Round Table, which he read first in a Ladybird Book and later in retellings by Susan Cooper, Rosemary Sutcliff, TH White and Mark Twain – even in Thomas Malory's *Morte D'Arthur*, where he first came encountered King Rience and his cloak of beards.

Not to put too fine a point on it, the teenage Jory modelled himself on those knights. His courage, especially on behalf of others, was exemplary, his sense of virtue archaic and honourable, his relations with girls… unusual. Even his Christianity came not from his parents, who were disinterestedly agnostic, but from his overenthusiastic immersion in the myth of the Holy Grail.

He was a strong student, and many universities would have been delighted to take him. When he learned, though, that one particular collegiate university boasted a Tournament Society, his choice of higher education establishment became pretty much inevitable.

***

Right now, a grown-up Jory whose sword and armour gleam, admittedly rather dully, in the sunlight, is confronting an enemy of the Round Table. He's thrown aside the wooden wall of Ribbens' garden shed as if it was a polystyrene packing sheet.

Ribbens blinks in the sudden inrush of daylight, his episcopal hostage dangling from the crook of his arm. Behind him in the shed, Jory can see a grim collection of objects – knives, lengths of wire and piping, a rounders bat with ugly stains, a pair of shears – hanging from racks where garden implements should rightly hang. A sewing machine sits demurely in a corner, like a maiden aunt at a biker rally.

Ribbens' cloak is more of a waistcoat, really – plain white cotton cut into a simple pattern. The tricky part must have been sewing on the beards.

In that later version of the legend, the one Malory Wendiman's namesake wrote about in *Morte D'Arthur*, Arthur's beard was meant to be the twelfth and last in Rience's cloak. Ribbens' scrappy patchwork covers his shoulders, but hardly reaches the small of his back. Evidently the facial hair of ancient kings was longer and more lush than modern bank managers'.

Still, the Beard Collector's a connoisseur – a completist, even. These sad stitched clumps of hair are all colours and textures: black, brown, blond, ginger, grey, white; straight, straggly, curly.

Ignoring the shouts from the newly-arrived police contingent, Jory reaches forward and plucks the kitchen-knife from Ribbens' hand. The maniac roars in anger and starts throttling the bishop, so Jory punches him hard. His head crashes into the shed's far wall, splintering the wood. Both bodies slump, dazed, to the floor.

Jory picks up the recumbent cleric, rips the gag from his mouth and checks his breathing before handing him to Thackett. Meanwhile, Paul hauls Ribbens upright and starts to handcuff him.

The police, it seems, have other ideas. Two of the constables, a black man and a white woman, take Ribbens' arms firmly and march him away from Paul. Jory shakes his head slightly as his squire glances questioningly at him. He turns to confront the inspector.

'Inspector Jade Kinsey,' she says, taking the initiative. 'What the fucking hell are you doing here? We get a tip-off that this James Ribbens is the Beard Collector, and when we arrive we find the Circle's taken over the whole operation. We've been after this bloke for bloody months!'

Jory gets embarrassed when women swear, but he keeps his head. 'Well, you can rest easy now – he's in our custody. The call was a courtesy – we thought you'd want to see the arrest, after all your work.'

'*You* tipped us off?' says Kinsey, unbelieving. She glares at Paul, who's standing, manacles in hand, ready to relieve the constables of their slowly reviving prisoner. Thackett has sat Bishop Crown down on the ground and is talking to him quietly.

The birds have shut up now, although the cat's still observing the scene intently. For the first time, Jory notices the pleasing smell of rose petals. Beyond the garden, he can hear more sirens on their way.

'A courtesy,' he repeats. 'I understand it was PC Jenkins who first realised there was a Beard Collector.' He nods towards the third constable, a reedy young man who's standing well back from the developing row. Jenkins swallows, then nods back. 'Your team's done excellent work on this case,' Jory goes on, 'but I'm afraid it's in our hands now.'

He shrugs. This isn't the kind of confrontation he enjoys.

* * *

At school Jory had been top of his class, but one of the drawbacks of attending a high-flying university is that everyone you compete with was top of theirs. When Jory discovered that, among his new study buddies, he was nothing special, academic work abruptly lost its lustre for him.

Stories still fascinated him, and he made the fullest use of the university's libraries, but what he learned from his tutors – about the only thing he learned from them, in fact – was that liking stories and appreciating texts are two very different things. Jory's only good trick in the critical arena was a strong line in interpreting stories as allegory, which was helpful when reading Chaucer or Spenser, but tended to produce strange results when applied to, say, Jane Austen or George Eliot. To his tutors, trained in schools of literary theory from post-colonial to Marxist-feminist, he might as well have stepped out of a steam-powered time machine.

He decided that a third-class degree would be perfectly adequate for his future plans, such as they were, and put all his energy into whichever sports clubs would accept him – and, in particular, the University Tournament Society.

He'd signed up with TourneySoc in his first week, striding towards their stall at Freshers' Fair with the resolve of a man on a quest. At their first social meeting, packed into a low-beamed pub named the Saracen's Head, he found most of its members to be indistinguishable from his school cohort – stolid, wealthy rugby-players with the upper-crust accent and manners which Jory had long since learned to mimic perfectly.

There were exceptions, of course, and if Jory felt more at home in their company, the sons of the gentry never seemed to hold it against him. Jory had always had the gift of making friends easily: it was what had enabled him to survive school, along with his knack of being able to beat up anyone who thought it might be fun to pick on him.

TourneySoc claimed to preserve the ancient traditions of chivalry practiced in the city since the Middle Ages (although with a modicum of research Jory had discovered that it was founded in 1973). The way the society taught it, medieval mock-combat was part contact sport, part historical re-enactment and – if you listened to some of the more pretentious members – part authentically homegrown English martial art.

Loaded with bequests from ex-members, the society maintained its own tiltyard for combat games and a huge armoury of replica weaponry, all of it rendered carefully non-lethal. If the students felt at all embarrassed by charging each other on horseback, pennants flying, lances tipped with giant lumps of sponge, they did their best not to admit it to one another.

Under the tutelage of the older members, Jory learned the art of jousting – how to angle his sponge to unseat an opponent, while gripping for dear life to his own horse's flanks – the skills of swordfighting on foot and horseback, the use of his shield for protection, and the application of other, more specialised weapons such as poleaxes, maces and flails. The blunted swords were flat and heavy and very different from the foils and epees he'd fenced with at school. When all weapons failed, he learned to grapple an opponent into submission.

The only area where TourneySoc failed him was archery – still a popular minority sport among society at large, and thus considered to be tainted by mass appeal. Indeed, the university had a thriving team which Jory joined, and he organised his own shooting sessions with a handful of likeminded TourneySoccers.

Endowments aside, the society paid for itself by mounting demonstration fights at historical festivals and appearing in period battle scenes on TV and film. A born re-enactor like Jory was in his element. Even so, historically authentic weapons, even non-lethal versions, don't come cheap, and he found himself spending his vacations covering the expense of membership with jobs from exam marking to pizza delivery.

There's no question that TourneySoc helped to prepare Jory for his work at the Circle, but it would be a mistake to think that it was all that was needed. After all, a dozen or so students joined TourneySoc each year, and very few of them ended up in Jory's position. Like the other upper echelons of British society, the Circle may owe a great deal to the past, but re-enacting it is one of the last things it wants to find itself doing.

TourneySoc was important, though, for one reason beyond the mere fact of training him up for Circle life. It was at TourneySoc that Jory met Malory Wendiman, his only lasting friend from this era of his life and now the Circle's resident psychological profiler.

It was Malory, more than anyone else, who set Jory on his post-university career path, and who must thus shoulder some of the blame for what's about to happen in James Ribbens' garden a few moments from now.

* * *

Inspector Kinsey's still angry. She's been angry, with Jory specifically, for some time now, and he's beginning to realise that this is her natural state.

'You're the fucking *Circle*!' she reminds him, loudly. 'You're like the Masonic wing of MI5! You deal with organised crime, terrorism, espionage — high-level shit. This guy may be a serial killer, but he's an amateur. We'd have caught up with him – we were *this close*.' She looks embarrassed for a second, perhaps recollecting that 'this close' wouldn't have been much help to his hostage. 'What the hell's the Circle's interest?'

It's a fair question. The Circle's remit is specific and precise, and it rarely involves its agents in straightforward criminal investigations. (It couldn't be more different from MI5's, either, though Kinsey's not to know that.) Just to understand its parameters, though, you need a certain specialist knowledge. If Ribbens had been just your common-or-garden sex-crazed killer, the Circle would have left pursuing him entirely in the Inspector's hands.

None of this is stuff Jory's allowed to discuss. The standard answer, true though it is, is hardly likely to satisfy Kinsey. 'I'm afraid that information's classified,' he says anyway.

'Bollocks!' snaps the inspector, shocking him again. 'It's because he's targeting establishment figures, isn't it? What, were they Masons too? If he'd been killing women – prozzies say, since that's who most of them like to kill – you smug, mystic, medieval bastards wouldn't have given a toss. Just because you've been around since the Stone Age and have Crown protection, you think you can come galloping in with your fucking *sword and shield* and –'

'That will do, Inspector.' The upper-class voice comes from the house, and the Inspector stops ranting straight away.

'Oh fuck,' she whispers, deflating. Jory's surprised to realise that underneath all that aggressive energy she's quite a small woman.

The Chief Constable isn't looking happy to have been roused this early. Jory assumes that Thacker's mate Clark, seeing Kinsey's attitude, took matters into his own hands and went over Jory's head with the problem. Then he sees Paul's expression, and realises that it was his squire who ordered this crass show of the Circle's civil authority.

'It's not the Inspector's fault, Sir Michael,' Jory tells the Chief Constable. 'She's worked hard on this case. I understand why she's disappointed, but as it turns out it falls within our jurisdiction.'

'You patronising bastard,' Kinsey murmurs, loud enough for him to hear. 'Sorry, sir,' she tells her superior crisply. 'I crossed the line. Heat of the moment. Won't happen again.'

Paul's smirk becomes more pleased with itself still. Jory feels his anger stirring, along with absurd feelings of protectiveness towards Kinsey. Given how capable the Inspector is, this has to be a chivalric response galvanised by his device.

Paul's distracted by his temporary triumph and isn't paying much attention to the police officers and their beard-bedecked prisoner. His look turns to alarm when he realises that Ribbens, now wide awake, has pulled his arm free from the woman constable's grip. Immediately the killer lands a violent punch on her colleague, then pulls his second arm free from the man. He pivots and elbows the first constable in her stomach, at the same time punching the black officer again.

He pulls a machete from the tool-rack and runs towards the house.

* * *

The turning-point of Jory's life was, in retrospect, the TourneySoc end-of-term banquet which marked the end of his final year as a student. The committee liked to make these events spectacular, and it had taken over a fourteenth-century dining room at one of the university's oldest colleges. The caterers were specialists who generally worked historical festivals and battle re-enactments.

The food was pretty much what you'd expect, assuming you were some kind of expert in medieval cuisine: jugged hare and capons, artichoke sauce, savoury blancmange, pease potage, frumenty, comfits, sugared plums – all accompanied by an antique ale brewed yearly by a local brewery to a meticulously recreated recipe.

The beer was dark and oddly spiced, tasting rather like cinnamon and figs. Jory knew from previous years that it guaranteed the kind of hangover best cured by beheading, but had nonetheless been appreciating it keenly.

The word was that all of this was paid for not by the society itself, but by its sponsor on the university faculty, one Dr Edward Wendiman. An elderly but vigorous academic whose specialism was obscure to Jory, Dr Wendiman never took any obvious interest in the physical skills the

TourneySoccers practised, confining his involvement to throwing them this annual knees-up. This very lavish gesture was, of course, enough to make him hugely popular among the members, but it also, Jory now realised, made him an unusually well-off university lecturer.

The good doctor was also the father of Malory Wendiman, one of TourneySoc's more dutiful members, who was sitting with him, Shafiq Rashid and a few others not of the society's inner circle at one of the long communal trestle tables.

'You won't get much of this sort of thing at Hendon,' Malory said now.

'Doesn't seem likely,' Jory agreed gloomily. He'd accepted, and was anticipating without much zeal, a place on the officers' fast-track programme at the police training college. It had been the best fit for a knight in service of the King that the university's careers advisors could come up with.

Malory broke off a corner of one of the huge slices of bread which were serving as their plates, and nibbled at it. 'My, these are almost inedible.'

'They're supposed to start off stale,' Shafiq said. 'They become softer by soaking up the juices. At the end of the meal you eat them, if you can still face it. Traditionally the leftover trenchers were given to the poor.'

'It's a shame we don't do that,' Malory noted.

Like Jory, Malory was a paid-up life member of TourneySoc, but it was generally assumed that she was humouring her father. As far as Jory knew she'd never participated in the society's rather perfunctory women's games (which always gave the impression of being an unhappy concession to modernity, one which might be withdrawn at any time). She was hardly built for it, being a tall, rather gangly woman who wore small round spectacles and her ginger hair in a bun. She was a postgraduate psychology student, only a few years older than Jory, but she spoke and dressed like an academic in late middle age.

'Mm. Good luck with the guys down at the shelter, then,' Shafiq said. 'I know I wouldn't want to turn up and hand them our leftover soggy bread.'

Shafiq Rashid's career path had been more or less parallel to Jory's, but with the added disadvantage of being visibly not a member of the traditional landed gentry. He was inevitably known as 'Radish' among the compulsive nicknamers of TourneySoc, a few of whom even had the wit to claim that it referred to his 'rad-ish' politics. As well as volunteering at a homeless shelter (to which he tithed some of his earnings via the city mosque), Shafiq had led a slightly rueful campaign to have 'any pub not named after a decapitated foreigner' adopted as TourneySoc's regular haunt.

Uneasy at first in one another's company, Jory and Shafiq had found themselves thrown together, partly by their shared passion for archery (at which the Asian lad excelled), but mostly through ending up in the same holiday jobs. It hadn't taken them long to unbend and realise how much they had in common. Malory, who for several years had been orbiting TourneySoc's social margins, attached herself to them soon afterwards.

'No banquets at Keele, either,' Jory noted, referring to Shafiq's offer of a postgrad chemistry place in the rural north.

'No,' Shafiq agreed. 'And no proper archery team. I'll be lucky if there's a chip shop,' he added, sipping his water. His religion wouldn't even let him drown his sorrows.

'Jory!' bellowed the incoming Social Secretary, who'd paused on his way back from the gents. He was swaying gently. 'Hendon, eh? Bloody good luck with it, old son! We'll make a Chief Inspector of you yet! Evening, Malory,' he added, raising his tankard but obviously stumped for anything further to say to her. 'Your dad's put on a fine spread as usual,' he eventually added.

She smiled shyly at him. 'That's good, Viv, I'm glad you like it.'

Viv gazed vaguely at Shafiq as if wondering why he'd never noticed him before, and staggered away.

'My father's swapped places to avoid him,' Malory noted.

After some time spent in his first year worrying that Malory had a crush on him, it had suddenly dawned on Jory that she was actually a rather attractive woman. He'd thought at the time that just wasn't interested in making anything of her looks, but in fact her dowdiness was conscious and deliberate. (When I asked her, much later, she told me that she externalised and projected her disinterest in romantic attachments, so that the men around her thought it was they who were disinterested. Honestly, academics.)

For Jory's part, though he'd had his share of girlfriends, he found most actual relationships a disappointment. For him, love was something pure and noble, holy even, which you pursued at a distance, and after which the mundane reality of everyday life with an actual woman could only ever be a comedown. He'd been glad of Malory, a platonic friend with whom – unlike all his male friends, including Shafiq – he was in no conceivable kind of competition.

'Really, though,' she mused then, still following Viv's unsteady progress back to the high table, 'TourneySoc could do more in that area. The whole university could. I mean, I dread to think how this kind of event must look to people like your friends at the shelter, Shafiq. For us it's an exceptionally posh meal, for them it would be an opulent orgy. Just because we're interested in history, it doesn't mean we have to act like the Roman nobility.'

Jory, by now more than a little muzzy-headed, realised that she'd reverted to their previous topic of conversation. 'Quite right,' he said. 'Re-enacting the past should mean we take an interest in the values of the past.'

Malory looked puzzled.

'Robber barons, droit du seigneur and scrofula?' suggested Shafiq, who regarded TourneySoc's hearty Englishness with a self-deprecating detachment which did little to lessen his commitment to the society. 'That doesn't really appeal, I'm afraid.'

'No no,' said Jory. 'I'm talking about proper chivalric values. What they preached, not what some of them practised. Charity, hospitality, beneficence. Nobility, in its most abstract sense. We ought to invite those chaps from your shelter to join us here.'

He might talk like a student (and a drunk one at that), but in most ways that matter, Jory really hadn't changed a lot over the past decade.

Malory gave him a studious look. 'This is your King Arthur fixation talking, isn't it?'

'No, he's right,' Shafiq said. 'In a sense, at least. Your medieval knights may have acted like thugs, but they bequeathed the world a pretty useful moral code. That's exactly what some people say about Mohammed.'

'Not you, though, surely?' Jory asked.

'Of course not,' Shafiq agreed. 'The point is, everyone in TourneySoc treats that moral code like fancy dress. We could be doing just what you said, applying its values to the world today. If we tried we could really help people, you know?'

Malory was looking at them with interest. 'How much do you both know about my dad's work?' she asked.

* * *

Paul begins to chase the charging Ribbens, but too slowly. Neither constable's in any state to follow. Jory moves to block the lunatic, guessing that his target is still Bishop Leonard, but a second later his trajectory resolves itself quite differently.

'*Fuck!*' shouts Inspector Kinsey, just as Jory realises

that the Chief Constable is also a gentleman of the bearded persuasion.

Two quick steps bring Jory within reach of Ribbens, but the madman's almost at Sir Michael's throat. The Chief Constable gapes at him, rigid with shock.

With no real awareness of the motion, Jory's hand goes to his sword-hilt, that righteous rage of his continuing to build with the mounting of the sun.

This tragic, futile little man, he thinks. *This midget with delusions of gianthood, this petty fool intent on razing better lives than his…*

His sword springs from its sheath. The impact of bone and sinew jars Jory's arm, but the blade has the strength of justice behind it. The blow bites cleanly through Ribbens' neck, detaching head from shoulders and flinging it forward with a powerful momentum. It flies past the Chief Constable and through the wreckage of the patio doors, coming to rest bloodily on the floor of the kitchen. Jory wishes, just for a moment, that the thump of a severed head colliding with a hard surface wasn't a sound he recognised.

The cat yowls and leaps away. The beheaded body collapses into Sir Michael's arms, blood spurting down its cloak, turning the ragged beards a muddy red.

What follows would be a shocked silence if it weren't for PC Jenkins being loudly sick into one of the rosebushes. It's a strange, reflective little pause in what's been a very odd morning. As he stares at the late murderer, Jory realises that there are nine clumps of hair on his pathetic cloak, not eight.

Malory must have missed a victim. With the Beard Collector dead, he may never be identified.

'Christ, what a mess,' mutters Kinsey.

Jory can only nod in agreement.

***

The morning after that final TourneySoc banquet,

Jory was sitting in Edward Wendiman's college rooms, wondering what Malory thought her father could contribute to his own nebulous career plans.

He'd moved on from ale to mead, and thence to some kind of fortified wine, and was now praying for a swift and merciful death. Failing that, his hope was that he hadn't done anything too visibly embarrassing in the academic's presence the previous night.

Dr Wendiman's rooms consisted of a flat occupying the top floor of a recent extension to one of the oldest colleges. His living room contained barely a single wall of books, and no oak-panelling whatsoever. It was dominated by a plate-glass window offering an impressive view across the medieval city, and by a large computer screen on which a mathematical model was slowly building itself. Jory had no idea whether this was some essential part of Wendiman's research or an elaborate screen-saver.

'Tea's the thing,' said Wendiman sympathetically, before Jory had even opened his mouth. 'Coffee's hopeless, it's a stomach irritant.' Jory suddenly developed another hope relating to visible embarrassment, which was that his stomach would let him get through the conversation without vomiting in the old man's waste paper bin.

'We'll put plenty of milk in it,' added the old man. 'Don't worry, I know how you feel,' he added, massaging his temples as he vanished into his tiny corridor of kitchen.

Jory had been surprised to learn from Malory that her dad, despite his obvious interest in matters medieval, was actually a futurologist. As she'd explained it, this was a branch of history whose students, rather than confining themselves to the past, tried to understand past, present and future holistically as aspects of a continuous process of change and evolution.

('According to him, we're living in history,' Malory had elaborated. 'It's our natural medium, like water for a fish. Which means your Round Table is exactly as relevant now as it ever was. Whether it existed or was just a fiction, its effect is on the whole pattern of history, not a single era.')

It all sounded a bit mystical to Jory – not that he had a problem with that, obviously – but apparently it mostly meant that Wendiman and his solitary research assistant spent their time analysing and extrapolating trends in order to predict the near and long-term future. According to Malory, they tended to get snappish if you compared this in any way to writing science fiction.

What this had to do with his own future, Jory still had no idea.

'I gather my daughter suggested you see me,' Wendiman said, returning with the tea. He was taller than Malory and as thin, his hair a white chrysanthemum trailing florets of beard. He spoke like the BBC World Service circa 1955. He must have been nearly fifty when Malory was born. It didn't take long for Jory to twig that his ivory-tower persona, like Malory's, was mostly an act.

'Yes sir,' said Jory. With his schooling, calling authority figures 'sir' came naturally to him. His tutors were regularly appalled, especially the Marxists, but Wendiman seemed the kind who'd appreciate it. 'She suggested I should approach you about something called the Circle.'

Though the mystery of this excited Jory, part of him hoped that the Wendimans were only trying to co-opt him into the Rotarians. The university had been a notorious recruiting-ground for the KGB during the last century, and there was talk that the British intelligence services had taken a more recent interest. Jory was willing to serve his sovereign in any way she'd accept, but spying – Ian Fleming's novels aside – had never very much appealed. The covert nature of the work troubled him.

Encouraged by Wendiman's friendliness, he said so. 'Never interested me either, I'm afraid,' Wendiman replied. 'All those acronyms. It's worse than higher education. No, for MI5 you'd be wanting Dr Jarvey over at Queen's. The CIA used to use Professor Dixon, before he went doolally and started threatening to send students to Guantánamo.'

'So the Circle's not a… spy ring?' Jory said.

'Ah,' Wendiman said, reminded of his train of thought's original destination. 'No, the Circle's a different proposition altogether.'

And he began to tell Jory of a body of men – ably assisted by the occasional woman – who serve at the command of the Crown, protecting the realm from threats domestic and foreign, who strive to safeguard the innocent and bring the guilty to justice, who stand firm – and yes, who fight when necessary – to preserve the way of life their ancestors held as right and noble and true, who see themselves as the successors to generation upon generation of brave and loyal knights.

It took the old man a while, but Jory sat rapt, his hangover forgotten.

'There's a Christian element to the ethos, as you might expect,' Wendiman added as an afterthought. 'Not sure whether that's your sort of thing. Certainly non-believers aren't barred. I've never really had much time for it, myself – bit of an old pagan really – but you can imagine the kind of thing, God and St George and so forth. Anyway, if Malory thinks you'd fit in I'm sure I can put in a good word for you. I don't know if that interests you at all?'

For perhaps the first time in Jory's life, he recognised and embraced life's tendency to work out exactly what it was he wanted most and drop it in his lap.

'Feel free to go away and think about it,' Wendiman said, misreading his silence. 'Not for too long, mind.'

'Oh no, sir,' Jory said at once. 'I don't need time. I'm interested.'

So far, he's never looked back.

* * *

Outside James Ribbens' house, the journalists are

massing. They're having to struggle through the residents to get there – it seems the entire neighbourhood has come out to watch.

Police cars and ambulances, including the Chief Constable's limo, are double-parked up and down Snowdon Street. Neighbours mingle with passers-by: the newspaper delivery men have stayed to watch, while the council worker peers down from his lamp-post. One family's brought bacon rolls and a thermos of coffee. There's a macabre carnival atmosphere brewing.

The Chief Constable's the first to emerge from Ribbens' house, his bloodstained jacket hurriedly ditched. Inspector Kinsey and her three subordinates follow. Sir Michael makes a short statement explaining that the chief suspect in a murder investigation has tragically died resisting arrest. He doesn't mention the Circle or the bishop, but – rather hearteningly for the Church of England – the cleric's recognised when he's carried out on a stretcher. As he gets photographed, the journalists' excitement mounts.

Pressed on how the Beard Collector died, the Chief Constable stays tight-lipped, tugging nervously at his own full-set. Kinsey's photographed looking furious, but she looks furious in all her photos, and the hacks think nothing of it. Besides, PC Jenkins causes a diversion by fainting as Ribbens' body-bag is carried past him. It, too, is swarmed about by photographers before being loaded into another ambulance.

The neighbour with the phone is talking to one reporter, and the news of what he saw from his back garden spreads through the crowd like a coughing-fit. As crime-scene officers, photographers and forensic scientists – all from the regular police, though their reports will be copied back to the Circle – troop into the house, journos and locals alike crane their necks to catch a glimpse of the knight in armour who took out their friendly neighbourhood serial killer.

In the bustle Bob Thackett emerges unnoticed and goes to join Johnny Clark in the van. They pull away, take a right past the shops then into the next road along, where they collect Jory and Paul, who've nipped out through a neighbour's garden at the back.

'Back to the Fastness then, sir?' Thackett asks once they're both aboard.

'Seneschal's been on the phone,' Clark adds laconically.

'I rather think we'd better,' Jory sighs. He gives Paul an irritated look. 'We both have some explaining to do.'

3. THE CASTLE

The Fastness is the Circle's headquarters, and its base of operations for London and the south of England. Officially known as Kelliwick House, it's a high-rise Thameside monolith which most passers-by take for a more than usually hideous 1960s office building. From the outside it's a reasonable assumption, the building being a blocky concrete plinth which climbs three storeys before it's even broken by a mirrored window.

The few who are allowed inside already know what to expect: a fortress whose design is to your old-school motte-and-bailey castle roughly what Jory's ceramic-polymer armour is to medieval plate-mail. Kelliwick House is no more than a concrete shell, a curtain-wall peppered with mirror-windowed guard posts. Its interior holds a courtyard and an honest-to-goodness moat, surrounding the tall cylindrical keep which is the true Fastness.

As Jory and Paul enter the lobby, they pass between slabs of metal which could stop a smallish tank. The burly men-at-arms who act as doormen wear collar-and-tie civvies which would fool only the most casual observer, but fortunately the London streets are full of those. Knight and squire pass through the open-plan reception area, exchange pleasantries with the receptionists (women trained in hand-to-hand combat and given the honorary rank of page), produce ID cards which they swipe at the security barriers, then key in their unique PIN codes. They pass beneath the unobtrusive channel in the ceiling where the portcullis hangs and mount the staircase to the raised parade-ground within.

A squad's being drilled by a sergeant-at-arms as Jory and Paul emerge beneath the high frosted-glass roof of the Fastness. At nearly noon on a hot June day, the smell of sweat is unignorable. Away to the right-hand side of the keep, six non-honorary pages are practicing swordsmanship in pairs, while opposite them two Knights are locked in what would appear to anyone less than an expert to be mortal combat. Jory gives them a casual wave.

Inside his own impregnable exterior, he's tense. He's spent the hour-long motorway journey trying to predict the Seneschal's reaction to his recent encounter, and he couldn't claim to be looking forward to it.

The keep stands like a pillar in the courtyard's centre, extending as far below ground as above. It's rumoured that the lowest storey's a tiny underground station last used during the Blitz, which you won't find on any Tube map. The building's current design may be post-War, but it's not the first Fastness to occupy this site.

Gun emplacements, never yet used but stringently maintained, stand ready to defend the central stronghold against any invader who penetrates the courtyard. The tower's summit peeks above the frosted-glass roof to house phone and TV masts, a flagpole flying the Union Jack, and some formidable, though disguised, anti-aircraft weaponry.

The Fastness is strong, but it wouldn't withstand the worst that modern warfare has to offer. Air defences or no, a serious aerial assault could reduce the above-ground structure to rubble, and even the deep bunkers wouldn't survive a direct nuclear strike. In theory a lone terrorist could obliterate the place – along with much of central London – out of his or her suitcase. But the effect of that kind of event on the British psyche would cripple the Circle anyway, however much of its infrastructure survived.

Jory and Paul circle the base of the keep, skirting the moat, walking together in less than companionable silence. The swing-bridge is open so they cross, submitting to the final security layer of biometric scans before the guards allow them access to the stairwell. (There are no lifts here. Disability equalities legislation, like equal opportunities, stops at the curtain wall.)

'Eighth floor, sir,' one of the guards tells Jory laconically, and his heart sinks. Sir Charles Raymond, the Circle's Seneschal, is in the habit of using the boardroom to introduce a little extra intimidation into selected debriefings.

Jory's in trouble, he knows. He left himself without a leg to stand on when he removed James Ribbens' head.

* * *

Even without Edward Wendiman's recommendation, Jory would have been an exceptional supplicant to the Circle – effectively combat-trained, and steeped from an early age in the ethos the Circle claims for itself. His career trajectory since his acceptance as a page has been appropriately meteoric. Even now, several years after his acclamation as Knight, many of his year's intake are still squires. Some of them feel rather bitter about it.

Jory doesn't feel guilty: he knows that he, like all his brother Knights, earned his promotions through merit. The only contemporary he feels bad for is Shafiq Rashid, whose supplication for pagehood was rejected despite his own commendation from Dr Wendiman. Shafiq's hardly done badly for himself – an Olympic silver medal has to come high on anyone's CV – but Jory's often wished he could have had his companionship on his quests. If the Circle had taken him on… well, who knows.

Jory does wonder sometimes how Shafiq might have felt, if it had been him rather than Jory who'd gone to Iraq during his final year as David Stafford's squire.

You don't see a civilisation at its best when you're there with an occupying military force. The lands we call Iraq used to be called things like Ur and Mesopotamia and Babylon: they've been continuously cultivated since the invention of agriculture, and their people invented many of your basic civilisational skills like writing, timekeeping and arithmetic. Mosul used to be the biblical city of Nineveh, where the prophet Jonah's buried.

Jory did catch glimpses – echoes perhaps – of the much later city of the Emirs, the medieval capital where those early feats of invention were refined into what we'd recognise as physics, chemistry and algebra… but mostly what he saw were the interiors of military vehicles, a lot of dust, a great many hostile faces, ruined buildings of recent vintage, Western corporate logos, various biting insects, explosions, his own and other people's bodily wastes, and dead bodies.

There weren't all that many dead bodies, in actual fact. But they were the first Jory had seen, and really, it only takes a handful to put you right off a place.

***

As he ascends the stairs, Jory considers Paul's role in their current predicament. His squire hasn't been talkative during the journey, but reading between the lines it seems he phoned Sir Michael Wills almost as soon as he met Inspector Jade Kinsey. That Paul saw Kinsey's robustly sceptical approach to authority (other than her own, obviously) as a personal slight, says more about him than about the Inspector, or the normal relationship between the Circle and the police.

In all honesty, Jory finds his squire a difficult companion. As his training's progressed, Paul's proven one of the most proficient fighters the present-day Circle has at its disposal, but his easy upper-class charm – and occasional frank snobbery – cover up a deeper insecurity. He'd never dream of saying that he resents squiring for someone of Jory's background, but he finds excuses suspiciously often to mention family members who preceded him into their country's service.

Jory wonders whether Paul's self-esteem issues stem from his strong sense of morality. Prigs are never popular at public schools, and as product of the system himself, Jory can readily envisage scenarios where calling in a higher authority to teach a bully a lesson would have resulted in social ostracism for the lad. Paul shouldn't have made that call this morning without consulting his Knight, of course… but Jory was flushing out a deranged serial killer at the time and has to admit he wouldn't have appreciated being asked.

Still. Calling in Kinsey's immediate superior, a chief inspector or superintendent, would have been regrettable, but justified if it kept her people out of harm's way. Summoning her force's Chief Constable served no purpose except as a show of strength. In turf-war terms, it's breaking out the nukes in response to a border incursion. Paul's only possible reason for acting this way was to teach Kinsey a lesson, and that suggests a thin-skinned self-importance which Jory can't condone.

Unfortunately, he's not in a position to criticise. Knights of the Circle are bound by an ethical system so complex and arcane it constitutes an area of legal study in itself. As well as such old favourites as loyalty, chastity and humility, this code contains stipulations about magnanimity and mercy towards defeated foes, which aren't usually taken to justify lopping their heads off.

Admittedly Ribbens was an escaped prisoner intent on killing, which mitigates matters considerably… but Jory knows, and Paul knows, and the Seneschal will surely learn if he hasn't already guessed, that Jory had other options open to him. A range of alternative assaults, leading to wounds of varying severity up to permanent maiming or paralysis, would have occupied Ribbens' attention even under the influence of his device, for long enough that the police and the Circle's men between them could have restrained him.

Because this ethical system also specifies, idiotically, that Knights – and squires, who aspire to follow the code though they aren't yet bound by it – should take blame on themselves when it might save the reputation of another, it's become standard protocol to circumvent this by placing them on oath before debriefing them. What Jory and Paul tell the Seneschal won't be subject to much discretion.

Being so hellishly complicated, the code of honour is impossible to remember in full, let alone observe flawlessly. But it's a basic tenet that for a Knight of the Circle in peacetime, killing should always be considered as a last resort.

(War is another matter, of course.)

* * *

The warlord who David and Jory were sent to Iraq to bring in or bring down wasn't just one of the most dangerous opponents a Knight of the Circle can face, but also much the most embarrassing. Clifford Chalmers was a renegade Knight who'd abandoned the Circle some years previously, taking his unique knowledge, skills and status into the job market as what's euphemistically called a 'private military consultant'.

Chalmers' most recent employers were a remnant of the Iraqi regime ousted by the British and US invasion forces, who had an interest in establishing a guerrilla resistance around the city of Mosul in the north. The mercenary had been enjoying great success in bombing buildings, equipment and personnel belonging to the allied forces and their perceived collaborators. He'd carved out a miniature empire in the foothills north of the city, where his arbitrary cruelty had earned him the ironic Arabic nickname of Al-Wasati, 'the moderate man'.

The blowing-up-Americans aspect of his work was viewed by allied command as unacceptable, and as soon as British intelligence had penetrated the fog surrounding Al-Wasati's background, the Circle had been alerted. They'd dispatched their bravest Knight, his squire and a squad of men-at-arms to close down Chalmers' Iraqi operation and put him out of action altogether.

The Circle's men had a dubious welcome from the locals. Al-Wasati was beyond a doubt a vicious, merciless bastard, and many people in Mosul had friends or family whose deaths were on his hands. On the other hand, he *was* working for Iraqis, and some took the view after the alleged war of liberation that while the late Saddam Hussein had been a vile, bloodthirsty dictator, he had at least been *their* vile, bloodthirsty dictator. This new world, of democracy and a constant Western military presence, was an unknown over which Iraqis themselves felt they had little control.

In other words, some of the Mosulites were open to the idea that Al-Wasati was the lesser of two evils even before David Stafford turned up.

* * *

Eventually Jory and Paul reach the eighth floor of the tower, the first with windows. Here, bulletproof, mirrored glass wraps the eighth floor's single room, commanding a 360-degree view of the courtyard beneath.

I've never seen the boardroom, of course – my privileged status only extends so far. I'm told, though, that the huge conference table can accommodate the full complement of Knights at times of utmost crisis. Jory's never yet seen it done, but he imagines there'd be very little elbow-room.

Instead of the Seneschal, to his relief, they find an altogether less forbidding authority figure. David is standing, slightly stooped, and peering through the window at the combat practice taking place below.

'David.' Jory smiles but sees the older Knight's sombre face as he turns. These days they're supposedly equals, but even in the Circle's upper echelons there are gradations.

'Jory,' David says. He explains, 'There's b-been a change of plan,' and Jory's upset to hear his stammer return. It's been a good few years now. He sees Paul's head cock with interest.

'Retho caused us a bit of bother, I'm afraid,' Jory confesses, as much to give his friend a moment to compose himself as anything.

'So I heard.' David shakes his head. 'Never mind that now, though. Something more urgent's come up. You're not off the hook, don't go thinking that, but… well, this can't wait.'

'Sounds pretty serious,' Paul observes obsequiously.

David grimaces. 'It is. The Seneschal's waiting for us in the briefing room.' There's little love lost between David and Sir Charles these days.

The briefing room's four storeys underground – back down twelve flights of stairs, in other words. You or I might groan a bit at that – Paul certainly winces.

Jory appreciates the climb.

* * *

David Stafford's a genuinely nice guy, as well as a puissant and noble Knight. He treated everyone in Mosul with all the courtesy, generosity and respect the Circle's code and his device would dictate.

Unfortunately, that device also proved something of a liability. In a modern combat zone – even a relatively informal one such as was in effect around Mosul at the time

– someone whose shield bears a white field quartered by a scarlet cross stands a significant chance of being mistaken for a well-protected paramedic. Some soldiers would see this as a tactical benefit and take advantage of it. The Circle being the Circle, David was under an honourable obligation to declare his combatant status before anyone made any such mistake.

Worse still, the emblem of a bloody cross brings with it some more unfortunate connotations, especially in the context of a conflict which many in the Middle East saw as the culmination of a history of Christian aggression running back almost a millennium to the First Crusade. Shafiq, with his quaint views on naming pubs after Muslim body-parts, might well have found a word or two to say on the subject.

When this issue was pointed out to the Seneschal before they flew out, he'd shrugged it off. 'So you inspire a bit of holy terror in the natives,' he'd told David. 'Do them good. Never did an occupying force much harm, either.' Even then, Jory was fairly certain this was a historically questionable assertion. David said nothing at the time, but his puzzled frown at the Seneschal's obtuseness spoke volumes.

As I say, David was as nice a bloke as you could hope to encounter in a war zone. From a Middle Eastern point of view, though, he couldn't have more obviously epitomised Western imperialism if he'd been playing polo while wearing a pith helmet and whistling 'Rule Britannia'.

The irony is that David himself is hardly anti-Islamic. Christianity's part of the package as far as his device is concerned, but it was the Crusaders who tainted the symbol, not the other way about. Not even the Circle is as militant as all that – Anglicanism may be its default for historical reasons, but as Wendiman told Jory, there are Circle employees who belong to other faiths, and some with no time at all for the whole religion thing.

(Not many, admittedly, especially not at the rank of Knight. And those there are tend to convert at some point during their career. But still, it would be absurd to suggest, for instance, that Shafiq – a fine swordsman, Olympic archer, accomplished athlete, and a keen proponent of all the values the Circle upholds as its own – was turned away when Jory's supplication was accepted, simply because of his religion.)

The point is, through no fault of David's, even the so-called friendlies among the local population treated the Circle's quest with hostility and suspicion. So it wasn't terribly surprising when their plan for capturing Al-Wasati got leaked to the opposition.

***

The briefing room's in the subterranean section of the keep, sharing a floor with the armoury.

Ranks of seats face a dais, where the Seneschal stands in front of one of those giant wall screens you usually only see in films. Those ones are generally displaying a map of the world or the United States, but Britain's a less convenient shape. At the moment it's just southern England, the midlands and Wales that are in view, with a tiny bit of Ireland visible to the upper left. A flashing graphic near the top right – Jory thinks somewhere in Lincolnshire – indicates what could be anything from a spate of ghost reports to a major terrorist incident.

Five other Knights, including the Seneschal, six squires, including David's and four sergeants-at-arms, are already present in the room. This suggests a level of seriousness towards the upper end of that scale.

'Sir Charles,' says David as they arrive. 'Jory Taylor and his squire are here.' The Seneschal is one of the few Knights who are habitually addressed as such, having been publicly re-knighted by the Queen in recognition of unspecified services to the nation. It's a distinction the Knights maintain for form's sake, except in their own private ceremonies.

'Taylor,' Sir Charles Raymond nods. 'Parsons. Sit down and pay attention.' It's a compliment to Paul that the Seneschal remembers his name – one which Paul certainly notices, although Jory thinks nothing of it. Raymond remembered Jory's name when he was a squire.

The Seneschal is the de facto leader of the Circle, in the Head's absence. Sir Charles has held the post for twenty-odd years now. His shield – which these days he uses purely for ceremonial purposes – bears the device of two silver keys on a blue background. Its bearer isn't automatically appointed to the Seneschalate, but it often seems to work out that way.

'Gentlemen.' Raymond addresses the room at large. 'You've all heard of the Saxon Shield. Some of you are aware of our interest in it. For the benefit of the rest, Stafford will recap.'

Jory has indeed heard of the Saxon Shield, a far-right organisation predictably known among its adherents as the SS, but not of anything that suggests it's the Circle's concern. In Britain an absurd number of groups (many of them absurd in themselves) claim the sanction of ancient tradition. It's usually nonsense, but even when it isn't, it rarely involves a device.

David taps a button on a remote, and the map of England is replaced by the image of a rounded shield, with a heavy central stud – a Saxon shield, in fact. It's painted black, with the chalk figure of the White Horse of Uffington emblazoned across it. More than one heraldry expert in the room winces.

'The Saxon Shield's a white supremacist group,' says David, his stammer firmly in abeyance now. 'Specifically they claim to be *Anglo-Saxon* supremacists. So in theory they don't just hate immigrants from the last century or two, but everyone from the Norman conquest onwards. Their political programme for England includes the restoration of the House of Wessex to the throne, devolution for the seven Saxon kingdoms, dual-language road signs in modern English and Anglo-Saxon, and closing down the Viking heritage centre in York. In practice that's mostly posturing – their primary focus is the usual racist nastiness against identifiable minorities.

'They're completely berserk of course, but even so they've amassed a surprising number of followers.'

This is sounding familiar to Jory. 'Presumably we know the reason for that,' he says.

David nods. 'It looks as if –' he begins, but the Seneschal interrupts him.

'Miss Wendiman will cover the psych background later,' Raymond says, and Jory remembers he's not the Circle's most popular Knight right now. 'For now, let's allow Stafford to spcak without interruptions.' Which is Jory told.

'The SS was founded around six years ago,' says David, 'by these two men.' The screen shows head-and-shoulder shots of twenty-something blond bodybuilders. One has that same White Horse design tattooed across his forehead, but otherwise they look eerily similar.

'They go by a whole directory of aliases,' David continues. 'Different rumours suggest they're brothers, twins even, or that they're homosexual lovers. One conspiracy site claims they're the results of a neo-Nazi cloning experiment. We've managed to rule that one out, at least.' There are a few polite laughs. 'Their real names are Colin Hill and Alfred Noake, and they're cousins and school contemporaries, originally from Canterbury.'

'The capital of the Anglo-Saxon kingdom of Kent,' an older Knight puts in. The Seneschal doesn't tell him to shut up.

David nods again. 'Noake and Hill each have a lengthy criminal record including multiple charges of assault and affray. Noake did time in a young offender's institution. They joined the BNP together in their late teens, but obviously they've moved on since.

'We've taken an interest in them,' David says, 'for a number of reasons. But the most direct connection between the Saxon Shield and the Circle,' he says with crisp precision, 'is that we've been backing them for several years.'

You might think the embarrassment of a line like that would make almost anyone trip over their words.

* * *

The Circle had been tracking Al-Wasati's movements for some time, using military spy planes and surveillance satellites. Chalmers' motley international mob of thugs was distributed across the mountains north of Mosul, and he made irregular tours of his command by armoured car. Their preliminary surveillance had revealed three remote locations which he occasionally passed through en route, where a carefully planned ambush might have a hope of succeeding.

Obviously the Circle had the firepower to destroy the armoured car outright, but this is where a close reading of the chivalric code comes into play. The vehicle was itself a weapon, and a churlish rather than a knightly one, so honour would permit the men-at-arms to disable it with grenades. After, though, things would get more tricky. Actually killing Chalmers with an explosive strike would be dishonourable, bringing disgrace upon David, his device and the Circle, so the scale of the assault would need to be very precisely calculated.

David's plan was, once Chalmers' transport was immobilised, to call him out and challenge him to single combat. Word had it that Chalmers still carried his own Circle-issue sword and shield, so he might actually be up for meeting him on equal terms. There was no doubt about David's own courage and honour, even among his enemies, but he was well aware that, given the device that shield of Chalmers' bore, the chances of the mercenary playing nicely in their fight to the bloody death were slim.

However – and this was the clever bit – the moment Chalmers deviated from the time-honoured polite etiquette for hacking your enemy to pieces, he would be dishonoured as a Knight, and there would be just cause for Jory to set the entire squad of men-at-arms on him – guns, grenades and all. With Al-Wasati down, there'd be no need for his backup to linger, so they'd likely run away to carry on their private war without the leadership of a Circle renegade. The Americans wouldn't be happy, but David and Jory's quest would be accomplished.

As you'll have guessed, it didn't quite go that way.

Al-Wasati had been tipped off, and planned his movements carefully so that the Circle forces had to opt for the least secure of their three ambush locations. Jory clearly remembers the crunch of the first grenade, lobbed up into their vantage point from a completely unexpected direction.

It took out two of the men-at-arms and stunned David, leaving him concussed and semi-conscious. Seeing his Knight in no position to direct his men, and the squad suddenly exposed in what was supposed to have been their strategically advantageous high ground, Jory ordered them to drop to the ground in a tight defensive formation, the wounded David in the middle, and used their radio to call for backup from the regular army.

For twenty minutes they fended off snipers and grenade-throwers, jeered at by a capering, sword-wielding figure whose Old Etonian accent immediately identified him as Clifford Chalmers himself. By the time Allied paratroopers arrived to relieve them, three men were dead, five injured; David was bleeding heavily and unconscious;

and Jim Feddon, a man-at-arms who had been away reconnoitring at the time of the ambush, was missing, presumed captured by the enemy.

Like I say, Iraq's not one of those tourist destinations Jory's desperate to revisit.

* * *

Now, David is explaining his employers' grotesque decision to support a neo-fascist paramilitary cell. He says, 'Dr Wendiman senior predicted some years ago that we could expect a flare-up of devicial activity within the fringe groups of the English far right. We identified Hill and Noake's organisation as a likely nexus for that activity, but we couldn't act against them until we had confirmation.'

The Circle's remit, as I've said, is clear and specific. It exists to police rogue devices. If it seems insular and inward looking, irrelevant in our unsuperstitious modern age, it's because how well it's doing its job can be measured precisely by how little it affects the rest of us. Devices which impact the undeviced are exactly what the Circle is supposed to predict and prevent. All other threats, however serious, it leaves for what it still calls 'the secular authorities'. Even in wartime, Knights of the Circle are only deployed against device-bearing agents of enemy powers.

'So Trevor Macnamara contacted the SS,' David continues, 'claiming to be a sympathiser inside the establishment who had to preserve his anonymity. I believe our friends in the intelligence services would call this a "deep throat" source.'

This sort of clandestine nonsense is exactly what Jory wanted to avoid when he rejected a career in spying. He knows that it's done, and even that the Circle might one day call on him to carry out a similar quest (though they'd be fools to, given his well-voiced opinions on the subject), but he's always been profoundly offended by this kind of duplicity. He looks around for Macnamara, who he knows mostly as a friend of David's, to see whether he'll be held accountable for his actions, but the older Knight's not here.

David goes on. 'The idea was to keep the group on a long leash and perhaps use them as an instrument against other manifestations of devices on the far right. This was to be done by passing them information occasionally, and a certain amount of money, and… um, equipment.'

That one nearly defeats him.

'What kind of "equipment"?' Jory asks aghast.

David shakes his head and presses on. 'Until last month,' he says, 'the SS were vocal and obnoxious, but rarely violent. We knew that they were stockpiling armaments, but Macnamara believed this was on survivalist principles rather than in preparation for an offensive. However, in the last few weeks there's been an increase in violent attacks on individuals in cities near the SS headquarters.'

More victims, then, thinks Jory.

'Around half the victims,' David says, 'have been people we'd think of as members of ethnic minorities – blacks, Asians, Chinese – but the police haven't yet correlated these with a second set, who are of recent Continental, Scandinavian or Celtic ancestry. The SS are our obvious suspects.'

When a rogue device goes uncontained, there are always victims. Ribbens' surrogate kings, the soldiers blown up by Al-Wasati's thugs, these ordinary men and women assaulted for their notional otherness. Even the impressionable yobs who Noake and Hill have gulled are victims in their way.

'As soon as we realised this,' David continues, 'Macnamara contacted Noake and Hill and asked for a meeting. He went to meet them in their usual rendezvous venue at midnight last night.' David swallows uncomfortably. 'H-he hasn't checked in since then.'

* * *

David recuperated in a Baghdad field hospital, insisting on writing personal letters of condolence to the families of his dead troops. It wasn't really what the poor sods had signed up for, for all they'd said they were willing to serve. The Circle's usual combat quests are limited and domestic, involving criminals or terrorists, and actual deaths are rare, let alone fatalities on foreign battlefields.

David set Jory to trying to locate the missing man, Feddon. He drew a blank right up until the point the video appeared on the internet.

Chalmers had remembered his chivalric etiquette. The Circle's code not only allows it to pay ransom for hostages, but when the hostage is a vassal of the Circle – or 'employee', as we'd have it nowadays – they're pretty much obliged to.

The Circle has its resources, and its reserves. Finding the ten million US dollars Al-Wasati demanded wasn't exactly routine, but it didn't present too great a challenge. Unfortunately for everyone, the warlord was stupid enough to add a condition at the last moment, insisting that the Circle leave him and his operation alone in future.

This – as Chalmers should have realised, if he'd remembered as much about his previous life as he thought – went entirely against Circle's very basis. The warlord was an ex-Knight bound to a hostile device: this made him the Circle's problem, and they were honour-bound to deal with him, rather than leaving him to regular forces who were entirely ill-equipped for such a threat.

Given this answer, Al-Wasati made his second, even more stupid mistake and executed Feddon. Two dozen Knights with their squires and pages were immediately shipped out to Mosul, with fully half the Circle's complement of men-at-arms. Under the command of Trevor Macnamara, who'd shared his pagehood with David years before, they took out Al-Wasati's network without a single casualty on their side (though plenty on his).

Clifford Chalmers killed himself as the Knights stormed his final bolthole. David was already in the private hospital in Norfolk where he'd spend most of the next year.

For most of last century it would have been called a nervous breakdown. Before that we'd have called it melancholy or apoplexy or possession or something. These days, even the Circle knows the proper name is post-traumatic stress disorder.

One of the milder symptoms of David's PTSD was the resurgence of the stammer which evidently plagued his boyhood. Shortly before he came back to active duty with the Circle, he managed to kick it for the second time. It took a series of intensive sessions with an intimidatingly prestigious Harley Street speech therapist.

If one of David's closest friends has been captured by the Saxon Shield, Jory thinks now, it's likely the Circle has another hefty therapy bill heading its way.

4. THE SHIELD

By now it's obvious to you, of course, that the Circle considers itself the spiritual heir of the Knights of the Round Table. That's clear even to outsiders: books have been written on the subject, sensational and serious both, although the Circle's reach means that libraries and bookshops just shelve them between the Ripperology and the UFO bestiaries.

Each Knight of the Circle identifies with one of those original companions of the High King at Camelot, and their shields bear those knights' heraldic devices. David Stafford's red cross derives from the legends of Sir Galahad; Trevor Macnamara carries Sir Percival's pattern of gold crosses on purple; Charles Raymond's twin keys are the arms of Arthur's foster-brother and seneschal, Sir Kay.

Even the men-at-arms know all this. The officer class, the successful supplicants for the status of page, are told the reasons for it.

The Circle, they're told, *is unbroken.*

The Knights don't just take their inspiration from the Round Table: they're literally part of the same order. Its Head is the Pendragon, King Arthur himself, his seat kept ever empty in the expectation of his return at Britain's time of greatest need. While he sleeps, the Circle serves at the command of the current monarch, on the understanding

– never yet tested, obviously – that he or she will yield authority to the High King on his return. (Quite how that would work these days, with sovereignty vested in parliament rather than the Crown, is something only bored constitutional scholars have ever considered.)

Since the order's creation back in foggy sub-Roman Britain, the devices of those first Knights have been passed down in succession, carrying the wisdom and the courtly mores of those Christian warriors – Arthur and Lancelot, Percival and Galahad, Bors and Bedivere and the rest – forward through history. The Circle's outlasted the Saxon kingdoms and the Norman baronies, defended the reigns of Plantagenets and Yorks and Tudors, held fast through Civil War and Commonwealth and Restoration, watched the growth of the cities and the invention of the industrial towns, made use of factories and railways and internal combustion engines as they each emerged, fought for God and Crown through two World Wars, and been bemused in turn by flower power, Thatcherism and the war on terror.

The pages work out fairly quickly that the enemies they deal with also carry symbols, ones associated with King Arthur's enemies. This, on the face of it, is pretty odd. It's hardly surprising that an esoteric martial-mystical order, especially with a prominent national security role, should identify with its country's most famous legend, but the idea that the criminal elements it guards against maintain a similar-yet-opposite tradition begs a few pertinent questions.

These get answered when these pages become squires, when they're told of the true nature of the devices – or as much as one can know such a thing, without carrying a device of one's own. That bit, within the Circle anyway, comes as the final stage of initiation – synonymous, in theory at least, with Knighthood.

That's why becoming a Knight of the Circle is a sacrament, not a promotion. It involves spiritual discipline, fasting, hours of meditation and a symbolic rebirth. The Circle are sticklers for tradition, and they take their rituals very seriously.

As I've said, they take secrecy seriously as well. Jory's acclamation as a Knight wasn't the sort of rite-ofpassage you invite your parents to. He'd told his mum and dad all he dared about his calling, but mostly this meant they knew he had to keep things secret. They assumed he was something in the intelligence services, were thoroughly proud of him, and worried constantly about his safety. This was more or less the right attitude anyway, so Jory let them carry on believing it.

The only friends at Jory's acclamation ceremony were those he'd made within the Circle itself. David was there, of course; the Wendimans, father and daughter; the Seneschal; a dozen other Knights, Macnamara included, who'd taken an interest in Jory or who just happened to be in the building at the time; most of Jory's peers within the ranks of the squires; a handful of the men-at-arms.

Oh, and the other kind of peer. It's a common mistake, though based on long-familiar tradition, that a knighthood can only be conferred by the sovereign. In medieval times being knighted by a lord was fine, and the Circle still keeps a tame member of the aristocracy for the purpose. The last member of the Circle to be granted a peerage – for unrelated services, of course – was the philanthropist Sir Jonathan Bullimore, bearer of the minor device of Sir Elyan, created Baron Northwood by Queen Victoria in 1867. His great-great-grandson, the fifth Lord Northwood, isn't a member of the Circle, but accepts this particular service as his inherited responsibility in that dutiful but slightly bewildered manner that members of the hereditary peerage do.

The acclamation itself was momentary, a tap on the shoulders with a medieval sword which (presumably) spontaneously generated Jory's knighthood. The Circle bulked it out with testimonials and other waffle, and rounded it off with a service of holy communion, but otherwise it was much like the trad graduation ceremony Jory had sat through a few years before.

It's the vigil that precedes the acclamation where most of the more significant ritual occurs.

The previous day Jory's hair had been shorn, then he'd been dressed by his envious fellow-pages in what looked and felt like white pyjamas and a red dressing-gown. (He wore old-fashioned armour for the ceremony itself, the only time in his career with the Circle that he'd dress in actual metal.) He'd enjoyed – if that was the word – a formal meal with Sir Charles, David, Edward Wendiman and various other Knights in the boardroom, which doubled as a dining-room on occasions of high ceremony.

Just as the haircutting was done by a Mayfair barber seconded to give the Knights-to-be the most expensive styling of their lives, the Circle had an arrangement with a caterers who specialised in upmarket gentlemen's clubs. As far as they were concerned, the Circle was just another. They cooked in a kitchen in the curtain wall, and handed the food to pages acting as waiters, without ever seeing the real inside of the Fastness.

The Knights and Knight-to-be ate at the boardroom table (which yes, now you mention it, is basically round.) The menu was English and achingly conventional: fish soup, a pheasant with roast potatoes, a treacle pudding. Afterwards over port, with the waiters dismissed, in conversation (slightly stilted in David's case, as he was in the latter stages of his therapy and couldn't always get the words out), the older men gave Jory one last chance to change his mind.

'Some squires never take the final step,' David told him kindly. 'There's no sh-shame in it.'

'Think carefully, Jory,' Dr Wendiman suggested. 'It's important to be sure of what you're doing. Nobody here would think the worse of you if you were to change your mind.'

'Certainly not,' grunted Sir Charles, not altogether convincingly. 'We can always use skilled men in secular jobs. Admin, HR, payroll, that sort of thing. Recruitment and contracts and procurement. Need a trusted pair of hands for it, but hardly worth a Knight's time.'

Jory, needless to say, wasn't having any of it. Nor did they expect him to. Like everything else, it was a formality they had to go through.

***

Back in the briefing room, the Seneschal's ceded the floor to the Circle's psych profiler.

'Colin Hill and Alfred Noake may be of pure Saxon descent, as they claim,' Malory Wendiman concedes. 'Of the fifty million people in England, I imagine a tiny number may be, not that that makes their crusade any less ludicrous. The important point, though, is that they believe it.'

In this company of Knights, Malory's confident and assured, without ever failing to be deferential. Whenever the Seneschal looks as if he might interrupt – which he does a lot, being a man who sees listening to others as an evil of limited necessity – she gives him the opportunity with a respectful pause.

So far he's mostly changed his mind and held his tongue, which may be the effect Malory's aiming for. It doesn't take many years of working with Charles Raymond to learn the workarounds.

'We were clear that the Saxon Shield's founders had bound themselves to a device,' says Malory. 'By all accounts they're electrifying speakers, and their success in recruitment speaks for itself. Their charisma, the atavistic savagery of their outlook, the oddness of their specific obsessions, are all highly indicative, but Mr Macnamara's reports of their conversations together enable us to pin it down precisely.'

Malory's here on sufferance, though Jory can't imagine how the Circle ever functioned without her. She holds no formal rank, not even the pagedom grudgingly afforded to a handful of women in the Circle's employ. Officially she's a secular counsellor on a highly lucrative secondment. Her primary employer's still Jory's old university, where she specialises in some rarefied subdivision of psychology. You can guarantee it's less obscure than her Circle work, even so.

'I'll circulate full briefing notes after the meeting,' she says. 'Although I'm sure most of you remember your Nennius and your Geoffrey of Monmouth.' She produces a brief flash of smile, mostly directed at Jory. Paul tuts.

In Wendiman senior's absence, Jory's the only person in the Fastness who knows quite how much of Malory's demureness is assumed. Her looks haven't changed since their university days – though as she looked prematurely middle-aged then, this is a bit of a backhanded compliment. Just as she used to do her spinster impression for students and faculty – and presumably still does – Jory knows she's also performing for the Circle. Not that her act's enough to win over the likes of Paul.

Malory goes on: 'The condensed version is that Hengist and his brother Horsa were noblemen from Saxony, heathen warriors who traced their ancestry back to the Norse gods. Although the literal historicity of the devices is none of our concern, their existence at least is confirmed in the usually reliable *Anglo-Saxon Chronicle*.

'The brothers were foolishly employed as mercenaries by Vortigern, the nominal king of Britain. In fact he was a Celtic tribal leader who'd usurped the throne from King Constans, the uncle of the then-unborn King Arthur. The author of the *Prose Lancelot* suggests that Vortigern had been his predecessor's seneschal. I'm sorry, Sir Charles, did you want to…?' she asks meekly, as the old man opens his mouth to butt in. He frowns more deeply and subsides.

Paul tuts again and shakes his head. Privately, Jory agrees that needling Raymond like that was strangely reckless of Malory. He can't approve of such disrespect, of course, but… well, it's Malory. He knows she's on the side of the angels. And though the old man's done plenty to justify his self-importance, pricking his ego hardly counts as sacrilege.

'Quiet,' he murmurs to Paul. 'I'm trying to listen.'

'Sorry. Forgot she's a mate of yours.' Today Paul's sailing close to the wind himself.

'Vortigern needed the Saxon brothers to consolidate his hold on the throne,' Malory continues brightly. 'But when they saw how ripe Britain was for conquest, they brought in armies from their homeland and demanded more and more land in payment for supporting his regime. Hengist even arranged for Vortigern to marry his daughter so they'd have a spy in his court.

'You'll notice two motifs here,' she optimistically predicts. 'Firstly, the myth's about the inadvisability of welcoming foreigners. Open the door to them and you'll let in a flood of immigrants who'll steal our jobs and land and women. Although the Saxons are the bad guys in this scenario, it's essentially the same xenophobic myth as the SS are now promulgating themselves.

'Secondly,' she says, 'the Saxons were recruited to shore up a king's authority, but ended up betraying him. My guess is that Mr Macnamara was acting partially under the influence of the brothers' device when he attempted to co-opt the SS as a tool of the Circle. He was, doubtless fleetingly and temporarily, playing the part of Vortigern rather than that of his own device, Sir Percival.

'The story ends unhappily, of course,' she goes on. 'The king and his allies quarrelled, and one of Vortigern's sons killed Horsa. Then Arthur's other uncle,

Aurelius Ambrosius, took back the throne and Hengist was captured in battle and summarily executed – by the Bishop of Gloucester, rather surprisingly. By then, though, their countrymen had settled a significant proportion of England. Aurelius' brother, Uther Pendragon, and his son Arthur fought some valiant campaigns against the Saxons, but eventually they drove out the Britons and became the dominant culture in what we recognise as historic times. At least until the Normans arrived in the eleventh century.'

This time Raymond does interrupt, before Malory can backtrack into the detail. 'Hence all their talk of Saxon racial supremacy,' he concludes heavily. 'We'll read the notes, Miss Wendiman, I'll make sure of that. Meanwhile, have you anything that might lend us an advantage in combat? I'd contact the Bishop of Gloucester, but I don't think the church would thank me for endangering another bishop today.'

The joke's as pointed as it is pedestrian. It elicits a few smiles nonetheless, but Malory's frowning seriously. 'Judging by his notes,' she says, 'Mr Macnamara couldn't decide which of Noake and Hill was bound to Hengist, and which to Horsa. He concluded that it didn't matter a great deal, as neither of the Saxon brothers has much by way of individual personality. I'd say they match Hill and Noake rather well in that respect. It's possible that the pair form a single device, which requires two closely associated subjects to bind themselves to it. If that's the case, then in a combat situation terminating one of Noake and Hill may well weaken the other. Though not neutralise him, of course, as Hengist fought on without Horsa. Does that help at all?' she concludes.

The Seneschal dismisses her, so the men can get down to discussing tactics.

Her eye catches Jory's briefly as she goes, and her eyelid flickers in the most fleeting wink imaginable.

***

The Circle's chapel is on the tenth level of the Fastness's keep, immediately beneath the roof: a big round room, its ceiling lower than most churches, but higher than those of the lower storeys. It's plastered in plain white and set about with twelve tall stained-glass windows. Opposite the doors to the stairwell is a large wooden altar with a plain wooden cross suspended above it.

It's a light, airy room during the daytime, with faint Londonish sounds always drifting in from beyond the curtain wall. At night, with only a huge altar-candle and the sodium echoes of the stained-glass to define it, it becomes a flickering, cryptlike shadow-space whose elevation only heightens its isolation from the world.

Naturally it was at night that Jory had to keep his vigil here, on the eve of his Knightly acclamation.

The vigil is listed fourth among the seven stages of ritual which make a Knight – preceded by the shearing, robing and feasting, accompanied by fasting and prayer, and followed by the acclamation itself. (The fasting isn't particularly arduous, particularly after the meal the Seneschal had laid on. Still, Jory was a big lad with healthy habits, and not used to staying up all night and skipping breakfast. By the time the ceremony itself rolled around at lunchtime, he'd be seriously peckish.)

The vigil is a time of meditation – technically a rather different thing from prayer – and Jory was invited to reflect upon the kind of knight he aspired to become. Another thing the Circle's big on is the discipline of vocation, so there was no guarantee at all that he'd be allowed to fulfil these specific expectations, but long experience had taught them that this period of reflection was essential for a Knight to discover his device.

In those generic olden days the Knights commemorate with these ceremonies, a squire would spend his pre-knightly vigil kneeling, or even lying face-down, before an altar. These days, while Jory was certainly meant to spend most of his time in contemplation, nobody particularly minded him walking about a bit to stretch his legs, or parking his arse in a pew for a few minutes.

The catch was, if he fell asleep, it meant an automatic disqualification from Knighthood. No one was keeping him under surveillance, of course, but he'd have been honour-bound to confess his failure, and then it'd be the procurement department for him. One thing you can pretty much guarantee of anyone in the final stages of becoming a Knight of the Circle is that they'll take their honour very seriously indeed.

Supposedly the reason for this condition was that, if you fell asleep, the devices wouldn't come. There were stories that for some people they came anyway, but that they were the wrong devices. How true that was, Jory didn't know – the squires were as prone to daft rumours as his school sixth form – but he was acutely aware that the device of Sir Mordred had lain unclaimed since the suicide of Clifford Chalmers. A Knight bearing the bends sinister sable on a field argent might be a trusted member of the Circle for decades – because that's the tradition, and the Circle always makes proper use of its resources – but everyone would know he was on borrowed time.

So Jory knelt, the building discomfort in his knees a welcome prompt to stay awake, directing his mind alternately inward in meditation, then upward in prayer. Stripped of his timekeeping equipment, the clocks of London's churches muffled and irrelevant beyond the curtain wall, he lost all track of time. His stubbled scalp felt cold. With only that weak flame and a glass-filtered haze of streetlamped sky to see by, Jory began to feel both tiny and enclosed in that echoing space, a Jonah in a sacramental whale.

At some point – he thought early in the night, though he was never sure – Malory came to him.

Jory had stayed friendly with the younger Dr Wendiman throughout his page- and squirehood, and she was almost the only friend from his pre-Circle life who he was still in contact with. Malory had begun the work for the Circle for which her father had long been grooming her, and during her sporadic London visits they'd visit museums and galleries, drink and eat the occasional meal together, just as in the old days. She'd even stayed, though rarely, at his flat, snoring in Jory's bed while he lay chastely on the living-room sofa.

With him she relaxed her severe intellectual persona, admitting to a love of seedy pubs and trashy films which took them to some unexpected corners of the capital. By now he saw her (he thought privately to himself, having never had a sibling) as a kind of younger sister, headstrong but needing more protection and guidance than she realised – despite being, in fact, several years his elder. He worried that she found him self-righteous and pompous, but if so she seemed to enjoy his company anyway.

The floors of the keep below the chapel contain accommodation, unluxurious but adequate rooms where Knights and other dignitaries – and, on occasion, visiting secular counsellors – can stay. Jory knew that Malory and her father were in the building (in her case largely because Wendiman senior was there supposedly to chaperone her), but he hadn't expected to see either of them until the morning.

She came to him that long night, though, shedding her nightgown in a heap by the chapel door, stepping barefoot through the shadows to where he knelt in silent prayer before that austere altar. To him she was a pale ghost, indistinct in detail, the hollows of her body wreathed in shade like smoke.

He looked at Malory, and recognised and desired her. He knew at once why she had come, which helpfully avoided an excruciating whispered conversation straight out of the rom-coms she'd made him sit through. She was his best friend, his pseudo-sister, and perhaps – though he'd never have admitted to it – the only woman since his mother who he'd considered an equal. And here she stood before him, naked at the altar, offering herself to him.

Now, Jory wasn't what you'd call experienced. It's true he was a good-looking boy who'd grown up at the turn of the twenty-first century, so he wasn't quite a virgin sacrifice. Not all his relationships at university had been consummated – you might imagine that was one reason they hadn't lasted – but a couple had. It had been a long time, though, since a nude woman was last in the vicinity of Jory.

As for the Circle… well, the Circle. You know what they're like by now. Chastity's a virtue, celibacy even more so, but even the best can fall. Back in Arthur's time, a nubile maiden throwing herself at a knight was enough for many of them to fall quite enthusiastically, and be forgiven later. Sir Bors, Sir Tristram, Sir Lancelot (twice), even Merlin – hell, even Arthur himself, and with his actual half-sister, no less. You can hardly miss it as a recurring theme.

But now? Tonight?

It was Jory's vigil. The one night in his life when he was obliged, not only by his morals and his honour but positively and absolutely by a sacred vow, to maintain his purity.

'Jesus, Malory,' he whispered – realising as he said it how unusual it was for him to swear by that name. 'This is… um, really flattering and everything, but really… you know, it's just… completely inappropriate. Um. Sorry.'

Malory sighed.

(Later, they'd talk about it. Oh boy, did they talk about it later. He'd ask her, 'But I thought you… well, respected the Circle's ideas of honour. Like chastity, and the sanctity of the vigil. The whole code. That's why you work for them – us. Isn't it?'

And she'd reply, 'I just wanted you to have an opportunity, that's all. We both know the Circle's work is indispensible, but that doesn't oblige me to sign up to its every tenet. I'm more of a twenty-first-century woman than you probably imagine, Jory.'

She didn't resume her offer. It was only her absolute refusal to be embarrassed by the episode which allowed them to stay friends at all.)

For now, though, she simply picked up her nightgown from the floor and walked back to her room, defiantly naked.

***

As the Knights are filing from the briefing-room, to make prayerful and practical preparations for the assault on the Saxon Shield, the Seneschal suddenly says, 'Taylor. Stay behind a moment, will you?'

Jory winces. Paul looks worried as he leaves the room, presumably wondering how his superior's disgrace will reflect on him. David looks back too, but they both know that Jory fights his own battles.

Raymond sits, without inviting Jory to do likewise.

This can't be the full debriefing Jory was expecting – there are protocols, Paul would need to be present – but it could well be a preliminary dressing-down, a warm-up before the main event. 'Sir Charles –' Jory begins, but the older man raises a hand.

'I'm not interested in any of that,' he states. 'I've a Knight captured or worse, I haven't time for your antics. We'll not forget any of it, I promise you that – but for the moment we've got a rescue quest to organise. Rescue or… well, as I say, we must be prepared for the worst. Stafford insisted we bring you in on this despite your behaviour of this morning, and I've decided he's right. He knows his men, Stafford, despite his… health issues.'

'I understand, sir,' Jory replies stolidly. He waits to be told what he's here for.

Raymond clicks his tongue as he gathers his thoughts. 'There's one aspect of this we didn't cover in the briefing. D'you recall the last time you carried out an extrajudicial beheading?'

It's possible that this is, in Raymond's head, a joke. Jory cringes internally, but remains outwardly calm.

'The Green Chapel?' he asks. 'Have they got something to do with this, sir?'

The Seneschal grunts. 'We don't know. It's a possibility, evidently. I haven't time to go through the reports, and you've encountered them personally, as well as having an association through your device. What do we know about them?'

Jory frowns. 'They're followers of a renegade device,' he says. 'The Green Knight. Our archives have records of earlier iterations, but this version seems to have grown up while our attention was taken up in the Middle East. They're violent eco-terrorists – Green anarchists with an anti-capitalist bent. Dr Wendiman believes they're neo-pagans, too.'

'Bunch of bloody hippies,' Raymond mutters. Though Raymond's no paragon of Christian humility, he still sees regular church attendance as a vital indicator of Britishness. Jory has his suspicions as to who vetoed Shafiq Rashid's supplication to join the Circle, although Raymond clearly makes an exception for Edward Wendiman, who it turns out – rather to Jory's surprise – is the Chief Druid of some neo-Celtic nature-worshipping sect. He doesn't let it interfere with his work in academia or his consultancy here at the Fastness, and Jory suspects it's just another carefully cultivated eccentricity.

The Green Chapel, on the other hand…

'They may not be,' Jory clarifies. 'Their ideology seems wilfully obscure. There may be elements of Marxism and

Luddism in there. Apart from the obvious, the name "Green Chapel" probably refers to a mixture of environmentalist and unionist ideology. We know they oppose wealthy businesses, industrialisation and the exploitation of the workforce. They support direct action against pollution and environmental damage – sabotage and sit-ins and that sort of thing. They also have a habit of, erm, appropriating business assets I suppose you'd say –'

'I damn well would not,' snaps Sir Charles. 'I'd say *stealing*. You almost sound as if you go along with them. Exploitation, my eye.'

'I'm just describing their position, Sir Charles,' says Jory. 'Of course I don't agree. Anyway, they use the proceeds to bankroll those of their supporters who can't support themselves – industrial accident victims, workers who've been made redundant, bereaved families and so forth.'

'And that's all we know?' The Seneschal isn't impressed.

Jory shrugs. 'Yes sir. We don't even know who replaced Shaun Hobson as their leader and device-bearer.'

'No racialism?' Raymond barks. 'Nothing that would suggest they'd sympathise with the SS?'

'Quite the reverse, sir.' Like its members, the enemies of the Circle tend to be predominantly white, but that's not true of the few Green Chapel members who've been arrested by the Circle over the years – nor indeed of Shaun Hobson. 'Do we have evidence that they do?' He can't really believe it. Malory would surely have mentioned it in her briefing.

'There are rumours,' the Seneschal reveals. 'Theories. Miss Wendiman's not our only secular counsellor, you know, *clever* though she is.' Sir Charles pronounces the word with distaste, though whether he disapproves of cleverness in general, or just in civilians and women, Jory couldn't say.

He can see where this is going. Obviously the Seneschal's read at least some of the reports. But Jory really doesn't want to talk to Jack Bennett.

Eventually he says, 'I suppose we have one possible source, sir.'

* * *

When Jory's device came to him, it was nearly the morning of his vigil.

It's very bad form, during a vigil, to think about which specific device you might end up with. The squires keep an obsessive tally of the ones which are known to be free, but of the hundreds of recorded Knights of the Round Table there are some whose devices are rarely out of use, even for a few years, and others – Sir Gwynn son of Nudd, for instance – who hardly ever appear. Wendiman senior probably charts the trends, but if so his extrapolations are shared only with the Circle's upper echelons.

Jory carefully wasn't considering, therefore, that at least one prize device, the red diagonal stripes of Sir Lancelot, was currently up for grabs.

He'd tried to restore his pre-Malory train of thought, to turn it back to the high places it had been traversing before her sudden undressed intervention had derailed it… but it returned continually to that moment of rejection, to the powerful allure of her naked body, to that very Lancelot-like conflict between his manhood and his knighthood. Rather than thinking on how best to be the noble, courtly, virtuous Knight of the Circle he knew he had it in him to be, his mind was running quite vigorously along lines of sexual desire.

He was troubled, also, on a question of honesty and honour. Just as he would have been obliged to report it if he'd fallen asleep, his involuntary response to Malory's nakedness had been a significant lapse. The blame on her part was far more obvious, of course, and there was no doubt that he was duty-bound to mention the incident.

The question was whether he could bear to. He was pretty sure the Knights would find him blameless in the matter, but it would mean disgrace for Malory. Her work with the Circle on the devices would be at an end.

The candle on the altar burned steadily lower. Jory's knees ached more and more, his head was chilly, and his white culotte things itched. Eventually he admitted defeat and did a quick circuit of the chapel. He banged his knee on a pew in the dark, and bit back a swearword. A nighttime siren briefly penetrated the muffled concrete womb from which he was to be reborn.

Jory wondered when the sun was going to rise. He thought about the different selves that women present, in daytime and at night. He wondered whether he should have just let Malory have her way with him.

The process of alliance with a device has been compared with various things. Falling in love with a character in a book is one; a dream so beautiful one awakes from it desolated is another. Most often, though, it's likened to religious inspiration.

Like a religious experience, different people will encounter it very differently. Some Knights claim to have long conversations with their devices, while others speak of a faint awareness of presence at the back of their heads. Some devices appear in blinding flashes of revelation, even visions, while others sidle in and change the mind in subtle ways. The relationship varies from bearer to bearer, as well as from device to device.

For Jory it was an emotional state, starting imperceptibly as he wondered whether he would have discharged his duty if he simply mentioned Malory's indiscretion to her father. It mounted as he wondered how it would feel to lose her friendship – and then it carried on growing and swelling until all at once it overtook his mind, and Jory, far from being the person feeling those emotions, became an all-but-imperceptible harmonic in their wild polyphony.

Lust was part of it, no doubt about that: and guilt, anger, and pride, all sometimes terrible in their intensity, but tempered with a humble humour which brought with it mercy and forgiveness – not merely to others, but just as importantly, to himself. The *person* who suddenly Jory was full of, was full of love – love for life, love for fighting, love for women – and, quite differently, love for men, for comrades and brothers – and finally, though ruefully aware of its absurdity, a love for self.

It built and built, this wave of feeling, until Jory felt that he would simply fall down on the spot and be discovered in the morning by the squires, ravished to death by the good humour of this wild demigod – and then it crested, broke, receded, and Jory was himself once more.

Though not, and never again, quite the self he'd been before.

When Jory spoke to Malory later about his encounter, his only way to put it into words was to remember it as such: as if a gruff voice had said to him out of the darkness, *Best you say nothing, laddie. You did nothing wrong, and she'll still be needing you tomorrow.* That was some of the substance, surely.

But really, no, that wasn't it at all.

That morning, before the acclamation ceremony, when Jory was strapped into his brightly polished armour, he asked for and was given a shield blazoned with the bright gold pentacle of Sir Gawain.

5. THE PENTACLE

The Fastness isn't set up for long-term prisoners. There are no dungeons or oubliettes, just a row of holding cells underneath the curtain wall. If Ribbens had lived – if Jory, caught up in the intemperate wrath of Sir Gawain, hadn't hacked his head off – he'd have been kept there while the Circle assessed the danger he presented, then transferred to the secular criminal justice system.

In what would have appeared, apart from the sensational nature of his crimes, to be a perfectly ordinary criminal trial, Ribbens would have been tried, found not guilty by reason of insanity, and hospitalised in a secure psychiatric unit on the North Sea coast. The Benwick Institute is funded by and notionally answerable to HM Prison Service, but governed by a retired Knight with a staff of medically-trained men-at-arms on constant call. Jory once overheard a page – not one who went on to become a squire – call the place 'Arkham', and had to google the reference. Malory does a lot of her research there.

Jack Bennett isn't insane, however. Before his arrest during a break-in at a prominent MP's house, rumour placed the former machine-worker as second-in-command of the Green Chapel's loose, supposedly nonexistent hierarchy, second only to the carrier of the Green Knight device. After his arrest he was assessed as being unallied to any known device – so, no more dangerous than any other violent criminal – and handed over to the police.

Bennett was charged with multiple counts of criminal damage, breaking and entering and assaulting a police officer (a piece of legal algebra, since in fact the arresting officers were Circle men-at-arms), and is now doing time at a Category B prison in the Midlands.

Now Jory's been ordered to call in on Bennett and grill him on the Chapel's connections to the Saxon Shield, before meeting up with David and the other Knights for their raid on the SS headquarters.

Jory last saw Bennett – interviewed him in fact, as part of his assessment process – during his brief confinement at the Fastness. The Chapel man's a giant bruiser, highly intimidating if you're less than, say, seven feet tall. Jory's largely immune to that, but during their conversation he also found him disquietingly articulate. A shop steward at a Derby car factory, sacked after an assault on a senior manager then adopted and radicalised by the Chapel, Bennett speaks eloquently and belligerently about whatever's currently at the front of his mind.

He's not a complicated man, but he's a formidable one. Capturing him was, in theory, quite a coup, but he's doggedly refused to give up any information about the Chapel's membership, operations or workings. If they do have some mutual arrangement with the SS, Jory hasn't many hopes of hearing about it.

'Oh. It's you,' Bennett says as Jory enters the interview room. 'Bloody Sir Galahad.' He's wearing a grey boiler suit with prison-stripe tags.

'Just "sir" will do,' Jory replies, unnerved already. He guesses the big man's just being sarcastic about his Knightly status, but he has no idea how much Bennett actually knows of the Circle's devices. The prisoner grunts contemptuously.

Bennett isn't in the mood for small talk – and if Jory was, he'd find someone more congenial than Bennett to have it with. 'The Saxon Shield,' he says, peremptorily. 'What can you tell me about them?'

Bennett's contempt deepens. 'You've got the wrong prisoner, pal. I'm Green Chapel, remember?'

'I remember,' Jory says. 'I want to know about the Saxon Shield. What do you know?'

The big man frowns, considers, shrugs. 'Only that they're fascist scum. They go on about our Oldie English heritage and that, like it's that they care about, but it's the same old Paki-bashing Nazi skinhead shite. Giving you trouble, are they?' he smirks.

'If they were, would you approve?' Jory asks curtly.

'You and the bloody SS scrapping instead of bothering ordinary folk?' Bennett laughs grimly. 'Aye, I'm not seeing any downside to that.'

'Would you help it happen if you had the chance?' asks Jory.

Bennett shrugs again. 'Might do. Only because it's good for your enemies to be at each other's throats, mind. Your Circle must be desperate if you're coming to me for advice. Do I get consultancy money, then?'

'So you're telling me the Green Chapel's not connected with the SS,' Jory concludes.

'What, *you're* calling me a fascist?' The big man's riled now. 'You saw our lads that time in Northampton. Did we *look* like white supremacists to you? Did –' he bites back a name and glares angrily at Jory, who says:

'I'm sorry about what happened to your friend that night.' He corrects himself. 'What I did to him, I mean. I wasn't myself at the time, nor was Shaun. And you can't say he wasn't asking for it. But even so, I'm sorry.'

'Aye, well,' mutters Bennett. 'He were out of control. Thinking he were the boss of us, like we were your lot. Thinking like a Knight. I still don't know what got into him.'

Jory decided to risk the truth. 'The SS have a Knight hostage,' he told Bennett. 'They won't want to ransom him, that's not their style. They're going to torture him to death if we can't rescue him. That's why I'm not interested in the Green Chapel, not today. I want anything you can give me on the SS.'

'There isn't anything, you daft pile of shite,' says the man. 'They've nowt to do with us, I keep telling you.'

Jory believes him. But for Trevor Macnamara's sake he has to be sure. 'So nobody in the Chapel talks about Saxons at all, then? That whole SS rhetoric of Saxon supremacy, that's a foreign language to you?'

He knows it's not, and from the way the prisoner's staring at him, Bennett knows it too. It's the second, and only remotely convincing, reason Sir Charles gave for believing that the two terrorist sects might be in cahoots.

'It's not like that,' says Bennett, irritated. 'It's not the same. Look, I never listened much in history at school.' He sounds as if he's launching into a well-rehearsed speech. 'But England were a Saxon land once, aye? Everyone living here were Saxon. Then the Normans come in and kill the Saxon king and say, "We're in charge now, we're the bosses, you've got to kowtow to us"?'

'That's quite an oversimplification,' Jory says.

'Likely it is,' Bennett concedes, 'but that's the story everyone knows. So then there's a time when all the upper classes, the rich noblemen and what-have-you, were Normans, aye? And the peasants, the working-class masses, *they* were Saxons. That's what us in the Chapel mean when we talk about being the Saxons now.

'So aye,' he continues, 'we want the Saxons to rise up against the Normans oppressing them. But that's nowt to do with *race*. It's all about class. You can be black or white or Indian or whatever you please – like I said, you saw our Shaun – but as long as you're trod down by rich bosses and police and bastard politicians, you're a Saxon to us. And if you're one of those rich bastards, whether you're white or anything else, then you're a Norman. We don't care where you come from, though – it's all about where you've ended up.' He stares at Jory as he says this, bringing back a memory of midwinter chill.

It makes sense, Jory thinks, ignoring his discomfort. Raymond's other argument about the SS and the Chapel, the stupid one, was that both organisations – when not resorting to guns – supposedly use 'Saxon fighting paradigms'.

In the SS's case, that means the short thrusting-swords, the throwing-spears and round, wooden shields used by the pre-Norman Saxons, aristocrats and peasants alike. The Chapel on the other hand favour daggers, fighting-staves and longbows – one of Bennett's arresting men-at-arms suffered a fractured skull from the wooden pole the big man was wielding. All of those were weapons of the Saxon peasantry after the conquest, when the Normans were developing their own more refined martial skills.

The fighting styles are as different as *Beowulf* and Chaucer, Jory thinks. It's like assuming that two groups who practice judo and karate must be colluding because they fight in Japanese.

'So what are you going to go and tell your Circle, then?' Bennett asks. 'You going to tell them we're in league with those Nazi scum bastards, just 'cause we use a word they do? Like your lot calling yourselves Christians makes you the same as the Inquisition or the IRA. No, you're not, are you? You're not a complete wazzock.'

His voice suggests that he remains unconvinced. He's right, though – Jory isn't a complete wazzock. It's obvious that there's no connection between the Chapel and the SS. Which means there's nothing he can learn here that'll help Trevor.

* * *

It took a while, after his vigil and acclamation, before Jory understood how belonging to Sir Gawain had changed him.

On a simple practical level, the difference was obvious. His strength, speed and agility had all improved. He could lift more, run longer, react faster. Combat skills and disciplines which he'd had to learn painstakingly felt suddenly like instincts.

He found he was aware of his own body, his opponents and their surroundings, in ways his Knightly trainers had always told him he should be, but which (he only now realised) had always slightly eluded him. Flashes of insight told him just where a sparring partner might attack next, or how they might parry some thrust, and these were nearly always confirmed by events. He suddenly understood the quantum leap in ability which had always seemed to yawn between the Circle's squires and its Knights.

Weirdly, he felt strongest – and actually performed better, in measurable ways – a bit before lunch.

Whenever he remembered his encounter with the device that was now his, Jory felt energised, renewed by that urgent inrush of humanity. Imagining his future as a Knight – their future together – he became fervent, light-headed and recklessly confident. With such a device as his patron, what mightn't he achieve?

His Christian faith had always been a quiet, restrained thing, free of the zeal which he saw animating some of his more evangelical fellows. Now, for the first time, he understood how it must feel to be so caught up in that intimacy with something suprahuman that the urge to tell others simply flooded over you. He became very cautious in his choice of words when he spoke to outsiders.

When, inevitably, this early ecstatic excitement started to fade, Jory remained awestruck, and quite often terrified, by the compact he'd made with this ancient spiritual construct.

Not that Sir Gawain, eldest son of King Lot of the Orkney Isles, was an unknown to Jory, the reader of Arthurian legend. The High King's nephew – though they're said to have been about the same age – Gawain turns up in great swathes of poetry and prose legend, as one of Arthur's first and best knights. Like all of them, he's praised for his strength, his fighting prowess and (with a couple of reservations) his virtue, honesty and courtesy. His loyalty to his uncle's second to none.

A lot of knights in the legends are either idealised to perfection (hello, Galahad), or let down by a single tragic flaw (stop that, Lancelot), but Gawain's a more complex character. He does his best to live up to the knightly code, but his short temper and his weakness for a pretty face – or, in one story, a repulsively ugly one – get in the way. He feels guilty when he makes mistakes, and tries to put them right. He's friendly, shrewd, a good judge of people and generous to a fault.

He comes across as the most likeable of Arthur's knights. You'd be glad to have, say, Percival or Palamedes on your side in a fight, but you wouldn't go for a drink with them down the pub afterwards, unless you wanted a long chat about exactly how chaste and temperate you'd need to be to be vouchsafed a sacred vision of the Holy Grail. Gawain is less ascetic hermit, more boozy reveller. He'd drink you under the table while regaling you with ruefully self-deprecating anecdotes about his exploits. If you're a good-looking woman, you might even persuade him back to your place for coffee afterwards.

And Jory? Well…

He'd always been a sociable lad, and you'll remember he was fond of a drink or two as a student. He certainly appreciated female beauty, though with him it had always been more aesthetic than passionate. (The incident with Malory kind of flags that up, of course.) He'd never had problems with anger management: even back at school, when discouraging the bullies, he'd been calm and methodical in the hammerings he'd handed out.

Now it was as if he was playing a role, method-acting like a natural in the part of a modern-day Gawain. He dragged the more convivial of his brother Knights (including those who bore the devices of Gawain's actual brothers, Sirs Agravaine, Gaheris and Gareth) out for drinks so often that eventually, used to the sudden excesses of the newly deviced, they asked him nicely to stop. His eye for the ladies grew sharper and more discerning, and his response a lot more – shall we say – concrete. He found himself more and more often blowing his top with strangers who'd done something to provoke him, and positively relishing the consequences.

These facts between them landed him in more bar fights in a month than he'd previously witnessed.

The Circle knows to do the right thing by its Knights, and of course counselling's provided for those experiencing a rocky time with their devices. Unfortunately, Jory was honestly unaware that anything in him had changed, except in the physical arena where he'd been looking out for it. He'd just been acting as he thought came naturally.

Eventually Malory had to sit him down and have a talk.

The devices might be spiritual in nature, she reminded him, but they're not *magic*. They turn ordinary men into heroes – or villains, of course – but not into superheroes or supervillains. Jory's increased strength – even the way it waxed and waned with sunlight, just like Gawain's in some of the legends – was entirely psychosomatic.

A device helps the bearer get the best possible performance out of their mind and body, but it charges a price. Few Knights of the Circle live long into old age, and in the meantime, while their fighting skills and knowledge may be enhanced, there's an accompanying loss of self-awareness. As much as they're anything, the devices are characters in stories, and having an allegiance to one of them means that you start acting out that story.

So, any woman daft enough to marry a Knight carrying the Sir Geraint device will be forever quizzed about who she's seeing behind his back. The bearer of Sir Lancelot's arms will, if there's someone it would be utterly disastrous for him to shag, predictably do so. And if you ask the holder of Sir Bedivere's device to do something for you, it's best to check a few times to make sure he's done it.

Obviously, this entails a certain story-blindness. These men all know that there are certain, quite specific things they really mustn't do, but still they somehow stumble into them, without ever quite realising until it's pointed out.

A really smart, strong-willed and well-read read Knight of the Circle can keep his device's tendencies in check most of the time – not, of course, *mastering* the device, but learning like a wise and trusted servant how its real best interests are served.

It would take years at best, Malory told Jory, to learn the trick of this. And even then, he could lapse all too easily.

* * *

David's waiting outside his temporary command as Jory arrives.

'Anything?' he asks. He's wearing the lightweight quilted coveralls the Knights sport underneath their armour. It makes him look like a fencing instructor. Since the Circle's current local base of operations is exactly the kind of place you'd expect to host fencing classes, this is innocuous enough.

Jory shakes his head. 'I said it was a long shot.'

'Well, never mind.' David leads the way through the wooden panel doors. Inside is Paul, armoured up ready, with Jory's coveralls and armour laid out for him to put on. Half a dozen other Knights and squires are there too, in various stages of the arming process. At the other end of the hall, several squads of men-at-arms are being issued weapons.

The hall was added on to a Victorian redbrick church sometime in the early 1900s. Its parquet floor's uneven, its leaded windows cracked, its plaster flaking. With what the Circle's paying for its use this evening, the Methodist congregation can afford to do it up nicely again. It comes with a view of the target building, and a secluded, remarkably unbuilt-on car park.

Jory took a look at their target on his way from the train station. Once upon a time – the mid-'80s, approximately – Thankaster Shopping Centre would have been impressive, an out-of-town complex that any city would have considered an asset. It's long since been superseded by larger, more ambitious retail projects, but it still attracts a steady stream of shoppers from the nearer suburbs. Certainly it dominates this undistinguished outskirt, once the village of Thankaster.

Conscientiously ignoring the security cameras – it's not clear from Trevor Macnamara's notes exactly what 'equipment' the Circle has been supplying to the SS, but it's unlikely it includes sophisticated facial-recognition software – Jory wandered round the lower two floors, mingling with the shoppers. The glass, chrome, paint and polish have faded to something nearly as seedy and depressing as this hundred-year-old hall.

The upper floors, whose stairwells Jory could only glance at without attracting suspicion, are given over to offices of various sizes. Over the past five years, according to Macnamara, every new business that's rented office space has been a front organisation for the Saxon Shield. For six months they've had those floors all to themselves, fortifying them heaven only knows how.

Well, assaulting fortresses is just another of the things the Circle does.

'How was your pal Bennett?' Paul asks as he straps Jory into his armour. 'Prison agreeing with him, yeah?'

'It doesn't seem to have changed him,' says Jory. 'He was still awkward and rude.' He buckles himself tightly into the synthetic-fibre shell, welcoming its hold on him. 'He doesn't know anything about the SS, though.'

'Bad luck for Mr Macnamara, then,' Paul observes.

It's late-night opening at the mall tonight, and there are civilian bystanders to take into account – shoppers, security guards and retail workers, some of them potentially in the SS's employ. One option would be to wait until closing time, but David has no way of knowing how long Hill and Noake will take to decide keeping Macnamara alive is a liability. (Nor does he know how much they might have learned from him about the Circle. In legend, Sir Percival the paragon would be able to stand up to any kind of torture, but Trevor Macnamara's a human being operating in the real world.)

Besides, one of David's assets derives its strength from sunlight. As far as Jory's concerned, there's no time to lose.

* * *

'The devices,' Jory remembers Malory telling him, ages ago now, 'aren't *spirits*, you know. They're not ghosts or gods, or any kind of objective psychic entities existing outside ourselves. That's a fantasy, although a lot of Knights of the Circle have found it convincing over the years.'

'But –' Jory said.

'Quiet. I'm the expert, remember? The devices,' Malory elaborated, 'are living patterns in the human mind. That's all a device is, in heraldry: a shape superimposed on a field. Jung would have called them archetypes, inhabiting the human collective unconscious and existing by virtue of our belief. I'm sure Dawkins would say they were memes, transmitting themselves like viruses from person to person.'

'A meme's not the same thing as an archetype,' Jory objected. He might not be in Malory's intellectual league, but he had a degree, and he wasn't going to let her ignore it.

'Of course not,' Malory agreed. 'But both models seek to explain how each culture ends up with a pool of shared concepts like – in our case – King Arthur, Camelot, the Holy Grail and so on. What I find interesting is that both Dawkins and Jung, with their very different perspectives, allow for the possibility that these ideas are somehow alive. Or at least analogical to life.'

'Dawkins isn't even a psychologist,' Jory objected. Like most Christians, even those of the least rabid bent, he had a particular aversion to the eminent academic, largely based on his going round telling the world at large that Jory was delusional.

'No,' said Malory. 'Nor's Jung, really, by modern standards. He was a mystic, not a scientist – he and Dawkins would have hated each other. It's taken a lot of work to integrate their views with proper academic psychology, which these days is all information processing and brain structure. It's certainly more intuitive to think of a device as a spirit that lives in your head and gives you inspiration – a daemon, in Socrates' terms. That's how it feels experientially; it just happens to be wrong.

'A device is similar to an archetype,' she continued, slipping into lecture-theatre mode (although surely she'd never delivered *this* spiel to her students), 'in that it takes different forms for different people, while still retaining the same core characteristics. Most of them are human figures, but others are animals or objects, processes even. The Grail Quest's certainly one. A human being can come to identify with one of them – Jung would have called that a neurosis – and that obsession simplifies the mental functions, making them paradoxically more efficient. We now know that consciousness is just one bodily process among many, which is why other physical functions can be affected as well.

'On the other hand, a device is like a meme in that it evolves. Its characteristics change from generation to generation, and with transmission from culture to culture, to suit its new mental environment. Our present-day devices have an ancestry, relationships, their own evolutionary tree. When a person changes their devicial allegiance, it's –'

'Good Lord, can we do that?' Jory asked, startled.

'Mm?' Malory was annoyed to be diverted. 'Yes, one person can be allied – bound – to more than one device. Certainly in their lifetime. Dad's linked to the Merlin device now, but he wasn't always. He used to serve Sir Menw son of Teirwaedd.'

It hadn't surprised Jory very much, given Dr Wendiman senior's personality, religious affiliation and role within the Circle, to learn that he was the current bearer of the Merlin device. Not being a knight, Merlin had no coat of arms, so traditionally the holder of his device gets to pick their own symbol. Wendiman used a trilithon of standing stones – as seen at Stonehenge, which the seer traditionally built.

'Menw? He's from the *Mabinogion*, isn't he?' Given the Welsh name it was an obvious guess, but it still took Jory a moment to place him. 'The one who casts the spells.' Heaven only knew what his device looked like – the Celtic ones tend to be incompatible with traditional heraldry.

'Exactly,' agreed Malory. 'He's one of Arthur's warriors like any other, but he can make their war-party invisible and transform himself into a bird. Dad's speciality used to be covert infiltration, you see, although you wouldn't think it now.' Obviously Jory had been nearer the mark than he realised when he assumed the old man was a retired spy.

'Anyway,' Malory said. 'The point is, the previous Merlin died, or retired – retired, I think – and dad, who'd been taken off active duty, had a second devicial epiphany. He says he nearly drowned – he was in the bath at the time. That was soon after he married mum, a little while before I was born. He's not the only one to swap devices by a long shot.'

'Who else?' Jory asked.

'Never mind that now,' she insisted. 'You might see that process as the patient detaching from one archetype and fixating on another, as Jung would – or you could see it as the meme mutating to ensure its continued survival in a changed environment. When dad was pensioned off, Menw was no longer suited for survival in his new environment, but Merlin was. A warrior-magician's not so different from a wizard.'

Jory knew just about enough Dawkins and Jung to know that they'd both find all of this profoundly suspect. Of course Malory was a highly respected academic psychologist, so she presumably knew what she was talking about far better than he did.

But still, he thought, real knowledge of the devices came through experience, and Malory was no Knight of the Circle. 'How can you be sure of all this?' he asked. 'I mean, however much you interview these "patients" of yours, or even counsel us Knights, you can't know what it feels like. Isn't all this stuff quite theoretical?'

Malory gazed at him with a kind of fond murderousness. 'For heaven's sake, Jory,' she said. 'You *know* it's not just Knights who carry devices. Yours choose to operate within the structure of the Circle, but a device can form a bond with anybody. They're not all evil – you've heard the Circle's legends of Knights finding women who bear the devices of their true loves, Iseult or Blanchefleur or Enid or whoever. Perhaps there's even a Ragnell out there for you somewhere.

'Occasionally, though, the Circle finds someone else with a device and, instead of fighting or marrying them in the traditional manner, you pay them to come and advise you instead.'

Jory was terribly confused. 'I'm sorry, what? You mean you –'

She sighed. 'Do you think they'd let me know so much if I didn't? My dad's been grooming me for this job since

I was eight. He gave me my own initiation ceremony when I was thirteen. I'm allied to the device of the sorceress Nimue.' Malory shrugged. 'In the Circle's terms, I'm the Lady of the bloody Lake.'

* * *

Paul hands Jory his sword and gold-starred shield, and he buckles them on. Finally, he's good to go. The other Knights are waiting patiently.

David still holds his helmet under his arm. He clears his throat. 'I'm not going to make a speech,' he tells the room at large. Everybody listens, even so. 'We're fighting for God and for the Circle,' he continues, his voice quiet but clear. 'Right is on our side, and we're going to win. You don't need motivational speeches to tell you that.

'Instead I'll tell you – quickly – who we're fighting to save. Not all of you know Trevor Macnamara, and probably few of you know him well. He's a brave Knight, an honourable man, a worthy successor to Sir Percival's device. But all that might be said of any Knight.

'Trevor's also my friend,' David goes on, 'and as such I know him better than nearly anyone. He's a kind man, a generous and loyal man, always willing to listen to other people's problems. He's never married – his device, like mine, usually precludes that – but I've seen him with his nieces and godson, and he's as gentle, loving and playful with them as he's ferocious with the Circle's enemies. Today we ride and march, not just to rescue one of the Circle's best and noblest Knights, but a good man, a much-loved man. It's not only God and the Circle who will thank you for that.'

The senior Knight's voice is steady, but his emotion's all too visible. Suddenly, Jory thinks he understands more about David Stafford – and, he supposes, Trevor Macnamara – than he ever has before. A similar, though more scandalised, comprehension is spreading over Paul's face too.

David nods, turns on his heel and leads the way past the ranked men-at-arms. The armoured Knights and squires clatter after him into the car park, where the grooms have been readying their mounts. Jory steps into one stirrup and swings his body up into the saddle, whispering soothing nothings all the while.

The Circle's tried various alternatives, since the beginning of mechanisation. There's hilarious photographic evidence of experiments with bicycles, motorbikes and, most recently, Segways. But there's a reason most urban police forces still use horses for crowd control, and in the end the Circle's needs are basically the same. Not only is there no substitute for the manoeuvrability, responsiveness and high vantage afforded by an actual living animal, but – well. An armoured steed and rider bearing down on you, hooves flashing, swinging a damn great sword?

It's just so awe-inspiringly, pant-wettingly *iconic.*

The Knights and squires give the men-at-arms a couple of minutes' headstart. From the viewpoint of the Saxon Shield's top-floor offices – where someone's surely keeping lookout – the infantrymen will look like a phalanx of riot police from some unsavoury dictatorship tramping down the sloping street towards them.

Then, at a signal from David, the Knights trot out of the car park into the street. Down the hill, across a road where even now the men are setting up roadblocks, through a flimsy hedge and over its own, much larger car park, the shopping centre awaits.

David raises his hand again, and the horses break into a gallop.

You see, what some Knights of the Circle forget... with all their talk of honour and virtue, and their sacred vow to serve the Head and Crown... is just how damn *cool* their job is.

6. THE CHALICE

The oldest, youngest and least observant of the local shoppers are hurried out of the way by men-at-arms as the Knights ride into Thankaster Shopping Centre. They gallop with their squires past Primark, their hoofbeats juddering the jewellery in the shopfronts of Goldsmiths and H Samuel. They wheel right at the Early Learning Centre, two outliers thundering diagonally through the shop's open frontage, sending a display of Thomas the Tank Engines flying.

The company charges down the wide central concourse, sending men and women scurrying into the neighbouring shops. In Currys' windows, TVs shake and crash from shelves. The pounding trips a circuit in the Disney Store's security system and a shutter descends, protecting the wares from this influx of unprocessed legend.

The horses round the dismal central fountain and advance, the Knights in an arrowhead formation behind David and Jory, the eight squires following behind. Their hoofbeats echo and resound from the high glass ceiling. The red cross, the gold star, the other six devices flashing green and silver and blue, then the grey shields of the squires, approach the wide flight of stairs that leads to the upper shopping gallery.

The Saxon Shield's watchmen meet them there. Four uniformed security guards, two cleaners in overalls, a shelf-stacker from Argos, a pair of shoppers in England football T-shirts and Doc Martens.

All have cropped hair, not all blond, and bulging muscles. A couple also have visible tattoos. They hold compact handguns – in fact, the same SIG P226s as the men-at-arms use. (The Circle will later learn that these were supplied for police use somewhere on the continent, but diverted somehow onto the Ostend-to-Ramsgate ferry.)

The Saxon Shieldsmen fire methodically at the rapidly-approaching horsemen. Their bullets make expensive-looking scratches in the Knights' armour. The screaming of the remaining bystanders redoubles, and they suddenly get a lot more cooperative about being evacuated.

The Circle's horses wear the same not-Kevlar as their riders, and their shoes are high-performance steel, laminated with a rubber contact surface midway between a running-sole and a tyre-tread. It helps them grip the hard, shiny floor, and cushions their hooves against its impact. These modern animals are smaller, slighter and more agile than their medieval counterparts, but just as well-trained. They barely waver as their riders spur them up the stairs towards the gunfire.

The SS men scatter as the horses reach them, the riders slashing at their gun-arms as they pass with steel-polymer blades. Those who can still flee run straight into the embrace of the men-at-arms. The Knights and squires spread out along the upper gallery, heading towards the access to the office space.

A lone SS sniper remaining in La Senza is picked off quickly by a Knight carrying the white-on-black lion of Sir Dinadan. He emerges, blood on his sword, red lace accidentally embellishing his shield, as he drags the miscreant out and throws him to the men-at-arms below.

* * *

One Saturday morning in London, Malory, still trying to teach Jory about the workings of the devices, took him to the British Museum. She indulged him for a while as they inspected weapons and armaments from around the world, then took him for a coffee in the basement cafe. She then found a discreet door behind an information desk, showed the curator on duty a membership card, and asked to take a guest to see the Nestine-Gull Collection.

'Sir Lionel Nestine-Gull was an eighteenth-century Knight, of the realm and of the Circle,' Malory explained, as they followed the curator down staircases and along corridors which – while perfectly ordinary – were cluttered, none too clean and obviously didn't see members of the public very often. 'He was the bearer of the device of Sir Lionel, by a coincidence so staggeringly dull even he didn't think it was worth mentioning. He used his family fortune to assemble one of the largest collections of Arthuriana in Europe, then couldn't work out what to do to with it. His son tried to sell it off to pay his gambling debts, but the Circle intervened and seized the lot. They couldn't think of anything to do with it either, so most of it ended up here.'

She stopped with her hand on a doorknob. The door was a wooden slab, repainted sometime in the twentieth century in battleship grey. A brass doorplate bore the Collection's name and nothing else. Malory waved the curator away with a thank you.

'Listen, Jory,' she said. 'What you'll see in there is... well, most people, if they ever got to see it, wouldn't give it a second thought. It's likely to impress you – understandably – but you'd better try to keep a sense of proportion.' She opened the door.

The room was full of open shelves, on which diverse antiques were set out. They were neat, but cramped: nobody expected this to be a public display. Weapons and armour formed the bulk of the Collection – Jory recognised most of them as medieval, but with a few older specimens thrown in. There were a lot of shields bearing familiar devices, old since long before Nestine-Gull's time but probably belonging to earlier Knights of the Circle rather than anyone authentically Arthurian. There were coins, medallions and brooches; moth-eaten scraps of clothing, any colour in them long since faded to brown; skeletons of various unfortunate animals, heraldic and otherwise; a few broken musical instruments; and even a few tattered books. 'The good ones all went to the Bodleian,' Malory muttered.

Everything was labelled on worn pieces of card, in handwriting which was also neat and cramped, and also long since faded to brown. The shapes of the letters were so old the labels had to be the originals.

Halfway along the right-hand shelves at chest-height, not in any prominent position, was a wooden drinking-cup. It was crudely shaped, little more than a bowl set on a short stem and base, and was grey-brown. It looked, as Malory had said, utterly unremarkable – the sort of thing a diligent but unimaginative kid might make in woodwork.

Jory gasped and sank, without conscious consideration, to his knees. His head was thrumming, with what could either have been a sudden rush of adrenaline or else the song of an infinite choir of cherubim praising the boundless magnificence of their maker.

The label, in Lionel Nestine-Gull's orderly hand, read '*Romano-Britiſh chalice. Nr. Chicheſter. Early an. Dom? S.G.*'

He had to touch it. He reached out his hand.

He dare not touch it. He snatched his hand away.

S.G. The San Graal. The Holy Grail.

'My God,' he said. 'Sweet Jesus. Is it really…?'

The question hung in the air.

'No.' Malory sounded slightly peeved. 'It really isn't. It's just a cup hand-lathed from Sussex wych-elm that got dropped in a field somewhere near Chichester. It's never been near the Middle East, and it's certainly never held blood. A farmer called Glebe found it while ploughing in 1766, and flogged it to Nestine-Gull for fourpence.'

'Oh.' Jory tried vaguely to remember whether he'd ever felt quite so foolish in his entire life before.

'The only thing about it that's even a little bit unusual,' Malory complained, 'is how we all react like *that* to it.'

* * *

By now the shoppers have fled down smaller stairwells and fire escapes, and the Knights briefly have the run of the upper floor. By now too, though, the SS have had time to respond to the attack.

A gang of men pour out of the stairwell and take positions in front of Miss Selfridge. They wear backpacks and biker leathers, and are armed with Heckler & Koch MP5 submachine-guns – sleek black things which look like someone's grafted a pistol grip onto a submarine. They're powerful enough to do some serious damage to the vulnerable bits of an armoured horse or rider – and, firing automatically, far more likely to hit them. The Knights prepare to scatter.

'Don't worry lads,' a voice says over the shopping mall's PA system. 'We're not going to use them if your boys don't.'

'That's right,' says a near-identical voice. This one comes from a slim, muscular blond man stepping from behind the machine-gun squad. He's wearing a blue boiler-suit, and carrying a shortsword and a round wooden shield. 'This isn't the time for shooters. Not this fight,' he pronounces, hefting the blade up to his shoulder.

Jory tries to remember which of Noake and Hill has the White Horse tattoo. Whichever, this is him, which puts his clear-skinned associate behind the PA mike. Both voices have strong Estuary accents.

'The lookouts didn't know you, see, but we do,' the PA says. Its operator must be listening in somehow. Either the CCTV picks up sound, or his friend's miked up. 'You're the fucking *Circle*.'

'You lads are the real deal,' says the swordsman. 'Not filthy Pakis, breeding like flies, then load the kids up with semtex and send them out to play. Not jigaboo street-gangs, pushing drugs to white kids to bling up their girlfriends. Not grasping chinks or scrounging micks or thieving pikeys. *Them* we use the guns on.'

'Pest extermination, innit?' the PA voice says. 'Them others, they're an infestation. Here today, gassed tomorrow. Like I said, we know who you are.'

'You lads, you've been here forever,' the tattooed man says. 'You're the ones we had to take these bloody lands from in the first place. For you, we keep the real weapons.'

His men carefully lay down their submachine guns, then each draws a throwing-spear from his backpack.

Behind them, the doors open and a torrent of Saxon warriors emerges.

I say 'warriors'. Most of them are dressed in leathers or boiler-suits, some wearing crash helmets. They carry swords, though, and some axes, and the wooden wheel-shields, and they're shrieking blue murder. Jory barely has time to think, *How come we're the Normans* and *the Britons?*, before the horde's upon them.

* * *

'We've put it through every kind of archaeological analysis we can think of,' Malory said. 'Carbon-dating, dendrochronology, amino acid dating. We've shown it to palynologists and palaeoethnobotanists, scoured it for scraps of human and animal DNA. We're as clear on its history as it's possible to be at such a remove.'

Jory's constant urge to kneel and worship at the shelf of the Grail had been hampering the free flow of conversation, so they'd left the Museum and walked the short distance to the Fastness. The boardroom was empty, and for some reason Malory had insisted on loitering there.

'It really is just someone's drinking-mug,' she said. She still seemed irritated at the goblet's persistence in seeming to be something it wasn't. 'It's old, yes, but this is Britain – we're living in history. If you spot a pointy stone in someone's garden wall, it's as likely as not to be a Neolithic arrowhead. Artefacts like that are buried under half the farms in the country.'

She sat angled neatly away from the conference table, while Jory paced restlessly. He was still disorientated by his instinct to venerate a wooden beaker. Beneath them in the courtyard, some pages were being given equestrian training by a weary squire. By the looks of things, a couple of them had never seen a quadruped before.

'It's another device, isn't it?' Jory concluded. 'The cup, I mean. The "Grail". In the same way I'm not Sir Gawain, but I bear his… identity, I suppose… the cup isn't the Grail, but it contains the Grail device.'

Malory smiled. 'It's very nearly that simple, yes. The Grail's the single most significant object in the mythic cycle – other than Excalibur, of course, but that's so closely associated with your Head that it's never reemerged in his absence. Oh, and the Round Table, naturally. I think we know where that device has ended up, don't you?' She gestured around the boardroom.

Jory nodded, absorbing the idea, and pulled out a chair of his own.

'No, not that one!' Malory snapped, urgent suddenly, and Jory froze mid-sit, remembering the legend of the Siege Perilous, the seat in which only the purest Knight could sit and live.

She gazed at him gravely, then smirked. 'I'm joshing, Jory.'

Jory breathed again, and sat. 'You're an evil witch.'

'The difference, obviously,' Malory continued, 'is that the cup and the table have no awareness. Their devices are attributed to them by others, rather than being a property of the objects themselves. Specifically, people with devices of their own perceive them in the objects, as inflected by their own devices. I don't get explicitly Christian overtones from the cup the way you do, but I feel reverence towards it as a repository of healing power, a kind of womb of rebirth. The Grail legend was based on earlier Celtic myths without the Christian component, of course.'

'Of course,' said Jory vaguely. The pagan precursors of the Arthurian myth don't hold much interest for him.

'Someone without a device – a man-at-arms, say, or a museum curator – would just see an antique drinking vessel,' Malory said. 'Nestine-Gull begged to differ. Whether he felt the phenomenon first, or just identified Mr Glebe's find as the Grail because he was a gentleman dilettante and didn't know any better, he went round telling the other Knights it was the Grail, and the idea spread from one Knightly device to the next. By the late twentieth century, when it became possible to interrogate the object's history, the belief was too entrenched to shift.

'For all the Circle's purposes, that *is* the Holy Grail, being kept securely incognito to prevent it falling into the wrong hands. Sir Charles still refuses to listen when I tell him otherwise, but he's an incorrigible romantic.' She sighed.

'A romantic?' The word sat oddly with Jory's perceptions of Sir Charles.

'You all are,' Malory said. 'All you Knights. But Sir Charles is old-school. He still believes the Pendragon device will manifest itself at the time of Britain's greatest need.'

'That's the official line still,' Jory pointed out. In the sesquimillennium of the Circle's existence, despite a number of pretenders, not one man has ever been accepted as bearing the dragon's head device of the High King. Nonetheless, the Circle's always held to the ancient legend which states that Arthur, though mortally wounded at Badon, is merely sleeping in some Avalon of the subconscious, and will return when the land he once ruled has most need of him.

'If so, he has lousy judgement.' Malory sounded annoyed. 'The Black Death, the Civil War, the Blitz… they were all the greatest peril in British history at the time. If none of them were enough, what *is* supposed to bring the Head back? Nuclear war? Environmental meltdown? Alien invasion?'

* * *

The SS charge against the Knights splashes out into a full-on melee, spattering through shops and onto escalators and into the gents' loos (both sets of combatants instinctively avoid the ladies'). Knights and squires parry and jab and thrust, some of them coming off their horses, while the men-at-arms stream in with batons and commando knives to join the affray.

Spears hurtle through the air: one of the squires – not Paul, thank God – is hit, and tumbles from his horse as blood blossoms from his armour's shoulder-joint. Unridden horses bolt towards the stairs, the fountain and freedom. A knot of fighting bursts into the Perfume Shop, and at once the sound of shattering glass and the reek of mixed discount fragrances permeate the air. Clinton Cards becomes host to a particularly vicious struggle, and soon the atmosphere is thick with shredded pre-printed sentiment.

Paul's horse is injured and he's pressed back through the doorway of Waterstones. Jory chivvies his own steed after him, scattering peasants as he goes.

...*Peasants?* he thinks, and realises he needs to get a grip, if he doesn't want a repeat of this morning's festivities. Knights are expected to use minimum force necessary in hand-to-hand combat against the undeviced, even in self-defence. The men-at-arms have more latitude, but they've been wrongfooted by the SS's refusal to use their guns. It would dishonour the Circle if they fired now, but they're not armed or properly trained for this kind of close combat.

The truth is, the Shieldsmen took them all by surprise. The Circle expected to be making a steady assault on the Saxon stronghold, not facing an all-or-nothing, do-or-die counter-attack. The SS headquarters must be wide open now, and Jory fears what that might mean for their prisoner. He just hopes someone on his side is taking advantage of the fact.

Inside the shop, he careers into a table, sending books flying to be trampled underhoof. Jory's mortified, but they're just reality-TV celeb biographies. Paul's in here – fighting with his back to the military history, which isn't coming out of the encounter well. His abandoned horse is leaning weakly off to one side of the action, wrapped in a signing-desk abandoned in haste by some terrified author.

Jory spurs his own mount into the fray, swinging his sword with devastating (but carefully non-lethal) force. Shieldsmen fall stunned or maimed on either side. One lurches wildly and scatters some comedian's collections of wry insights everywhere. Paul's hard-pressed but apparently uninjured. Jory wheels his horse around, kicking a Saxon supremacist in the head as he passes. He reaches down and gathers Paul up in his left arm, huffing. His squire's a wiry man, but with his armour on he's no small burden for Jory's ebbing strength. Jory hefts him up anyway, to perch in front of his own saddle.

'Crouch down a bit,' he snaps, since Paul's nearly as tall as he is. Paul does so, transferring his sword to his own left hand so they can inflict damage on the SS men to both sides as they flee.

Jory's sword clashes with a Saxon fighting-axe and sparks fly, singeing the covers of a nearby stack of childhood abuse memoirs. The man's bulk is unexpectedly solid, and Jory feels himself toppling. If he grabs Paul he'll have them both off, so he clutches a nearby bookshelf for support. The horse canters out from under him, and Jory drops into a crouch. He's still got his sword, which he swings in a far-reaching arc as the burly Shieldsman approaches him. Paul tries to rein in the horse, but she's spooked at losing Jory and bolts for the door.

The Saxons dart in warily at Jory, two at a time from different directions, splitting his attention. He manages to wrest a spear from one of them, and then is better able to defend himself from the pairs. The spear's a thrusting weapon, though, and he doesn't always know where to point it. Besides, the sun's low in the sky outside. A couple of the Saxons get a stab or two in before he manages to hit them, and one manages to penetrate the armour at his elbow, drawing blood from the soft tissue.

The flaw in the SS's overall battle strategy, brave though it is, is that a troupe of infantry have very little chance against a disciplined mounted force with superior weaponry and footsoldiers of their own – a fact which only changes when firearms of some kind are involved.

Outside, a sudden roar from the Heckler & Kochs signals that Hill or Noake has finally acknowledged the inevitable.

Jory hopes Paul isn't in the immediate line of fire – he should have had time to get clear, he thinks. The spear-throwers' submachine-guns are overwhelming in the mall's echoing acoustics, and his assailants are momentarily deafened. Pushing past them as they reel, he reaches the door and steps out – just in time to run back and throw himself behind a display of young adult supernatural romances.

He's heard the dull thump and seen the smoke-trail.

They're followed moments later by a colossal crash, far louder than the gunfire, a wave of heat and smoke and the disintegration of all Waterstones' windows. The Circle's men-at-arms, freed from the honourable obligation to abstain from using modern munitions, have taken out the SS's entire submachine-gun squad.

While Jory's ears are recovering – and while he conscientiously tramples smouldering copies of *The Teenage Mummy's Survival Guide* underfoot – a scrap of floral chiffon drifts forlornly past and down into the lower gallery, suggesting they've taken care of Miss Selfridge as well.

* * *

'All of which explains why the Circle tends to favour bladed weapons made of steel.'

Malory was concluding her tutorial – Jory couldn't help but think of it as that – on the devices as they applied to inanimate objects. 'Doesn't it?' she added, rather confirming his impression.

He stared at the boardroom table and considered. Given the Circle's willingness to use contemporary armour and shield materials, he had occasionally wondered why they were so conservative in the sword department. He'd seen some modern knives, whether or not designed as weapons, which used titanium or cobalt alloys or even ceramics in their blades. Some of those must surely have potential for use in swords, but as far as he knew no experiments had been done.

'It's the iron,' he hazarded. 'Magical creatures, faeries and witches and so forth. They don't like it up them, traditionally.'

'Exactly,' Malory replied. 'An iron alloy has a greater effect on someone carrying the device of… oh, Sir Esclados the Red, say, the otherworldly guardian of the forest of Brocéliande… than a blade made of some other substance.

Its presence will bother him. He'll be distracted when he tries to evade it; he'll tense up when you cut him so the wound tears badly; his stress will make him slower to heal. All device-led, and all psychosomatic of course, but no less real for that.

'Don't look so pleased,' she added. 'You should see the damage he could do to you with a weapon made of wood.'

'How could he tell?' Jory wondered. 'Steel looks the same as any other metal when someone's swinging it at your face.'

Malory beamed. 'Good question. Our best theory is that it's vestigial human magnetoreceptivity, enhanced like the other senses by the presence of a device.'

Jory shook his head. 'So what you're saying is that objects have power,' he concluded. 'Just like in the legends.'

'No,' sighed Malory. 'Haven't you been listening? Objects are just objects. The way we perceive them gives them power.' She leaned back, put her feet up on the archetypal descendant of the Round Table of Camelot. 'If you live and move in the world of the devices, you'll inevitably perceive some objects as having power over you, whatever they actually are.

'I'm telling you this,' she said, 'because the Circle doesn't. It's stuff you need to know.'

***

Jory emerges from Waterstones onto the somewhat charred tiling of the upper gallery. The air is laced with smoke, strong perfume and horse-piss.

The men-at-arms' grenade has brought down the tiled ceiling, which crunches underfoot. A pile of bodies, few of them intact at a swift glance, lies in front of the blackened shell of Miss Selfridge. They're not the only dead or injured people lying around – but no horses, which presumably means Paul got clear.

A sergeant-at-arms runs up to Jory, relieved to see a conscious Knight. 'He's done a runner, sir,' he says. 'The leader, I mean, him with the tattoo. Ran over one of our field medics driving out of the car park.'

Behind the bodies, the doors to the stairwell leading to the SS headquarters hang askew from their hinges. 'I'll be with you in a sec,' Jory tells the man and takes them at a run.

The stairs are littered with groaning Shieldsmen clutching at their various limbs, a few of them no longer attached. Jory follows the trail up and through the broken glass doors to the top-floor offices.

This evening's not the time for Jory to be a hero. Tonight he's to be a supporting character in someone else's legend. That's OK. The devices are nothing if not an ensemble cast.

These rooms are open-plan, the latest thing in motivational workplace design when this complex was built. They look only marginally less welcoming with all the desks and soft partitions taken out and replaced with weapon-racks, map-tables and a cabinet displaying Saxon artefacts. There's a crude bar, barrels sitting on trestles, and even a portable dancefloor, which Jory guesses they've been using as a miniature parade-ground. The alternative is too hideous to contemplate.

The lights are off, the windows shuttered, with tiny slits which he presumes you can stick a gun through. There aren't many SS men left around, and those who are seem to have been injured. A couple are feeling well enough to have a go with their swords as Jory passes, but despite his wounded arm and loss of strength, he doesn't find much effort's needed to get them to drop it.

In the very centre of the space there's a platform. Mounted on it is a large white object – or possibly an assemblage of small objects, depending on how you count things.

It's been posed carefully to echo the cantering figure of the Uffington White Horse (which hangs, white on black, on banners all along the two long walls). The stylised hill-figure makes more sense as a skeleton, Jory realises, though it's far from naturalistic even so.

The horse's bones have been decorated with ribbons, and piled up in front of them are fruit and cured meat, tins and bottles, paper money and coins, like some macabre harvest festival.

'Hello?' a voice calls, and Jory suddenly recalls the urgency of his quest here.

At the far end of the mead-hall – Jory's no longer thinking of it as an office – are two closed-off rooms, an outsized wooden shield emblazoned with the Horse hanging between them. Beneath it stands a podium, for Hill and Noake to take turns fulminating from. The voice is coming from the left-hand door. 'Jory, is that you?' He runs.

Inside are David and two bodies. The room's a mess – upended chairs, scrambled paperwork, a computer on the floor with its casing cracked. A display of press cuttings relating to the Saxon Shield has been ripped from the wall by the force of a falling frame.

The other SS leader – the tattoo-free one – is lying slumped across a desk, David's sword still buried in his chest. He seems to glare his hatred at Jory as he enters, but a second glance tells Jory the man's been dead for minutes.

David's crouched over Trevor Macnamara, whose naked body is a map of cuts and bruises. He's breathing, weakly, but around him is a dark red puddle. With a revolting lurch, Jory realises that David's holding him – gently, lovingly even – by the throat.

'They c-cut him open,' David says. 'Left him to d-d-die.' Trevor's hands are still tied behind his back.

Jory crouches by David, puts a hand on his shoulder. Trevor's still conscious. His expression is weak and confused, but he, like David, looks at Jory imploringly. Though clamped in David's hands, blood trickles from his neck-wound at an alarming rate.

'I'm using both hands,' David says. 'Please, c-call an ambulance.'

Jory stands, heaves the dead terrorist off the desk and uses its landline to dial 999.

* * *

The Circle has its own library, of course, located in the bowels of the Fastness, and its own literature going back well over a thousand years. Its archives contain hundreds of retellings of the Arthurian myths, many of them unique to the Circle. Most are relatively recent, historically speaking: romantic epics, pious propaganda by the Knights of the Circle themselves. A few are genuinely ancient.

Although the Circle's justification for its existence relies on there having been a real King Arthur with actual historical events surrounding him, it's grudgingly acknowledged that the diversity of variant versions of the legends is one of the devices' strengths. Some, though, are judged to be inappropriate for the public domain.

There's one writeup of the Grail myth which Malory recommended to Jory as particularly interesting reading. It's medieval, she says, but she believes it's a transcription into Latin of a much more ancient oral tradition.

It goes – and when I say 'goes', of course I mean 'translates approximately into modern English' – something like this.

In King Arthur's youth, when he was newly come to his High Kingship, there was a knight of the Round Table named Sir Pelles, as young as the High King and as handsome. He could run as swift as a hart, and swim as lithe as an otter, and fight as fierce as a wolf, all for three days and three nights without calling for food or drink. In addition he was devout, and served Christ and his mother Mary with all the devotion not due to his King.

A day came when Sir Pelles rode forth from the King's court at Camelot to seek adventure. He rode alone for many days, through villages and fields and moors and marsh, until he came to a forest, where a castle stood upon a high hill overlooking a bright lake.

The castle was overgrown with creeper, until the white of its stone could hardly be discerned among the green, and guarding its gates were two men bearing shields of a blazon vert. But when Sir Pelles looked more closely, the green of the shields was not a tincture but the colour of the metal itself, which was an ancient weathered bronze, and the knights' swords were of the same verdigrised hue.

Sir Pelles said to the gate guards: 'Greetings, in the name of Christ Jesus our Lord, and of Arthur His High King. Pray tell me, whose castle is this and whom do you serve?'

'Our master is Sir Bertilacus of Hautdesert,' answered the first man, 'who can run as swift as a stallion, and swim as lithe as a salmon, and fight as fierce as a lion, all for five days and five nights without calling for food or drink.'

'A formidable master indeed,' replied Sir Pelles coolly. 'I myself am not unknown for my feats of endurance and fortitude. However, I have been riding for many days, and I long for a kind host's welcome.'

'Then enter, sir,' said the second man, 'for our master is a devout man. He serves the gods of these isles, Lugus and his mother Brigantia, with all his devotion, and takes not his duty of hospitality to strangers lightly.'

'A strange allegiance,' mused Sir Pelles, 'for did not Christ Jesus die to save us from our sins?'

'We know not,' said the men. 'We know only what Sir Bertilacus will have us know.'

They bade him enter, and within, in a hall all hung about with holly and with mistletoe, he found Sir Bertilacus of Hautdesert. He was as tall as a tree, and his hair and beard were as green as his bronze sword and armour, as green as a tree's leaves. He greeted Sir Pelles warmly and promised him meat, wine and a bed for as many nights as he wished to break his journey. And Sir Pelles thanked him heartily, though his host was strange, he thought, and his ways were stranger.

That first evening, Sir Pelles ate and drank well of Sir Bertilacus' bounty and slept in a bed as soft as a lamb's fleece. And during that first night he had a dream.

Sir Pelles dreamed that he was awoken by a bright, golden light. And he arose in his dream and followed the light down stairs of wood and earth, until he reached a cave far beneath the castle, its roof girded and gnarled with tree-roots. And there in an alcove stood a great bronze cauldron, and it was from the cauldron that the light shone. And when Sir Pelles saw it, he awoke at once.

The next day he arose, and rode out hunting with Sir Bertilacus, and on that first day the giant caught and killed a hind. And as they rode home with her carcass, Sir Pelles asked his host, 'Sir, if I may ask, why do you make your home in this forest, so far from the world of men?'

And Sir Bertilacus replied in his giant's voice, 'There is a holy duty which keeps me in this forest of Hautdesert with my servants, and until that is lifted we cannot return to the company of other men.'

That evening after feasting on the hind, Sir Pelles lay down on his bed as soft as a lamb's fleece, and once again he dreamed of golden light. And once again he followed it down the stairs, and into the cave, and to the alcove whence the light was pouring. And in place of the bronze cauldron on that second night he saw a wooden cup, and it was from the cup that the light shone. And when Sir Pelles saw this, he awoke at once.

The second day he again rode out hunting with Sir Bertilacus, and their quarry was a stag, and Sir Pelles had the honour of killing him. And as they rode home with their kill, Sir Pelles asked Sir Bertilacus, 'Pray tell me sir, if it does not offend you, what is this duty of yours which keeps you here in the wilderness, so far from the company of men?'

And Sir Bertilacus answered him, 'I guard a treasure, and this keeps me here, away from the dwellings of men.'

That evening, after feasting on the stag, Sir Pelles dreamed for a third time, and on that third night he followed the light to the underground cavern and found a chalice all of gold, full to the brim with blood-red wine.

And he heard a voice, which told him: 'This is the cup from which my beloved son Jesus Christ supped at the last meal before His death, when He exhorted His disciples to drink wine in memory of Him for ever more. And it is the vessel which they used also to catch His holy blood as it flowed from His wounds on the Cross. You are to be its custodian, Sir Pelles. The Grail will be your glory and your undoing, and the glory and the undoing of the Round Table.' And Sir Pelles knew that the voice he had heard was that of the Blessed Virgin herself.

When Sir Pelles heard the voice, he awoke at once. And he arose immediately, although it was the darkest hour of the night, and lit a candle and walked the halls and corridors of the castle of Hautdesert, seeking out the staircase from his dreams.

He found it darkened, with no trace of the golden light. Carefully in the candlelight he followed the steps of earth and wood down into the cavern far beneath the castle. The roof above him was girded and gnarled with tree-roots, and before him in an alcove stood a drinking-vessel, its form unclear in the candle's half-light.

Sir Pelles wrapped it in his cloak and carried it back with him, up the stairs and to his bedchamber, where he lay down once again but did not sleep.

The next day was the third, and once again Sir Pelles rode out to hunt with Sir Bertilacus, and he carried with him the Grail, wrapped up in his cloak. And as they rode home with the carcass of the great wild boar whom Sir Bertilacus had killed, Sir Pelles asked the giant, 'Sir, if it is not impudent of me to ask, what is the treasure which you guard here in the wilderness, so far from the dwellings of men?'

And Sir Bertilacus replied, 'From another man I would consider your question impudent indeed, but you have slept in my house for three days, and hunted with me, and drunk my wine, and so I shall answer you.

'The treasure is the cauldron of the Lady Brigantia, from which any man, be he so sick he be nearly dead, may drink and at once be whole and healed, unless he be the keeper of the cauldron himself. It was placed here by the Lady Brigantia, and she has appointed me to be its holy protector.'

'You lie,' cried Sir Pelles indignantly. 'For it is the Holy Grail, the drinking-vessel of our Lord Jesus Christ.'

'I know nothing of this Christ,' replied Sir Bertilacus.

'Then you are not worthy to have the keeping of it,' Sir Pelles swore and drew his sword to strike the giant.

They fought, then, and Sir Pelles was sorely wounded, and he felt the verdant poison of the giant's green sword working away in him. And like a wolf injured by a lion, who in desperation turns on his attacker and mortally wounds him in his turn, he thrust his iron sword into the giant's chest and felled him.

Sir Bertilacus lay dying, and said, 'Now I am dying, wretched man, and Brigantia's cauldron will have no guardian. What will become of my holy duty now?'

And Sir Pelles replied, 'I have been appointed custodian of the Grail by the Blessed Virgin herself. See, I have it here.' And he drew out the cup from his cloak. In daylight it was a poor thing, a jar of clay, and the wine within it was but brackish water.

Sir Bertilacus said, 'Then let me drink from it, and I shall be restored. For none are left unhealed save the guardian of the vessel himself, lest he grow too strong and become the invincible High King of all the world. If you are now the cauldron's appointed keeper, then I am no longer, and I may drink. But you must return to my castle and take up my place there, and never return to the world of men until your duty is lifted. And until that day, your wounds will never heal.'

And so it came to pass. Sir Pelles returned to the Castle of Hautdesert, and took the Grail with him, and he kept it there for many years. And during that time, the wound made by the giant's sword of wood-green metal never healed, and Sir Pelles spent those years in great pain. And when at last the High King's knights came searching, with their own prophecies about the Grail, they did not recognise him, for they were young knights whom he had not known at Camelot, and he had grown old and twisted from his wounds. And he did nothing to remind them of his former renown.

And before Sir Pelles died, the guardianship of the Grail passed to another, the bravest and purest of King Arthur's knights, and Sir Pelles was permitted by God's grace to die healed and whole. But that is another story, and one which would take many days in the telling.

But whether Sir Pelles allowed Sir Bertilacus to drink of the Grail and to return whole and healed to the dwellings of men, asking only that he embraced Christ as his Lord thenceforth, or whether he allowed the giant's life to ebb away there in the forest of Hautdesert and buried him within sight of his ivied castle, no tale will say.

7. THE CHAPEL

It's mid-evening in June. The sun's nearing the horizon and Jory's device-borrowed strength is ebbing fast.

He and Paul have stayed behind at Thankaster with a couple of other Knights and their squires, to help the emergency services with the mopping up. Jory's in no hurry to see the Seneschal again tonight, and he urgently needs the brownie points.

The gallery outside the burnt-out wreckage of Miss Selfridge looks like a butcher's counter after a fire. Away from the immediate blast-zone, men-at-arms and squires are helping the fallen on both sides, some of them looking rather dazed themselves. Others are escorting paramedics up the stairs, or carrying the body bags.

'Thanks, you know, for the heroics back there,' Paul says to Jory as they tour the carnage. 'You saved my life, probably.' He sounds marginally resentful.

'You might have been safer where you were,' says Jory, 'what with the gunfire and grenades and so on.'

'Even so, yeah?' His tone's flippant now. Whatever his flaws, his own safety's a minor concern to Paul. He'll make a brave Knight, if not a forgiving one.

Inside Curry's, some TVs are still working. Averse though the Circle is to publicity, it's a reasonable rule of thumb that you can't have a pitched battle involving cavalry inside a crowded retail centre without incurring a certain amount of media attention. When the same organisation's started the day by decapitating a serial killer in a suburban street in broad daylight, it's fair to say connections may be made.

The Circle reluctantly employs a PR firm to take care of such eventualities, and currently a 'spokesperson' is on every screen, explaining that this evening's raid, which has successfully curtailed the activities of a dangerous paramilitary group intent on stirring up racial violence across the country, is unrelated to this morning's action of protecting the public from a murderously violent psychopath.

In related news, Chief Constable Sir Michael Wills is taking 'extended compassionate leave,' following the traumatic events of that morning.

A police forensics team arrives, demanding access to what they call, with constabulary understatement, 'the crime scene'. They throw up their hands and act aghast when they see how much it's been interfered with.

Jory has a word with Superintendent Leibniz, the man in charge of the civil clean-up operation, and after much protesting the officers turn round and go away. The Circle – and that's Jory, as temporary emissary with full local authority – gets to write the report on this one.

Leibniz is a fretful man, but thankfully more pliable than Inspector Kinsey. He tends on the whole to disapprove of violent racist maniacs, and to feel that anything which prevents them using their machine-guns on innocent members of the public is probably a good thing. That said, eighteen of the maniacs in question are dead and thirty or so injured, and this involves an awful lot of report writing.

The remainder of the Shieldsmen – another twenty-odd – are only bruised or dazed, and have already been handed over into the custody of Leibniz's men. It seems vanishingly unlikely that any of them carries a device, but a Knight will visit each of them over the next few days to assess the possibility. A squad of men-at-arms has been parcelled out to guard the local hospitals where the injured have been taken, though they, too, will hand over to the secular police as soon as Leibniz locates the manpower.

Allowing for spin, everything the PR firm's spokesperson – actually an out-of-work actress wearing what looks like an abbreviated Joan of Arc costume – says is true. It's also true that the Circle only intervened against the SS because one of its own was in danger, and that it had previously been extending its aloof patronage to the group, who wouldn't even have come to the attention of the Knights if there hadn't been reason to suspect there were devices involved.

It would be wrong to say that these facts don't trouble Jory, but he's more concerned right now for Trevor's health and David's sanity. When they left in the ambulance – Trevor seeping through his emergency sutures, David hurriedly delegating his operational authority to Jory as the doors slammed shut – they both looked terrible. There's no certainty here: no legend about Sir Percival meeting Hengist or Horsa, who weren't even his contemporaries. Indeed, Percival's a figure whose death is rarely mentioned even in legends. Like a successful player character in a computer game (not an analogy Jory would use, of course), he fades out after completing the Grail Quest.

Even if Trevor's fine, Jory worries about David. Of all the Arthurian devices, Galahad is perhaps the hardest to lay claim to.

'All quiet on the northern front,' says Stephen Mukherjee suddenly, poking his head around the door of the Body Shop branch where Jory's set up a temporary base of operations. 'Evening, Taylor. Battling the dreaded monster paperwork, I see.'

Jory sighs. 'It's fearsome, but I think I'll vanquish it.'

Stephen's in civvies, with his chequerboard shield slung over his shoulder. As usual, his choice of summer clothing involves cricket whites and a cravat. Being a Brideshead stereotype doesn't seem to bother the young man, any more than the fact that the device of the Saracen Sir Palamedes falls to him, a Knight of British Asian origins, by lazy default. (It could have been worse, after all. Palamedes had two younger, obscurer brothers.)

'Need a hand with it?' Stephen asks. 'Otherwise, I'd rather like to be back at the Fastness before the wee smalls.'

He's angling for Jory's permission to leave, which technically he needs, without actually saying so. Jerry Transom, who carries the device of Galahad's dull uncle Sir Lavaine, asked for it two hours ago, and has left for London with his and Stephen's squires.

'Give the Seneschal my best,' Jory agrees. He's had one of the pages book a hotel nearby for tonight, in the hope he'll be allowed to clock off at some point. With Stephen gone, it'll only be him, Paul and a brace of men-at-arms, plus a handful of policemen here.

Just like this morning, in fact. 'Oh. Actually, Stephen,' he adds, as his fellow Knight turns to go, 'take Paul with you, would you? He's done more than enough for one day.' As has Jory, of course, but duty of care's a one-way obligation.

'Stint of childminding?' Stephen grins. 'Of course, old boy. Who's the babysitter and who's the toddler?'

The Palamedes device is notorious for getting sidetracked by its obsessions, which in Stephen's case is likely to involve organising a late-night cricket match with some of the youths from the local council estate. It'll all end in sweary fighting and the odd hospitalisation, so on the whole it's best avoided. Some of his predecessors have had less innocent compulsions.

Jory returns his smile. 'See you back in London, Stephen.'

'Cheerio, then.' And Stephen breezes off to collect Paul, leaving Jory to carry on fretting.

* * *

Jory's first major solo quest as a Knight of the Circle was to escort a lorryload of artwork from London to Edinburgh. A Scottish gallery was hosting a special exhibition of Pre-Raphaelite art to celebrate some sesquicentennial, and the London galleries had clubbed together to loan them a consignment of paintings.

The Circle doesn't normally involve itself in the art world, and its more conservative members haven't quite got over their Victorian predecessors' reservations about the Pre-Raphaelite Brotherhood and their dissolute lifestyle. Even so, Arthurian subjects were a particular favourite with the movement, and the Scots – conscious that one of the capital's major tourist spots was called 'Arthur's Seat', even if nobody's quite sure why – had decided to run with this as a theme of the exhibition.

It was this concentration of subject-matter that set the Circle's alarm bells ringing. The devices, both the Knights' own and the renegades they combat, are primarily symbols – and sometimes (obviously not always) they favour symbolic statements over mere violent conflict. Here was the potential for both: the self-declared enemies of the Round Table might effectively critique the acceptance into high culture of the Victorians' romanticised interpretation of Arthurian values by, say, nicking the paintings and burning them.

Clearly the lorry needed a Circle presence to be truly secure, and Jory, who'd had a poster of Waterhouse's *The Lady of Shalott* on his wall for three years at uni, volunteered to take time out in the run-up to Christmas, the first he'd spent as a Knight, to guard the real thing in its journey up the M1.

It was, to start off with, a very boring assignment. Jory rode in the secure lorry's cavernous trailer, its floor space barely encroached upon by the paintings carefully strapped vertically around its edges, with a curator who was too busy worrying about the artworks to let a triviality like conversation divert him, and two uniformed security guards who were so freaked out by Jory's presence that they barely said a word which wasn't about the job. Being on duty, he hadn't brought a book or radio or any other form of entertainment.

The trailer was heated to a moderate temperature, to preserve the paintings against the December chill. Even so they were wrapped and padded, though clearly labelled for reference at the far end, so Jory could sit in his canvas chair and stare at, for instance, one particularly tiny cardboard rectangle, and know that it was Rossetti's obscure watercolour *The Damsel of Sanct Grael*, which as far as he could remember he'd never seen and would have rather liked to.

They were travelling overnight, the need for discretion outweighing Jory's concerns at not being able to draw on his device's reserves of solar strength. The lorry belonged to a popular haulage company, too common a sight to arouse unwelcome interest.

At a service station somewhere outside Northampton the driver stopped for a loo break, and Jory's fellow guardians left him one at a time to visit the facilities, coming back blowing into their hands and complaining of the cold.

For Jory to have gone in full armour would hardly have chimed with their inconspicuous agenda, so he had to hold it in as he'd been trained to. It's a man's life in the Circle.

When the second guard came back from the loo and banged on the rear doors of the trailer, something pricked at Jory's mind for a moment. Three quick knocks were followed by another a moment later, then a shouted 'Oi!'. The first guard wandered over to unlock the door from the inside. Jory was tingling – galvanised, in the way he was now getting used to, by his device.

(When he'd first described it in these terms to Malory, she'd smirked, and he'd sighed and asked why. She told him that Luigi Galvani, the bioelectricity pioneer, had had as his surname the Italian form of 'Gawain'.

'It's just a word.' He'd been annoyed. 'It doesn't mean anything. I mean, of course it *means* something, but – oh, you know what I mean.')

'Wait a sec,' Jory told the first guard now, a moment too late to stop him releasing the lock.

An instant later a very large man in a hoodie shoved through the door, pushing the guard back into the trailer. The second guard dangled helpless in the crook of his enormous arm.

Half a second after that, Jory – who'd started moving before he had any real understanding of why – cannoned into him.

It was like hitting a wall, but not a structurally sound one. The big man had been standing on the rear step of the lorry, with no room to build up his momentum, whereas Jory had run half the length of the trailer. A moment after he and his armour rammed into the intruder, all three of them – Jory, the big bloke and his hostage – were crashing down onto the pitted tarmac.

As they fell, the short-term memory replaying in Jory's head went *Knock knock knock*, another *knock*, then a muffled shout. Three shorts, one long – then an interruption. The guard had been trying to bang out an SOS before his captor thumped him.

Meanwhile, Jory faced a confused present of sudden midwinter cold, of muscled bulk, of dark-green man-smelling fabric and loud northern swearing. His assailant's face was shrouded in the hood of his garment, tugged tight by drawstrings. The man let go of the guard when they hit the ground, and all three of them began to struggle to their feet.

The would-be-thief had grabbed a wooden pole from the ground and used it to lever himself upright. For some reason he wore a string of silvery Christmas tinsel as a sash. The guard scrambled, then ran for the front of the lorry and the driver's cabin. Jory stood and fumbled his helmet visor shut. He heard the other guard and the curator slamming and locking the trailer doors behind them.

A moment later the vehicle's engines started up. The giant was swinging his pole, as thick as Jory's arm and as long as his entire body, and laughing. Jory drew his sword and stepped back, aware that they were standing such as to prevent the lorry reversing out of its space.

'Back off, mate,' said another voice then, calmly. 'I told you, I get the Knight.'

Jory looked out into what he'd thought was the deserted freight park and realised that he, the huge man and the lorryload of priceless artwork were surrounded by a rough circle of hooded figures.

* * *

'A skeleton?' Malory's voice is distorted by the tinny earpiece on this elderly shopping-centre payphone and by some stuttering of the mobile phone signal wherever she is now. 'That's peculiar. You're certain it's a horse?'

She also sounds obscurely annoyed, though he can't imagine why. It's sunset on a balmy summer night, and Jory's imagination, while fertile, has the occasional blind spot.

'It's a horse all right,' Jory repeats. 'I thought it was odd, that's all.'

'This isn't a particularly good time, Jory,' Malory says. He wonders what she's doing, exactly. Some kind of academic conference?

'Hang on,' he says, and shovels a few pound coins into the machine's slot.

It's not that the Knights aren't allowed mobile phones – the Circle even provides them for bone fide work purposes, although taking them into a combat situation (as Paul did this morning) is discouraged. Still, Paul recovered their clothes from the church hall before leaving, and Jory's back in his civvies – smart jeans and open-necked shirt, with his wallet and keys and penknife present and correct in his pocket. It's just the routine of having a phone – remembering to keep it turned on and carry it around with him, charging it up with actual electricity and all that stuff – that consistently defeats him.

(He once asked Malory whether she thought this was one of the cognitive handicaps of having a device. She laughed shortly and said, 'No, I'm afraid that really is just you.')

'Oh, never mind,' she sighs now, slightly muffled. 'Let me try and remember the background. There's a theory that Hengist and Horsa are late versions of a much older mythic archetype. *Hengest* meant "stallion" in Old English, if I recall, and –' Malory's voice cuts out momentarily, then resumes: '– obviously a variant of "horse". The association's pretty much vanished in the literature, but the Uffington White Horse has been associated with them for centuries. It's possible they originally represented ancient Indo-European horse deities.'

'Really?' Once again, this pre-Christian stuff simply confuses Jory. 'I thought they worshipped the Norse gods.'

The pause is longer this time. '– chronicles, yes. But a lot of other Germanic tribes had legends of twin horsemen as their founders, and there are similar dyads –' another break '– ancient cultures from India to Ireland. That suggests it's a very old ur-myth of the Aryan peoples, which would obviously appeal to your neo-Nazi chums.'

'Trevor's chums,' Jory feels obliged to point out, although he knows full well that Trevor could still die from his injuries. The late Colin Hill – it turns out Alfred Noake's the tattooed one – cut his throat deeply and savagely.

Jory hears a man's voice over the line, an indistinct grumble that becomes (he thinks) familiar for a moment, then cuts out. What on earth can she be up to, he wonders.

'Malory?' he asks, before she comes back on the line.

'– go now, Jory, I'm sorry,' says Malory, and Jory's left listening to the phone's null tone.

* * *

'I found him first,' the huge man Jory didn't yet know as Jack Bennett complained, that midwinter night in the Northampton service station lorry park. 'Any road, we should be grabbing the stuff, not ballroom-dancing with this armour-plated ponce.'

'He's mine,' repeated the second voice. This one wasn't northern, but Jory could only narrow it as far as 'Midlands, not Birmingham'. 'He's my oppo and I fight my own battles. Or are you calling me a coward?' it asked rhetorically.

The man stepped forward from the rough ring of hooded figures. All were wearing tops with hoods drawn tightly over their faces, nearly all dark-green like Bennett's.

Two of them held the guard Bennett had captured, two the lorry's driver. (In what could have been seen as a significant design flaw, the trailer was secure but not the driver's cab.)

These figures varied in size and shape – Jory was sure there were women among them, one of them wearing the only red hoodie on view – but all were similarly shrouded. Surreally, all wore Christmas decorations – some had strands of fairy-lights draped around their shoulders like a stole, some pairs of baubles hanging from their drawstrings, some a star mounted atop their hood.

The effect should have been merry, but it managed at that moment to feel oppressive, dangerous, like Macbeth being menaced by a plantation of Christmas trees. The fact that most of them also carried weapons – spears, bows, long wooden staves – augmented the effect. It was the sort of nightmarish incongruity Jory had learned, even then, to associate with the workings of the devices.

Even if he hadn't, he would have been left in little doubt as the new speaker stepped forward.

He was burly, but not built on Bennett's scale. He carried a heavy long-handled axe, of the kind Jory imagined men using to fell trees. It was twined about with tinsel. Over his hood, the man wore a pair of rubber Christmas reindeer antlers and a holly wreath.

In theory, he looked ridiculous. To Jory, his tawdry headgear looked as regal as a crown.

The device-bearing stranger plucked off the festive hat and pulled his hood back, showing himself to be a black man of about Jory's age.

'Nice sword, pal,' he said. 'Where's your horse?' When he laughed his face creased as though he did it often, but when he stopped it became grim.

There'd been laughter from the other figures, too – again, more challenging than cheery. Jory could see about twenty – more than he could take on alone. He rather hoped the two men locked in the trailer had thought to phone the police.

'What's your name, then, chum?' the man asked.

'Jordan Taylor,' Jory replied, still gripping his sword. He'd left his shield back in the trailer. 'I'm a Knight of the Circle.'

'A Knight of the Circle,' the man said. 'And you're here just for me. Or I'm for you – not that it makes much odds. You see, you fight my teeny-tiny friend there –' the man nodded at Bennett '– then it's just a punch-up. Nothing wrong with that, but it's not what we're here for.'

'We're here for the goods,' Bennett scowled. It wasn't the answer the man had in mind.

'You and me fight,' the black man continued to Jory, 'it's not just any old scrap. You and me – we each brought a guest, didn't we? A special guest. You and me fight, it's your imaginary friend against mine. It's a *contest*.'

Raising his sword slowly, Jory looked around at the man's ring of followers. 'Somehow it doesn't look like a fair one to me.' *I'll give you a contest*, he thought. He felt his anger rising like a wind-fanned fire.

'Right,' the man snapped back, 'and the filth aren't on their way to back you up, eh? Never mind about all that.

If I say so then it's just you and me, and I'm saying let's you and me have it out. Blow for blow, eh? Knock for knock, like in the old days.'

'We're wasting time,' Bennett complained.

The man placed his axe carefully on the ground and stood, loosening the drawstrings on his hoodie further. Come on then,' he taunted. 'Game of buffets, they used to call it. You can go first, if you like.' He placed the cheap antler-wreath back on his head.

Another voice said, 'What is this, improv?' It came from a tall, wiry man who barely filled out his narrow hoodie. An American accent of some kind – Jory was hopeless with those, but he thought the man's vowels sounded Anglicised, as if he'd lived here for some time. 'You know this is not how the story goes. Plus, I hate to remind you, but he's got a *goddamn sword*.'

'Goddamning well noted,' said the black man. 'Come on then, Knight of the Pentacle. Let's see what you've got.'

'Stop pissing about, Shaun,' Bennett snapped. 'We've got a job to do, and you're playing chicken with this… canned twat.'

'Fuck off, Jack,' said the man, still smiling. 'And let's leave the names at that, eh? Mister Taylor's the King's man.'

Jory stared, through the helmet still on his own head, at the sword still in his own hand. 'Your friends are right,' he told the man Shaun. 'You're being ridiculous. I could kill you.' He thought, *And wouldn't that teach you a lesson, you cocky ass.* He found the prospect quite invigorating.

'Maybe,' the man said, 'and maybe not. You never know until you try, do you, you bastard? Come on, you horsefucker,' he chuckled. 'Come and slice me open, if you think you're enough of a man.'

* * *

Jory wanders the aisles of Thankaster shopping mall, watching the Circle's specialist subcontracted cleaners – among the best-paid members of their profession in the British Isles – scrubbing at the walls, floors and (being also among the most thorough) the remaining ceilings, to remove all stains of battle from the building. They're making good progress, although the soot- and bloodstains around the ruins of Miss Selfridge are proving stubborn and hard to shift.

The physical damage to the building and its contents will take longer to put right. The Circle has already offered ample compensation to the businesses impacted by the action, and the mall's owners have their builders tutting over the wreckage. The Saxon Shield's mead-hall and its satellite offices have been sealed, and will be thoroughly examined by the Circle's own rarely-deployed forensics team over the coming weeks. Still, with the exception of the taped-off areas where the greatest damage has occurred, the mall itself should open more or less as normal tomorrow morning.

Or rather, as Jory realises, this morning. It's gone midnight now by the clocks, and is approaching one o'clock in the morning. In British Summer Time, that's solar midnight, the weakest time of day for the Gawain device. On the other hand, it's the morning of Midsummer's Day, and a scant few hours to sunrise.

'Sir, there's a phone call for you,' says a policewoman, approaching Jory with a radio to her ear. 'On the Super's mobile, apparently.'

She leads Jory to Leibniz, who's staring moodily at another troupe of cleaners as they sweep up scattered pills and medicines in Boots. Wordlessly, the Superintendent hands him the phone.

Jory's assuming that Malory's thought of something else, something that couldn't wait till morning. To his surprise though, it's Stephen Mukherjee's voice that greets him, sounding uncharacteristically tense. Jory sighs, dreading to think where his device's wandering attention has led him this time.

'Taylor.' A distorted list of stations tells him that Stephen's on a train, at least. The Knight waits for the announcement to finish. 'They're trying to reach you from the Fastness,' he says. 'Came through on my mobile. Said I'd tell you myself. Hope that was the right thing.'

Jory feels his own throat-muscles tightening. 'Tell me? Tell me what?'

'It's Macnamara,' Stephen says. 'I'm frightfully sorry, Taylor. They couldn't get him stable at the hospital, and he just...' Jory can almost hear him searching his lexicon of gung-ho euphemisms, before finally surrendering to: 'He died.'

'But –' Jory tries to say but finds himself horribly voiceless. He tries again. 'They've been gone hours, though. Why didn't David –'

Jory's not close friends with Trevor, never has been. There's a hearty brotherhood between all the Knights, as you'd expect, a camaraderie backed up by oaths of loyalty. Jory's upset by Trevor's death, but no more than he would have been by Stephen's, or Jerry Transom's, or some of the others whose devices he can never remember without looking them up. To Jory, Trevor's just another brother Knight.

To David, though...

'Yes, well,' says Stephen. 'It seems Stafford didn't report it straight away. He's quite cut up about it, evidently. Well, you heard him earlier on. They must have been... close, I suppose you'd say. Jolly good friends. It's a damned shame for him.'

Even with Trevor gone, Jory could have guessed that David's speech to the men earlier this evening wouldn't go unnoticed. There's no question of him being expelled from the Circle – the devices choose their hosts, and it's not for human beings to question that – but David's standing among their fellow Knights may never recover.

Like I say, Galahad's pretty much the most demanding device the Circle has access to. Among the Knights of Round Table, he's almost a Christ-figure, as his emblem would suggest. He was the one the Siege Perilous was waiting for: celibate, sinless, uniquely worthy of that hotseat, and of the mystical union with God embodied by the Grail.

Jory only has to stand around in the sunlight for a bit for his device to start enhancing his strength. If he went and lived in the Arctic Circle, he could keep it up for months at a time. The Sir Galahad device draws its power from abstinence and austerity. *His strength was as the strength of ten*, as Tennyson said, *because his heart was pure.*

How's any actual human being going to live up to that?

* * *

In retrospect, it should have been obvious what was happening – but Jory, like all Knights, like all bearers of devices, was if not blind then at least very short-sighted when it came to his own story.

Even so, in that midwinter midnight, when he was furthest from the sun and his device's strength was at its lowest ebb, he should have seen it. But he was still quite new to his device, and tired, and frankly he needed a piss.

'If I strike you down,' he pointed out quietly and reasonably to the man with the antlers, 'your friends here will tear me to pieces. Armour or no armour.'

'If you strike me down…?' the man Shaun grinned. 'Didn't have you down as a *Star Wars* fan.' His face became lugubrious again beneath his wreath, and he looked around at his followers. 'Listen, all of you,' he said. 'Whatever happens, this is on me, right? No comeback for Darth here. Just tie him and his mates up, do the job, then leave them be. Everyone good with that?'

'For fuck's sake, Shaun,' the woman in the red hoodie,

a Scot by her voice, drawled. 'What're you playing at? We can take this wanker easy. Christ, six of us could hold him down while the rest of you take the paintings and smoke the van.'

'That's enough,' the black man barked. There was an angry silence.

'As it happens, Shaun, I have seen *Star Wars*,' Jory said, keeping a tight lid on his seething anger. 'And if you think me killing you will mean you come back as something more powerful, you're insane. I mean in an actual medical way. That's understandable, it's a consequence of the… arrangement you've made. But whatever your protector's telling you, he can't heal a mortal blow, or bring you back from the dead. The devices can't work miracles.'

'Devices?' Shaun snorted. Some of his fellows tittered. 'That what you think they are? Personal accessories? Your friend's a Swiss Army Knight then, is he? Mobile phone with the powers-that-be on speed dial? Holy satnav guiding you along your spiritual path? I don't think so, chum.'

'That's not –' Jory snapped, then shut his mouth. It was futile to argue. The police would be here at any moment – he'd been trying to dampen his fast-raging fury by calculating how long they'd be, but there were too many variables. (How quickly did the lorry's remaining occupants call them? Had there been patrol cars already out on the motorway? Were they waiting for armed backup before coming in?) It would be humiliating for a Knight of the Circle to be bailed out by the secular police force, but far less humiliating than failing in his quest completely.

'You've bought into everything they've told you, haven't you?' Shaun snapped. His rubber antlers wobbled in a way which might, in other circumstances, have been comedic. 'You're so grateful to be allowed into their bloody gentlemen's club that you just lap up whatever they say.'

Jory gripped his sword until his gauntlet bit into his fingers.

'Oh, I can tell you're not one of them,' the man Shaun

sneered. 'Even if I was wrong about *Star Wars*, I can see *that* plain as day. It's the way you stand, the way you talk. You come from working folk, like me and Jack here. Like the lot of us. No silver spoon in your mouth, Mr Knightly. You're one of us, a poor bloody Saxon yeoman.'

If he'd been calmer, Jory would have noted the black man's claim to be 'Saxon'. It might have saved him some tedious clarification a few years later. But he was barely keeping his wrath in check, and was in no position to be noting anything.

'Oh yeah, you're one of us,' said Shaun. 'Started off that way, at least. But it's not about where you've come from, is it? It's about where you've ended up. You were one of us once, but you've gone over to their side. The bosses, the management, the fucking barons. You know what you are, Taylor? You're an executive thug. You're a collaborator, a scab, an Uncle Tom. A bastard traitor is what you are.'

Sir Gawain stepped in then. That's how it felt to Jory, as if the device literally walked into his body and moved it like a suit of armour. He lifted Jory's sword, and swung his arm, and struck the head of the insolent churl from his shoulders. Shaun's features gaped in pantomime astonishment as the blow connected, then his head spun away to hit the tarmac with a sound that would remain with Jory for a very long time.

After that, the situation became rather heated.

* * *

Jory steps outside into the shopping centre's car park. He's told Leibniz he's going for a cigarette. He's never smoked, even at school, but right now he'd take it up for real if it would give him an excuse to be alone for a few moments.

He stays there for long minutes. Every so often there'll

be a movement or a rustling of the bushes at the far edge of the car park, and he looks up out of now-instinctual habit. It's always some clubber walking home from a night on the town, or an insomniac dog-walker. The SS has been comprehensively broken, Noake has fled, and any Shieldsmen stupid enough to be still hanging around will be no threat at all. That isn't what's disturbing Jory.

What's disturbing him is this. All his attempts to remember the obscurer details of the legends (Did Hengist or Horsa ever kill a notable knight? How did Vortigern die? Did Galahad outlive Percival?) were academic. Worse than that (since one of his best friends is, after all, an academic), they were actively deceiving.

It's easy to forget, when you live like Jory in a world saturated with the devices' influence, that these iconic meme-archetype things don't dictate reality. In all the time Jory's been with the Circle, he's never seen anything done by a device-bearer, friend or foe, which hasn't fallen firmly within the laws of physics. Not only those, but also those of anatomy, even, he gathers, of clinical psychology.

All the devices can do is guide the minds and bodies of those they protect, and even there that guidance is far from binding. They motivate and hint and persuade; they never coerce. It's far more like divine inspiration than demonic possession.

Jory hasn't always thought so, of course. That night in Northamptonshire, he was certain that Sir Gawain himself had literally taken charge of his body. But that's the seductive thing about knowing the devices: you can define part of yourself as other. The devices are, as Malory's often told him, aspects of our selves, bundles of our best and worst instincts, suppressed or disowned or never-quite-fulfilled, given identity and personality within our minds. It's why they're so very dangerous.

Even at school, even when the less safety-conscious

of his peers jeered at him for his clothes or his accent, Jory never let his anger show. He harnessed it systematically, directed it into actions which made it known he wasn't the kind of person who would be bullied. Externally, and before very long even consciously, his fury was undetectable.

Before his binding to the Gawain device, he would have said he wasn't an angry person. Afterwards, that it was his device who was prone to wrath, not him.

But that repressed rage, the fire of humiliation, of being the butt of taunts about his class, his parents, his home – it hadn't gone away. It was there all the time, beneath the threshold of his conscious mind. And with the arrival of his device, it had an outlet.

It's taken Jory years to realise this, but now he knows that everything he does – from his wandering mind at his vigil to his current slacking-off, from Shaun Hobson to James Ribbens – happens on his own recognisance. Being under the influence of his device no more absolves him than if his mood had been altered by drink or drugs. It's only the extraordinary authority which the Circle wields that makes him an executioner and not a murderer.

Unlike Colin Hill, God rot him.

Never mind Percival and Vortigern, Hengist and Horsa. Hill and Macnamara had quite enough history of their own. Noake and Hill had trusted Trevor – had, indeed, seen him as their man on the inside, in the Romano-British-Celtic-Norman-Jewish-Asian-African mongrel establishment – and he betrayed them.

If Hill wanted to kill Trevor, which very obviously he did, he didn't need his device's permission. Hengist and/or Horsa might try to dissuade him, and Sir Percival would urge Macnamara to defend himself to the utmost… but if Hill chose deliberately to slit the throat of a tied-up prisoner, then neither his nor anyone else's device could possibly have stopped him.

What good, then, are the devices? They don't turn

people into gods or devils. They don't even turn them into storybook knights and ogres, though their hosts may do their best to act out those roles. What they undoubtedly do – what, in fact, Malory's entire academic interest in them is based on them doing – is turn more-or-less sane people (though admittedly unusual enough to bind themselves to a device in the first place) into wildly dysfunctional ones.

However marginal David Stafford's future career might be now, Jory knows his friend's mental balance must be even more precarious. His – the choice of word doesn't come easily to Jory, but he supposes his lover – is dead, and Jory knows from his passionate speech at the church hall how terribly that will have taken him.

For David to recover from this, after all his earlier troubles, would need a minor miracle, and that's something the devices can never provide.

Another shape moves in the distant bushes, and Jory glances up disinterestedly. Sir Gawain must be sleeping on the job, because he's actually looked away before it registers that this is no stray late-night hedonist, no sleepless pet-owner. Not unless they have a very good reason to hide their face inside a hoodie, or to wear stag-party antlers from a joke shop, or to wreathe them about with strands of Japanese knotweed.

Or, for that matter, to be carrying a bow made from a treebranch with the leaves still on it, and a quiverful of arrows.

The figure steps forward from the bushes, the unseen eyes within his cowl fixed upon Jory's.

* * *

You might think that the members of the Green Chapel, having seen their friend and de facto leader cut down before their eyes, might respect his dying wish and final instruction, not to take any action against his murderer.

Not if you actually knew them, though. One yelled,

'Stop! Let's leave that idiot and take the valuables!', but this was obviously not the majority view.

The moment after Jory had decapitated Shaun Hobson, he was being set upon by a crowd of hooded figures, many of them spangled with baubles or sparkling with fairy lights. There was frenzied shouting and repeated being-hit-with-things.

Had any of his assailants had a gun, they could have done for him there and then, but apparently Hobson had insisted on carrying out this raid the old-fashioned way. All Jory's armour had to contend with was spears and cudgels. Even so, Bennett's flailing quarterstaff succeeded in cracking two of his ribs. He wouldn't have lasted five minutes against so many, if the Northamptonshire Road Policing Unit (who'd been observing the situation from a distance while they waited for an armed response team) hadn't belatedly decided that the situation called for intervention.

The melee dispersed at once, and the Green Chapel's members scattered. The police gave chase, but their quarry had already melted away into the nearby scrubland, and presumably thence to the farms and villages beyond. They left behind both meaty cuts of Shaun Hobson's carcase, but seemed – based on the later inventory of the crime scene – to have taken his woodman's axe away with them.

Jory, the body, the guard and driver (both badly beaten up themselves), the other guard, the gallery curator and the lorry full of priceless art treasures had to wait inside a police cordon while three more Knights of the Circle were dispatched from London: one to take charge of the clean up and containment quest at the service station; one to protect artworks as they proceeded (with a police convoy, this time) up the M1 towards Edinburgh; and one to escort Jory back to the Fastness for medical attention and what's still his only disciplinary debriefing.

They were stern, the Seneschal and the panel of senior

and retired Knights, including Edward Wendiman, who heard his case, but in the end he was surprised and mortified by how easy on him they went. He was suspended from active duty for three months, his pay was docked to cover a small fraction of the Circle's additional expenses, and he was sent on a penitential pilgrimage to Tintagel.

All of them understood exactly why Jory had behaved as he did, although he needed it spelled out explicitly before the obvious facts managed to penetrate the fog of story-blindness clouding that corner of his mind. Shaun Hobson had been carrying the device of the Green Knight, Sir Gawain's antagonist in one of his most legendary starring roles.

In the original Middle English poem the Knight turns up, literally green from the curls bobbing above his green hood down to the hooves on his horse, at King Arthur's New Year banquet, and insists – demands, in fact, quite forcefully – that someone cuts his head off for him. The not-unexpected catch is that anyone who does must agree to the Green Knight doing the same to them at his Green Chapel, the same time next year. Brave Sir Gawain rises to the challenge of course, and follows through with a clean neck-severing, whereupon the Knight picks up his head and gallops off with it. Next New Year it's Gawain's turn, and hilarious hijinks ensue.

In the written-down version, the Green Knight's a man enchanted by Morgan le Fay, the evil sorceress, to look and act the way he does. Considered as a myth though, he's obviously a nature-spirit, a symbol of the annual rebirth of greenery, conceptually descended from some Celtic god of crops or woodland.

If Hobson really thought the Green Knight device would help him re-enact the universal myth of death and rebirth, he was embarrassingly mistaken. His body was impounded by the police, lay for a few months in a Northamptonshire morgue and was eventually cremated.

(The Circle arranged it while Jory was on his long walk to Cornwall, to stop him turning up at the ceremony and moping.) Hobson had no living relatives, and unsurprisingly no one from the Chapel stepped forward to claim his body.

A year or two later, a new and rather young member of the Green Chapel happened to have a conversation with a member of another eco-activist group, who was sleeping with a member of a third eco-activist group, who was in fact an undercover policeman, and the information reached the Circle that the Chapel were planning to break into the mansion of a certain influential businessman-turned-MP with a notoriously bad environmental record, steal his stuff, kidnap him and hold him to ransom.

When they tried, a detachment of men-at-arms was waiting for them, and in the ensuing fight Jack Bennett was taken into Circle custody. At the Seneschal's order, Jory's involvement with this quest was confined to the post-arrest assessment process.

Both then and since – until now, in fact – Jory has been unable to establish whether the Green Knight device has chosen a new carrier from among the Green Chapel's ranks. He's sure that any new host will do his best to reciprocate the fatal blow that Jory landed on Shaun Hobson.

And now? Right now there's a new Green Knight and he's directly in front of Jory, no more than twenty metres away. Before Jory can even properly process what he's seeing, Hobson's successor nocks an arrow, draws and shoots.

His movements are fast as lightning in the forest, as unstoppable as a tree's slow upgrowth.

Jory's still in his civvies. With no enemy to fight but bureaucracy, he discarded his armour hours ago. The night's so mild that not even his thin jacket impedes the arrow's progress as it thuds into his upper arm.

It's of a strange design, the wood spliced with tough plastic. There seems to be a hollow outer barrel, and an inner shaft. It looks as if the arrow compressed when it hit him. As yet there's no pain, but his arm's experiencing a strange and spreading chill.

A hypodermic arrow? Jory thinks. He's tireder than he realised. 'That's… unexpected,' he says aloud.

The Green Knight approaches him – no, Jory reminds himself, trying to suppress his rising panic, not the Knight, but just a man bearing a device, no different from Jory himself – the stranger approaches him across the car park. He seems to stride with inhuman speed, but perhaps Jory's eyes are just working slowly. His brain certainly is.

His own legs feel a bit wobbly, so he sits down.

The antlered man arrives in front of him and towers overhead. When he was over by the bushes, Jory remembers, he didn't look so tall – a bit shorter than average, if anything. Perhaps it's the antlers. Or perhaps Jory himself is shrinking, collapsing down into nothing at all. That seems plausible.

A voice arrives, as if from a great distance. For a moment, Jory mistakes himself for a radio-telescope array picking up signals from some distant star. This one reads, 'Hello, Jory.' *Little green men*, thinks Jory.

This man's not actually green, though his skin's darker than Jory's. His face, like his voice, is familiar, though Jory must have somehow missed him taking off his party horns and pulling back his hoodie.

Jory tries to beam back a response signal, but his array's losing power. His lips won't move, and he just can't muster up the energy to vibrate his vocal cords and say *Hello, Shafiq.*

He decides to rest his eyes as well.

8. THE OAK

Jory ascends slowly from the bedrock, drifting like a bathyscaphe through depths where branching forms slumber and twitch, to lighter realms where arrows dart like eels and shields flick past him in heraldic shoals, then at last to the surface, where he passes ghostly through a wooden hull, into a sunlit cabin which creaks and sways, and wakes.

His dream evaporates, and he opens his eyes to find himself inside a creaking, swaying, sunlit room.

He's lying on a mattress – clean enough, though bare and none too luxurious – against one wooden wall. The room's small, the mattress taking up a full third of the floor. The wooden walls are straight, with no shipshape slopes or curves, and a window – square, not a porthole – in the furthest.

There's a trapdoor in the centre of the floor. His arm hurts like a bastard.

The room's gentle motion, which he rather hoped was an effect of waking, doesn't go away. Nor does the creaking, nor the gentle lulling whoosh of waves.

It takes a while for him to process all of this.

Someone's left him a tumbler of water, which he gulps down gratefully, and a cheese-and-pickle sandwich on a plastic plate. He'd prefer something meaty, but he's famished and wolfs it up. The bread is home-baked and delicious, the cheese mature and rather too salty. He wishes he'd kept some water back.

His upper arm's been dressed and bandaged – and the cut in his elbow redressed as well – but the pain is more than he'd have expected. Still, he's never been shot with an arrow before, and has no idea how it's supposed to compare to a bullet wound.

Rehydrated and recarbohydrated, he decides to try out his legs. They threaten to buckle at first, but he calls their bluff and they co-operate. Standing upright, he finds his head only just clears the wooden ceiling. He peers out of the window and blinks in disorientation.

Oak-leaf branches rustle in what must be a stiff breeze. His floor is swaying with the tree-trunk they spring from. Beneath the canopy of leaves below him, he sees grass.

Oh, he thinks, *that would make sense.* He feels foolish, yet still slightly seasick.

Between the branches he sees tents, a woodchip path and what he thinks must be a tepee, or possibly a yurt. Beyond them more trees, mostly conifers – they're in a semi-clearing in what must be a reasonably sized wood. A woman in a tough brown dress walks past, glancing up reflexively at the oak-tree he's in. She doesn't seem to notice him.

In all his time with the Circle, Jory's never been captured by an enemy before. It's not easy to keep the panic at bay, but his reason tells him sternly that the Green Chapel evidently want him alive. He settles for cursing his own carelessness at Thankaster instead.

Would he be jumping to conclusions to assume this encampment is the Chapel's headquarters? As far as he knows, the Circle's never had a location for them. His guess now would be that that's because they move around. Is there a physical Chapel, he wonders? Has there ever been? Or is the Chapel wherever its members build it?

He tries the trapdoor. As he supposed, it's bolted from the outside. He suspects that if he did force it open he'd see a sheer drop to the ground, and a ladder lying there.

He gives it a try anyway – kicking, stamping, even jumping up and down on it. It helps ease his feelings a little. The wood creaks, splinters slightly, but the hatch and its mounting have been made sturdy, and it holds.

He looks around for something to sit on, eventually settles on folding the mattress in two. He waits.

* * *

When he hears scraping beneath the trapdoor, he stands back and readies himself. There's a sound of one, two, three bolts sliding aside, and he prepares to stamp down hard on whoever's head appears in the gap.

Instead, a spear pokes through. Not jabs – it's a precaution, not an attack. Changing tactic, Jory drops to his knees and seizes the weapon's shaft, but he can't keep his grip through the pain in his arm. The spear twists away from him, the hatch flies open and a man's head and arms emerge.

He keeps the point towards Jory – again, a warning only – as he climbs into the boxy room and closes the hatch.

'Sleep well?' Shafiq Rashid asks.

Jory fumbles at him, but Shafiq bangs him on the shoulder with the spear and his arm flares up again. Jory staggers over to the folded mattress and sits down.

'The sedative won't have completely worn off,' Shafiq says. 'Besides, this stuff's all made of wood.'

Shafiq wears one of the Green Chapel hoodies, with no adornments this time, and black denim jeans. There are a few more lines around his eyes and mouth, and he's grown a modest goatee which rather suits him, but otherwise he looks much the same as when Jory last saw him, shortly after Jory's acceptance and his rejection by the Circle.

They promised that day to stay in touch, the two of them and Malory, but in practice Jory's lost contact with almost everyone he knew before his supplication. Knighthood just seems to work that way.

For a while he followed Shafiq's career – not his unremarkable scientific research, but his involvement in British and international competitive archery. It's not a high-profile sport, or one in which Great Britain excels these days, but Shafiq enjoyed some brief and very minor celebrity after a spectacular Olympic match which gained him Britain's first silver medal in the sport in about a century. (Since the 1908 London Olympics, in fact, when three-quarters of the archers participating were British and, oddly enough, won most of the medals. This sort of thing was deemed acceptable back then.)

Since then, Shafiq's dropped out of view rather. Jory hasn't heard his name for ages – not in an archery context, certainly not through Malory, who he supposes has lost touch with him too. He's been assuming that his old friend's found a lectureship somewhere, perhaps settled down with a nice Muslim girl, had kids. On the rare occasions he's given it any thought, Jory's rather envied him. He's certainly been keeping no tabs on him.

What was it Shafiq just said? Something relevant. 'Yesterday morning,' Jory begins, then realises can't be sure that it's still the day after his confrontation in Snowdon Street. Never mind. 'I pulled the side off a shed,' he says. 'A wooden one.'

'Yes.' Shafiq laughs. 'I saw photos of the shed afterwards. They were in the paper. But you were out in the sun trying to get inside, not shut in a wooden treehouse wanting to force your way out. And you hadn't been shot with a wooden arrow, either.'

The Circle has certain issues with wood, Jory knows. In its proper place, furniture for example, it's fine. The big round boardroom table at the Fastness is made of wood.

(Plastic tables look far too common, and you try making something that size out of glass or metal.) The Nestine-Gull Grail's wooden too, though the Circle don't think of that as being exactly theirs.

But the Circle – and its Knights, and most especially their devices – work better with other materials. The Circle's arms are iron, its fortresses stone. Well, steel and concrete these days, or various durable plastics, but it's the same principle. Its buildings are solid, definite things, made of edges and corners. They make their boundaries known, just as their weapons leave you in no doubt when you've been cut with one. They last, and remain useful, long after organic stuff like bodies has disappeared.

Wood to the Circle is alien, insinuating, ambiguous. It belongs *outside*. It comes with no straight lines, with porous boundaries. It curves and bends and sprouts and makes more of itself. It springs up from the earth of its own accord, unbidden by human technologies. It warps and sags and rots, and then returns to being part of what it came from.

Worst of all, it's alive – first with its own life, then with moulds and insects, then as a life-giver to other things. How can you exert a decent level of control over that?

People who build with stone, and fight with metal, build and fight for keeps. They want their position to be secure and unassailable. They cleave earth and flesh alike in clean, flat planes. They impose order on the world, lay down foundations for generations yet to come. When the stone-builders come to the forest, the forest yields.

People who build and fight with wood have seen life cut short. They construct, they inhabit, they move on. They take their dwellings with them, or leave them to biodegrade. Like their materials they're pliable, adaptable, transplantable: their seed springs up everywhere. Like trees, they enter castles only after they've fallen.

* * *

'So,' says Jory. 'You got yourself bound to a Knightly device after all.'

Shafiq smiles thinly. 'That's not how we'd put it here. We're not so keen on Knights, or binding for that matter. But yes, it's true in your terms.'

'But it's a rogue device,' says Jory. 'A renegade. What's the point of that?'

Shafiq sighs. 'All *that* means is that it falls outside your control. It's a point outside your Circle, that's all. And since I wasn't welcome inside... well, what else was I to do?'

'Not that. Really... just... not that.' Jory isn't feeling at his best just now. A simple confrontation might be reviving, but arguing moral absolutes seems suddenly like an overwhelming challenge. 'Listen, I don't know how you got involved with the Green Chapel, or how this device chose you. But taking on a rogue device isn't just an alternative lifestyle. This isn't some hippie commune you're running, it's a terrorist cell.'

'Is it really.' Shafiq looks distinctly less friendly now.

'Of course it is,' says Jory. 'You use intimidation to further a political agenda. That's terrorism in my book. You sabotage nuclear power plants, you steal and vandalise corporate property, you *certainly* assault security staff. You tried to steal those Pre-Raphaelite paintings, remember? I was there. You kidnap MPs...'

'You stopped us doing those last two things, of course,' Shafiq says. 'But yes, we try.'

'Well, then,' says Jory. Frustratingly, that that doesn't seem to be the end of the argument. 'Look, we're friends... or we used to be. I know I haven't been in touch for ages, my life's so hectic nowadays, you wouldn't believe... sorry. The thing is, I'm bound to the Sir Gawain device.'

'I know,' Shafiq replies. 'That pentacle's a dead giveaway.'

'But you know what that means,' says Jory. 'You must have read the literature.'

'Of course I have, Jory.' Shafiq sounds angry now. 'What I can't work out is why you see it as some kind of binding contract. Why do we have to be enemies, just because a fourteenth-century manuscript says so? Aren't we better than that?'

'We could try,' Jory admits. There are other devices, Knightly figures firmly within the borders of the Circle, whose legends speak of deadly feuds. Their bearers are expected to put that aside and work together as professionals. 'But it's an uphill struggle. A needless one, if you hadn't been so reckless in the first place. And frankly, while you're running the Green Chapel I'm not inclined to try.'

'So what, you'll just chop my head off?' Shafiq snaps. 'Like you did Shaun Hobson's? Fuck you, Jory, I was there, I saw what you did.' The four-letter word gives Jory a nasty twinge. Shafiq has changed more than he realised.

'I get the pressure you were under, I know Shaun was provoking you, but... honestly man, I felt sick, just really physically sick that someone I thought was my friend would do a thing like that,' Shafiq says. 'I tried to stop the others piling on you afterwards, but frankly I felt like stabbing you myself.

'You killed a man, another friend of mine, just because you thought you and he were... what, destined to be enemies by some medieval legend? You...' he struggles for control. 'You, of all people, you have *no right* to judge me!'

Angrily, but not dropping his guard, never looking away from Jory, he squats, picks up his spear and opens the trapdoor.

'Merry thought,' he says, bizarrely. 'Hell, I thought... Well, never mind. The Circle will pay a good ransom for you, that's the thing to remember. Maybe they'll even exchange you for Jack Bennett. They won't have realised he's worth ten of you.'

With all the dignified rage any man can muster when backing cautiously down a ladder, Shafiq leaves.

* * *

It's a hot day, and although the planks of Jory's treehouse are loose enough to allow for ventilation, the air quickly becomes stuffy and oppressive. He wishes he'd asked for some more water before antagonising Shafiq. Outside the angle of the sunlight changes, casting the shape of the window on the wooden floor. Jory's worked out from its slow creep that it must be late afternoon, by the time the hatch opens again, and a white woman of about twenty appears. She's wearing jeans, a green top and something that could be a hijab or just a headscarf. Her face is pretty, her expression fixed in neutral.

She's carrying a gun, which she keeps casually trained on Jory. He can tell at once that she knows how to handle it. Someone beneath her on the ladder passes her a ceramic jug of water and a plastic tumbler, which she brings up and hands to him.

He smiles at her. 'No glass? No, I suppose not.'

She doesn't answer, doesn't smile, but hesitates slightly before reaching down again, and bringing up a pile of clothes. He wonders whether her first language isn't English.

She nods and goes, closing the door behind her – but not before, to his considerable relief, adding an empty bucket to his prison inventory. It's not the arrangement he'd have preferred, but right now he'll happily take what he can get. Once he's finished, he changes into the clothes – black tracksuit, no hood. He's been sweating into his civvies since sleeping in them, so he's not going to be precious about that either.

He hears occasional voices from outside – men and women talking, even children playing – but they're muffled by the wood and by the window's glass. He's considered breaking it and climbing down the tree outside, but the noise would attract attention and at the moment he can't trust his arm to support his weight.

Still, maybe once it's dark he'll give it a try. It can't be *that* far to the ground.

The afternoon wears on. The room becomes steadily more stifling.

Later, a man – no, a boy, a teenager – comes with a tray and to refill his pitcher. He speaks, but tersely, introducing himself with an 'All right.' Again, he carries a gun, though he holds it with less confidence, making Jory instantly more wary of him.

He's brought a plate of pasta with tomato sauce, a fork and spoon to eat it with, a lump of the salty cheese, an apple. The boy takes away the bucket without comment, replacing it with an empty one. Jory refuses to feel embarrassed – if you hold people prisoner, then there are certain things you have to deal with. 'Need your clothes too,' the lad says, and takes them. 'Later' he says – a neutral farewell, not a threat – and slams and bolts the trapdoor.

As Jory eats, the sun gets lower still, and eventually the sky starts to darken. The muffled voices from outside become more numerous and less occasional, until they're convivial and continuous. Someone puts some music on, but all Jory can hear is a thumping bass beat.

After a while, Shafiq comes back. Wordlessly he takes the tray and contents and passes them down the ladder, peers into the still-empty bucket, refills the pitcher.

Then he says, 'If I let you out to stretch your legs, will I have your word of honour you won't hurt anyone or make a run for it?'

'You still trust me, then?' Jory answers. He's obscurely pleased by that.

'I'm not sure I even still know you,' Shafiq says flatly. 'But I know you're bound by a code of honour. So do you want a walk or not?'

'All right, then.' Jory selects the right words. 'If I can leave this room with you, I give you my word that I won't attack anybody or try to escape as long as I'm out there.'

'Nicely equivocated. Let's say until I've closed the hatch and taken the ladder down.'

Jory nods, and Shafiq throws back the hatch. Jory steps forward, but he stops him with a hand.

'One thing,' he says. 'You'll meet people out there – my people, Green Chapel people. They know that you're a Knight of the Circle, and that you and I go way back. They also know, because most of them were there, that a Knight named Jordan Taylor killed their friend Shaun Hobson. What they won't know is that you're him. The only one who got a good look at your face that day was Jack Bennett, and you've got him locked up.'

He sees Jory's expression, and he sighs. 'I'm not asking you to lie, idiot. I'm saying that if you volunteer the truth, they're likely to kick the shit out of you. Hardly anyone here uses their real name anyway. I've told them yours is Dan. Do you think your code of honour will permit you to answer to that?'

* * *

Out here, the sound of festivity is unambiguous. Voices of all ages are chatting, arguing and singing along to the music, around what seems to be a camp fire. It's all a lot louder than Jory realised.

At the bottom of the ladder there's a tall, muscular woman in her thirties. She has dyed-scarlet hair, wears boots and combat trousers and carries a gun in a shoulder-holster. She looks as if she's been on guard.

'It's all right, Scar,' says Shafiq. 'I've got him on his best behaviour.'

Scar nods and says, 'OK.' She puts her hands in her pockets, nods again and says, 'I hope a tree falls on the fucker, then.' She turns to go.

'I thought you said they didn't know who I am?' Jory protests as she stalks off. He recognises her voice as that of the Scotswoman in Northampton.

'Scar? No, she doesn't,' Shafiq says. 'She just hates the Circle. More so since Shaun, but before then, even.'

'Right,' Jory says. He'd expected being a prisoner to be uncomfortable, humiliating, possibly agonisingly painful. He hadn't realised that it would be so socially awkward.

'You don't need babysitting,' Shafiq says. 'When you're finished, I'll be over there.' He points across to the centre of the clearing, where Scar's gone and where the party's clearly happening.

Instead Jory walks the dark perimeter of the encampment. Beyond, pines and spruces loom against a starry sky, untainted by the orange light of any city.

As Shafiq surely realises, his temporary promise doesn't mean that Jory's not going to note the lay of the land, or map out mentally the best escape routes. There's no fence or stockade: the whole camp – a small village, really, of tents and treehouses, as well as various exotic tentlike structures – is open to the woodland. There'd be very little danger under normal circumstances – the fiercest animals left in Britain now are foxes, and even those tend to be more aggressive in the cities. Still, Jory thinks, if they're trying to hold a prisoner, their security arrangements can only be called lax. Despite his promise, he's sorely tempted to make a dash for it right now.

Then there's the question of defence, of course. The Circle will gladly arrange a ransom for him – those are its normal rules of engagement – but to exchange a Knight for a convicted criminal is out of the question. They'll give Shafiq very little grace to contact them, either, before they decide it's time to mount a rescue quest, and Jory knows how efficient that would be. This worries him, now he knows that there are children here.

The settlement's larger than he thought – there must be fifty separate dwellings, some of them big enough for whole families. As he passes one of them a baby cries, before being shushed by a woman's sleepy voice. From several more he hears over the music the sound of quiet conversation, or of… well, things better kept private.

The site's a thinning of the forest rather than a true clearing, and it's still dotted with trees such as the oak which bears his prison. As he passes around the perimeter a man emerges from the silhouette of a birch tree, startling Jory. He's out of practice with woodland combat protocols.

'Hi,' says the man, as he walks out from under the tree's shadow. He grins at Jory with an unnerving self-confidence, and Jory sees he's wearing a clerical dog-collar.

He's also wearing khaki cargo pants, a T-shirt with the words 'CLAXTON AND THE RANTERS' – a band's name, Jory guesses – and a number of facial piercings, so it's possible that the collar's just another fashion statement. Still, Jory's met enough eccentric Anglican priests that he can't take that for granted.

'Evening,' Jory says guardedly.

'You're Dan,' the man says, 'is that right? My name's Cantrell,' he adds before Jory can answer. 'But these good people call me Rev.' He's the American, the one who warned Shaun Hobson about Jory's *goddamned sword*. It turns out that he's in his fifties and scrawnily thin.

Jory frowns. 'So are you really…'

'An ordained pastor of the Episcopal Church?' Cantrell's grin is asymmetric, with a worrying glint of teeth. 'Yes I am, though currently without a parish placement. Or superiors. Or a salary, sad to say. I like to think I'm on permanent secondment.'

'You belong to the Chapel?' Jory asks.

'Just call me the Green Chaplain,' agrees Cantrell. 'No, don't, that sounds terrible. Cigarette?'

'Thank you, no,' says Jory. Cantrell shrugs and takes a long puff on his own. 'You're not like the other American priests I've met,' Jory ventures.

'I'm sure that's true,' says Cantrell. 'The US churches serve Jesus in their own particular way. I wanted to serve him in his, which is why I moved to England in the '80s. That and London's thriving gay scene.'

He's not being ironic, although the line's certainly self-aware. 'You wanted to convert them?' Jory guesses.

Cantrell laughs for a while. It sounds like a vulture coughing. 'No, Dan,' he says when he stops. 'No, mostly I wanted to fuck them.'

Jory carefully isn't shocked. He owes that much, he thinks, to David and Trevor. 'Perhaps you *are* like other US pastors,' he deadpans, and Cantrell laughs again.

However marginal his beliefs, Jory thinks, there must be some way to use this man's borderline Christianity to his advantage. But then if that were true, why would Shafiq let Jory walk where he might meet him?

'I'm surprised they make you welcome here,' he tries. 'We thought the Chapel was a neo-pagan organisation. Or is it Muslim now? I'm actually rather confused.'

'We have pagans and Muslims here, sure,' says Cantrell. 'We've got atheists and miscellaneous and couldn't-cares as well. Everyone needs spiritual support some time. You can't have a Chapel without a holy man.' He uses the term without embarrassment, as if it's a professional designation.

'I'm surprised they all accept that.' Jory has trouble imagining it.

'Yeah, they're a tolerant bunch once you get to know them,' Cantrell says. 'Come on, let me introduce you.'

* * *

Over by the giant bonfire, the heat and music are oppressive. A babble of noise from what must be forty or fifty men, women and children barely manages to be heard above the thudding beat. A second rhythmic thrum, slightly off the musical beat, turns out to be the noise of a portable generator.

Jory follows Cantrell into the crowd, picking his way through standing, sitting and recumbent bodies to a makeshift bar, staffed by a girl who can't be more than thirteen. Nearby, a young black man's doing conjuring tricks for the appreciative partygoers.

Cantrell claps him on the back and introduces him to the barmaid as 'Dan'. She's 'Bonnie', apparently. She smiles and hands them each a bottle of what must be homebrewed beer. No money changes hands, but Jory hardly imagined it would.

He sips the beer. It's surprisingly decent.

'All right,' says the teenage boy who brought Jory his supper earlier, joining them at the bar. He leers hopefully at Bonnie, and she passes him a can of lager. 'Rev show you round?' he asks Jory, who has to strain to hear him.

'It's a lovely place,' Jory shouts in reply. He adds inanely, 'All these trees.'

'Miss the city, me,' the boy says.

'Dan, this is Squig,' says Cantrell. He offers Squig a cigarette.

'*Squig*?' Jory repeats, before he can help himself.

Luckily the boy doesn't take offence, although he does take the cigarette. 'I do graffiti,' he says. 'Squig's me tag, see? Ess queue you eye gee. Big danglers, nice and loopy. I do them up on buildings, bridges, railway cuttings… I can get anywhere, me.'

'He isn't boasting,' says a man standing nearby. He's nondescript, but Jory thinks he might look faintly familiar. 'He may not look like much,' the man smiles, 'but point him at a building and five minutes later he'll be holding the door open for you.' Squig grins.

'That must be useful,' Jory says. For a group of thieves and saboteurs, it really must be.

'So,' Squig says, 'one day me and me mate went up on this old factory to tag it. Abandoned steel mill, it were. Me dad used to work there long time back when he were a lad, told us the way in. We climbed up really high, up onto this bridge bit. Conveyor belt thing it were. Then security came and we legged it, and then me mate fell down. He died.'

'Oh,' Jory said. 'I'm sorry.'

'Yeah,' said Squig. 'Me too. 'Cause they reckoned I pushed him, didn't they? That's what they said, anyway. Didn't want to have to pay his family anything, I reckon. Hey, Zara, you met Dan, yeah?'

The young woman who brought Jory his water is at the bar now, collecting two drinks. She nods, still unsmiling. 'He prisoner, Rev,' she reminds Cantrell. Her English, as Jory suspected, isn't good.

Cantrell shrugs. 'That's not up to me. Shaf let him out.'

As if in explanation, Squig tells Jory, 'We don't usually like your lot here. King's men, all that. You lot've got Big Jack locked up and all. But Shaf reckons you're OK.'

When did he say that? Jory wonders. Before their altercation earlier, presumably.

'You are Circle?' Zara asks. She pronounces it with an initial 't'.

'Normally, yes,' says Jory, remembering how she handled her gun earlier. 'Just at the moment, like you say, I'm your prisoner.'

Zara nods curtly. 'Don't forget,' she says. He sees her cross over to the Scottish woman, Scar. She hands over one of the drinks, and Scar draws her in closer for a kiss.

'Oh,' Jory says. 'I thought perhaps Scar was Shau – Shafiq's girlfriend,' he says, catching himself just before committing to something outrageously stupid. 'Her or Zara, anyway. She's not, though, is she?'

'Ah, no,' Cantrell says, lighting his third cigarette since Jory met him. 'That's not where her interests lie.'

'She's got a will on her, that one,' says the third man. Jory frowns, trying to place him. 'A will and more. Shaf's girlfriend's rather merrier. But then aren't we all?'

'Stop teasing our guest,' Cantrell tells him. 'Or I'll have to take him back and tuck him in.' The comment's met with disproportionate hilarity.

They must be drunker than Jory realised. That or worse. He can certainly smell marijuana here, although he hasn't seen any of the three partaking of it.

'Drink any more and you'll be barred!' Squig tells their friend, and collapses in giggles.

That third man… Jory stares surreptitiously at him. He's not especially tall, not especially old, not especially good-looking, just… reminiscent. His clothes are shabby, and he could do with losing weight. He should get his hair seen to as well, it's been months. Somehow he always ends up having more important things to do with his time.

'Dan, this is Dale,' Cantrell says. 'He's just passing through.'

'A bit like you,' I tell Jory. 'Only not so much of a prisoner, obviously. Great to meet you.'

I shake his hand.

***

All right, I realise a bit of elaboration may be needed here. Although I did say I'd be turning up in the story. And that I go everywhere, within limits. There's a special licence for the likes of me. It comes with the job.

I'm a storyteller, you see. Well, obviously. I'm telling you this one, if you'll just let me finish explaining and get on with it. And traditionally we storytellers – bards, skalds, troubadours, what-have-you – we've had what's called a privileged outsider status.

We're wanderers. We go from kingdom to kingdom, town hall to tavern, castle to croft, telling our tales in exchange for our bed and board. Along the way we meet up with each other, greet old friends, look out for new faces, learn each other's tales. Sometimes we make up new stories of our own. Sometimes we see them in the world around us.

The job's evolved down the years, and these days it takes in more music festivals and children's parties than it used to, but it's still possible to make a living this way. More or less.

Jory's met me more than once, as it happens, at some of the less formal Circle events where wives and other outsiders are invited, and even at a couple of the banquets of his TourneySoc. He's just never really noticed me as a person. Usually I'm part of the entertainment, like the sound system.

At this point I don't know Jory, either, not as anyone special. (Historic present, remember? All this is happening a few years ago.) I'll get to know him and his story much better later on, but at this moment none of us knows quite how interesting it will turn out to be.

Oh, some of us have plans, that's true. But what are plans?

I'm not partisan, and I'm not proud. *Will narrate for food* is pretty much the job description. You can't afford expensive tastes in my line of work, and to me the Green Chapel's victuals are just as good as the Circle's.

Hell, I'd have happily drunk the Saxon Shield's mead if they'd have had me over. Wouldn't tell those bastards my favourite stories, mind, but they'd be wasted on them anyway. The best stories are the ones which teach a moral we've known all along, but never really realised it. I wouldn't have had anything to say to them they'd have wanted to know.

So yeah, the Green Chapel let me know where they are, and I'll visit sometimes. They're an awful lot friendlier than the Circle, I can tell you that. None of this *You'll find a meal waiting in the kitchens, then be on your way*. The Chapel know the proper meaning of hospitality.

'I used to be in a folk group once,' I tell Jory now. 'You wouldn't have heard of us. I don't mean you particularly, someone who actually liked folk music probably wouldn't have either. We were a bit shit. But that's what got me into all of this. I wasn't a good singer, frankly, and my string-plucking was never quite the works. But when it came to writing lyrics, I was good. Not tunes, I sucked at those. Perhaps with a good collaborator, but… well, as I say, we were all pretty rubbish, really. The others all went back to taxi-driving or running a pub or teaching or whatever, and I ended up doing this.'

It's all true. What would be the point of lying about something like that?

We all chat for a while – Rev, Squig, Dan (as I'm thinking of him at the time, although I know he's got another name) and me. After a while Scar and Zara come over and join us, though they pointedly don't talk to Dan. The other people of the Green Chapel mill about all round us – cursing, bantering, flirting, all the other things that people do when got together in a group and given alcohol. It's all pretty congenial, and I'm happy, though I can tell Dan's uncomfortable still.

The lad's a prisoner here, after all.

* * *

'So,' Shafiq says to Jory as they walk back to his treehouse cell. (I'll hear about this much, much later, of course.) 'What do you think?'

Shafiq's wearing the green hoodie – the only one he's seen tonight, Jory realises. Even Scar wasn't wearing her red one. His anger's gone now, and to Jory he seems strangely excited, impatient even. Jory wonders whether he's looking for some kind of affirmation.

'Of your friends?' How can Jory possibly answer this? 'They seem… well, nice. Apart from Zara and Scar – is that short for something? They seemed quite aggressive. Not that I'm stereotyping. I mean, I liked Cantrell, and he's gay. Or was he having me on?'

'Right,' Shafiq sighs. 'And apart from making a checklist of their sexual orientations, what did you notice about them?'

'Well,' Jory racks his brains. There's obviously something specific that his friend's waiting for him to say. 'An ex-priest, a young lad, a folk singer, two... probably perfectly nice women once you get to know them... and everybody else having a good time. They hardly seem like natural criminals, if that's what you're getting at.'

Shafiq gives him a look. 'That sounds like progress.' They've stopped now, at the trunk of his oak. The ladder's still set up, the trapdoor still open. Jory's glad to see the room's been getting some air.

'Not really,' Jory says, 'since they *are* criminals. They're all involved in this subversive enterprise you're running. Yes, "terrorist" is too strong a word, probably, and I'm sorry I used it before. But you're industrial spies and saboteurs, and thieves and – well, kidnappers. It's all terribly wrong, Shafiq. You need to put this right.'

'What are you talking about, Jory?' Shafiq's angry again now, too angry to keep up the 'Dan' pretence. Luckily there's no-one within earshot, outside the tents at least. 'Put what right? You know our principles, and you know what we do with our proceeds.

'It's true we take what we need to live and to fund our future actions, but the rest we give to our victims' victims.' He counts on his fingers. 'Employees who they've laid off, industrial accident victims who were never compensated, communities suffering from pollution or environmental degradation... if we get a ransom for you, it'll go to better causes than if we let the Circle keep it.'

'But it's not yours to spend,' Jory says stubbornly. 'Look, you're these people's leader –'

'That's bullshit too,' Shafiq insists. 'We take decisions corporately. We discuss everything –'

'But you're the one who's carrying a device!' Jory blurts, exasperated. 'The Green Chapel only exists because of the Green Knight! I'm sure they'll all *say* you're not the leader, that everything's done democratically or anarchistically or whatever it's supposed to be, but none of that changes the fact that you're their device-bearer. You're the one with the charisma, the leadership skills, the…' he searches for the right word. 'The glamour. We have a responsibility to use that wisely.'

'You really don't get it at all, do you?' Shafiq says. 'What on earth makes you assume that I'm the only one here with a device?'

That brings Jory up short. There's something…

For a moment, he thinks he knows what Shafiq's talking about. But then it's gone.

'This is the Green Chapel,' he repeats. 'You're carrying the Green Knight. What other devices would be…' He tails off, lost.

'That's what you call him,' Shafiq says. 'It's one of his names, but it's not the one we use. We don't call them "devices", either, but lots of us have them. Everyone you were talking to tonight does, for a start.'

Jory stares at him. 'Everyone?'

'Well, not Bonnie. Did you talk to her? Not her, but all the others. Rev, Scar, Zara, Dale, even Squig,' Shafiq insists. 'Jack Bennett's got one too – and no, I know your intake procedures didn't pick up on it. You didn't know what you were looking for. Obviously you still don't.'

'I… no, obviously not.' But there *is* something.

Something's been nagging at Jory all evening, something about not only the people he's met but about this whole encampment. Something that, now he comes to line the concepts up together, reminds him very much of the Fastness, and of the people within it. Something…

'Come *on*, Jory,' Shafiq says. 'You never used to be this obtuse. Do you really not recognise us?'

And then – not suddenly but in a slow and gradual wave of realisation – Jory does.

The people here… they've put themselves beyond the law, one way or another. They live outside the city, miles away from anywhere, probably moving around to avoid being found.

Their identities… no, their descriptions… no, not that even, their *affinities*… are familiar.

The millworker's son. The foreign warrior. The minstrel.

The laughing priest. The bruiser in scarlet. The giant with the quarterstaff.

The hooded archer.

He realises that everyone was punning, earlier on. That's what the inane giggling was all about. Teasing the guest.

They wear green, and they live in a forest. They steal stuff from the rich and powerful, and then they give…

They give…

'Oh dear Lord,' Jory says weakly.

They give it to the poor.

'Welcome to the 'hood,' Shafiq says.

II
THE GREENWOOD

9. THE HOOD

Jory and Shafiq stare at each other.

'I'm sorry – you're telling me you think you're *Robin Hood*?' Jory repeats.

Shafiq sighs, annoyed. 'Only in the sense that you "think you're" Sir Gawain of Orkney. You know perfectly well how all of this works.'

'But what about the Green Knight?' Jory wants to know.

'What about Sir Guy of Gisbourne?' Shafiq counters.

Jory blinks. 'The Sheriff of Nottingham's henchman?' he says, after a moment spent ransacking his memory. 'What about him?'

'He was the King's man,' Shafiq says. 'A knight sent to capture Robin as an outlaw and bring him in. When he first turns up in the ballads there's a contest of arms, a severed head…' he shrugs. 'If you think your myth should define my ally, why can't mine define yours?'

'But… Gisbourne's a villain, surely.' Jory's still trying to muster his thoughts. Aside from one evening at university, which he spent pointing out to a girlfriend and her decreasingly tolerant flatmates the multiple historical inaccuracies in their rented Kevin Costner DVD, his specific knowledge of the Robin Hood corpus comes from his boyhood reading of adventure stories.

Even during his literature degree he never read the Middle English ballads where Robin's exploits are first recorded. And while the Merry Men – along with Romans, Vikings and pirates – are a staple of boys' historical fiction, Jory always judged their stories rather harshly, finding them insufficiently full of magic, quests and jousting. Ask grown-up Jory about this folklore cycle and he'll... well, try to bluff it, basically.

'Look,' he says now. 'You've got the whole myth back to front, you must have. Robin Hood's a hero. I mean, an outlaw, yes, but a noble one. He protects the weak and upholds what's right, and is brave and generous and self-sufficient, and... well, generally the good guy.'

Shafiq's expression could be disgust or just exasperated pity. 'That's right, Jory. And that's what we strive to do. Not by your lights, I'm sure, but by our own. Nobody's a villain to themselves – not even Guy of Gisbourne. Surely you realise that?'

In point of fact, much of Jory's Knightly career has been spent tracking down and punishing people who identify explicitly with villains. There's little moral ambivalence about Mordred in the myths, or Retho, or the Black Knight of the Black Lands, whose protégée Jory hacked into submission last April at West Bromwich bus station. He's seen no evidence that their present-day device-bearers think of themselves as anything other than evil.

* * *

Jory sleeps badly on his mattress, hindered by the pain in his arm, the continuing steam-hammer thump of music from outside his prison, and the heat inside it. For ages he waits for the revelry to quieten down, so he can make his escape. For ages it continues not to, till he realises his captors are quite determined to make merry – ha! – right though to the morning.

Realising that their stamina must be more persistent than his own right now, he decides instead to wake up early, and make a break for it while the partygoers are sleeping it off.

(He knows full well that there are Chapel members who gave the party a miss – he heard them variously chatting, shagging and snoring in their tents the night before – and that these types are likely to be up at the crack of dawn doing yoga or eating organic yoghurt or whatever, thus maintaining an effective ad hoc shift system. Even so, he has to try.)

After a short, fretful night of difficult sleep, he awakes with the sunrise at about quarter to five. The twilit campsite's quiet now, and from his limited vantage through the treehouse window, he sees no movement.

His plan's also best described as ad hoc: it's to break the window (quietly) then crawl out (carefully) into the tree's branches, then lower himself (painfully) using his legs and his good arm, then stumble off (as purposefully as he can manage) into the forest, hoping it won't be too long before he hits a road or someone's house. He must still be in England, and we haven't had a wilderness you can get properly lost in for centuries.

Just for the sake of thoroughness, though, he gives the trapdoor one quick tug before attempting the window. As expected it sticks, so he tugs harder – and then it flies open, sending him flying back onto his arse with an almighty crash.

Shafiq must have been upset by their argument, Jory realises with a pang of affection. He's forgotten to bolt the damn door behind him.

He rights himself. If he lets himself down by his good arm, and drops the remaining distance to the ground… well, now he's climbed the distance up and down the ladder, he's pretty sure he can do it without serious risk of breaking a leg. He peers down through the trapdoor.

He can't quite believe what he sees then, although overall it's considerably less unlikely than being held captive by Robin Hood and his Merry Men in the first place. Shafiq's left the ladder in position, too, and as far as Jory can see there's no guard at the bottom of it.

Quickly he climbs down to the forest floor, the early-morning birdsong surrounding him like a battalion of arcade games. There's no sight of human movement, though a couple of the tents are rustling.

Jory orients himself in what looked last night like the likeliest direction for a road, and starts to run. The grassy floor is springy under his feet. It's a crisp summer morning without a cloud in the sky, promising a welcome scorching later in the day. With luck he can be back at the Fastness by –

Oh, Jory thinks, shambling to a halt just as he reaches the perimeter of pines. He's just remembered something from last night. 'Oh, balls,' he says aloud.

At the time the exchange seemed like a sensible, if petty, precaution on his captor's part, but he now realises that it may have been rather more cunning than he gave it credit for. He gave his word last night not to attack anybody, nor to try to escape, until Shafiq closed the hatch of his treehouse… and took the ladder down.

'Bloody *balls*,' he says again.

Shafiq's plan – his message to Jory – is all at once clear. Jory's not a prisoner in the treehouse, in fact he has the run of the camp if he wants it, but he's stuck with the Chapel as surely as if they'd chained him in a dungeon. Until they – specifically Shafiq himself – see fit to lower that damn ladder, Jory's constrained by a prison far more robust than any flimsy wooden structure.

Shafiq's just met him on his own terms, and bested him in a contest of wits. It's just the sort of dishonourable trick you'd expect from a merry outlaw.

'Curse you, Robin Hood,' Jory groans and goes back to bed.

* * *

'Well,' Shafiq says later that morning, 'you're certainly nearer Gawain than Guy. Gisbourne would have been out of here in moments, honour be hanged. By now he'd be back with a small army.'

'You were testing me.' Jory's quite offended.

They're sitting at a trestle table in the communal area, drinking tea. Others are sitting nearby, several of them nursing ostentatious hangovers. A mingled breakfast smell drifts over from the open-sided cooking tent.

At the near edge of the clearing, some of the less worse-for-wear adults have roped off an area to use as archery butts. A man and woman are sparring, surprisingly energetically, with quarterstaffs. A flock of children are playing an unnecessarily riotous game involving sticks, pebbles, daisy-chains and a pair of small overexcited dogs.

Shafiq nods. 'We need to know who we're dealing with.'

'Well, lucky you,' Jory replies sourly. 'I still have no idea.'

Although the Circle has certain uneasy ties with analogous organisations in other countries, he's never even heard of a British device which owes nothing to the Matter of Britain – that lineage of kings and heroes of which Arthur's just the best-known member, running from the earliest, entirely imaginary Trojan settlers of these islands down to the beginning of proper written records under the Saxons.

Cadwallader, the last king dealt with in Geoffrey of Monmouth's *Historia*, died in AD 689. The tales of Robin Hood and his Merry Men are conventionally set a good five centuries after that. If they survive into the twenty-first century as devices, who else has? Lady Godiva? Dick Turpin? Jack the Ripper?

'You know us,' Shafiq says. 'We're the Merry Men, plus sundry unallied comrades. We're the motley band of followers who've grown up in time and legend around the Robin Hood archetype, who himself has many names – Robin-in-the-Wood, Hobbehod, Jack-in-the-Green, the Green Knight, Robin Goodfellow. We're Little John, Friar Tuck, Will Scarlet, Much the miller's son –'

'That's not the point,' Jory interrupts gracelessly. 'Legend or no legend, you're criminals. You take the law into your own hands. You set yourselves up to judge who deserves to keep their property and who doesn't, and you redistribute it through theft. The kindest word I can think of would be vigilante – except that having money isn't a crime.'

'That's a matter of opinion,' Shafiq says.

'I think you've taken these legends out of context,' Jory persists. 'Robin Hood's a rebel, yes, but against a corrupt regime.'

Shafiq smiles. 'All regimes are corrupt.'

'But the stories are set in a specific historical era.' Jory's been thinking about this during the night. 'King Richard was away at the Crusades, and Prince John was squeezing everything he could out of his regency. It was *John* who was the criminal – killing noblemen and seizing their lands, taxing the poor extortionately, appointing corrupt thugs as his officials.'

Shafiq nods. 'Well, quite.'

'Society was in disarray,' Jory argues. 'The Sheriff, Gisbourne, the wicked Abbot – there is a wicked Abbot, isn't there? – they're all symptoms of a country gone rotten. It's the old "wounded land" motif – in a realm without a king there's no rightful order, no rule of law. Even the church can't be trusted, which is why they won't tolerate an honest cleric like Friar Tuck.' He pauses for a moment, thinking of Cantrell. The ex-priest has honesty in his favour, at least. 'The only moral response to that is to become an outlaw – especially if, like Robin, you're loyal to the true king.'

'Ah,' Shafiq says. 'You've heard *that* version. Robert, Earl of Huntingdon, unjustly dispossessed of his lands and waiting for the Lionheart's return to restore him to his rightful place? Yes, that's one interpretation. It's not the one we favour.'

'So I'd deduced,' Jory says.

'Even dating Robin to John's regency is a later tradition,' Shafiq says. 'As you say, it's a period in which it's acceptable to be a rebel. The early ballads are very vague about who the king is. They don't seem to think it makes much difference, and they're right.

'Robin was an agitator,' he insists, 'a rebel against authority. His men leave the peasants and yeomen unmolested, and molest the fat and powerful instead. He'd have said that John's particular abuses were irrelevant, that the real crime was human beings having that much power over one another at all. His objections to the barons, the church and the king's officials were *political*. What else do you call redistributing wealth and siding with the serfs against the aristocracy?'

'You think Robin was a revolutionary?' Jory says. 'A twelfth-century Che Guevara? That's ludicrous.'

Shafiq grimaces. 'Do you really think there haven't been dispossessed in *every* society who knew how unjust the status quo was? Tens of thousands were prepared to march with Wat Tyler in 1381. In Walter Raleigh's defence at his trial for treason, he listed past insurrectionists. The four he picked were Tyler, Jack Cade, Robert Kett and Robin Hood. Why would he have classed Robin with three men who led popular revolts against the Crown, if he thought he was an aristocrat victimised by an unpopular regent?'

At university, when Shafiq overcame his natural reticence and started sounding off on one of his pet subjects, he could keep going for hours. Even as Jory cuts him off, he realises how much he's missed that.

'So everything you've done,' he says, '– which, let's be clear, includes theft, vandalism, trespass, kidnapping, assault and bodily harm with multiple offensive weapons against those both with and without devices of their own to draw on – you stand by this on the basis that it's what Robin Hood would have done?'

Shafiq sighs. 'I think you forgot possession of a class C controlled substance.'

'I'm serious, Shafiq,' Jory snaps.

Shafiq shakes his head. 'You're the one who's got things back to front. I was allied to the figure of the Saracen long before the position of Robin's ally became vacant. I joined myself with Robin because of my beliefs, not his. I stand by it all because it's what *I* would have done.

'You think I've changed a lot since TourneySoc,' he continues, animated again, 'but really this was always where I was heading. This country of ours is *riven* with injustice. Nearly a thousand years since the Norman conquest, and our class system's still fundamentally feudal. Whoever's in power, the country's ruled by rich public schoolboys – denying ordinary people their rights and dignity, colluding with the corporations to maximise their profits, and screwing the workers, the consumers and the unemployed.

'And what else can you expect,' he asks rhetorically, 'when hereditary privilege is central to our constitution?'

'Well, you certainly never said any of that back at uni,' Jory observes drily, hoping at least to stave off a tirade against the monarchy.

Shafiq snorts. 'It wouldn't have made me very popular in TourneySoc.'

'Mmm,' says Jory. 'It's interesting you bring up TourneySoc, because I thought you understood the concept of fair play. Shaun Hobson died before those Olympics of yours, Shafiq. Was it really you who won that silver medal – or was it Robin Hood?'

Shafiq stares at him, shocked. 'I –' he says. 'You think that *matters*? I made sure I put in the best performance I could. The allies are aspects of ourselves, that's what – I mean, that's the theory as I understand it. If Robin brought out the skill in me, it's because the potential was there.' He seems genuinely upset by the idea that his Olympic performance was an enhanced one.

'Honestly, Dan,' Shafiq says stiffly, and Jory remembers with a start that that's supposed to be his name here. 'Call me a terrorist if you must, but I don't appreciate being called a cheat.'

Jory feels an overwhelming sense of sadness. He's left so many of his friends behind.

* * *

On the morning of his third day in the Green Chapel encampment, it occurs to Jory that the Circle isn't coming for him. There were no witnesses to his abduction from Thankaster Shopping Centre, and the car park had patchy CCTV coverage. Assuming Shafiq had the sense not to appear on camera, there'll be no evidence that Jory was even kidnapped, let alone that the Green Chapel were involved.

In fact, with Alfred Noake still at large, the obvious assumption will be that a remnant of the Saxon Shield has taken Jory. The Circle will be hunting the wrong quarry.

He's been considering plans for fooling Shafiq into taking down his ladder, but he keeps discarding them. The trouble is that Robin, at least in his ballad incarnation, is a trickster figure, whereas the same can't be said of Gawain. (Rather the reverse, in fact, in that it's Gawain who's gulled by the Green Knight.) The chances are high that Jory will come out worse from any exchange of trickery.

With escape forbidden, at least for now, and no rescue to look forward to, Jory's options are limited. It's not in his nature to make himself a nuisance without good reason, so he tries to fit in with the daily arrangements of the Green Chapel as best he can and hopes they soon stop thinking of him as a threat.

Since he's proved he isn't about to run, there's been no nonsense with buckets and food-trays. He's allowed to move around the communal areas, eat the communal food and use the communal latrines. He has two changes of clothes – identikit black tracksuits plus underwear – and access to laundry facilities. The treehouse is still at his disposal and is more comfortable than some of the other accommodation on offer.

Offering to make himself useful, he's set to help repair the weatherproofing on some of the more solid structures. Given his height and strength, this seems like a popular move. (They're missing Jack Bennett's brawn, of course.) It's hard work, and he has to be careful not to strain his wounded arm, but he's grateful for the exercise. Some of his captors are reserved with him, or actively hostile, but others treat him with friendliness.

He spends his days in maintenance, carpentry, cooking, sewing, laundry – all pooled tasks here. The work isn't segregated by sex, which suits the skills Jory's learned as a bachelor soldier. Eager to learn a new one, he volunteers to help out with the childcare, and discovers yet another aptitude he wasn't previously aware of. His energetic approach to play makes him quite a favourite with the more rambunctious children.

While some children have two parents in the encampment, he notices that others have one or – in some cases – none at all. A few appear to have three or more. Relationships between the adults seem equally varied, with the heterosexual monogamy Jory's used to being a popular minority option.

He spends time with Squig, who extends the same teenage mixture of garrulous moodiness to him as to everyone else, and with Cantrell, and me when I'm around. He treats Zara and Scar with an unfailing courtesy that's hilarious to watch, until they're finally forced at least to be polite back to him. He meets new Chapel members, men and women either without allies or allied to the more obscure Merry Men: Will Stuteley, Gilbert Whitehand, Arthur a' Bland. He doesn't meet the Green Chapel's Maid Marian.

After a board-book which he reads some of the youngest children turns out to feature Robin Hood (alongside Jack and Jill, Cinderella and various others), Jory thinks to seek out the Green Chapel's library.

It's a small bookshelf in Cantrell's tent, stuffed haphazardly with books, CDs and DVDs, plus a laptop for playing the discs on. Most of what's there is popular bestsellers from recent decades, but as Jory hoped there's also an eclectic shelf full of versions of the Robin Hood legend. It's nothing systematic, ranging from a dog-eared collection of medieval ballads, heavily annotated, to ex-rental discs of various TV and film adaptations.

Methodical as ever, Jory works his way through the books during his spare time spent sitting in the treehouse. There aren't many of them. The ballads aside, the oldest material here is an Everyman paperback of Walter Scott's *Ivanhoe*, and although there are straight retellings from later on (as well as a painfully earnest Marxist reimagining from the 1930s), he feels like he's missed out on several centuries' worth of cultural development.

Jory takes stock and remembers how baffling the sprawling permutations of the Arthurian myths can be for the novice. Even so, there are certain core texts, from the *Mabinogion* to the *Morte D'Arthur*, which are definitive, and to which modern versions, even revisionist ones, always return in some form.

In these books there's no clear consensus on Robin Hood's real name, let alone his class, age, background or reasons for being outlawed. It's frustrating. Seeking further clues, Jory plunges into the visual media – and that's where I find him, the ninth day after his arrival in the encampment, staring at people in green moving about the laptop's screen.

'Ah,' I say. 'You've worked it out, then.' I've been away for a bit and come back again. When I left, Jory (or Dan, as we're still calling him) was just starting on the ballads.

'Worked out what?' he asks. 'I'm seeing how much I can gather about the legends from watching these. But they're all over the place.'

Cantrell's tent's a gigantic, family-size, all-weather affair, surprisingly luxuriously furnished. You could almost call the thing I sit down on a sofa. 'All over what place?' I ask.

'There's no consistency,' says Jory. 'Not in the story, the politics or even the characters. The boy Much, for instance – is he a childish simpleton or an experienced warrior? Is Will Scarlet a foppish dandy or a murderous thug? This Saracen chap doesn't even have the same name twice, and half the time he's a Moor instead. In this one he's a woman.' He nods at the screen.

'And in the Disney cartoon they're all talking animals,' I say. 'It's all about what makes for a good story.'

'Yes, I see that,' Jory replies. 'But they're all making up their own stories, whereas what I'm trying to find is the basic legend. I'm sure I could access more public-domain texts on the internet, but Cantrell only lets me use the laptop for playing discs.'

'You've got the self-control not to arse around on the internet instead of working?' I say. 'They breed them tough, your Circle.'

'He made me promise,' Jory says, as if this settles the matter.

'You're approaching all this the wrong way round,' I tell him. 'You're thinking like a literature student. Yes, I know,' I add as he opens his mouth. 'Shaf told me. So when you think about the Arthurian myth-cycle and its importance to the world – the world outside the perimeter of your Circle, I mean – what do you think of?'

'Well,' says Jory defensively, 'I suppose it would be literature, mostly, yes. I mean, it's been massively influential on the whole Western canon. There are poems, plays and prose accounts from every period, all kinds of major writers creating their own versions of the legend or referring to it in other works. Not just in English, either – there are important renditions of the story in all the major European languages and others, even Japanese, I think. But then there are also paintings, operas, ballets…'

'Exactly,' I say. 'All of the above. That's not just you; I'd say it's a pretty good description. Meanwhile, what does Robin Hood get? A few forgotten plays by contemporaries of Shakespeare's and a cameo in *Ivanhoe*.'

'It's very frustrating,' Jory agrees.

'Yeah,' I say. 'That *is* just you, though. King Arthur's a product of high culture, always has been. Poems about kings and queens and knights, carrying on in various lordly ways and being sung about by bards to noblemen and courtiers. Monks copying it all down, Caxton fixing the whole thing indelibly in print. Arthur belongs in universities and libraries, just like he does in palaces, cathedrals and opera-houses.

'Meanwhile, we have a robber with a mob of peasant followers sleeping rough in a forest, eating whatever they can kill or steal, smelling of God knows what, and taking all the rich people's stuff. That's story's not so appealing to your gentry, somehow. While your man Arthur's hobnobbing up the high end of British culture, our Robin's slumming it with the rustics. Those stories end up in tavern ballads, May Day dances, mummers' plays and pantomimes. Nobody bothers writing most of that stuff down. Nobody prints it, till upper-class Victorians start getting interested in folklore. It's not until the 1920s that people start making the really *lasting* versions of the Hood legend.'

Jory's given up trying to interrupt, poor lad.

'And who's the key figure in that?' I ask rhetorically. 'Some poet or artist? No, it's Douglas bloody Fairbanks.'

Jory looks sideways at the shelves. 'We haven't got that one,' I say. 'Not many ex-rentals knocking about. We've got the Errol Flynn version, though, the Technicolor one. Plus a whole season of the '50s BBC series. Richard Greene, not Patrick Troughton. You know…' I sing the famous bit from the theme tune. 'Lots of people think those are definitive. And how many films and TV series since then? There's *Robin of Sherwood*, *Robin and Marian*, *Maid Marian and her Merry Men*…'

Jory's nodding. You know how I don't like to bang on, so I let him talk.

'You're saying I've gone wrong,' he says, 'in trying to use TV and films as a guide to the authentic legend. Because popular culture's where the Robin Hood myth actually *lives*.'

'Bingo,' I say. 'I mean honestly, how many successful films about King Arthur can you name? There's *Excalibur*, obviously. *First Knight* perhaps. *Monty Python and the Holy Grail*, *The Fisher King*, although it's pretty tangential… you run out pretty quickly, though. Robin Hood has *dozens*.'

Sorry – exaggerating slightly, I know. Bit of a hobby-horse of mine.

'Disney did *The Sword in the Stone*, too,' says Jory, a tad defensively.

* * *

He's splitting logs for the wood-burning stoves when Shafiq comes to see him. He's been at the camp now for two weeks.

'Hello, Dan,' Shafiq says. 'Just wanted to say thanks for all your work.'

Jory shrugs. 'I'm eating your food.'

'I know,' says Shafiq. 'You'd be surprised how few of our guests are so community-minded.' He upends a log with his foot and sits down on it.

They're at a small clearing close by the campsite, where a handful of spruces and larches have been felled. Jory can't imagine this is legal, unless the Green Chapel have a wealthy protector who actually owns the woodland. He's not yet met an avatar of Sir Richard of the Lea, and somehow he doesn't think these Merry Men would be keen on his patronage. From the number of trees down, and the amount of wood the Chapel burns, Jory guesses that they've been camped here a couple of months. He gets the sense that some of them are restless and wanting to move on.

This would, of course, entail lowering Jory's ladder, unless they leave both it and the treehouse in place – and that, he guesses, would be taking the joke too far for Shafiq's taste. Robin is a trickster, but not usually a vicious one.

Whether this explains why they haven't upped sticks yet, he doesn't know. Apart from anything else, he's interested to see how they do it – green principles or no, he can only imagine some form of motorised transport is involved. The Chapel surely use motor vehicles to get to and from their… what would they call them, operations? Demonstrations? Merrie jests? He presumes they keep them somewhere within walking distance of the campsite – he's been keeping an eye open for people nipping into the woods and coming back an hour or so later, but so far they've mostly been doing it in pairs. Shopping arrives, as well as unpackaged farm produce, but he hasn't yet managed to observe it happening.

Once camp is struck, and Jory's free from his vow, he can't see how the Chapel will stop him escaping – unless they tie him up or lock him in a van or something, which would be a definite backward step.

'I was wondering,' Shafiq says, gesturing for Jory to join him, 'whether you'd be interested in doing something else for us? For me, really.'

Jory sits warily. 'What sort of thing?'

'We have a direct action coming up,' Shafiq says. 'It's a bit of a departure from our usual line. Something you'll be interested in, as it happens.'

Jory stands up again immediately. 'Forget it, Shafiq. While I'm here I'll help out with domestic stuff, because I understand you're a community. That doesn't mean supporting your politically motivated programme of criminal activities. As soon as I'm back with the Circle I'll be doing everything in my power to ensure that you and the other decision-makers here are taken into custody. If I haven't been clear about that… well, actually I think I have been,' he concludes, slightly bathetically.

Shafiq's still sitting on his log. 'You've been practising that,' he notes. 'I'm not expecting for a moment that you'll participate, naturally. I know you too well. I was going to invite you along as an observer. As you say, sooner or later, one way or another, you'll find your way back to the Circle. When that happens, I'd be a fool not to consider that some of us may end up standing trial. Or whatever it is the Circle gives its prisoners instead of a trial.'

He shrugs. 'I also know that you're fair and honest, and in that event I'd be a great deal happier if you were able to give an accurate account of us.' Shafiq looks carefully around, seeing nobody in earshot. 'It would be a personal favour, Jory.'

Jory's device is twitching inside him, warning him that this is another trick. 'What sort of "direct action"?' he asks, sitting gingerly again.

'It's superficially similar to the last one you saw,' says Shafiq. 'We'll stop a certain group of people who we know are travelling with a valuable cargo, we'll attack them and we'll… liberate their goods. It's more or less our job description. This time, though, I guarantee you'll agree with me that our victims are the bad guys.'

'Really,' says Jory flatly. 'And will I agree that this "badness" of theirs invalidates their basic legal right to property?'

Shafiq looks grim. 'Nobody has the right, legal or moral, to own this kind of property.'

'What is it?' Jory asks. 'Drugs? Guns?'

Shafiq shakes his head. 'Human beings. Specifically women.'

'Women? You mean…' Jory pulls back abruptly from saying '…prostitutes?', realising first that it's the wrong thing to say to Shafiq, and immediately afterwards that it's the wrong reaction altogether. He's always had trouble navigating this kind of conversation with Malory, too. He considers and rejects '…illegal immigrants?', then takes the vocal plunge with '…migrant workers?', and wishes he hadn't.

'I mean *young women*,' Shafiq snaps. 'Women from Eastern Europe or the Balkans or the Middle East, brought here against the law and their will, to "work" in the sex industry. By which, just so we're clear, I mean that British men will pay for the privilege of raping them repeatedly. I don't think anyone who holds that kind of "property" is entitled to keep it, do you?'

'Good God, Shafiq,' says Jory. 'What are you planning?'

'They bring them in by lorry, on a ferry,' Shafiq says. 'We'll carry out the same kind of hijack as on your art consignment, obviously trying not to mess it up this time. Given that we very much don't want a hostage situation, we'll have to take them unawares. We need to overwhelm them as quickly as possible, without giving them time to react. We'll take the women to a secure shelter Scar knows, and we'll leave our best women fighters there to keep them safe. We may place some men nearby as backup too, but of course we don't want the women to feel intimidated. We can't rule out the possibility of some attempt at retaliation, though, until they've been rehoused.'

'That sounds…' Jory begins. It sounds incredibly dangerous. The Circle could pull it off, he knows – though they'd only do it if the criminals bore devices, and they'd certainly target the ringleaders directly, rather than these small fry – but surely Shafiq's group don't have the firepower to take on an international crime syndicate. 'If you know where they're taking these poor women,' he says, 'why on earth don't you contact the police?'

Shafiq sighs. 'We're not exactly on best terms with the police,' he points out patiently. 'But assuming we were and they believed us, it wouldn't do any good. This gang's been running the same operation for years, with someone somewhere along the line keeping them safe from prosecution – if not the police, then lawyers, judges, perhaps even MPs. We know we don't stand any chance of actually bringing them down, but if we can save this one group of women that's still to the good.'

Jory's device is still on the alert, the hairs of his two weeks' growth of beard tingling. It's clear now what Shafiq's doing – he hopes that if Jory comes along as a spectator, he'll be so moved by the plight of these women that he'll get involved. He may not be able to help himself: Sir Gawain's known as the maidens' champion, and as I've said he's a sucker for a pretty face.

Maybe he'll emerge from it convinced that the Chapel is doing good, perhaps even defect from the Circle. He's started to realise that it's this, not a Knight's ransom, which was Shafiq's object in capturing him.

Unfortunately Jory can't fault his strategy. If he does attend the 'direct action', then the first of those things may well happen. He doesn't know whether he'll be able to stop the others following.

'It's not,' says Jory, 'that I don't sympathise with these women or detest their traffickers. Of course I do. It's loathsome that things like that go on and that so many people stand by ignorant of them. But this isn't the right approach, Shafiq. It's a gesture, that's all. You know it won't address the root of the problem, you don't have the muscle to do that. Instead you're salving your consciences with a quick, easy fight. These people don't have devices, do they? The criminals, I mean.'

Shafiq shrugs. 'There's no reason to suppose so.'

'Then you'll make mincemeat of them,' he says, hating how this sounds. 'You're talking about killing them, Shafiq. I understand the impulse, but that's not the way. It's…'

'What?' Shafiq's angry again now, suddenly. 'What is it, unfair? Unsporting? These women are being kept in conditions of unimaginable misery – a kind of misery you and I will never need to imagine, thank goodness – and these worthless swine treat them like livestock. Like freight. And you won't get involved because it wouldn't be a fair *contest*? Fuck that, Jory. That's not chivalry, that's collusion.'

'It's not that,' says Jory, remembering Shafiq's silver medal. (Why silver? Surely – *surely* – Robin Hood would be a good enough archer to win the gold.) 'It's just that there are proper authorities –'

'Oh yes, *authorities*,' Shafiq says. 'Authorities like your Circle, no? Authorities who sit back and allow this kind of thing to happen on exactly that basis. Let the police deal with the ordinary criminals, provided they leave the extraordinary ones to us! Like I say, fuck that. It's complacent, it's paternalistic and it's elitist.'

'The Circle –' Jory begins, then stops.

The Circle bears the authority deriving from its Head, he wants to say. *But only in theory. Without the true High King, what are we? The sovereign and her ministers and servants put up with us because they need us. We'll never have the popular support she does, let alone the universal loyalty Arthur commanded. We're an anomaly, an anachronism: an undemocratic remnant whose sole purpose is to deal with the crimes of the deviced. As long as we fulfil that role, we're tolerated by state and people alike. But if we started throwing our weight around in matters of state, they'd try to abolish us, and then…*

Well. Never mind rogue devices, imagine the whole Circle going rogue. Civil war would be the least of it. Britain's very psyche would be torn apart.

But all of that's… not even classified, as such; among the Knights it's barely even spoken of. Whispered, perhaps, between friends who trust each other implicitly.

'The Circle does its part,' is all he can say.

'The Circle *enables* this shit,' Shafiq spits. 'And you wonder why we see you as the Sheriff's man.'

* * *

For the rest of the day, Jory finds himself less at ease in the encampment. The Chapel members he's been friendly with are suddenly nervous or withdrawn around him, and those who've always seemed hostile become more so. Scar, who actually tolerated a conversation with him yesterday about martial arts, now glares at him and dares him to approach. Zara spits on the ground as he walks past.

Either he and Shafiq were overheard, Jory thinks, or Shafiq was asking on behalf of all of them, and has reported back. Worse, if he was too angry to keep their exchange private, he might have finally told them the truth about their friendly prisoner and his past history with the Green Chapel. For the first time in weeks, Jory suspects he might be in immediate danger.

He finds a refuge in Cantrell's tent. The ex-priest's palpable disappointment in him is far more congenial than outright enmity. Jory accepts his grudging offer of an extremely small Jack Daniels, and sits nursing it moodily.

Squig calls in later. 'Merry's coming –' he says, then breaks off when he sees Jory. 'Oh,' he says. 'Look. King's man after all then, hey?'

'Squig, what's the matter?' Jory asks. 'Everyone's being very odd suddenly.'

Squig doesn't meet his eye. 'Direct action soon,' he says. 'Big thing for us. Not that you care. Later, Rev,' he says and leaves.

'Merry?' Jory asks Cantrell, who's using the laptop for some kind of chat program, typing in short directed bursts like a sniper with a machine-gun. Jory hasn't liked to look at the screen.

Cantrell shrugs.

'Rev, who's Merry?' Jory asks again. He's well aware he hasn't met Maid Marian, still. Over the past week it's been bothering him increasingly. 'Is she Shafiq's girlfriend?' he asks.

Cantrell responds with a pointed flurry of typing. Jory drains his glass, gets up from the sofa and goes out.

Outside, he walks around the perimeter of the encampment, telling himself he needs the exercise. He runs into Lee, the middle-aged biracial guy whose ally is Gilbert Whitehand, carrying two hardy cloth bags of shopping in from the wood. Jory realises that the rest of the encampment will be having supper.

'Supplies,' says Lee, who has a Brummie accent but doesn't use it much. 'Merry's coming.'

'Is Merry Shafiq's girl?' Jory asks, but the man just keeps walking. He's wearing his green hoodie, the first time Jory's seen one since the night he was abducted.

Jory walks some more. He paces and frets. Cantrell comes to the encampment's edge for a smoke, and Jory hangs around irritating him. The cleric's wearing his hoodie too, and when Jory looks inward to the communal area where supper's being eaten he's surprised to see a throng of green-clad figures, with one scarlet shape among them.

'Who's Merry, Rev?' he asks again. 'Is she Maid Marian?'

Cantrell shrugs. 'Is that really what you want to ask me?'

It's not. But Jory's real question isn't one he can articulate just yet, not even to himself.

An hour before sunset, on Jory's thirty-fourth circuit of the clearing, Shafiq leaves the encampment, his hood drawn up over his face. For a moment Jory contemplates following him, but he can tell Shafiq's well aware of his gaze.

Besides, he'll be back soon. Jory sits, leans back against a tree-trunk and waits for the inevitable.

A half-hour later, two figures approach along the worn path through the woodland. Both are dressed in green, hoods shading their faces in the dying light. One is taller than the other.

They break the treeline, walk towards where Jory's sitting. The shorter figure has a gait he remembers from long ago, and has come to know better over the past two weeks. The taller one's walk, he discovers now, he'd recognise if he saw it anywhere.

He stands as she approaches, sticks his hands awkwardly into his black tracksuit pockets. He's aware of how his clothes now mark him out as an outsider, the Sheriff's man among the outlaws.

He calls her name before she reaches him. He isn't letting her have her moment of revelation.

She lowers her hood, shakes out her long, free-flowing ginger hair. 'Hey, Jory.'

She grins at him – a cheerful expression, conspiratorial as ever, but freer, he thinks, than he's ever seen on that face.

10. THE SARACEN

Jory walks with Merry and Shafiq to the communal circle in the centre of the encampment, where the camp fire's being built and speakers set up for the evening's feasting. The people of the Chapel give a cheer when they see Merry, and Jory realises it can't be something that happens often, what with the demands of her official job and her other covert one. It's a contrast with the stiff reception she gets from some Knights of the Circle, anyway.

'Hello everyone,' she calls in answer to their greetings. 'It's glorious to be back here. I miss you all every moment I'm away.'

As Jory hears her say it he knows it's true. He knows Malory Wendiman well enough to distinguish between her deferential academic persona and the bolder, more irreverent woman who's her private self. Merry is something different again – a third persona, and whether it's a different performance or a deeper insight into her true character he couldn't say – but she's still Malory, and he could tell if she was lying.

'I'm even more pleased this time,' she says, indicating Jory, 'because while I've been away you've collected one of my oldest friends. Shaf tells me you've been calling him Dan, and I respect that, but I've know him for years under a different name. I know it's been difficult for some of you to accept him, and believe me, I understand why. But he's a good man, brave and honest, and I'll always trust him to do what he thinks is right.

'That doesn't mean he hasn't done things he regrets, just like the rest of us,' Merry adds. 'Like us all he's still trying to figure out his place in the world.'

Jory glances sidelong at her, only to see that Shafiq's doing the same. Neither man says anything.

She says, 'It would make me even happier if you could all accept him as a friend as well. Can you make him welcome here – try to forgive his past, understand the dilemmas he's facing now, and hope for his comradeship in the future? Can I ask that much of you?'

There's a general rumble of assent – grudging in some cases (and Zara in particular scowls as she nods), but heartfelt in others. Jory's always had the knack of making friends, and his time among the Chapel's been no exception. Still, it's Merry's influence that's dispelling the taint that's settled on him today.

Charisma and eloquence are qualities often lent by the devices, and he's seen them at work many times, in speakers as diverse as Shaun Hobson and the Noake-Hill duo. There's nothing inherently sinister about it, any more than the enhanced strength and fighting prowess. Frankly, if you want to coerce someone into doing something they don't want to do, brute force is usually more effective than persuasion.

There's no denying, though, that if for some reason you wanted to create a cult of personality around yourself – or even just a cult – then a device would be a very useful tool to have available.

Merry beams. 'Thank you all, that's wonderful. Now, I know we have a lot of preparation and a lot of planning to do – but before that, there's a party to be had, and I'm parched. Shall we open the bar?'

The Lady of the Lake's an ambivalent figure in Arthurian literature. Depending who you read, she may be one woman or several, Nimue's identity overlapping with those of Viviane, Elaine and others. Around the edges she starts bleeding into the figure of wicked Morgan le Fay, as if there's really only room for one beautiful young witch-woman in the legends.

She's most famous for brandishing the royal sword Excalibur from beneath the waves, providing Arthur with one aspect of his claim to kingship and Monty Python with some of their better lines. Sometimes she becomes the High King's closest counsellor after Merlin's retirement, although it's usually Nimue herself who forces that retirement by enchanting and imprisoning him. It's she who reclaims Excalibur while Arthur's dying, once Sir Bedivere's stopped faffing and thrown it into the water.

All this is Malory's area of expertise, though, and Jory never imagined he'd need to give serious consideration to psych-profiling his best friend. The idea appals him – and besides, just at the moment, as she vanishes into the crowd, hugging green-clad men and women as she picks her way towards the trestle-tables, with their various sources of liquid refreshment and some manic fiddle music playing on the stereo… it's not the Arthurian legend which seems to be inspiring her.

Cantrell and Squig come over and shake hands with Jory, Squig muttering an apology, Cantrell just smiling his predator's grin and clapping him on the back. Others come and join them, eager to make Jory welcome, to forgive and forget. He still doesn't know if they realise what it is they're forgiving.

Jory urgently needs to talk to Malory, or failing that Shafiq, but one is inaccessible among the throng and the other has turned moodily away from Jory, still unbending, immune to Nimue's – or even Marian's – charm.

Disturbed, upset, confused, emotions wildly orbiting the knot of betrayal at the centre of his mind, Jory allows the others to draw him into the party, and eventually into a state of desperate, drunken oblivion.

* * *

…Or nearly so. In years to come he'll have one memory of that party, and it will be of Merry's voice.

> *'Through drinking too much vodka before I went to bed, strange dreams came to my slumber: strange thoughts came in my head.'*

She's singing, unaccompanied, the stereo silent for the moment, and the folk of the Green Chapel, aside from the odd disrespectful dog or baby, listening appreciatively.

> *'This world seemed topsy-turvy, and persons of renown were humbled at the people's feet as the world turned upside down.'*

It's an old folk song, or something like. The tune's hauntingly simple, her voice clear and firm, the words… not original, clearly, but somehow authentic nonetheless.

> *'I saw the merchant bankers, the princes, dukes and queens, all standing on street corners and selling magazines.*
>
> *'I dreamt that politicians were honest and ill-paid, and lived the consequences of every law they made.'*

Jory listens, propped up against a tree with a beer-bottle in his hand, poleaxed by the purity of the sound and sentiment.

'I dreamt that news reporters, and media barons too,
stood up with no agenda and told us what was true.

'I dreamt the churches practiced no rationing of love,
and worked to build a heaven in this world, not above.'

The song's a Green Chapel favourite, incidentally, continually evolving like all our best songs, based on a nineteenth-century ballad which grew out of a much older idea. Given his biochemical state, it's not surprising that Jory won't remember all the words later, but – equally unsurprisingly – I shall.

'I saw the soldiers ordered back to their homes and lives,
to bring peace to their children, their husbands and their wives.

'I dreamt all men respected their women, strong and proud;
their children, never troubled, walked through this world unbowed.'

(I can also tell you that Merry isn't the only person who'll perform a capella tonight, or even the best, good though her voice is. She'll clearly make an impression on Jory, though.)

'The homeless slept at the palace, and sold the sceptre and crown
to fill themselves with beer and bread as the world turned upside down.'

In all the time he's known Malory, Jory manages to remember through the thick fog of alcohol poisoning his brain, he's never heard her singing voice before.

* * *

He awakes in his treehouse, naked under a sleeping-bag on his mattress, with no clear idea of how he got there. He really hopes it wasn't Cantrell who undressed him.

Malory is sitting beside him, holding a halogen lantern. Her shadow looms huge behind and above her. Jory considers leaping up in alarm, but frankly it seems like too much effort.

'Malory,' he tries to say, but his throat's too dry. He grabs the bottle of water someone's thoughtfully left for him and drains it. He tries again. 'Malory, what the *absolute hell* do you think you're doing?'

She smiles. 'In your bedroom, you mean?'

He sits up. 'No, I bloody don't.' His head objects, though less strenuously than he might have expected. 'I mean what are you doing *here*.' He gestures widely, realising as he does it that he's still drunk. 'And what the godforsaken… almighty *sod* are you doing being involved with the Green Chapel?'

He's not a naturally creative swearer, our Jory.

'I'm sorry, Dan,' says Malory sweetly.

He considers the merits of swearing again, then just says coldly: 'Don't you *dare* call me that.'

'I'm sorry, Jory,' Malory repeats, looking genuinely contrite. 'You must be feeling shitty at the moment. I came to explain. I'm sure you have a lot you need to ask me.'

In the background, Jory can hear the faint beat of music, indolently slow now. They're not the only people still up in the encampment. Beyond being dark, he has no idea what time it is.

The drink's still dancing in his head, muddling his thoughts. 'Are you sleeping with Shafiq?' he asks, surprising himself. There are rather more substantial questions to be addressed, after all.

She gives a tiny laugh. 'Notionally, I suppose. Marian and Robin are lovers, usually. But there are many versions of the legend where her guardian forbids her to marry him, and they live chastely together. Which is why she's called "Maid", of course. Sometimes she's even a nun. And whatever else he gets up to, in matters of romance Shafiq's still a well-behaved Muslim boy. You two have a lot in common, you know.'

'Thanks,' says Jory. 'But you *have* still been in touch with him. All these years.'

'Oh yes,' she says. 'The Circle rejecting him was one of the reasons I revived the Green Chapel. It seemed like such a waste of potential. He was the Saracen at first – one of the Merry Men I brought in to join Shaun Hobson. Shaun was already the Green Knight, but he was angry and undirected. I helped him to find the Robin Hood facet of his device, in the same way I'd been able to find the Marian aspect of mine.'

Jory tries to remember what he's learned about Maid Marian. She has connections with the court – in many stories her guardian's the Sheriff himself, after her parents die or are killed – but she lives among natural things, out in the greenwood. As a nun she'll be a member of an otherworldly sisterhood; but she's young, usually, and attractive – definitely a sexual being. (The thought slightly arouses him, for some reason, and he rumples the sleeping-bag up awkwardly over his thighs.) She knows about healing and sometimes has more esoteric skills as well. She's not a perfect fit for Nimue, but Jory can see the parallels.

'The devices aren't separate entities, not really,' Malory's saying meanwhile. 'They're more interconnected than anyone in the Circle realises. Like leaves on a tree which you can trace back to a twig, then a bough, then the trunk itself. It's possible they all originate from one ancestral monomyth.'

'You and Shafiq,' Jory says, processing all this. 'And Hobson. Which others?'

Malory says, 'Big Jack and Rev were in from the beginning as well, both with the allies they have now. We had a different Will Scarlet to start off with, and nobody seems to stay as Much for long. Our first one left to live with a girlfriend, and I got the second a place on the computer games design course at the university. Squig's the third. The others, allied and otherwise, accreted around us.'

Jory considers. This must have started while he – and later the majority of the Circle – were busy quelling the Mordred device in Iraq, like King Richard on his crusade. He supposes Malory must have been at a bit of a loose end. 'The really big question though, Malory, is why.'

'I wish you'd call me Merry while we're here,' she says. He glares at her.

She sighs. 'All right. I believe in the Circle, Jory, really I do. Not quite in the same way you and the other Knights do – nobody's ever made me swear fealty, I'm just an employee – but I think it does a great deal of indispensible good. Nobody else could have stopped Al-Wasati or the Beard Collector, not without taking far longer and endangering the public much more. In all likelihood they'd simply have stayed uncaught and faded away, becoming new legends. Devices have a tendency to do that. I think it may be how they reproduce.'

Jory knows all this. Well, not the last bit, which is faintly mindboggling, but all the stuff about the Circle. 'So presumably you now tell me where the Circle's gone wrong.'

'It's not wrong,' she says carefully, 'as such. Just… insufficient. There's so much evil it can't fight, because of its ethos and its constitution and its position within the state. If the Knights had the will, they might step outside those boundaries, but the Circle's natural recruitment constituency is old-fashioned and entrenched in its politics.'

Jory says, 'Whereas yours are… what, progressive? Radical? Revolutionary?'

Malory shrugs. 'Don't forget that my dad basically pressganged me into the Circle. I respect his intentions, and I know he was acting as he thought right, but how many adults do you know who share their parents' views on everything? You know I'm not naturally subservient to authority. I'll submit when it's the right thing to do, but when authority itself is in the wrong, the right thing is to defy it. The Circle is necessary, but not sufficient. It needed an opposite, a counterbalance. A devicial group driven not by obedience, but by rebellion.'

A mistily-remembered fragment of poetry comes back to Jory. *Neither way is better. / Both ways are necessary. It is also necessary / to make a choice between them.* TS Eliot was one of the few modernists who interested him at university, and not just because of the Grail symbolism in *The Waste Land.*

'Hang on,' says Jory. 'Does that mean you were sleeping with Shaun Hobson?'

'Oh, for Christ's sake,' Malory snaps. 'We're finally getting to talk freely about mythopolitics and suddenly you're obsessed with who's been inside my fanny. No Jory, I wasn't sleeping with Shaun either, not that it's any business of yours. He became the Green Knight after a gas explosion killed his wife and daughter in their home. He blamed corporate negligence, and he wanted to avenge them. He grieved for them until the day you cut his head off. He wasn't interested in anyone else.'

They're quiet for a moment. The music outside has stopped. A subdued voice shouts goodnight, is answered. Then silence.

'So you betrayed us,' Jory says, half-heartedly, aware that he's not been defending his moral high ground all that successfully. 'Betrayed the Circle. Did you betray me?'

She frowns. 'What do you mean? Jory, we never –'

'Did you tell Shafiq where I was going to be that night?'

'Oh.' For the first time, Malory looks a little ashamed. 'That. Yes, I did. I thought it was time you saw the Chapel for yourself.'

'I'd already met them once,' Jory says. 'They beat me up, remember?'

Malory clicks her tongue. 'Well yes, because you killed Shaun. An armed robbery was never going to be the optimum situation for social bonding, even if your devices hadn't responded so atavistically to each other. Although it was only to be expected, I suppose – devices of divine origin tend to be volatile, especially in combination. That's why I had to let Shafiq bring you here, so you could see us on more peaceable terms. I wanted you to experience our life as a community, get to know the people here and how they see the world.'

'But why?' says Jory. 'What are you trying to achieve, Malory? Sir Gawain making an alliance with the Green Knight? Guy of Gisbourne joining the Merry Men? Are you trying to create a new myth?' He wonders what you could do with a completely new device – or with a forgotten one, revived. Is that what Malory's doing here?

He realises how little he knows her. A witch inside an activist inside a counsellor inside a researcher… how many lives can one woman lead?

How many are the names of the Lady of the Lake?

Malory looks at him. Her eyes, enormous in the half-light, are steady, slightly sorrowful. Her hair, gloriously released from its habitual restraints, has the russet lustre of copper-beech leaves.

'I've known Knights of the Circle all my life,' she says. 'I've only known one Jory Taylor. Everything I said was true – you're good and brave and honest, just like the rest of them – but you have a perspective the others haven't. You're self-aware, you doubt yourself and question others in ways they try to weed out at recruitment. That's not Gawain, Jory, it's you.'

'So…' Jory's trying to understand. 'You thought I'd be more easy to, what… turn?'

'It's not about your loyalties,' Malory says. 'It's not about myths or politics. It's not about your device. I just wanted you to be a part of this with me. I'm tired of always having to hide something of myself from everybody. I wanted to have someone I could share it all with.'

She shrugs again. 'I wanted it to be you.'

For a woman who works so hard to protect herself from unwanted attention, she has no qualms about making herself utterly vulnerable when she feels the need to.

'Oh, Malory.' Jory feels an incredible surge of affection for his friend. He's known her longer than anyone, his parents excepted, and they've shared more than most friends do in a lifetime. Her arrival today, after he's been alone in hostile territory, cut off from everything familiar, has come to him as an overwhelming relief. Whatever she's done, whatever she is to these people, to him she's just Malory.

Besides, her confession just now has brought back vividly the last time she exposed herself so nakedly to him – literally, on that occasion – and his body's responding keenly to the memory.

In this moment, Jory forgets more or less everything.

His reservations about the Green Chapel, for example. The need to keep friendship and romance separate. Thoughts of the future, even of the hangover which will inevitably blight his world tomorrow morning. Shafiq, whose feelings for Malory, he could see from one glance earlier, are stronger than her airy denial would allow.

Plus, at the number one spot, his vow of chastity.

For the moment, he's a student again, no Knight and owing nothing to any chivalric code. And Malory – the woman who he surely should have been with, all those years ago – is here, his if he wants her. Whatever happens later – and a great deal will – in this instant, he loves her.

Like I said, Sir Gawain. Always a sucker for the pretty face.

He pulls her to him, sliding the sleeping-bag aside, embracing her as nakedly as she once came to him, and…

…Well. I'm sure you don't need me to describe the rest.

* * *

Jory cries out in the middle of the night, waking then both.

'Hush,' Malory tells him sleepily. She's draped across him, naked too now, the warmth of her more welcome than any sleeping bag. 'Go back to sleep.' She strokes his side.

'But...' Jory struggles to remember. 'Morgan le Fay,' he blurts.

Malory shifts. 'What?' Her voice is sharper.

The drink has mostly gone from Jory's head now, but in its place is sleepy fuddlement and an incipient headache that's just as incapacitating. 'She came to Arthur. Used magic on him. Forced him to sleep with her. She was his half-sister. It's how Mordred was conceived.'

Malory rests her head back on his chest. 'Sweetheart, that was his *other* half-sister, Morgause. Gawain's mother.' Her voice is muffled. 'Well, usually. And I don't imagine he needed much forcing.'

'They're all the same, though.' Jory's grasping at an insight, but sleep's tentacles are steadily pulling him back into its jaws. 'All those sorceresses. Their roles shift around from legend to legend. Aren't their devices all part of the same... branch?'

'Oh, absolutely,' murmurs Malory. 'All the same, that's us women. Listen, I'm not Morgause, and you're definitely not Arthur. I am on the pill, though, so there's no danger of accidental bastard heirs. Can we go back to sleep now?'

'Mm,' Jory says. 'Can't imagine why I was worried.'

As he drifts back into whatever fathoms his unwelcome revelation pulled him from, it occurs to him very briefly that Malory didn't deny being Morgan le Fay.

The thought's gone by the morning, though.

* * *

When he wakes up, she's gone, and he realises that this development in their relationship isn't something she can be open about here, where her status as Robin's maiden bride is sacrosanct.

Probably not at the Fastness, either, supposing Jory ever finds his way back there. It's one more thing Malory needs to hide – only this time from everyone except him.

He goes through the day dazed and bewildered, a feeling not helped by his hangover, yet also prone to bursting out in an irrepressible grin of euphoria. He finds it difficult to believe that he and Malory have finally slept together, even though the fact of it – the memory of it, in fact, flashing vividly erotic in his mind even when he's helping mend the communal latrines – keeps overwhelming his attempts to think through its consequences. He knows that it's not only their friendship that's changed – his relationships with both the Chapel and the Circle have undergone seismic shifts as well.

He's longing for that night, but neither of them can acknowledge any of this during the day – which in any case Merry needs to spend in planning to which Jory isn't privy. That afternoon she arranges for him to talk to Zara.

The foreign woman's been consistently unfriendly to Jory since his arrival in the encampment, but her response to him after yesterday's conversation with Shafiq took the hostility to a whole new level. He's been guiltily suspecting that this was something intensely personal for her, and he's right.

'You won't come with us for direct action. That right?' Zara says. He's learned that, while her vocabulary's limited and her English broken in places, she's an articulate, intelligent woman, perfectly capable of making herself understood. 'You know who we fight, yes?'

Jory swallows and nods. This isn't going to be an easy conversation. 'People-traffickers,' he says. He guesses he doesn't need to elaborate.

'That right,' she says. 'So Merry tell me talk to you. Tell you what you let happen.'

'I'm listening,' says Jory.

'I was young girl in war, in Sarajevo.' Her pretty, hard-set face takes on a faraway look, as if this is a story she's told many times. 'You don't know anything of war, in UK. Not anything.' He doesn't know whether she means the Bosnian war specifically, or war in the abstract. He knows it's not the time to mention his own combat experience.

Zara continues. 'There was siege. Serbs surround city, fight us with shells, snipers, bombing. My friends, children like me, die walking on street. My sister lose both hands in shelling, then later shot in head by sniper. We thought they would come into town, kill all men, rape and kill all women, take children away, nobody know for what, but rape and kill after for sure.

'My brother teach me to use gun, and to defend with knife if I have no gun. Where on man to stab to make most pain, most bleeding. I was six.'

She stops, breathes deeply. Jory's not going to interrupt this kind of testimony. He listens with respect.

'Then NATO men come. Siege end, war end. Serbs go home to other part of Bosnia. They Bosnians now, Bosnian Serb. Always Bosnians, they say. We forgive and forget now, OK? War is over.' Her tone is bitterly sarcastic.

'My father fight with Republic Army. We hear nothing from him for year. After siege they tell us he died in Srebrenica. We go live with my grandfather in Tuzla. I go school, learn politics, history, some Arabic. I learn to fight, too – to fight well. War is over, but more fighting will come. I know this. My grandfather not happy, but there was siege in Tuzla too. He know even good women need to defend.

'When I eighteen, two boys ask me to party. I know these boys. Already then I think I like girls, but for Muslim woman in Bosnia this isn't possible. In autumn I go university – think maybe I meet foreign girl, American maybe, go home with her. Stupid dream.'

Zara pauses. Her eyes are wet now. 'I tell you this only for Merry, yes? Only because she say I tell you.'

Jory swallows. 'I understand, Zara. Go on, please.'

'I never go university. I go with boys to party. No other girls there, only some older men. I want to go but they lock door. I have knife but there too many of them, with gun. They take it away and hold me down, put gun on head. They make boys rape me. One of them cry, tell me sorry, but he do it anyway. They laugh – at him more than me, I think.'

'They give boys money and they go. I think they let me go too, but oldest man says no. He lock me in bedroom. Later he rape me too, and some of his friends. I try to fight them, but always they have gun. When I fight they beat me.

'Then other men come, tied my hands, take me outside to van. I bite one and try to run, but I fall and they catch me. They throw me in van and drive me to flat, I think in Sarajevo. There was other girl there, and older woman. Girl sit in bedroom and cry, woman hit her and she cry more.

'Another man come, with two bodyguard. They stand with gun and he rape other girl. Then he rape me. I think he was… assessor? Testing goods?'

'Oh God.' The exclamation comes without conscious thought on Jory's part.

Zara looks scornfully at him. 'You think these things not happen, Dan? All the time? In Bosnia, Moldova, Ukraine? In UK, even? You don't know anything.'

He says, 'I realise that. I'm very sorry. Carry on, please.'

She nods, accepting his ignorance. 'It rare in Bosnia,' she concedes. 'I was unlucky. Not rare in other place, though.

'The bodyguard drive us to Albania, then take boat to Italy. They lock us inside cabin with no water. Other girl scream and cry and they hit her and beat her till she stop.

'In Ancona they put us in van and drive us again. We pick up other girls in other cities – Moldovan girls, Romanian girls, Bulgarian girls. We can't talk to them. We stop where lots of factory and warehouse, outside big city. I look on internet after, I think it was Milano. They have lorry and many men now, all with guns. I try to run again but they… they hold gun to other girl's head. Other girl from Sarajevo, Mahira. They tell me come back or they will kill her.

'I come back, but… they want to show. Tell us not to run. They shoot Mahira in head. Some men put her in trunk of car. Then they beat me and we all get in lorry. They drive us for very long time, all in dark. Sometimes stop for food and water and to take away shit-buckets. One girl kick over shit-bucket and lorry stink until men clean it out. Then they beat us all.

'After long driving, engine stop but nobody come. We hear other lorries outside, men talking, loud voice like loudspeaker, talking English maybe. I can't hear words. Then loud engine noise, and we feel moving like sea. I think how long we on lorry, guess we on boat to Britain, Ireland, maybe Sweden, Norway. Nowhere else make sense.

'When boat stop, I asleep. I wake as lorry drive onto land – then I hear voice, not like other voices. I know it isn't real person, or voice I hear with ears. It sound… We see American films in Bosnia, you know. Even with Kevin Costner. American films are everywhere. That voice sound like Morgan Freedman.'

The incongruity of this startles Jory. 'Morgan Freeman?' For a moment he thinks he remembers something about a different Morgan, but it eludes him.

Zara looks defiant. 'I tell you how it sound. You know about allies, you know how they come to us. I hear Morgan

Freedman speak to me. He say, *Salaam, daughter. You have come to England: a strange, barbarian land, it is true, but a land where you have a place, if you should seek it. However, it is not the place these men have in mind for you. When you are able to, you must run, and run quickly, for your life will depend upon it.*'

Her face is set still, but there's something about the corners of the mouth that's changed. It makes her look – not happy, but ecstatic, in the strictly mystical sense.

'I say, *But if I run men will kill other girls.* And the voice which sound like Morgan Freedman say, *Not if* you *kill all of the men first. Lend me your strength, daughter, and I will show you how it should be done.*

'Next time we stop, I wait with full shit-bucket for men to open door. I empty bucket on one man's head and throw it at other man. Other man has gun and I take it. I shoot them in heads, then other men come so I shoot them too. One run away and I shoot him. Then I run fast, like voice said. I leave other girls in open lorry with dead men outside, and run and run until I find place where there Muslim women, ask them help.'

'And you ended up here, with the Green Chapel,' says Jory.

'Scar find me,' Zara says. 'In women's shelter. She know my ally belong here.'

'What happened to the girls?' asks Jory.

'Police arrest them. Send back to their homes. If they have problems there, they deal with there.' Zara is clearly pleased with the outcome.

'And this direct action…' he says. 'It's your idea? Is it the same people-trafficking ring?'

Zara nods.

'You want to rescue other women in your situation,' Jory surmises. 'Like you did before.'

'Yes,' says Zara. 'I want that. But more, I want to kill more of bastard men who bring them here.'

'Yes, I see,' says Jory.

***

Sir Gawain had a complicated relationship with women. He took a dim view of wives who betrayed their husbands, especially his mother (who had complicated relationships with just about everybody) and Queen Guinevere – but when he was on the receiving end of a married woman's favours (we'll get to her later) he didn't get angry until he found her husband had put her up to it.

Despite this chivalry-with-benefits approach, he was well-enough known for defending the honour of women that he was nicknamed 'the Maiden's Knight'. In some stories he has a fairy bride, but it's his other marriage, as told in a couple of medieval poems and numerous modern retellings, where he emerges as a proto-feminist.

The story goes that King Arthur, for some contrived reason or other, would die if he were unable to lift the curse on a particular knight – the key to which was to answer the question, 'What do women truly want?'. Naturally he took pains to interview a number of women on the issue, but the one who claimed to have the definitive answer was Dame Ragnell the Loathly Lady – an old, wizened, grotesquely ugly woman, who declared that she would only reveal it in exchange for marriage to one of Arthur's best knights. In some versions, she asks for Sir Gawain by name and he agrees: in others her ultimatum's open-ended, and the game lad volunteers.

In any event, Gawain gladly sacrificed his own marital happiness to save his uncle's life. Throughout their betrothal, despite the cruel taunts of his fellow knights and their ladies, he treated his bride with perfect courtesy – until their wedding night, when Ragnell revealed that she was actually a lithe, sexually voracious young supermodel who'd been cursed with a serious dose of ugliness.

One imagines that Gawain, however chivalrously he may have acted towards her, was rather relieved by this.

There was a catch, though. Ragnell had been cursed by the same tricksy enchanter (and if it wasn't Morgan le Fay, it should have been) who'd cursed the other knight, who turned out to be her brother. Now she was married to a good knight, Ragnell's curse was only half lifted: she could either be beautiful by night and ugly by day, or vice versa. Gawain had the choice between parading his trophy wife around Camelot all day, but being stuck with a gorgon in the bedroom, or keeping her beauty a secret for his own nocturnal satisfaction.

Wisely, he ducked the question, and told Ragnell it was up to her – which was all he needed to do to lift the curse altogether, and he discovered you really can have your cake and eat it. By all accounts, the couple then lived happily ever after, or at least until the kind of early, unpleasant death that characters live until in this sort of story.

You may have guessed the answer Ragnell gave Arthur, which uncursed her brother: it's that *What all women want is to be given their own way.*

It's advice that Jory first read when he was thirteen, and which has stood him in good stead for much of his adult life.

11. THE MAIDENS

At ten o'clock the next evening – and very much against his better judgement, as nearly everything he does seems to be these days – Jory is lying on a warehouse roof and watching for the arrival of a particular lorry from the ferry-port nearby.

These docks are interchangeable with all docks everywhere – bleak, blocky, functional, inhabited by giant metal dinosaur-skeletons and spattered everywhere with graffiti and seagull-shit. As it happens, they're not far from the tree-lined suburban idyll where Jory killed James Ribbens, which might tell you something trite about human nature.

At Shafiq's strict instructions Jory's still an observer here, black clothes emphasising his non-alignment. Shafiq's reminded him that he's still pledged not to run away from the Chapel, but now Merry's joined them, Jory's desire to be anywhere else has dropped considerably. Shafiq's been acting more friendly since Jory agreed to come along on this criminal jaunt, but there's still a coldness to him that began with Merry's arrival.

She came to his bed again last night, tense after her day of planning, with bunched muscles he helped smooth out of her. The two of them had a strained, absurd conversation where he agonised over her going into a combat situation without him to protect her, and she laughed heartily and reminded him how long she's been doing this.

She didn't travel here with him. Jory was driven here by Cantrell, along with a dozen hoodied Chapel members. Squig and Lee sat either side of Jory, trying not to look as if they were guarding him. Shafiq and Merry were in another van, Scar and Zara in a third, all taking different routes to their destination.

Squig scouted out Jory's route to the roof, which involved a row of rubbish skips and a fire escape. Jory saw the boy pull out a spray-can on his way back down, and add a modest tag to the building's already deeply-layered graffiti.

Now Jory stays low on the near-flat asphalt slope, his head a little lower than his ankles, presenting a minimal profile. It's hardly likely the traffickers will be expecting an ambush, but he doesn't want to draw the attention of the docks' security patrols. (In fact he's considered putting an end to this nonsense by accidentally-on-purpose doing just that thing, but he knows the Chapel would blame him for their failure to rescue the girls. Besides, he might get Merry arrested, and however he might feel about this whole unwise enterprise, Jory can't countenance that.)

'Taylor?' hisses a voice from further along the roof, and he starts. He clutches to the roof, although its slope's so shallow he was never in much danger of rolling off. 'Is that you?'

He knows before he looks that it's no Knight of the Circle. Their voices are all male.

A figure, far smaller than him but also dressed in black, laden with binoculars, a radio and various other police-issue paraphernalia, is shimmying prostrately across the roof towards him.

Her next words are 'What the fuck are you doing here?', which would narrow it down even if he didn't recognise her face.

'Inspector Kinsey,' he says weakly. 'I might ask you the same question.'

Occasionally, in Jory's line of work, the clichés are all you've got to fall back on.

* * *

You may, I suppose, be wondering where I am. The fact is, I'm not much of a one for these direct actions. Shaf came to me last night, just as I was packing up my tent, and asked me, 'So Dale, what are your plans for tomorrow?'

I said, 'Well, you know. I'm a balladeer, not a hero or an outlaw. You lot fight crime – or, you know, commit it, if that's what seems reasonable – and I'll write it up afterwards.' These conversations always make me nervous, which is why I was trying to sneak off quietly before this one happened.

You see, the thing is I see myself as a story*teller*, taking command of the stories rather than following them. I like to think the minstrel characters in these legends of ours – Allan a'Dale, King Arthur's bard Taliesin, all the skalds and scops and troubadours – are above all that. We're meant to be observers… not neutral, exactly, because of course we praise the heroes of our tales and express certain reservations about the villains… but dispassionate. We may get tangled up in the edges of the action (in fact it's important, it lends us the veracity we need), but the stories we tell can't be about us.

At heart we have to remain outsiders, as aloof and uninvolved as a Greek chorus or a Shakespearean prologue or… well, an omniscient narrator I suppose.

I may have made it sound as if I'm a paid-up member of the Green Chapel, but my loyalty's to the friends I have there, not to the institution. Originally, Allan a'Dale wasn't even a Merry Man.

Shafiq was still looking at me quizzically, so I added: 'You know me, Shaf – not much of a fighter, am I? I can hold my own in a pub brawl if I have to, but on the whole I'd rather have a quiet drink.'

'Especially if someone else is paying, eh?' Shafiq said quietly.

I shivered. Don't get me wrong, Shaf's a mate. I know he'd never hurt me, physically anyway. But he – or more likely his ally, Robin or the Green Knight or whatever you want to call it – has this way of looking at you which makes you feel… well, looked at. Examined. Judged. Found wanting.

Oh, I'm a hypocritical coward, I know that. But most of the time everyone around me's too nice to make me face up to the fact.

Then Shafiq clapped me on the back. 'Good lifestyle if you can keep it up,' he said, all smiles again. 'Good luck with whatever you're up to.' In fact I had a Circle gig booked later in the week, but I wasn't going to tell him that. 'Don't be a stranger, OK?'

And off he wandered, going to do the right thing as per usual.

* * *

The Green Chapel's hard-gathered intelligence, from its people on the ground and those they've paid for their knowledge, says that the lorry's bound for Sheffield and an expensive hotel with unimpeachable security, where the captive women are divvied up among brothel-keepers before being taken away and whored out to customers.

Whatever Jory's reservations about the direct action, thinking about their experiences – and indeed Zara's – makes him feel sick. Captive, alone, wounded and brutalised, in a country whose language they barely speak, and forced into degrading sex with strangers… the very idea makes him shudder in sympathetic horror.

The hotel effectively belongs to the crime cartel, and assaulting it is beyond the Chapel's current capabilities. However, between leaving the ferry from Antwerp and arriving at the hotel, the lorry will make one single stop. It'll loop around behind these warehouses for a brief check-in with the bosses' agent at the docks, before proceeding to the nearest motorway junction. Its short halt here – the moment when Zara made her escape two years ago, although they've changed their procedures since then – is the Chapel's only real chance to waylay it en route.

Green-hooded men and women are already distributed around the open area, occupying entrances, lurking behind skips, hiding in the shadows. If all's gone according to plan, they've already grabbed the agent and stripped him, after finding a Chapel member who looks enough like him to wear his clothes. Jory hasn't been told any further details of the plan once the man's flagged down the truck, but it's obvious that violence is going to be involved.

It's also likely to happen any minute now. Just as Kinsey accosted him, Jory saw a lorry with the branding he's been told to look out for, turning the otherwise deserted corner which leads from the ferry terminal to this out-of-the-way storage complex.

'What the hell is the Circle's interest here?' Kinsey's hissing at him furiously. 'This is a police operation! Or are you bastards muscling in on all my cases now?'

Something's very wrong here. Kinsey has to be waiting for the lorry too – it's far too big a coincidence otherwise – and she won't be here alone. She knows enough to be watching for it *here*, the one place prior to Sheffield where anything's likely to happen to it. Shafiq was wrong to say the police had no interest in the traffickers, thinks Jory.

Unless, of course, their interest is in the Chapel itself.

The lorry's steadily approaching the stretch of road beneath them. Thinking quickly, Jory realises he's going to have to make himself obnoxious. Again.

'Oh, we absolutely have an interest, Inspector,' he tells her crisply. 'I'm going to have to ask you to tell me now exactly what your people are doing here.'

'Fuck *you*,' snaps Kinsey. 'I've been trying to set this up for years, but that bastard's always blocked me. Oh – sweet bloody Jesus, I've just realised. He's brought you in to stop me, hasn't he? You're colluding with him.'

Him? wonders Jory. He doesn't say it out loud – suddenly he seems to be back in quest mode, and his device's canniness is interposing between his brain and his mouth. 'The Knights of the Circle don't "collude", Kinsey. I insist you tell me right now what the police operation here is.'

Below, the lorry's trundled to a halt while a wide, muscular man in a boiler-suit approaches it. Jory thinks he recognises him as a Chapel man called Twink, one of the unallied ones. *He's taking a risk*, thinks Jory, before remembering that this is supposed to mean the fight's a fair one. Twink is probably armed in any case. That said, the lorry's cab holds three men, and Jory imagines they are too.

One of the men leans out to talk to the newcomer, but Twink beckons him down. The man shrugs, opens the door and climbs out onto the cracked tarmac. An arrow takes him in the shoulder, whirling him around like a rattle, and he cries out in surprise.

'What the *fuck*?' cries Kinsey.

Hooded women and men pour out from the background, suddenly visible, as Twink jumps into the cab and wrestles the second man out, grasping his gun tightly. The driver drops the handbrake and accelerates, pitching both men onto the hard road surface. As he does it he wrestles with some kind of phone – and Kinsey's radio crackles into life.

'*Shit, boss!*' it says. '*I mean mayday! We're being attacked! There's hundreds of the bast – ungh.*' A Chapel man with a bow – Jory recognises the stance as uniquely Shafiq's – has fired an arrow through the moving lorry's open door, burying it in the driver's thigh. The lorry, which has moved scarcely three metres, trundles to a halt again. Jory hears cries of pain over the radio, sees the driver clutching at his leg.

'Shit!' Kinsey's shouting. She turns to Jory. 'You've got men here! Get them on this now! Mine are setting up in Sheffield. This was supposed to be the easy bit!'

'No men,' gasps Jory, shocked the sudden reversal of expectations. 'There's only me.'

The driver's dragged bleeding from the cab as a distinctive red-hooded figure turns the engine off and retrieves the keys. Scar leans out of the window and throws them to another woman at the van's rear. Jory's too dazed by this turn of events to tell, but he presumes it's Zara. He can't spot Merry among the figures beneath him.

'Kinsey,' he asks. 'The women on that lorry –'

'Armed undercover officers. The illegals are all on the ferry with Europol.' She barks into the radio, 'Ticia, we're under attack, repeat, under attack! Some kind of rival gang. If they let you out –'

'Belay that!' Jory shouts, aware that they're not currently on a ship but unable to think of a better phrase.

Kinsey continues, glaring, '– just shoot the fuckers. We'll sweat the paperwork later.'

Unthinking, only knowing that he must prevent a massacre, Jory stands. At his device's bidding he runs, unfailingly firm-footed, to the corner of the roof nearest the melee, then leaps.

He's lighter without his armour. As he hurtles through the cold night air, he hears a rapidly receding chain of expletives from Jade Kinsey.

He hits the lorry's roof spreadeagled, all the wind forced from his lungs. Ignoring the pain of impact and his breathlessness, he clambers to his feet, stumbles to the lorry's rear and drops again. This time he lands mostly upright, but staggers sideways and nearly falls.

Zara has the key in the lock and is staring at him, her mouth a lower-case 'o' in her inexpressive face.

'St…' he gasps, but without breath he can't complete the word. He shakes his head, waving his hands frantically at her. 'D…'

Zara realises what he's saying and is disgusted. She gives him a look of utter contempt, then tuts, and throws open the rear door of the truck.

* * *

Jory lunges at Zara, grabbing her and knocking her to the ground as the woman in the doorway opens fire. They hit the tarmac hard, and he's reminded strongly of his first encounter with Jack Bennett. He gasps with the impact, his first breath since he left the roof a minute or so before. It tastes of exhaust fumes, salt air, Zara's cheap deodorant.

His head whirls. The nearby Green Chapel members are already scattering like leaves. Scar appears above the two of them, crouches down and drags Zara to her feet. Behind them the policewomen's guns roar. Scar turns away with Zara on her arm, hesitates momentarily, then turns back to offer Jory her other hand. He grasps it gratefully and pulls himself up. The three of them run, Scar pulling him and Zara along with her momentum. Bullets spang after them along the asphalt.

Kinsey's standing on the roof now, talking into a compact megaphone she's managed to produce from somewhere. 'Police!' it shouts. 'You are ordered to put down your weapons and surrender! That means *you*, Taylor!' He's thankful that Kinsey herself isn't armed.

The Chapel's people have worked it out already, alerted by the throng of young-looking women with easily-concealed weapons pouring from the van's rear doors. Everyone's running, diverging as if by instinct, diving for the shadows, climbing for the roofs. If there's one thing they all do well – and Jory thinks this has to be a device thing, shared out somehow among the Chapel's unallied followers in their capacity as generic Merry Men – it's blending into the scenery.

Jory risks a glance back and there's nobody in green visible – just the policewomen, some of them still trying to give chase, some standing still and peering around in confusion, some hanging back to help their colleagues – and the three policemen, bleeding into the cracks in the road.

He hears sirens. Whether they're ambulances or police reinforcements, he doesn't know.

* * *

'OK,' says Shafiq later, drinking from a giant bottle of water. 'This hasn't been one of our better days.'

They're back at the Chapel's campsite. The last minivan rolled into the nearby concealed clearing half an hour ago, to be driven away by Chapel affiliates who Jory doesn't recognise. Everyone's made it intact, though there are a couple of superficial bullet wounds, a lot of bruising and a cracked wrist sustained through an unwise choice of escape route.

Although it's the middle of the night and those who stayed behind are – well, were – sleeping, the direct action party have lit up the camp fire and amped up the music. Some of their fellows, though not all, have emerged sleepily to join them.

'Too right,' says Jory. He was too tired and stressed when he got back to refuse a beer, and its tawny, spiky taste – and content, presumably – is mellowing him. 'You screwed up a police operation which could have broken the entire trafficking ring.' He's with what he's come to recognise as the core of the Chapel – Shafiq and Merry, Scar and Zara, with Squig, and Cantrell hovering nearby but mostly watching the dancing. Twink's getting a lot of attention from the women for his bravery, and Cantrell's watching him with some appreciation too. The young conjurer, whose name Jory now knows is Burn, is shuffling a deck in preparation for a turn.

'Might've,' says Scar. 'If it worked. Those women might've never made it through security at the other end.'

'Even so,' Jory affirms. 'We only wanted to save a lorryload of kidnapped women. Inspector Kinsey wanted to stop the kidnappers for good.'

'One gang,' says Zara. 'One gang of kidnappers only.'

'Even so,' Jory says again and shrugs.

He sees that Merry's giving him a knowing smile. *Oh bugger*, he thinks belatedly. *Did I just say 'We wanted'?*

'Our intentions were good,' says Merry. 'Our intelligence obviously wasn't. Perhaps I could have found out at work what Kinsey was planning, but there would have been no plausible reason for me to ask. Even we didn't think there was one.'

Shafiq says, 'The Circle could certainly have taken on the cartel bosses, Dan, but the Chapel's not that kind of organisation. We've got the will, but we're not powerful enough. The Circle have the power, but not the will.'

Neither way is better, thinks Jory again. *Both ways are necessary*. 'Your intelligence was fine as far as it went,' he says. 'It was just incomplete. You're right, the police haven't done anything about the trafficking up to now. Officers like Kinsey must have wanted to, but they've been blocked at a very senior level. As luck would have it though,' he says, 'Kinsey's Chief Constable had a bit of a run-in with a crazed killer a couple of weeks ago. Headless bodies jumping out at him, that sort of thing. Partly my fault, I'm sorry to say.'

Squig laughs at that. The others smile, at least. The Chapel like stories about authority figures being discomfited.

'He's been on gardening leave ever since,' continues Jory. 'Kinsey must have seen it as her chance to act at last.

If she arrested someone at a high enough level, she might even have been able to get Sir Michael on a corruption charge. Probably not, of course, but a girl can dream.'

'You like her,' Merry observes, out of the blue but casually enough.

'No,' Jory says. 'She's arrogant, she hates me and everything I stand for, and she swears a lot. But that's career women for you, I suppose.' That gets another laugh from Squig, although he didn't mean it to. 'I do admire her, though. She's got nerve and she cares about her officers. She's got a clear idea of what her purpose is.'

'What're you getting at?' Scar wonders.

'Between us,' says Jory, 'we injured three of her people and aborted an operation she's going to have to account for, probably to the same Chief Constable who's been blocking it for years. We seriously ruined her day, and probably became her case on an official basis as well. I've a feeling she's going to come after us mercilessly, and she won't be wrong to either. Which is a pity,' he adds, 'because otherwise, if you'd approached her tactfully, she could have made rather a good inside contact.'

Shafiq looks thoughtful. Squig looks drunk. Cantrell laughs heartily, either at Jory's suggestion or Twink's dancing.

'She call you "Taylor",' Zara observes neutrally.

'Leave it, Za,' says Scar.

* * *

Everyone's late to bed that night, Jory included. The sun's already threatening to rise when, as he hoped, Malory comes to him a third time. She kisses him and takes off her hoodie.

'I knew you'd understand us,' she says as she undresses, 'once you saw.'

'To understand,' says Jory, 'is not necessarily to condone.' He means it to sound mock-sententious, but realises immediately that the mockery was lost in transit. Malory smirks.

'Your instincts were good, though,' she says, shedding her blouse. 'When it came to a crisis, you sided with us, not with the police.'

'I intervened,' Jory admits. 'I'd promised myself I wouldn't. I was just trying to stop people getting killed, though. I didn't side with anyone.'

'Of course you didn't.' Malory hits him with the knowing smile again. She's only wearing knickers now, and he finds the effect strangely mesmerising. '*We* know that.'

Jory struggles to continue. 'Also, what you said earlier, about good intentions? I don't agree. I think you all took your lead from Zara, and I think that what she wants is revenge. Utterly understandable, of course, and nobody has any business telling her not to feel that way, but still… as motivations go, it's not a good one.'

'I can think of certain Knights of the Round Table who'd disagree,' Malory says. 'Budge up.' Naked now, she climbs into bed with him. 'Didn't Gawain and Agravaine hunt down and kill Sir Lamorak when they thought he'd killed their mother? Bad example possibly, since the murderer was actually Gaheris, but still, they obviously thought it was the right thing to do.'

'Not if you're not sure of your target, it's not,' says Jory. He's going to say more about the injured policemen, but he's distracted by the thought of Gawain's mother, Morgause. 'All Lamorak had done to Morgause was have an affair with her. And by all accounts she had sex with anybody.'

'Lucky woman,' murmurs Malory. 'At this moment I don't seem to be having sex with anybody.'

'No, but…' Jory's losing his train of thought again. 'Today was a mess, Mal. It was an almighty cock-up.'

Jory's embarrassed, for a moment, to have used that word to a lady, but then he tells himself to get a grip. A moment later Malory does just that, and Jory doesn't think about anything for quite a while.

* * *

'Mal,' he asks her later. 'What you said the other night, about devices of divine origin. Did you mean because the Green Knight used to be a nature-god?'

'Bingo,' Malory agrees sleepily. 'Got it in one.'

'But you implied mine was too,' he says. 'The way Gawain's strength waxes with the sun – is he supposed to have been a solar god originally?'

'Mm, that's the theory,' she replies.

'Then why are they enemies?' he wonders, his mind drifting. 'I mean, the sun and the forest aren't opposing forces… not really… the sun nourishes the forest, shouldn't the forest embrace the sunlight…?' A concern grips him suddenly. 'Malory, you don't… I mean, people here don't…'

Awake now suddenly, he's not sure how to broach the subject without giving offence. He's met a few neo-pagans in his life – historical re-enactments tend to bring them out in modest numbers – but he's always avoided discussing their beliefs with them. Or indeed his.

'Does anybody here *worship* Shafiq?' he asks now. He's heard of rogue bearers venerating their own devices, but they tend to be the demented ones, the Beard Collectors of this world, rather than anyone with the presence of mind to run an organised activist network like the Chapel.

Malory laughs, then catches his look. 'You're serious.'

'Well –' he begins, embarrassed now.

'We don't encourage it,' she says. 'Worshipping the devices is a bad idea, for purely pragmatic reasons.'

'Well, it's wrong, of course,' he says. 'Mistaken, I mean. But pragmatically?'

'Get some sleep,' she tells him, and she won't be drawn further on the subject.

Outside, the sun rises.

* * *

They're both awakened by a knock at the trapdoor. Jory's lying on the left-hand side of the mattress, nearest the hatch, pincered between Malory's cool, smooth thighs. He starts awake, and his involuntary jolt wakes her.

She's immediately alert. 'What was that?' she asks.

'I think it was –' Jory begins, then the knock comes again.

'Oh, *hell*,' Malory hisses. She looks about them for a moment, but it's perfectly obvious that there's nowhere in Jory's wooden box where she can hide.

'Shall I pretend not to be in?' It's the best Jory can think of on the spur of the moment.

Malory gives him a withering look as she grapples with her underwear. 'Don't be silly, dear. We'll have to brazen it out and take the consequences. Put some pants on, for God's sake.'

Jory puts on last night's pants, checks to see Malory's decently covered (mostly with his sleeping bag), and opens the hatch. Shafiq puts his head up through it.

Seeing them Shafiq flinches, pauses for a breath, then nods to Malory as if he'd fully expected her to be there. 'I wanted to let you know,' he says '– both of you – that we're striking camp. You're right about Kinsey, Jory. We should expect her to be looking for us. We have to move.'

The news has obviously reached other parts of the camp, because now Jory listens – and now the trapdoor's open – there are hammering and rustling noises suggesting tents are being dismantled, and distant squeaks of things with wheels being pushed along.

'Naturally your promise doesn't hold once we've moved on,' Shafiq says quietly. 'After yesterday you've earned our respect, if not our trust. ' His eyes flicker towards Malory again, then back to Jory. 'All we ask is that you give us an hour's head start before you leave. We're used to being hunted, and we know how to cover our tracks. Or,' he says, 'you're welcome to come along with us. If you like.'

He doesn't quite look into Jory's eyes as he says it, and without quite meaning to Jory finds himself looking into Malory's, as if for confirmation. She's found a scrunchie somewhere, and is tying back her glorious autumn-coloured hair, the sleeping bag precarious around her breasts.

She says, 'Oh, I'd have had to go today anyway. I'm expected back on campus. My head of department thinks I've been at a two-day conference on the role of cognition in visual response.'

'So when are you back at the Fastness?' Jory asks.

'Not for a week or two,' she says, 'barring any sudden urgent need for my input. Shaf will let me know where the new hideaway is.'

'Listen, I've got things to do,' Shafiq says. 'I'll let you think it through between you.' And he withdraws.

Jory and Malory are still staring at each other. 'Well,' says Jory slowly, 'I think he took that *relatively* well.'

Malory pouts. 'I told you, Shaf and I aren't together.'

Jory's perversely pleased – or would be, if he didn't fear its consequences for his friend – to have found what seems to be Malory's one blind spot.

'It could change the group dynamic, though,' she muses. 'Certainly if he tells anyone else. Marian's other suitors always turn out to be villains who are coercing her. There'd be a lot of suspicion, and it could well alter the relationships between the Chapel's devices. I'd have to do some modelling.'

'Well, at least you're dressed for it,' says Jory.

She throws the sleeping bag at him. Then she pounces on him and drags them both down onto the mattress.

12. THE AXE

Jory stays behind, of course. He and Malory have already said their goodbyes (then chosen a discreet moment for her to exit the treehouse), when she makes her hearty farewell to the rest of the Green Chapel and walks away, alone, towards where she's parked her rental car.

Jory helps demolish the treehouse, using a large axe that someone brings him. He doesn't feel much sentiment about the wooden box that's been home by default during the past few weeks. In fact he finds it thoroughly liberating.

He helps with some of the other bigger structures as well. The wooden struts and poles he gives back to the local ecosystem by leaving them to rot among the pines. Manufactured or non-biodegradable components he loads into the variety of wheelbarrows, hand trucks and shopping trolleys which seem to be ferrying the campsite's essentials to the vehicle park.

Again they've been brought by people he doesn't recognise, not Chapel regulars, and he wonders whether this is a favour the Chapel asks from the beneficiaries of its stolen largesse.

Shafiq's own people are also leaving in dribs and drabs – now in their motley civvies, green work clothes packed away in rucksacks and duffel bags. He's said goodbye to Lee and Burn and several others by the time it's Cantrell's turn to go.

'Look after yourself, big fellow,' the ex-priest says, loading the last of his things onto a barrow with the help of one of the anonymous handlers. He claps Jory on the shoulder and grins his wolfish grin, then takes out a folded scrap of paper and tucks it into the pocket of Jory's tracksuit top. 'If you ever feel the need of a little *spiritual direction*, you get in touch, OK?'

He picks up the barrow and heads off into the woods, leaving Jory half shocked and half amused by his audacity.

Over the next few hours he says goodbye to Squig (who leaves him with a heartfelt 'See you round.'), to Zara (who shakes his hand coldly and flicks him a curt half-smile) and, he thinks, to all the other friends he's made here.

In the end, it's just Shafiq and Scar, doing a final sweep of the area. They're not looking for evidence that there was someone here – because there's plenty of that – but for anything that would identify who it was, or worse, give any sign of where they've gone. The axe is still lying at the foot of the oak, among the shards of Jory's treehouse, and Shafiq collects it.

'I think we're finished here,' he tells his lieutenant. 'Head over to the car, and I'll join you shortly. I just need to talk to Jory.'

'You mean Dan,' Scar reminds him sternly.

'I'll see you in a few minutes,' Shafiq repeats.

'And I'll see *you* never, right?' the Scotswoman tells Jory levelly. 'Yeah, that's the way it should be. You bugger off and get yourself killed defending the realm from scary bastards like me.' She punches him on the shoulder and walks away.

'She likes you,' Shafiq observes as they watch her march across to the treeline. This comes as a surprise to Jory. 'You have quite the talent for that. Scar doesn't usually like anyone. So, is that what you'll do?'

'Go back to the Circle?' Jory shrugs. 'Of course. My job's there. The Circle suppresses a lot of evil in this country, you know. There's domestic terrorism, organised crime, petty thuggery and murder… Obviously we can't stop all of it, and sometimes a man with a device does less harm than one with a sawn-off shotgun. But still, we stop some of it. That's important.'

Shafiq nods. 'And us?'

Jory shuffles his feet in the fallen leaves. 'Listen, I'm sorry about how I was when we arrived here. I didn't understand, back then. When I got here, I thought you were just the bad guys.'

'We had just kidnapped you, to be fair,' Shafiq concedes.

'The Circle thinks it has a monopoly on heroism,' he says, 'but they – we, I mean – we're trying to be one particular kind of hero. Knightly heroes, I suppose. Whereas you in the Chapel are –'

'Churlish ones?' Shafiq suggests.

Jory smiles. 'When I get back, I'll see if I can manage to deflect the Circle's attentions away from you. I'm not sure. I'll have a careful think about what I can get away with.'

'You do that,' Shafiq says. He nods at Jory and starts walking away towards the treeline. After a few paces he pauses and turns back, unwilling suddenly to leave. 'I suppose Merry will help you with that,' he says. 'Malory, I mean.'

'I guess so,' says Jory again, uncomfortable with his sudden change of tone.

'You'll be seeing each other again, I imagine,' Shafiq elaborates.

'Well, of course,' says Jory. 'Even before… what's happened, she was my best friend.'

Shafiq leans on the axe-haft. 'Mine too,' he says. 'Mine too. And more than that, of course.'

'Well, yes,' says Jory. 'In terms of your devices, you mean. Your allies, if that's what you call them. It's not like you and Malory are married.' He thrusts all the confidence he can muster into the assertion.

Shafiq laughs. 'Of course not. Nor were Robin and Marian, in most stories. But still, if someone asked you in a pub quiz to name Robin Hood's wife, what would you say?'

'Well, OK,' Jory says. He's dismayed, but not really surprised, that Shafiq wants to have this out with him after all. 'But you know, I don't think the devices dictate our actual romantic lives.'

Although he once again invests it with every sign of conviction, he's not entirely sure of this. As I've said, the Circle has stories of its Tristans finding their Iseults, its Gereints their Enids. There are even accounts of women who bear the device of Queen Guinevere, having to choose between an abstract faithfulness to the eternally absent Head or the ardent attentions of a disastrously present Sir Lancelot.

Shafiq snorts. 'I wouldn't have to look far to find a story where Guy of Gisbourne's trying to seduce Maid Marian.'

Jory has to concede that one. 'OK,' he says. 'But one where she accepts him willingly? Malory's free to lead her own life, never mind what Marian would have done. It doesn't stop her being your… what, symbolic bride?' He's thinking now of the church's relationship to Christ, he realises, although the analogy won't mean much to Shafiq.

Shafiq says, 'I'm serious, Jory. You've been a guest here. It's hardly fair to help yourself to your host's… good nature. Take advantage, I mean. Of your host's… generosity.'

Shafiq's brow is furrowed, as if these thoughts he's having are unfamiliar ones to him. And however he phrases it, Jory knows that the idea of a woman as property is alien both to his old friend and to the man he's come to know again over the past few weeks.

Jory's seen this confusion before, sometimes in Knights newly bound to their devices, sometimes in rogue device-holders who can't quite square the self they think they remember with the promptings of the device. In these cases it's almost invariably the device that wins out.

'Frankly, that's not acceptable behaviour,' Shafiq says sternly. He lifts the axe up to his shoulder.

Belatedly Jory realises the danger he's in.

***

It's a killer, that story-blindness. I mean, I'd have twigged ages ago that there's trouble brewing, here in this abandoned encampment. I bet you have too, sitting there while I tell you about it, even if you're not au fait with the story of Sir Gawain and the Green Knight.

In the poem, after Gawain rides off that next midwinter to find the Green Chapel, meet the Green Knight and have his head cut off, he gets sidetracked en route and ends up staying with a charming couple called the Bertilaks. While his lordship's out, Lady Bertilak gets *surprisingly hospitable* with their houseguest, although the poet would have us believe that this goes no further than chaste kissing.

Unfortunately, Sir Gawain and Lord B have made the slightly strange bargain that Bertilak will give Gawain the spoils of his hunt in return for the proceeds of Gawain's time spend lounging round the house all day. An unembarrassed Gawain passes his hostess's kisses onto his host, but he 'forgets' to hand over the quite-possibly-symbolic green sash which Lady Bertilak gives him on the third day.

Lord Bertilak turns out to be, as is the way in these stories, none other than the Green Knight, and he and Gawain proceed to the Green Chapel and their long-awaited decapitation date.

Jory's dismay now arises from recognising suddenly that he, Sir Gawain's stand-in, is standing in the Green Chapel right now – assuming Shafiq's comrades haven't managed to set up another one yet – and that he's here with: a) the Green Knight, who's upset to discover that his guest has been accepting sexual favours from his notional wife behind his back, and b) a bloody great big axe.

I hope that's all clear now.

* * *

'We agreed on a game of buffets,' Shafiq says. 'As I recall it's my turn to play.'

Shafiq was there, of course, when Jory had his fatal contretemps with Shaun Hobson. There's nothing surprising about him being able to pick up that conversation where Hobson left off. That doesn't stop it being eerie to hear thoughts that by rights belong to Hobson coming out of Shafiq's head.

'Very funny,' says Jory. 'The joke's over now, though.'

'Oddly enough, I agree,' says Shafiq grimly. He hefts the axe.

'Shafiq,' says Jory, in his best negotiating-with-loonies voice. 'You don't want to do this, do you? I'm your friend. I'm unarmed. Surely you don't want to kill me while I can't defend myself?'

'Oh, the irony,' Shafiq says flatly. 'How many defenceless men have you hacked down, Jory? Or was Shaun just a glitch? Now, stand still and don't try to weasel your way out of this.'

Jory realises he has indeed been backing away, even while the device within him urges him to stand his ground and face his fate like a man. To be fair even Gawain flinches once in the poem, the first time the Green Knight swings his axe in his direction – but after that he stands 'still as the stone' while the Green Knight takes his blow. Jory's human, though, and he can't help his reflex.

At least his voice is calm. 'There was no deal, Shaf. The contest was Hobson's idea, not mine – I never accepted his terms. It wasn't a game, it was…'

There's no good place for the sentence to go. Jory swallows, and says: 'It was murder. I killed your friend. I was on Circle business, so the law let me off, but it was still murder. I'm sorry. Kill me for revenge if you must, but don't fool yourself that that's not murder too.'

Shafiq's face twists uglily. 'Don't quibble with me, Jory. Merry's not safe with you around.'

In *Sir Gawain and the Green Knight*, you'll be relieved to know, Sir Gawain's humiliated but lives. The Green Knight deploys his axe twice, deliberately missing Gawain's neck, then on the third swing gives him a shaving-cut. The whole thing's revealed as a test, or a game, or a seasonal ritual – it's all a bit vague, but essentially Morgan le Fay's behind it all. If it's a test, then keeping the girdle means Gawain hasn't got the top score, but luckily it's still a pass mark. He goes back to Camelot chastened and wearing the sash as a reminder of his imperfections.

Jory has no faith that Shafiq will follow this merciful precedent. Apart from anything else, he suspects he's scored much lower in the test.

His steady reversing brings him up against a tree – he daren't look up, but he thinks it's the birch where he met Cantrell, his first night here in the encampment. He can't retreat any further without actually running away, and that his Knightly honour rebels against.

'Just think for a moment, Shaf,' he says. 'How's Malory going to feel about this? If you think chopping off her boyfriend's head is going to make her finally fall in love with you, you really have lost your marbles.'

Shafiq shrugs. 'It seems to have worked for you.' He raises the axe above his shoulder. Jory grits his teeth and steels himself to stand his ground and face the coming blade.

Just as Shafiq swings, a yell comes from the edge of the clearing. His aim's thrown, and Jory, startled from his resolve – well, ducks. Again, it feels instinctive, and he hears his device's roar of rage as he does it.

The axe cleaves deeply into the birch-trunk, and very slightly into the top edge of Jory's left ear. He flinches from the blade, feeling the blood well up and drip at a surprising rate from the tiny nick.

The shout comes again. 'Shaf!' The voice is northern, gruff, familiar. The speaker, visible now as he strides across to them, is tall and broad, an old-fashioned suit of armour built from flesh and bone. A man with legs like that has little need to run. He's with them in moments.

He's wearing a soiled tan raincoat, frayed corduroy jeans and what Jory, who knows what he's looking for, recognises as a shiny new pair of prison-issue boots.

'Jack?' Shafiq lets go of the axe, which stays quivering in the tree. He and Jack Bennett ignore Jory and embrace in a manly bear-hug. The big man actually lifts Shafiq off his feet, apparently unawares.

Jory feels like a chess pawn, wielded desperately by a beginner in a game against a grand master. The situation in his immediate vicinity keeps changing drastically, in ways which make no sense from where he's standing.

'What's that posh bastard doing here?' is the next thing Jack Bennett says. 'And where's everyone else?'

'Hello, Bennett,' says Jory.

Shafiq appears confused at the reminder of Jory's presence. Then he looks defensive. 'He's… It's complicated,' he says. 'We struck camp today; you're lucky to catch us. Jack, never mind him, what are *you* doing here?'

Jack Bennett laughs. 'Last-minute transfer, weren't it? Screws told me this morning I'd got my upgrade for good behaviour. Said they were taking me somewhere down south. The daft bastards put me in a low-security transfer van, just the one guard in the back with me. I cracked his head and kicked the doors out while we were doing seventy down the M6.'

'Good grief,' says Jory. Bennett has a cut over one eye, and his hands look bruised, but there's nothing else to suggest that he recently threw himself out of a fast-moving vehicle.

Shafiq stares at Jack. 'You jumped?'

'No.' Bennett grins. 'I banged and shouted till the driver started slowing down. Waited till he got to about thirty, *then* I jumped. Made a break for it into the woods. This was first thing mind, it's taken me all day hitchhiking to get here.'

'That's brilliant, Jack.' Shafiq is happier to see his friend than Jory can remember seeing him. 'Scar's over at the clearing with the 2CV. You can come with us to the new site. The others will have got most of the tents up by now. We'll get you cleaned up and find you a change of clothes, eh?'

Bennett nods. 'Suits me very nicely. These ones stink. I found them in someone's shed on an allotment.' There's certainly a strong smell to him, weeks-stale sweat with hints of manure. He reaches out one-handed, and pulls the woodman's axe from the tree like a knife from a cake. 'We'd best bring this, though.' Then he stares closely at it, recognising it. 'Hmm. Did I interrupt something?'

'Nothing important,' says Jory. He can hear something, very distantly, a sound like a rainstick being shaken fast and rhythmically.

'He coming with us, then?' Bennett asks. 'I don't want him running and telling those toffs of his where I've been.'

'I may not need to,' Jory says, with something like regret. The noise is building gently, bass notes mixing in with the steady percussion, and all at once he understands the grandmaster's game plan. Shafiq's heard it too, he can tell.

'I know what Kinsey's done,' Jory says. 'She's called in specialists. They gave you those boots fresh this morning, didn't they, Bennett? You should have ditched them with the uniform.'

Bennett stares at him. 'What? These are good boots, these are. What, was I supposed to tramp through this bloody forest barefoot?'

Shafiq groans. 'Jack, you idiot.' The sound's getting louder by the second, a throaty tiger roaring at its whip-cracking tamer. 'We need to go! Get to the car, quick!'

'But what –' says Bennett, then falters as the sound they all now recognise becomes too loud to speak over.

The helicopter looms over the treetops, a giant twin-rotored RAF Chinook like the thunder-god's hammerhead, swinging around the clearing, its vicious downdraught stripping trees of leaves and needles wherever it passes.

Birds shriek inaudibly and scatter. Bennett and Shafiq try to do likewise, but are disorientated by the noise, the buffeting gale from above, and by the sudden appearance of the troops.

The helicopter's personnel deployment doors are open, and as it circles the clearing it deposits men. They abseil down on nylon lines, wearing full Circle armour, bearing their shields aloft. Jory sees a lion, a double-headed eagle, stars and stripes, a three-pronged banner: gold and black and red on green and purple and gold.

Sir Tristan, Sir Gareth, Sir Lionel, Sir Bedivere… the devices of the Round Table have come to take Jory back.

As their feet touch the grass which was so recently the floor of the Green Chapel, each Knight lets go his line and draws a sword. There are no men-at-arms here – this is an all-Knight party, though not the kind this clearing has been used to recently. Powerful voices yell Jory's name, just audible over the Chinook's thudding thrum.

Gawping in amazement at this overly melodramatic show of the Circle's strength, Shafiq and Bennett stumble to the treeline, a part which the descending Knights – the shields of Sir Sagramore, Sir Ector and Sir Gaheris appearing now – haven't yet reached.

Their nearer comrades are reaching Jory now, taking him by the shoulders, their faces smeared hints of eyes behind tinted polymer. Their devices proclaim Sirs Palamedes, Bors, Lucan… to his shock he sees the silver-on-blue keys of Sir Kay. The Circle are really taking Jory's abduction seriously, if the Seneschal's in the field with a troupe of Knights. That hasn't happened since the Cornish independence riots in the early '90s.

Bennett has dropped the axe in favour of a sturdy plank of wood, which he swings powerfully at the Knights nearest him. The three red lions of Sir Agravaine crash to the forest floor. Shafiq pulls him away, shouting unheard advice, and Bennett reluctantly allows himself to be dragged. Other Knights pursue them, but the fugitives are in the woods now, where the Merry Men have the advantage.

Well, assuming Bennett has the sense to lose the boots.

Jory sags into the arms – a gold lion *passant* on black – of Sir Leondegrance. The man clumsily tries to catch him. Jory tries to recall his name to thank him, but at this moment he knows only the devices. The hammering of the helicopter blades begins to fade in Jory's ears, although its shadow's still huge overhead. He tries to stand, but something in his head is stretched to breaking-point.

Scar is back suddenly, over by the treeline. She's cut around away from the path to the car park, and the Knights are thinner there. She stares at Jory, shaking her head grimly as he collapses. Gun in hand, the woman turns to fend off Sir Segwarides, but her shots bounce from the black mountain on his gold shield, and he disarms her with a sweep of his sword.

From behind her, Sirs Aglavale and Caradoc run to take her in their grasp and force her to the ground.

Jory's vision narrows down, contracts into a circle the size of a clock-face. For a moment, to his inexpressible relief, it's filled with a red cross on a white background… but then it hinges open, and he's staring at the contents of an RAF standard-issue first aid kit.

'Where's Galahad?' he struggles to ask. 'Where's…?'

But he can't remember, and David Stafford isn't here to watch as he slips slowly into unconsciousness.

* * *

Many, many stories have been told – and sung and acted, broadcast and released – of how Robin Hood came to be an outlaw. As Jory noticed, there's not much these origin stories have in common: certainly not their settings, their plots or narrative details, their religion or morality or politics.

Though individuals naturally have preferences, the Green Chapel embraces all of them. They understand much better than the Circle the strength that's to be found in diversity. These stories were created by quite different people, singly or in groups, in very different places and times, each with their own intentions and audiences, each with their own ideas about who Robin Hood was and what he stood for. As with the books of the Bible, it's hardly surprising if they contradict each other.

Over the ages, though, one version of the story has evolved – changing, of course, from one generation to another – until it has become the Chapel's favourite account of the outlawry of Robin Hood.

The way I always tell it, it goes like this.

'In the old days of England, before Robin Hood became an outlaw and dwelt in the greenwood with his beloved Maid Marian and their merry band, there were two wicked princes.

'In time, each would be king. The older, Richard Lionheart, would sacrifice the lives and lands of many of his countrymen in his vendetta against the Muslims of Palestine, while his brother John Lackland would become so renowned for his cruelty and avarice that even the barons would turn against him.

'That, though, was still to come, and for the moment both were young men, not yet crowned.

'Robert of Locksley was also a young man, though of a lower station by far. He was the steward to the Earl of Huntingdon, a young man indeed to hold such a responsible position in a noble household. His father, also named Robert, had stewarded before him, and on his death it was agreed by all that his son, young Robin, had learned his father's work to such a degree that he could be trusted with it at once.

'The Earls of Huntingdon were of Saxon stock, and had held their title since before the Conquest a hundred years before. For their part, Robin's ancestors had been yeomen in Locksley since the Saxons first arrived on these shores. From childhood Robin had had the run of the nearby forests, and in them he learned his first woodcraft – building shelters, tracking animals and setting traps for game, although he was of course always careful to avoid hunting the deer, which everywhere in England belonged to the king.

'Robin had learned bowmanship from an old retainer of the earl's, a man named Stuckley who had fought for King Stephen against the Scots. The boy's gift for the weapon had quite amazed the old man, and soon Robin had begun to add arrow-making and bow-hunting to his forest skills, although naturally he would never have used his skill at archery to bring down one of the king's deer.

'Not when meat was plentiful for the household, anyway, and definitely not when anybody might find out.

'Robin had been the earl's steward for two years when a man arrived with the news that Prince John was travelling the countryside near Locksley, hunting his father's deer, and that he and his party would be staying with the earl that night. The earl was dismayed, for the prince and his men had a reputation for eating their way voraciously through any household that would put them up – and any man who refused would be lucky to keep his head, let alone his lands.

'"Thank God he's only coming for one night," the earl groaned to Robin.

'Even more dismayed, of course, was Robin himself, to whom it fell to lead the household in provisioning the prince's hunting-troupe. Herbs must be gathered, pigs and chickens slaughtered, vegetables dug up and water drawn from the wells before the feast could be cooked, the table set, the wine-barrels readied, the minstrels given strict instructions on the prince's taste in ballads. The earl and his family needed to be dressed, the halls garlanded with leaves and flowers, the privies emptied. Even for Robin, a man who others always loved to please with their work, the task of organising it all was almost impossible.

'Robin reserved for himself the task of bringing up from the cellars and polishing the household's best silver, which the earl's father had bequeathed to him and which had passed from earl to earl for generations before them. Each platter and salver, each cup and goblet, had to be cleaned and scoured into a perfect gleam, until the earl's daughters might have plucked their eyebrows by them.

'The pride of the set was a jewelled cup, splendidly engraved, and inlaid with coloured glass and gems in a fine silver filigree. This was, of course, to be Prince John's drinking-vessel at supper.

'The prince arrived – a sallow, peevish youth, already sporting a remarkably ominous beard. He accepted the earl's welcome with ill grace, and retired at once to his room where he insisted, despite the well-known health hazards, on being given a bath. Robin, who knew John's reputation, ensured that only the plainest and most matronly of the earl's serving women attended the prince at toilet.

'Perhaps this was why, when the young man emerged for supper, he was in a fouler temper than ever and spent the evening criticising the meat ("pale and stringy"), the bread ("tasteless, stale") and the wine ("thin and sour as an old woman's evening piss"). Robin, who as the steward had the honour of serving the prince himself, accepted all these calumnies with a murmured "Yes, my lord", and resisted the temptation to have the earl's old nurse, who was eighty-two, ensure the truth of the prince's words.

'"But perhaps," John said, noticing the cup in which the wine had been brought to him, "we may salvage something from this visit after all. This is a fine cup, my lord earl."

'"It is indeed, my lord," the earl replied. "It has been in my family for hundreds of years. My grandfather remembered *his* grandfather telling him that it was already old when –"

'"Yes, yes," the prince snapped. "A venerable piece, no doubt. I would take it most graciously, my lord – and even forgive the insult of the vile fare which you have laid before us – if you would make a gift of it."

'The earl fell silent, shocked at the idea of giving away an heirloom that his great-great-grandfather had known, but unable to think how to refuse the prince such a request. Seeing his confusion, Robin stepped in smoothly.

'"My lord prince, I fear that to accept such a present would be most unwise. The cup is subject to an ancient spell, placed on it by a wise woman. While it remains here at Locksley Hall, the cup will bring health and prosperity to all who drink from it – yourself included, of course – but if it is removed, disease and calamity will follow it, and its new owner rue the day it came to him – whether bought, stolen or given freely. It's said the old woman was worried that the Earls of Huntingdon might move their seat elsewhere, depriving Locksley village of its livelihood."

'Now this was nonsense, naturally, made up by Robin on the spur of the moment, but lying with the very conviction of truth was another skill he had learned from a young age. Not that he would ever have used this skill at dissembling to get away with shooting one of the king's deer.

'The prince was no fool, then or after, but he had not yet learned the arrogance which he would have in later years, to laugh in the face of such superstitions. He looked shrewdly at Robin and said, "Then here it must remain, of course. Although it is a shame that I cannot therefore forgive your master's slight. Given the prosperity this cup must have brought to him, assuming all you say is true, the insult of this poor fare looks all the more calculated."

"'Yes, my lord," Robin replied again, and went to seek out the earl's nurse after all.

'Before retiring that night, John announced that he and his men would stay another day, to recover from the arduous rigours of the hunt. "It's a ploy, my lord," Robin told the earl. "He knows that we have given him our best victuals tonight. If he stays longer, the provision will only grow worse, and he can demand anything he likes in recompense – the cup, the rest of your silver, your youngest daughter. I wouldn't put anything past that conniving snake of a man."

"'You will not speak of the king's family that way," the earl ordered him sharply. "But… I'm afraid you're right."

'Sure enough, the next night the prince found his food less satisfactory than ever, and renewed his request for the cup, which Robin once again refused on the earl's behalf – inventing a story about a thief who once stole the cup and reappeared a week later missing an ear, suppurating with boils and begging to be allowed to give it back. The prince looked at him more shrewdly than ever, but he kept his counsel, announcing only that he would stay a third night.

"'This prince will bankrupt us all," the earl complained, prophetically enough.

'On the third night fish was served, and the prince made a great play out of choking on a bone, eventually bringing it up (from his sleeve, Robin noted) and recovering his breath enough to accuse the earl of trying to kill him. Robin's master apologised abjectly, but the prince was unrelenting. Eventually, in desperation, the earl offered him the cup.

"'My lord prince," Robin began, having an elaborate lie ready this time, "the cup was given away once before, in the time of the Empress Maud. The poor recipient –"

'"That is enough, Robin," snapped the earl. "My lord," he told the prince, "we must allow the yeomanry their superstitions, I suppose – but you and I are educated men, and I dare say we both know that such things as curses rarely live up to their reputations. The cup will leave here, and my family's safekeeping, with you."

'"My lord –" Robin protested, then fell silent. He could see that his silver tongue would do no good here.

'The next day, with great pomp and ceremony, the prince's party left, to continue its hunting. That day, Robin asked leave to be away from Locksley Hall for a few days, to visit his aunt who lay dying in a nunnery a day's ride away.

'The day after that, Prince John was struck by an arrow while hunting, and his party was robbed, with only the jewelled cup taken.

'The prince lay abed and groaned for a week, and it is said that he never truly recovered from the pain of this wound, the first he had been given in his pampered life. In later years, when King John acted in a way which even by his standards seemed callous, arbitrary or mean, his servants would say that his old arrow-wound was troubling him.

'Two seasons later, the prince returned to Locksley Hall, bringing Prince Richard with him. Together the brothers accused the earl of plotting to murder a prince of the realm, and declared all his property forfeit – including the cup, which somehow had returned to its rightful place in his cellars. He and his family were permitted to keep their lives, provided they gave the name of the man who shot and robbed Prince John – a name which the prince, of course, had long since guessed.

'And so it was that Robert of Locksley was declared an outlaw, with a wolf's bounty on his head – and so he fled, taking only old Stuckley with him, into the greenwood, where in time he would find new friends and a new name.

'The jewelled cup was taken and locked up in the royal coffers. And there it sat unused, admired by no-one, until the day the prince had all his silver melted down to pay off part of his brother's ransom.

'But it is said that he kept back a small amount of that silver, and sent it to his man in Nottingham, to be cast into an arrow and used as bait to catch the notorious and wicked outlaw, Robin Hood.

'But that's another story, for another day.'

13. THE BARS

Jory spends fourteen weeks at Tud House, the Circle's recuperation facility on the Norfolk coast. His second-floor room is two doors away from the one they gave David during his recovery after Iraq.

During that time, Jory did his best to visit David once a week. He's a great deal less keen on being here as a patient. He protests repeatedly that his injuries are superficial, that he's really feeling quite himself now, that he's fit to return to work, but it seems his superiors have certain reservations.

During his conversations with the consultant therapists – experts to a man, of course, among the most expensive in the country and their field – it emerges that what worries the Circle most is not his physical and mental collapse, while they were extracting him from the abandoned campsite at what turned out to be Kielder Forest in Northumberland. Nor is it the health of his device, whose presence Jory hasn't felt directly since said collapse. It's not even his chronic tendency to get caught up in situations which involve the attempted severing of human heads – an issue which, in point of fact, bothers Jory himself quite a bit.

No – what's troubling his bosses, it seems, is the small matter of his having been seen and identified by a senior police officer acting in concert with a known criminal group to sabotage a police investigation through violence, a criminal act which resulted in several officers being injured and an expensive operation aborted. It wasn't just concern for Jory's welfare which prompted the Seneschal's personal intervention at Kielder – though there was that too, of course – but the very real worry that the Circle had a rogue Knight on its hands, and on British soil.

Jory's doctors are sympathetic by the Circle's standards, carefully avoiding unhelpful words like 'renegade' or 'traitor'. One of the older ones uses the un-PC phrase 'gone native', but the usual term, uttered with a confidence that threatens to drive Jory considerably more barmy than he was before, is 'Stockholm Syndrome'. His doctors believe that his experience of abduction and imprisonment at the hands of the Green Chapel has led him to empathise, and even to identify, with his kidnappers.

As a description, that's actually quite hard to argue with – Jory just doesn't see it as any business of a psychiatrist's. It turns out the Chapel are decent people – admittedly with the exception of their leader, who tried to kill him – and that's all there is to it.

His doctors, briefed by their Circle paymasters, refuse to accept this on principle. The options remain that Jory is deluded or has turned to the dark side. He rejects both suggestions. There's something of an impasse.

Although there's space for up to twenty Knights at the facility, the only other patient is Harold Lenton, the Knight carrying the device of Sir Griflet. He lost a foot in a recent raid on the headquarters of the separatist Sons of Gore, and is adjusting to life with a state-of-the-art prosthetic. Jory, who's only met him once before, finds him reserved and morose.

Tud House has a well-equipped physiotherapy gym to which Jory adapts his daily workout. He varies the times of his exercise sessions and notes uneasily that the sun's elevation isn't enhancing his performance as much as usual. Jory eats the superior hospital food, chats to the nurses (trained men-at-arms, for the most part – the only woman here works in the admin office), exchanges glum pleasantries with Harold, and does his best to avoid talking to the doctors.

His room isn't a cell. All the building's windows are barred, but he gathers from the attendants' tactful comments that this is because some of the facility's patients are considered a suicide risk. He has the run of the house and grounds, and is allowed to walk into the nearby town, to visit shops or promenade along the pier, although there's always a plainclothes man-at-arms coincidentally strolling along the same route at the same time.

His device is quiet – Jory's tempted to think dormant. Since their early, heady days together, Jory and Sir Gawain have maintained a necessary distance, with the device becoming involved mostly in situations of direct conflict (which Jory's faced on a frequent basis, of course). But Jory can't imagine the Orkney prince bearing this enforced seclusion calmly, and the lack of protest from that quarter troubles him.

One of the therapy exercises they give him is transparently intended as a diagnostic instrument for his device. (He wonders briefly whether Malory devised it: it seems too facile for her quicksilver mind, but it's possible that's just elegant simplicity.) He's given a piece of fibreboard cut to the size and shape of a medieval shield, and a collection of pots of paint corresponding to the traditional heraldic tinctures. One of the younger doctors suggests that he uses the shield to paint 'whatever comes into your mind', then leaves him alone in the white-walled room.

Jory contemplates the red and the gold paint-pots, but finds himself stubbornly unwilling to recreate Sir Gawain's pentacle. The star's five points, according to the anonymous *Gawain* poet, symbolise particular cardinal points of knighthood: the doctors will doubtless examine his rendition obsessively, searching for asymmetries and imbalances. He ponders the alternatives for a while, briefly considering some defiantly non-heraldic and potentially obscene motif, but eventually decorum wins through.

He cracks open the white paint – they've chosen the cheaper alternative to silver – and rustles up an alberia, the blazon argent sans device worn by knights who'd yet to earn their arms, or who wished to stay anonymous. The doctor looks at the unadorned white shield, grunts in amusement, and gives it back to him. It sits around his room gathering dust.

He has the occasional visitor. Paul comes to see him, awkward and stiff, not knowing whether Jory's betrayed everything they both stand for but not much inclined to give him the benefit of the doubt. He tells Jory he's now squired to William Posnett, bearer of the stolidly reliable Sir Galagars device, but that his own forthcoming elevation to Knight has been announced. It seems he did valiant work hunting down stray members of the Saxon Shield (although to his chagrin Alfred Noake's still at large), before the Circle discovered who Jory's real captors were.

Jory knows that Sir Charles has taken an interest in the lad, but even so, this progress is more meteoric even than Jory's own. He congratulates him heartily, and the Knight-to-be accepts it with obvious unease.

Jory asks after Malory, and David Stafford, and Paul clams up at once.

Stephen Mukherjee comes too, bringing Jory grapes – he's not one for originality – and talking with a friendliness that's far more sincere, though more or less devoid of content. Jory asks how Malory is, and Stephen says she hasn't been around the Fastness much: he supposes she's probably quite busy with her other job. Jory asks about David, and Stephen prevaricates then changes the subject.

Jory begins to fear the worst. David's never been the most stable of the Circle's champions, and how he may have reacted to Trevor's passing – not to mention how others may have responded to his self-revelation – is anyone's guess. Sir Galahad, Jory remembers, was granted one gift by God, as a reward for his service in the Grail quest. Alone among men, he was permitted to choose the time of his own death.

Jory begins to worry that David's taken a grimmer route to the same end.

Sir Charles doesn't visit Jory, which doesn't surprise him. He's more disappointed not to receive a visit from Edward Wendiman, not least because Malory's father could surely give him concrete news of her.

Malory herself he didn't expect to see – she's an academic, not a therapist, and isn't involved in this part of the Circle's work. Though he yearns for her with an ache which, like the patients' needs Tud House services, is physical as well as mental, he has to concede it's a good idea for her to stay away. It might look mildly strange that she isn't visiting an old friend – assuming anyone's paying any attention – but there's far more danger of their revealing something damaging if they meet in such an unprivate place.

He can't phone her, for similar reasons. More than once he considers calling Cantrell instead – the piece of paper's still in the pocket of the washed, pressed tracksuit in his wardrobe, and the ex-priest's mobile number is still just about legible – but he can't imagine what he'd say. *You bastards, you've ruined my life? Missing you all, wish you were here? Defecting effective immediately, require extraction asap?*

In any case, there's no phone he can use. Even if the communal one isn't tapped – and if they've had Knights in his position here before, he can't imagine that it isn't – the soldierly orderlies are always making their rounds. There's always one following him when he's near a payphone outside, and he doesn't have a mobile.

So, Jory reads a lot. Thrillers mostly, detective stories and spy novels from Tud House's moderate library. Nothing very challenging; nothing, certainly, that relates to the legends of King Arthur or Robin Hood.

In the early evenings, while he reads, the shadows of his window's bars prowl across his room, creating diagonal stripes across the plain white shield: bends sinister sable on an escutcheon argent.

* * *

They let him out for Paul's acclamation. Two men-at-arms apologetically (but very firmly) accompany him throughout the train journey to London, and then the taxi ride to the Fastness. He seriously entertains the idea of banging their heads together and giving them the slip, but he's not ready to burn his bridges with the Circle.

The Fastness looms above him with the authority of centuries – albeit ones this particular building has never seen – as he passes through the heavy iron doors between his minders. The receptionists nod them through, and they walk into the courtyard, round by the curtain wall and over the swing-bridge into the chimney-stack of the keep. It's early August, and the heat beneath the glass is blazing.

Acclamations, like the vigils they follow, take place in the chapel near the top floor of the tower, which fortunately is air-conditioned.

Lord Northwood is there when Jory arrives, preparing to do his ceremonial duty. He gazes vaguely at Jory as he enters, but considering the rate at which Knights pass beneath his dubbing sword it's hardly surprising that he doesn't recognise him. He nods with well-bred pretence, in any case.

Although Jory's own status at present speaks of suspension from duty on health, rather than disciplinary, grounds, it's been made clear to him that he's not expected to wear his ceremonial armour today. Instead he's in a suit and tie sent over from his flat. He's also not been invited to give a public testimonial to Paul. William Posnett will, of course, but to omit the Knight who Paul was squired to for longest is a very public snub. Jory's left in no doubt that, for now at least, his loyalties remain officially undecided.

Along with Paul's fellow squires and the usual complement of men-at-arms, a score or so Knights are here – more than for Jory's own acclamation. They stand up front in full armour, gleamingly unbattered, with swords sheathed and shields slung. Jory recognises a high proportion of the devices he saw descending from the helicopter, some four weeks ago now. Sir Palamedes – Stephen – is among them.

There's still no sign of David Stafford.

Other faces prominent by their absence include those of the Wendiman family. Again, Jory hardly expected Malory to be here – there's never been any love lost between her and Paul – but he's starting to worry now that the older Dr Wendiman's avoiding him too.

Sir Charles is here, of course, to welcome his protégé to full Knighthood, and he can hardly avoid talking to Jory. Not when Jory shrugs off his escort and walks up to him, anyway, thanking him loudly for his personal hand in saving Jory's life.

Raymond glances nervously at the minders, and Jory senses their hesitancy. He's bargaining on the latitude shown to a mental patient to protect him from a scene, and sure enough Sir Charles' sense of propriety keeps him polite.

'Taylor,' he nods. 'It's good to see you up and about, at least. Glad you could make it for young Parsons' do,' he adds, although his tone sounds anything but.

'Of course, sir,' says Jory. 'I wouldn't have missed it for the world. I'm rather surprised more people aren't here, in fact. Paul's a popular fellow.'

Raymond exchanges a look with Stephen, who's standing nearby. 'Let's find you a seat, old chap,' the latter says kindly.

'I know that David Stafford's very fond of him, for instance,' Jory lies. David was never so rude as to pass comment on Jory's squire, but Jory's always got the sense that he finds him prickly and judgemental. Maybe Jory's just projecting. 'I hoped I'd see him today. Where *is* David today, Sir Charles?'

Raymond looks shocked at Jory's directness, not to mention mightily pissed off. His eyes stray to the door, and Jory sees him weighing up how long he's got before Paul and his sponsors arrive and the ceremony begins. He sighs and puts a hand on Jory's shoulder, drawing him discreetly aside.

'What's the matter, sir?' asks Jory, innocently. 'Is David in some kind of trouble?'

'Nothing to the trouble you're in,' Raymond hisses, 'as soon as those quacks say you're fit to face it. This isn't the moment, more's the pity. Since you ask, Stafford's… elsewhere. For now we've no way of contacting him, so we could hardly ask him round for a buffet lunch and a glass of wine.'

Jory's startled. 'David's gone errant?'

'I'd be obliged if you didn't make a song and dance about it,' snaps the Seneschal, quietly. 'It's hardly a fitting subject at an acclamation.'

Errancy is the Circle's equivalent of AWOL, though somewhat more respectable. The lonely wandering of the Knight in search of some unspecific adventure, with associated journey of self-discovery, has gone in and out of fashion with the Circle down the years. For some generations of Knights, a year errant has been de rigeur: these days it's seen as terribly self-indulgent. Though frowned on, it isn't actually punishable except when tantamount to desertion.

Jory ignores him. 'Was it because Trevor died? Or was David being frozen out after you discovered he was gay?'

The Seneschal's aghast. 'For God's sake, Taylor. You may be missing half your marbles, but that's no way to speak of a brother Knight. No, if you must know, it was you.'

'Me?' Jory stares at him.

'You may recall the first time he broke down was after he lost Feddon,' Sir Charles says. Jim Feddon was the man-at-arms kidnapped and killed by Clifford Al-Wasati Chalmers. 'Macnamara's death upset him, of course, but it was your disappearance that tipped him over the edge. He blamed himself, for leading you into that shopping centre, and for abandoning you there to mop up afterwards.'

Jory feels chastened. All this time, the effect of his abduction on David hasn't even occurred to him.

Raymond shrugs. 'He wouldn't even join in with the rescue quest. He just… upped and went. I just thank God he's no way of knowing what you got up to during your *captivity*.'

All the same, Jory's convinced that Sir Charles isn't telling the whole story. He's about to probe some more, but Raymond nods at one of the nurses, and the burly man grasps Jory's arm. Stephen takes his other, lightly but with the promise of force.

The Seneschal says, 'Now get back to your seat. And I suggest you try *extremely* hard not to provoke me any further today.'

* * *

'I don't think there's much danger of that, actually,' Paul Parsons is saying, in response to another Knight's teasing. 'I've never had time for, you know, romance and stuff? Women aren't one of my weaknesses,' he adds pompously. 'Not that I'm… you know.

'Oh. Taylor,' he adds, as Jory arrives to congratulate him on his elevation. He's Jory's equal now, and not likely to forget it. 'Glad you could make it, yeah? What with everything.'

'Wouldn't have missed it,' Jory says again. 'Congratulations, Parsons, you've netted yourself the big one.'

Paul's in the burnished metal worn by Knights only at their acclamation (in fact, the Circle only owns three sets, in medium, large and really *very* large, which are fitted to the exact measurements of acclaimees by expert metalworkers). His helm is bright and feather-plumed, and his sword gleams impractically bright.

The shield he bears – three red diagonal stripes on a white background – is that of the most famous Round Table knight of all: the brave, strong, upright, noble, chivalrous and calamitously romantic Sir Lancelot du Lac.

'No Guinevere for you, then – yet, at least.' Jory smiles. If Paul thinks *that* device won't affect his behaviour, he's got a steep learning curve ahead. Pleased though he is for Paul, Jory rather relishes the idea.

(He wonders afresh how David would feel if he were here today. Lancelot was Galahad's father, after all. The Circle don't make too much of family relationships between the devices – the relative ages of the holders get too confusing – but a certain degree of affinity's expected between devicial families. Jory gets on well with the older Knights who hold the devices of Gawain's younger brothers Agravaine, Gaheris and Gareth. He sometimes wonders how he'd respond to Clifford Chalmers if he met him now, Mordred being Gawain's youngest half-brother and all. Not to mention his half-cousin, incest-born bastard that he was.)

'No fear,' Paul replies decidedly. 'You won't catch me out that way. It's a bit of a bad idea, actually, bringing women into the whole Circle thing. Not that I'm, you know, sexist or whatever. But in the legends, having them involved is usually really bad news. Makes total sense their devices won't be much help to us.'

On second thoughts, Jory wonders whether Paul's already found his common ground with the Lancelot device. The noble knight's often portrayed in later life as a bitter misogynist, blaming all his ills on the women he's fallen for.

'What about the Lady of the Lake?' Jory asks. He regrets it at once, but soldiers on. 'She's on King Arthur's side.' He doesn't know how widely Malory's affiliation is known among the Circle, but clearly Sir Charles must know of it. He suspects that means the members of his inner circle as well.

'Depends on the legend, doesn't it?' Paul looks at him with amusement, and Jory sees at once that he knows. 'She locks Merlin up in a tree, for a start. I've been taking your advice, yeah, and catching up on my reading?

'And speaking of the fairer sex,' Paul says. 'That woman we captured with y – I mean, when you were rescued? I interviewed her when they brought her in.'

Scar, thinks Jory, and he's ashamed once again to realise he hasn't thought of her during the past six weeks. *The Circle have Scar.* If she's talked – and there's no good reason why she shouldn't have – then they already know everything about him and Malory, and about Malory and the Chapel.

'Yes?' he says, keeping his tone casual.

'Appalling woman,' says Paul. 'You wouldn't *believe* what she called me. I pity her boyfriend or whatever. I don't know how you managed all those weeks.'

Jory bids Paul goodbye, waves at Stephen, and tells his attendants he's ready to go home.

* * *

Two weeks later, Dr Wendiman arrives at Tud House.

Jory's in the library, crammed into a leather armchair with a Raymond Chandler, when the old man's brought in. He recognises Wendiman's voice as it protests, rather weakly, the orderlies' handling of him. The academic doesn't sound like himself at all.

'Dr Wendiman?' he calls and goes to follow – to find his way blocked by a politely immobile nurse-at-arms.

'Sorry, Mr Taylor,' the man says. 'Dr Wendiman's overtired. He's not to be disturbed.'

The old man stays in his room, overtired and not to be disturbed, for twenty-six hours. Before supper the next day, the big nurse allows Jory in to see him.

Wendiman is sitting on his bed, wearing pyjamas and a dark blue dressing gown. The effect is at once more wizardly than his usual studied ensemble of corduroy and tweed, but Jory can tell at once – as if his presence here wasn't enough – that something's wrong.

As the old man looks up, his eyes flicker in panic for a moment, then settle into a general-purpose expression of avuncular fondness. 'It's you,' he says. 'So they're letting me have visitors, are they? Splendid. How have you been?'

He bluffs well, but not well enough to fool Jory. 'It's Taylor, Dr Wendiman,' he says. 'Jory Taylor.'

'Of course it is,' Wendiman replies. 'Jory Taylor.' He nods as if committing the name to memory. 'Splendid. How have you been?'

'I'm perfectly well, sir,' Jory replies. 'I've no idea why they're keeping me here, to be honest.'

Wendiman nods. 'To be honest, neither have I. I've never felt better. Fit as a fizzle. A fickle.' His eyes panic again for a moment. 'A fiddle. I'm fit as a fiddle.'

Jory sketches out his next sentence carefully. 'Do you remember what they said was wrong, when they told you you were coming here?'

'Ah well, where's *here*?' Wendiman observes with brittle cheerfulness. 'Philosophically speaking, I mean,' he adds casually.

'We're at Tud House,' Jory explains. 'The Circle's facility in Norfolk. It's a kind of hospital,' he reminds the old man, seeing his confusion continue unabated.

'Ah well, there, you see,' says Wendiman. 'A hospital. Which is absurd, of course, because there's nothing at all wrong with me. I'm as fit as a fuddle, Trainor.'

There's silence for a moment. Jory tries to think of the best way to fill it, but he's drawing a blank.

'So, they're letting me have visitors, are they?' Wendiman observes anew. 'That's splendid.'

'You've said that already, Dr Wendiman,' says Jory. 'You've also told me you that don't know why you're here, because there's nothing wrong with you. What I'm wondering is what the doctors *think* is wrong with you.'

'Well, as for that, that's easy,' snaps Wendiman, furious suddenly. 'Isn't it *totally fucking obvious?*'

The outburst's so wildly out of character that Jory physically flinches, and the academic looks mortified. 'I'm sorry. I'm sorry, I'm so sorry, that was wrong of me. I didn't mean to –'

He's almost crying.

'It's all right, sir,' Jory reassures him. 'It's very understandable. You're under a great strain. But what did you mean was obvious? What is it that the doctors think is wrong with you, Dr Wendiman?'

'Well, as for that,' Wendiman says, more quietly this time, the catch in his voice still. 'They think I'm senile, you see. Alzheimer's or something. They're wrong, of course, if only I could think why. I just can't seem to follow things through probably. Thoughts. Properly. I meant properly. I'm just… maybe that's why they think I'm senile. The doctors. They think I've got Alzheimer's or something. They're wrong, of course. Aren't they? They're wrong, aren't they, –?'

The sentence hangs in the air as he tries to remember Jory's name. Tears flow forgotten down his cheeks.

* * *

Jory finds Malory outside her father's room, sitting in a chair and crying silently. He gathers her up into a silent hug, and she soaks his T-shirt shoulder with salt tears. For a moment all the alienated dislocation he's been feeling for the past six weeks is lifted from him, and he realises with relief that yes, this is home.

Then, 'Old friends,' she whispers, almost silent, through the sobs. 'Here, we're old friends. Remember.'

He's hurt for a moment, but he recognises that all of Malory's responses, however heartfelt, come with this element of reservation – some eternally objective Malory, overseeing and evaluating her emotional self. Some people would see that as calculating, he knows, but it's just Malory. He can't tell how much of her distress is an act, but if he was – ridiculously – forced to quantify, he'd say no more than twenty per cent.

He pats her on the back. 'Shush,' he says. 'It's going to be OK.'

She disengages, wipes her eyes, waves a hand for both of them to sit. 'Somehow I doubt that,' she says. She reaches out to clutch his hand, her grip like a wolf's jaws. 'Alzheimer's isn't something you recover from. He's nearly eighty, Jory.'

'And still working,' Jory says. 'He's still on the faculty, isn't he? As well as advising the Circle. People don't just go down with Alzheimer's overnight. It must be something else. A stroke, or… Are there such things as curses?'

He feels ridiculous even saying it… but if a device can enhance someone's thinking, couldn't some application of them achieve the opposite effect? Jory has no idea.

He longs to hold her again, but through all her grief she's being more prudent than he could be.

'It's Merlin,' Malory says. 'The device has been holding him together all this time. Now something's happened to him – it, I mean, the device – and it's stopped working. He's gone back to how he would have been without it.

His synapses must have been degrading for years. I hadn't realised… it's so horrible. Alzheimer's isn't supposed to come on suddenly. We're meant to have time to prepare ourselves.'

'It can't be Alzheimer's,' says Jory, aware that his conviction's rooted in nothing more than a naive faith in the general goodness of the universe, but feeling it nonetheless. 'It has to be curable. He's *Merlin*.'

Malory sighs. 'Merlin's the device. It can always find another host. But Jory… this is part of Merlin's legend too. He always goes away. Arthur has to do without his mentor's advice, so that he can –'

She chokes up. *So that he can grow up*, Jory silently completes for her.

He can't quite forget, though he hates himself for it, who it is that's always – in the legends, anyway – responsible for Merlin's disappearance.

* * *

Malory takes him back in to see Wendiman. 'He's sleeping, Miss Wendiman,' the nurse says. 'And it's one visitor at a time, I'm afraid.'

'Nonsense,' Malory replies. 'Mr Taylor's a family friend. And, I might add, the only thing that's holding me together just at the moment. I'm not going in there without him.'

'Miss, I can't authorise –' the man-at-arms says, but Malory replies brusquely, 'Then don't,' and pushes past him into the room, dragging Jory behind her by the elbow.

Edward Wendiman does indeed appear to be asleep. He's lying down and breathing deeply, rhythmically and nasally – quite unconscious of his surroundings, although his eyes are disconcertingly still open. Malory fusses around his bedside table for a moment, making sure he has his watch and glasses to hand, as well as a handkerchief and a glass of water. Then she turns to Jory and says, 'This room won't be bugged. They have too much respect for him for that.'

Jory's about to embrace her again, but he holds back. Her demeanour hasn't changed – she's still tearful, and her voice's timbre is fragile – but it's clear she means business now.

'I've had email from David Stafford,' she says. 'Three weeks ago. It was sent through an untraceable anonymous remailer, but it was him.'

'From David?' Jory didn't know that his two friends were close. Now, after all he's discovered about them both, he wouldn't be surprised to learn that Malory knew about David and Trevor all along. 'What did it say?'

'It was for you, primarily,' says Malory. 'He'd heard you'd been rescued, I imagine, and he knew I'd be seeing you. He trusts me.'

'He could have written to me at my flat,' says Jory. 'They'd have forwarded it.'

Malory tuts. 'They'd have read it first. The same with your email, not that you ever check it. Luckily, I've got a research address at a partner university in Canada that no-one's monitoring, as far as I know. David doesn't want anyone to know where he is, especially not if they're being held in a Circle facility.'

Jory's boggling at these clandestine tactics. For all the need to keep what he and Malory know of the Green Chapel secret, the idea of conspiring against the Circle – which he supposes must be what they're doing now – is shocking to him. Though not as shocking as the idea that David, of all people, considers it necessary.

'What did he say?' he asks.

'He warned you to be careful,' she replies. 'Both of us, but you especially. Oh – he doesn't know about us, or about the Chapel. This is a different issue entirely. He doesn't think we can trust Sir Charles.'

'Sir Charles?' The Seneschal has many flaws, which Jory would happily list given the opportunity, but it's never occurred to him to doubt the man's honesty. 'Trust him with what?'

'David says something's going on,' says Malory. 'He's worried you'll find out, and go to Sir Charles about it. He thinks that would be a very unwise move.'

'What sort of thing?' A thought occurs to him. 'This is all sounding very melodramatic, Mal. Are you quite sure David was in his right mind when he emailed you? He's had a hard time recently, and he's not always –'

'Sweetheart,' says Malory dangerously, 'which one of us is the psychologist?'

'Ah,' Jory says. 'Fair point.'

'David was perfectly lucid,' she says. 'He told me Trevor had been having… reservations… about the Circle's clandestine involvement with the SS. It's been going on for a while, you know. David thinks they may have sent him to Iraq to keep him out of the way when it was first being discussed. He wasn't supposed to know, but Trevor confided in him. It was David who alerted Sir Charles when Trevor didn't get home that night.'

'So Sir Charles already knew about David and Trevor?' Jory says.

'Not knew as such,' Malory says. 'The Circle's highly skilled at institutional denial. But everyone knew they were best friends. Anyway, Trevor was worried that his quest might end up lending the SS respectability. It troubled him, David says. He was worried about what we were supplying them with, too. He thought we might help their cause in ways we didn't intend. He took his concerns to the Seneschal…'

'…and Sir Charles did nothing,' Jory supplies. 'I can't say I'm surprised.'

Malory shakes her head. 'David's worried that Sir Charles *did* do something,' she says. 'Trevor died because Noake and Hill found out that he was a Knight of the Circle. That information must have come from somewhere.'

It takes a moment for that to sink in.

'And David thinks...' Jory says, aghast. 'Sir Charles, selling out one of his own Knights to the Saxon Shield? I can't believe that. That's sheer paranoia.'

'Once again, love, not the psychologist,' says Malory. 'David could be mistaken, but I'm certain he's not deluded. That's a professional opinion. The point is, he urges you not to investigate it. It's too dangerous, he says. You're young, you've got a promising career. David's made his choice, but you can hang in there. Charles Raymond won't be Seneschal forever.'

But what if it's not Raymond? thinks Jory. *What if the Sir Kay device itself is plotting*... he can't even bring himself to finish the thought. In all the stories, Kay is utterly loyal to his foster-brother the King.

'If David really believes this,' he says, 'I *have* to investigate. It's too important not to.'

Malory smiles sadly. 'I know that,' she says, 'even if David doesn't. He's a good man, but he doesn't know you the way I do.'

'I should hope not,' says Jory. 'That would be extremely awkward.'

In his sleep, Edward Wendiman gives an eerie high-pitched giggle.

***

It takes a further eight weeks for a fully co-operative Jory – who now renounces the Green Chapel's politics and actions, acknowledging his earlier truculence as an aberration caused by that pesky Stockholm Syndrome – to be returned to active duty. After the doctors declare him cured – or, at least, as presenting every sign of recovery as compellingly as if he'd been schooled in them by an expert psychologist – he has to face his second disciplinary board.

Sir Charles presides, of course, over a panel which would normally include the bearer of the Merlin device, or in his absence the bondsman of St Dubricius, Arthur's archbishop and chaplain. Neither of Raymond's colleagues today is the Monmouthshire vicar who bears Dubricius' twin croziers, however. Nor is Malory here, although she's filling her father's shoes at the Fastness – strictly, everyone insists, as a temporary arrangement. The Seneschal's decreed that her presence on the disciplinary panel, as a friend and contemporary of the defendant, would present a conflict of interest, and Jory has to admit it's truer than Sir Charles knows.

Instead, the Seneschal's joined by the elderly director of the Benwick Institute – an avatar of King Pellinore, one of Sir Gawain's traditional enemies, which calls the 'conflict of interest' excuse into question – and a third man, not as old as the others, small and bearded and wearing a precisely tailored suit. He's introduced as Mr Lister, a secular counsellor to the Circle, with no further information as to what qualifies him as a stand-in for Wendiman.

The three older men grill Jory for four days, not just about his conduct at the docks and in Kielder Forest, but about the death of James Ribbens – a reckoning which Jory was promised, but had very nearly forgotten. Raymond and Lister seem particularly keen to determine his state of mind at the time, making him wonder whether it's his device they're trying to incriminate.

They seem little interested in the whole business with the Green Knight – which is as well, since the less Jory can manage to say about that, the better. Although he wishes Shafiq had been able to resist his device's urge to lop Jory's head off, he's not enough of a hypocrite to bear a grudge over it.

On the off chance that they already know Shafiq's identity, he claims that he never saw the Green Knight with his face uncovered. ('I hardly saw him at all, in fact,' he claims. 'And nobody used their real names.') He holds back on the Robin Hood connection, too, unwilling to give the Circle anything that might provide a tactical advantage.

He does, however, explain the Chapel's attack on the lorryload of police, playing up the rescue-of-fair-maidens angle for all it's worth.

During the course of the interrogation, he learns that Scar is being held, under the name Marianne Millar, at a women's prison here in London, convicted of assault and obstructing the police in the execution of their duty. As with Jack Bennett, the Circle's belief is that she bears no device, and Jory tries to give them the impression that they've exchanged the Chapel's second-in-command for a minor footsoldier, scarcely worth the trouble of holding. He has to tread a fine line between failing to support anything the police witnesses will have seen during their mutually bungled operation, and inadvertently incriminating her further.

The Circle has a tradition of forgiveness. Also of bloody vengeance, of course… but the annals of Arthur's original knights are full of quarrels and misunderstandings, renegacies and feuds, and most of the knights involved are accepted back into the fold, generally for pragmatic reasons to do with maintaining the security of the realm. Indeed, a number of the later Knights of the Round Table were villains who the original complement had had violent fights with, before persuading them to reform and join Arthur's cause. It's not a standard recruitment method in the present-day Circle, but the memory remains.

Eventually, the tribunal concludes that Jory has been influenced by the notoriously ungoverned passions of his device: the temper which got the better of him when confronting Ribbens, and the susceptibility to female charms which allowed him too easily to be led by the Green Chapel, with whose leader his legend is in any case intimately entangled.

As judgements go it's too accurate for comfort, but it has the merit of excusing nearly everything Jory's done. As before, at the hearing following Shaun Hobson's death, they dock his pay and send him on a penitential pilgrimage, this time to Caerleon. To his surprise, they don't impose a further period of suspension.

He shakes their hands and leaves for Knightsbridge, to collect the armour in which custom dictates he is to walk from the South Bank to South Wales. He'll be restored to full Knightly status, they tell him, as soon as he gets off the train back from Newport.

As he takes his leave of the tribunal, Jory asks the Seneschal whether Dr Wendiman's expected to recover. In the two months since the old man arrived at Tud House, there's been no improvement in his condition: if anything, his intellect's getting weaker, requiring continual reminders of where he is and why. Jory's stayed at the Fastness during the hearings and hasn't seen him since leaving Norfolk the week before. Protocol demands he set out on his pilgrimage at once.

'Leave that for us to worry about, Taylor,' Sir Charles tells him sternly. 'Dr Wendiman is our responsibility. If I were you, I'd be considering how he might have got this way.'

Jory is indeed considering – considering who might stand to benefit from sowing doubts about Malory's loyalty, who might consider her intellect, her knowledge and her scientific curiosity to be a threat to them – so much so that they were prepared to sacrifice the wisdom of the Merlin device to rid themselves of her. He has to admit it would be a pretty drastic decision… unless Wendiman himself was also becoming a threat.

He shakes his head, convinced by this conclusion that he, too, is going down with a touch of the paranoia.

'Poor fellow,' tuts Mr Lister. 'It's as if he were a prisoner inside himself. It must be a *living purgatory*.' He shakes his own head with undue emphasis.

14. THE HORSE

'What's at Caerleon?' Scar asks Jory.

'Not a lot,' he admits.

There's little to choose between this prison visiting room and the one he interviewed Bennett in, though some superficial effort's been made to make it feel less grim. Matching curtains and linoleum, marginally more comfortable seats. It's probably some Home Office apparatchik's idea of the feminine touch.

'Roman remains, mostly,' he says. 'Some museums, a war memorial. A village green. It may have been the site of Camelot once – or not, probably – but there's nothing to show for it now.'

'Why'd you even go?' Scar demands. 'You could've sat on your arse for a week then got yourself on that train. They check up on you, aye?'

'That's not the point,' says Jory. 'It's about an ideal. Honour, obedience, duty. That sort of thing.'

Scar rolls her eyes. 'It's all masters and servants with you bastards.'

'Says the class warrior,' smiles Jory. She grants him the tiniest quirk of a lip.

'That's just us telling it how it is,' she says. 'You're talking how you think things should be.'

She's wearing jeans and a sweatshirt, less humiliating than Bennett's prison clothes but still looking like a uniform.

The dye's gone from her hair, and the natural dirty blonde that's replaced it makes her usual crewcut look harsher and more institutional.

She's had no visitors, except an aunt who she sent away with a flea in her ear. Jory knows this from the prison governor; Scar hasn't discussed it with him. Neither of them wants to use names, but Jory guesses she's missing Zara and the rest of the Chapel. He also guesses, just as correctly, that she has no need of his sympathy.

'It's like, see your allies,' she says, elaborating. 'Your – what d'you call them? – devices. You reckon they're your masters, so you serve them. You think they want the world to be like King Arthur's times, so you try to make it that way.'

Jory shrugs, although his own device remains conspicuous by its silence. Scar, on the other hand... prison's made her talkative. She barely said this much in a day back at the encampment.

'Isn't that what you do, though?' he asks. 'Surely you fight the things you do because Will Scarlet tells you to?'

'Fuck, no.' Scar's scornful. 'He's no the boss of me. We're *allies*, don't you see? They lend us strength, they don't control us.'

Jory raises his eyebrow. 'You think you can control them, you mean?'

'I didn't say that, you daft shite. There's no controlling. It's a partnership. We want the same things, so we work together. Hey, why d'you think Rev's so scrawny, eh?' she asks suddenly. 'It's no because he doesn't like his food. He smokes, he drinks, he shags, why wouldn't he eat? It's to show his ally it's no in charge. If he eats, he puts on weight and turns into Friar Tuck. Rev knows how this stuff works, you ask him about voodoo sometime. He needs Tuck to see he's his own man.'

'I see,' says Jory. *Voodoo*? he thinks.

'It's like – you beg your knights for help, you *supplicate* them, like they're your patron saints or something.' Marianne

Millar, as Jory now knows from her prison file, was brought up a Catholic. 'All your swords and horses and castles and look-at-me-I'm-high-and-mighty, and you're bowing and scraping to stuff that's in your own mind.'

'But you know they're real,' Jory says, trying to clarify.

'Oh, aye,' Scar says. 'They're real because people believe in them. That's what reality means, for them. Take that away and there's nothing left to them. Just like a country, or money, or God.'

Jory frowns. There's a question he ought to ask here: *So if Will Scarlet wanted you to kill somebody just because of whose device they were carrying, you'd coolly weigh up the pros and cons before reaching for, say, a great big woodsman's axe?*

But he doesn't want to rake up the occasion in the Chapel's past when he himself failed to do more or less that. Not with Scar, anyway.

The conversation's getting away from him, in any case, and he had a purpose in coming here. He tries to steer it back to what he wanted to say.

'Look, Scar...,' he says awkwardly. 'Are you OK here?'

She shrugs and coughs a laugh.

'I mean,' he persists, 'is there anything you need that I could get you?'

'Out of here?' Her look's defiant. It's a challenge, not a plea.

But there are no strings Jory can pull at the moment. Even fully exonerated, his influence within the Circle – and especially with its authorities – in insufficient to the task. He shakes his head. 'I really don't think so.'

She smiles grimly. 'Then no, there's nothing.'

'OK. Then hear me out.' He takes a breath. 'I'm sorry they caught you. You came back for me, didn't you? Even if you didn't, the Knights were only there because of me. You're here because you know me, and... you must be quite upset about that. I know I am. I feel it's my responsibility.'

'Oh,' Scar says. 'Right. So if you'd got shot helping Zara out at the docks, you'd have blamed her, aye?'

Jory sighs. 'Of course not.'

'Don't be a prick then,' Scar says baldly. 'If I came back for you, that's my call. Whatever happens is on me. But that's no why you're feeling bad. It's 'cause it was your pals arrested me on the Circle's say-so, and you know in their place you'd have arrested some other poor bugger. I'm no going to absolve you for *that*.'

'No.' Jory shakes his head sadly. 'I didn't really expect that you would.'

* * *

As Jory leaves the main doors to the prison, he sees a man-at-arms hurrying across the car park towards him. It's October now, an overcast day, and grey clouds swell above the brick-red buildings like sails.

The man-at-arms is new, recruited during what Jory's peers are tactfully calling his 'sabbatical'. Jory met him a week ago at the Fastness. 'Mr Taylor,' he gasps. Jory's not surprised that the Circle knew where to find him, although he didn't tell them he'd be here.

'Doherty, isn't it?' Jory hopes he's got the name right.

'Delany,' the man says, looking fleetingly annoyed. 'Mike Delany. Sir, you're needed urgently. Seneschal's orders.' Jory hasn't been assigned a new squire yet, or they'd have sent him.

Jory shrugs. He guesses he's in for another bollocking from Sir Charles. Obviously the Circle's keeping him on a tighter leash than he realised. It's hardly unusual, a Knight visiting a prisoner whose arrest he was involved with – you could even see it as a chivalrous obligation, especially with the convict in question being a woman – but he supposes he should have mentioned it to somebody, if only to avoid the appearance of secrecy.

'Have you got a car?' he asks. He came by tube.

Mike Delany nods. 'Spare armour's in the back, sir. And a shield in your blazon.'

A *formal* bollocking, then. 'Back to the Fastness, then,' says Jory.

'Ah no, sir, sorry,' Delany explains. 'I should have said. You're needed at St Pancras.'

'The station?' Jory's strides purposefully towards what he now recognises as a Circle limo. You can't let the men-at-arms see you're not on top of things, even when you're floundering.

'Yes, sir. The Eurostar terminal,' says Mike. 'They've found that Alfred Noake.'

Jory stops up short. 'Noake?'

'Yes sir. You know, the SS man?' Delany's tone betrays a certain irritation at Jory's obtuseness.

'I remember him well, thank you Delany,' Jory says sharply. 'Is he in custody?'

The man-at-arms pulls nervously at his lip. 'Well, no, sir. It's all a bit complicated. Somebody saw him at the station. The police are there now. They say he's got a device.'

Jory frowns. 'Well, yes. The warlord Hengist. Or was it Horsa? I'm not sure we ever established, actually.'

'Ah no, sir, sorry again,' Mike says. 'Not our sort of device. The other kind.'

The police say... Jory stares at him for a moment, thoughts rough-and-tumbling through his head until his comprehension gets the upper hand.

'You mean an explosive device,' says Jory. 'You're talking about a bomb.'

* * *

The police have cordoned off the portion of the lower concourse serving the Eurostar trains by the time Jory arrives with Delany. Confused international travellers are milling around the shops and cafes, arguing with police and station staff, and getting in the way of irritated Londoners.

The barriers to the platforms are locked, and trains are being held outside or diverted to King's Cross.

'What the hell are all these civilians still doing here?' Jory asks rhetorically. 'Get them out, Delany.'

A platoon of men-at-arms and a lost-looking Knight stand next to the M&S Simply Food. Jory's pleased to see specialist sappers among the men, but his heart sags as he recognises the red cockerel's head on the officer's shield. Those arms belong to Sir Dagonet, the jester knight, and their current holder is a drunk and a buffoon, with all the bravery of any other senior Knight but none of the judgement, wisdom or tact. The rumour runs that Desmond Wigsby was as promising as any other squire before the fool's device was imposed upon him… but Jory fears that does the man too much, and Sir Dagonet too little, credit.

Of all the Knights to have at his back in a crisis, Wigsby would be his last choice. He'd feel safer disarming bombs with the White Knight out of *Alice in Wonderland*.

'Taylor!' says Wigsby, passing Mike as he hurries over with his squire. He skids momentarily on the polished marble floor, but the squire, obviously well practiced, steadies him discreetly. 'Thank God you're here. Tricky situation, this. I say – this one could really blow up in our faces, eh?' He guffaws.

'That's very funny, Desmond,' Jory lies.

Noake stands, an isolated figure, between the rows of pillars in the middle of the cordoned-off marble floor. At this distance his White Horse tattoo is a dark smear across his cheeks and forehead. A handful of frightened travellers kneel on the floor around him, hands clasped behind their heads, while two security staff are laid out nearby, dead or unconscious. Beside him on the ground lies the long raincoat he was using to conceal his bulky inner garment.

'That's what I call a bomber jacket,' Wigsby observes unhelpfully. 'Eh?'

Jory examines the vest as best he can, comparing it with the last customised waistcoat he saw worn by a renegade device-bearer. This one's shorter on the rustic psychosis, but heavy on the paramilitary chic. It's black, made of some tough canvas-like fabric, and slatted about like a Dalek with blocky rectangles the size of thick paperbacks, whose function is depressingly obvious.

'Fuck me,' the Shieldsman shouts up at the panelled ceiling. 'Looks like someone with half a brain's turned up at last.'

Delany and his comrades have started – with the police's help – to clear the station of potential massacre victims. Many take offence at having their lives saved in such an officious manner, so progress is slow and loud.

'Everyone else is out of town,' Wigsby's saying. 'Some flap about a mafia boss up north somewhere. They left me minding the shop. I don't think they were expecting something like this to flare up. Bet they're kicking themselves now.' He chuckles again, then suppresses a hiccup.

Jory guesses that the 'mafia boss' must be Willie 'the Emperor' Macari, a Glasgow gangster of nth-generation Scots-Italian descent. Macari's believed to bear the device of the legendary Roman Emperor Lucius Hiberius, who Arthur defeated at the battle of Saussy. The Circle's been planning a raid on his operations for months now. Jory's not especially surprised he didn't know about today's raid – the Circle tends to operate on a need-to-know basis – but he feels that leaving Wigsby in charge is rather a lapse of judgement on the Seneschal's part. 'Is Miss Wendiman available?' Jory asks the sergeant-at-arms.

'Out in the field with the Seneschal, sir,' the man replies. Obviously the old man's taking a more active role in marshalling the troops these days.

This is, thinks Jory, the worst possible moment for Alfred Noake to have lifted his rock and scuttled out into the world.

In his right hand, the Shieldsman holds a vicious-looking sheath-knife. In his left, a mobile phone. His thumb hovers ominously over the 'send' button.

'They caught him trying to buy a ticket for Paris,' hisses Wigsby. 'I always said those prices were steep, but I didn't know they literally cost –'

'I'll bet he wasn't going all the way, though,' Jory interrupts, sparing himself the horror of Wigsby's punchline. 'He'd have blown himself up in the Channel Tunnel.'

It makes sense, as much as any of the actions of the device-driven ever 'make sense'. Noake's hankered-for golden age of Angle-land for the Angles was destroyed in the centuries after 1066, by mass migration from France. What other venue is he going to bomb? The devices are all about symbolism, and as a grand gesture, this would have been hard to top.

Also as a mass murder, of course.

Unfortunately, as a symbol, the Eurostar's London terminus has its own possibilities. For Noake it will be a definite second choice (well, third perhaps, after the Gare du Nord in Paris) but still adequate in a pinch. And while the potential for expensive destruction and loss of life is probably, on balance, rather less, it still has to be classed as pretty high.

* * *

'Are you lads really the best the Circle can do?' Noake wonders, loudly. 'You've come down in the world since the old days. Still, what hasn't, eh?'

'Can't you shoot his phone hand off?' Jory asks Johnson, the sergeant-at-arms.

There's no question of treating Noake as an honourable combatant, but Jory knows from Iraq that it's all but impossible for even a highly-trained combat unit to disarm a suicide bomber before he or she self-detonates. As far as he's aware this is the first time the Circle's faced such a tactic on British soil.

Johnson sucks air in through his teeth. 'Doubt it, sir. Not in one shot, and not so's to be sure the bullet wouldn't trigger the phone.'

'Why not just shoot him in the head?' Wigsby suggests, altogether too loudly. 'Or are you worried you'll miss his brain?' Noake cocks the appendage under discussion and lifts his mobile menacingly.

'It's a bigger target, sir,' the sergeant-at-arms admits, 'but we'd still only get one shot. And if he has a muscle spasm while he's got his finger on the button… well. It's your last resort, sir, I'd say.'

'Really?' Wigsby snaps. 'That's a shame, I'd hoped to make it down to Brighton this weekend. So it's over to us, is it, sergeant? How do you suggest a *man with a sword* takes out a suicide bomber?

Clown though he is, Wigsby has a point. How does a soldier with a strictly short-range weapon incapacitate an enemy who can devastate a large area at the touch of a button, who by definition has no fear of death and nothing to lose?

The only way that's obvious to Jory is terribly risky. All credit to the Dagonet device, Wigsby should be able to mount an effective distraction – the idiot can be entertaining enough when he actually tries. Given the audience, a few off-colour jokes and racist impersonations should be pretty much sufficient. Meanwhile, if Jory can get out onto Pancras Road and back in past the police cordon, there's some chance he can use the cover of the pillars to approach Noake from behind and…

…well, presumably sever the connection between his hand and his head, in some way. At one end or the other. Preferably without the mobile falling on the floor.

Much though the idea of yet another decapitation nauseates Jory, it might at least wake his device up.

No. There's a better way. A bloodless way.

So Jory chooses it.

***

'Noake!' Jory calls out. 'I'm coming over. We need to have a chat.'

'What are you doing, Taylor?' Wigsby hisses. 'I thought I was in charge of this quest.'

Noake shouts back, 'Not with that kit you're not. The sword and shield, leave them.'

'Agreed,' Jory yells and lays down his shield.

'What the hell are you up to?' Wigsby repeats.

'Negotiating,' Jory says, 'with terrorists.' As he unstraps his sword belt he calls across, 'Noake, I'm disarming!'

'Let's hope so,' Wigsby mutters. 'Charm's all we've got going for us now.'

Gingerly, Jory lifts the police tape and steps beneath it. The world doesn't explode, so he walks slowly over to the man wearing the bomb. Pillars topped with departure and arrival screens surround him like idols to the dead gods of teletext.

'I mean you no harm,' Jory says as he approaches. 'I swear on my honour as a Knight.'

'Yeah, right,' says Noake. 'That's close enough.' Jory stops a couple of metres from the hostages. 'Keep your hands where I can see them,' he adds.

'Of course.' Jory, turns his palms to face the SS man. 'So, suicide bombing. That's a bit of a departure for you, isn't it?'

'I recognise you,' says Noake, nodding over to where Jory's left his shield. 'That pointy star of yours. You was at Thankaster. You're a big lad for a yid.'

'It's a Christian symbol,' Jory says. 'Well, more often a neo-pagan one, these days. Count the points.'

'Nah.' Noake sneers. 'Better things to do with my time. If you're not an ikey you're a vikey. Or a droody or a norm or what-the-fuck-ever. Every fucker is nowadays.'

It sounds like something from *A Clockwork Orange*, but Jory knows enough to parse the terminology: Viking, Druid, Norman. He's impressed by the Saxon Shield's single-mindedness, inventing ethnic slurs for ethnicities which haven't existed for centuries.

'It hardly matters,' he sighs. 'Let's accept my blood's tainted and move on. Look, I know you've had bad experiences with us Knights. One of us deceived you, one killed your friend… If you know anything about us, though, you know we keep our word. That's why we're parlaying now. In your eyes I imagine it's a weakness – following the laws of chivalry, taking our promises seriously. Nevertheless, you know it's true.'

'Alright.' The scrawl of the White Horse bucks and dives as he nods. 'So what?'

Time to give him the spiel.

Jory takes a deep breath. 'I'm here to negotiate with you, Noake. I know there must be something you want.'

'Yeah?' Noake looks scornful. 'I don't think so, pal.'

'I think so,' Jory says. 'If there was nothing more you wanted from life, you'd have pressed that button as soon as security noticed you. You'd be in Wealhall or whatever you call it, getting sloshed with your forefathers, and we'd be here, cleaning bystanders off the ceiling.

'You didn't do that, which means there's *something* that still means more to you than a glorious afterlife. You know how powerful and wealthy we are: if it exists, we can offer it. And given the potential loss of life, that's obviously the better option from our point of view.'

'Bollocks,' Noake says. 'More of you mongrel scumfuckers I can take out with me, the better. Like Cols said, it's pest extermination.'

Cols. Colin Hill. That's our 'in', just there.

'I've never heard of a rat-catcher gassing himself along with the rats,' says Jory. 'Not deliberately, anyway. Do you think that's what Cols had in mind?'

Noake spits. 'Don't you *dare* talk about Cols Hill. It was your gay bumfucking poof of a mate Stafford killed him, wasn't it? Too pansy to come and face me himself, is he, eh? Cols Hill – you're not fit to say his name.'

'Fair enough,' says Jory. 'But did you never wonder why he died?'

Noake twitches. 'You deaf as well as queer? Your bent arsebandit –'

Jory speaks loudly, keen to forestall another tour of the homophobe thesaurus. 'He was killed by a Knight of the Circle, we both know that. In an attempt to rescue a fellow Knight who Mr Hill was torturing to death, as it happens. That much we both understand, however angry it might make us both.

'I'm asking,' he continues, 'why we all ended up in that position. Hill, Stafford, Macnamara, you, me.'

Noake spits again. 'You'd know all about that, wouldn't you? Your oh-so-honourable Circle stitched us up. Macnamara came to us, said he wanted to help us, but he was one of you fuckers all along. That slag was lucky to die. He deserved worse.'

'So why,' asks Jory, 'do you think the Circle targeted the SS for infiltration? We could have raided you and broken you years ago, just like we did in June. We do it to terrorist groups all the time. Instead Macnamara played you – very effectively, I might add – and your friend died. Aren't you at all interested in knowing why?'

Noake glances over to the Circle's party, who are still standing by an electronic information point. As long as they talk quietly, they're out of earshot.

'Alright,' says Noake finally. 'You tell me. It'd better be good, though.'

'That's just the thing. I don't know,' Jory admits quietly. 'It doesn't make any sense to me, and it didn't to Macnamara. He was just following orders. What our bosses were playing at, I've no idea. But I want to find out.'

'That's it? ' Noake bursts out. 'What the fuck good's that supposed to be?'

'Quiet, Noake,' snaps Jory. *Careful now.* 'You're missing the point. I said I want to find out. If we can talk about what happened, we can try to work it out together. But we need to sit down calmly, without this kind of… distraction going on. We both lost a friend that day in June. We both deserve…' Justice? *No.* 'Revenge.'

The White Horse contorts as Noake's brow wrinkles. 'They gave us some gear. Never you mind what. Said it would put us in charge again,' he says bitterly. 'Fuck knows what they really wanted, but that's what they told us. Our shot at power, it was supposed to be – absolute power, they said. A proper homeland for us at last, just like the old days in England – no, before that even – Saxony, or back in the Aryan fatherlands. Imagine that eh, Cols Hill and me in charge of your precious kingdom?' He smiles wistfully. 'Oh, we'd have made Hitler look like a Jew-loving hippy, I can tell you.'

Jory's beginning to wish he hadn't dismissed the beheading option quite so hastily.

Never mind that now. Stay focussed.

Noake's face clouds over again. 'Your lot didn't act like they believed it, though. It was like some bleeding experiment to them.'

…It's not as if Jory hasn't heard the like before, though. What shocks him here is the idea that the Circle might have actually assisted the SS's ends in some material way – although come to think of it, he's heard that one before too. He remembers David talking about 'equipment' back in the briefing-room, after Trevor was first captured.

'This "gear" that was supposed to put you in charge,' he asks. 'What was it?'

'Oh, I'm not thick,' Noake says. 'That's your free sample. Do right by me, you get more. Very tasty story, you'll find it. Now show me what you've got.'

'I've got your life,' Jory says. 'Keep this up and there's no way out for you. One way or another you die, and that's an end of it.'

The Saxons – the barbarian raiders of Hengist's time, at least, if not their settled, civilised descendants – were all about the glory and the renown, the killing and the dying in battle. Jory can't imagine that civilian lives meant much to them. But what Noake's doing isn't combat. It's breaking down a dam to flood a village, setting a dragon on your enemy's mead-hall. Even knowing you'll die in the process, that hardly seems the sort of thing that gets you celebrated by the skalds. A suicide bombing would very likely have seemed as cowardly to Beowulf as it does to Jory.

'You can trust me,' Jory repeats. 'Come with us and you'll live. Were not like you – we don't put our prisoners to death. Again, you may think that's a weakness, but it's to your advantage.'

'Prison?' Noake looks scornful again. 'Oh no, pal, I'm not doing that. Screw you.'

'Listen to me,' Jory says. 'The Circle has a facility for people like you. The Benwick Institute. I'm not claiming it's comfortable – although personally I'd rather go there than a secular prison –' *And may well get my wish if I mess this up.* 'The point is, it's under the Circle's jurisdiction, and I'm a Knight.'

He swallows. *Just say it.* 'Give me time, and I'm certain I can get you out of there. Get you abroad, if you like.' The SS, he knows, has paradoxically good relations with similar fringe groups in Germany and the Netherlands, the original Saxon heartlands. 'You'll be alive, and free, and you'll find out – because I'm going to make damn sure that *I* find out – what happened to get both our friends killed.'

'You'd do that for me?' Noake scratches his stubble. 'Bollocks,' he concludes, but there's a doubtful hope there now.

'Not for you, Noake,' Jory tells him honestly. '*You* I want to see neutered and in pain, and your ugly little cause torn into shreds. But this is more important. I'll do this, I give you –' *Don't hesitate, say it:* '– my word as a Knight.'

There's a long, long pause.

'Yeah,' Noake says, 'alright.'

He takes his thumb off the phone, then quickly opens up the casing with the sheath-knife and pulls out the batteries. That done, he carefully removes the suicide vest and puts it on the ground.

'Horrible thing,' he says. 'I always hated those. Filthy raghead trick. Well, what you waiting for?' he shouts at the hostages. 'Get lost, you whingeing wankers.'

They scatter. Noake turns back to Jory, knife in hand. 'Just you see you keep your promise, Knight,' he says. 'Or I'm gonna track you down and fucking *flay* you.'

He reverses the knife and passes it to Jory.

***

As the men-at-arms frisk and cuff the unnervingly compliant Noake outside Foyles, the sappers swarm around the discarded explosives, and Wigsby fusses back and forth alternately congratulating and scolding Jory, the latter wonders exactly whose instructions he's been acting on for the past ten minutes. If it's his device, then it's the first sign of life Sir Gawain has shown since their inglorious confrontation with Shafiq and the Green Knight.

It didn't feel like him, though. Its communications – without being truly verbal, as such – felt more specific than the vague but overwhelming sense of personality he's always found in Gawain's presence. Besides, resolving a situation with diplomacy and guile is hardly the bluff Orkneyman's usual style.

How guileful was he being, exactly? Jory doesn't know. If he keeps his word – which he supposes he has to – he's committed to springing Noake from Benwick, which won't be easy and is liable to get him cashiered. If not, he's just unthinkingly forsworn himself in order to… well, save a number of lives and considerable damage to the property of London and Continental Railways, but still.

While he was with Noake, though, none of this felt like a consideration. He said whatever would pacify the man, with a close eye on how he, Jory, might benefit later. It doesn't feel to him likely knightly behaviour – at least, not that of an honourable knight.

Which naturally turns his thoughts to Sir Guy of Gisbourne. Jory read everything he could on Guy, the flipside of the Sir Gawain device, while he was detained at the Chapel's pleasure. The Sheriff's man's a treacherous plotter, certainly, but rarely a successful one. He's also a violent thug, far more inclined to find some excuse to fight and kill an outlaw than to take him in unharmed. In that respect he's more like Gawain than Jory's happy to admit.

But these two between them make up the faces of his device, obverse and reverse. If neither of them seems to fit with what's seen here, does that mean there's some third element he hasn't yet discovered? Or is Jory's device mutating, like Wendiman's shift from Sir Menw into Merlin?

Who might he be becoming? Which device falls nearest to Gawain's on Malory's taxonomic family tree?

Bends sinister sable on an escutcheon argent…

A sudden burst of noise brings him back to St Pancras. It's loud, but Jory quickly realises it's not the bomb going off. If an explosion, it was much smaller and much more contained. Shouts follow.

'What's that?' he asks Wigsby, who gives a rueful clown shrug. There's a commotion among the men-at-arms – not the sappers, but the party who've been dealing with Noake – and Jory races over to Foyle's to find out its source.

Behind him there's a thump and a muffled curse, as Wigsby makes to follow but falls foul of the floor-polish.

He finds the men-at-arms standing in a ring around Noake's body. The Saxon Shieldsman lies on the floor, a gaping chasm in the back of his head leaking angry red and grey in a spreading splurge. The White Horse on his forehead has been given a red eye like a fire-pit.

Two of the men-at-arms are gripping Mike Delany in an armlock. The man is thrashing and struggling.

The sergeant-at-arms holds a handgun limply in one hand, the shock on his face mirrored in his colleagues'. 'I'm sorry, sir,' says Johnson as he sees Jory. 'I didn't know – we couldn't, sir. We couldn't have stopped him.' He's sweating.

Delany calms as he sees Jory, or at least gains a focus for his defiance. 'You stupid bastard, sir,' he says. 'Why didn't you kill him? Why the hell couldn't you have just *done* it? Why did you make *me*? It's not like he didn't deserve it. What the hell is *wrong* with you, sir?'

* * *

'It was his sister, apparently,' Malory says loudly, over the insistent guitaring of Led Zeppelin.

She's back from Glasgow, having flown down with the Knights sent to follow up the St Pancras incident. The Seneschal and his primary war party are still in Scotland, mopping up the smashed remnants of Willie Macari's busted crime-ring.

'Half-sister,' she adds, 'if you want to get technical about it.'

The pair are huddled close together in a dim, loud, crowded pub in a grimy side-street near the Fastness. The rest of the clientele appear to be motorcycle couriers, who are making the fullest use possible of the juke-box. Malory maintains that a constant background roar of '70s and

'80s heavy rock hits is the ideal guard against covert aural surveillance, but Jory suspects she just wanted an excuse to come here. It's the kind of dive she takes an unassuming delight in – an obsession which makes more sense to him now he's met the people she must have been meeting in such places over the years.

The beer is terrible, naturally. Still, Jory sips it manfully as Malory continues: 'Delany's stepmother is British Chinese. His half-sister, Leanne Delany, was one of the civilians the SS assaulted shortly before your raid on Thankaster. Remember them? The ones Trevor was going to confront Noake and Hill about, but they decided to take him prisoner instead?'

'I remember,' Jory nods. 'Did she die, though? I thought…'

'None of them died,' says Malory, 'but three were permanently injured. Leanne was training to be a dancer. They beat her with a steel crowbar, and now she'll never walk again.'

'That's horrible,' says Jory.

Malory shrugs. 'You tried to make a deal with the bloke who ordered it.' Then, seeing his face: 'Sorry, I've had a frustrating day. It was the right thing to do, arresting Noake peacefully. What happened afterwards wasn't your fault. I'm proud of you.'

'The Seneschal will blame me, though,' Jory reflects moodily.

Malory looks at him through narrowed eyes. 'Do you think?' she says. 'Surely Desmond Wigsby was the one in charge?'

'Well, yes,' Jory acknowledges, 'but I… well, didn't disobey him exactly; he didn't give me any orders. But I took things into my own hands.' *And that, at least, was what Gawain would have done*, he realises.

'You did,' Malory agrees. 'You successfully arrested Noake and freed his hostages, and then you handed him over to Desmond's men-at-arms. This didn't happen on your watch, Jory – it's not as if you're the one who killed him.'

'I was tempted,' Jory admits. 'But I realised I didn't have to.'

'Hurrah for you,' she says gravely. 'As I say, I'm proud of you. I knew you had it in you… but given your track record, others in the Circle may be rather surprised. I doubt there's anyone who'd have predicted you'd bring in a suicide bomber, of all threats, alive. It's just unfortunate that there was someone else there who was guaranteed to kill him if you didn't.'

Jory's beginning to realise what she's saying. (*Why didn't you kill him?*, he remembers Delany asking. *Why did you make me?*) 'And when you say "unfortunate", you mean…'

She nods grimly. 'I mean "planned", of course. Who came to fetch you to St Pancras?'

'Well,' says Jory. 'In fact it was Delany.'

'On Wigsby's orders?' She obviously knows the answer, but she wants him to say it.

Uncomplaining as ever, Jory lets himself be treated as a tutorial. 'No,' he says. 'It was the Seneschal.'

'And who,' she inquires after a brief pause for Motorhead to launch into 'Ace of Spades', 'ordered the raid on Willie Macari today, after weeks of leaving him alone while we kick our heels? Who insisted that I come along in person to advise, despite the fact that I never come on combat quests, then spent all day telling me where to stand so I wouldn't get killed? Who left Wigsby – the Dagonet device, for Heaven's sake – in charge of the Fastness while we were gone, thus ensuring that the only real authority you'd have to act on would be your own?'

Jory sighs. 'The Seneschal.'

'So, who do we think Alfred Noake might have incriminated,' she asks, 'if Delany had left him alive so you could interrogate him?'

The question's so rhetorical it goes unanswered. Instead Jory says, 'Noake said Trevor passed them some kind of special equipment. Actually, he said "they". There was something "they" gave Noake and Hill that was supposed to put the Saxon Shield in charge of the country. What could that be, some kind of weapon?'

'I suppose it would have to be,' Malory says.

'But then why didn't they use it?' Jory wonders. 'When we attacked their headquarters, for instance. Unless they were storing it elsewhere, I suppose.'

'Or unless it isn't that kind of weapon,' Malory speculates. 'Some weapons work too slowly to be tactical. Biological ones, for instance.'

Jory looks at her in utter horror. She shrugs. 'Just covering all the possibilities.'

Jory shakes his head vehemently. 'That's just impossible. The Circle would never have supplied the SS with anything like that. Nothing biological... or nuclear, or chemical.'

'Which leaves one other option,' Malory says. 'The Circle's speciality. Could it have been something to do with the devices themselves?'

'*Devicial* weaponry?' Jory finds the idea appalling on a number of levels. 'Is that even possible?'

Malory pouts. 'In a sense every device is a weapon, or can be used as one. Besides, what else might have had the potential to give the SS that kind of power?'

'But Noake and Hill already had devices,' Jory points out. 'Although....'

'...Their followers didn't,' says Malory, completing his thought. 'Perhaps they were promised an army of the deviced. There are plenty of Anglo-Saxon heroes to choose from, after all: Alfred, Offa, Hereward the Wake... Perhaps they even hoped to tap in to the Saxons' Germanic roots, and summon up the devices of Beowulf and Siegfried.'

'Can that be done?' Jory asks. He adds, 'Noake said "our lot" were treating it as some kind of experiment...'

She sniffs. 'It would be highly experimental, yes. But there's no reason in theory why it couldn't work.'

'Would it be worth doing?' Jory asks. 'From a scientific perspective, I mean?'

Malory looks thoughtful. 'It would be useful to see what did happen, I suppose. Experimental ethics aside. But whatever it was, it was sensitive enough for somebody to want to eliminate all the evidence. Trevor, the SS... Noake must have been the last loose end.'

There's an appalled pause as Jory considers the magnitude of what she's proposing. He asks, 'So what happens to Delany?'

'He'll be court-martialled, obviously,' says Malory. 'I imagine the sentence he's given will tell us whether he was working for them knowingly or whether he was a dupe.'

'You don't suppose –' Jory stops. 'No, we'd never get him to talk. If he is a dupe he doesn't know anything, and if he isn't he'll be holding out for that lighter sentence. We've got all we're going to out of him.'

They sit still and let the crashing of electric guitars break over them for a while. 'Mal,' he says eventually, 'how much did you know about this? Obviously you'd never authorise that kind of experiment, but it's your area, and it must be the Circle behind it. Didn't they tell you *anything*?'

Malory pouts for a moment. 'I had an idea that something was going on,' she says. 'It's not as if device studies has a journal of record. I only know a few others working in the field – mostly overseas – and there's no formal forum for sharing our results. I guessed some time ago that the Circle had other researchers on the payroll, which meant they were deliberately keeping our lines of enquiry separate. But no, in answer to your question, they left me completely out of the loop.'

'When you say some time...?' Jory asks.

'A few years,' she says. 'It was one of the reasons joining forces with the Green Chapel seemed... defensible.

If it turns out that the Circle's working to an unacceptable agenda, the country's going to need to call on an alternative deviceplex to counter it.'

'To *counter* it?' Jory breathes in sharply. 'You think it could come to that? An actual war between the Chapel and the Circle?'

'Between the Merry Men and the Round Table?' Malory sighs. 'I don't know. I really hope not. But sometimes, these days, hope doesn't feel like a firm enough anchor.'

In one of those coincidental sudden silences, the whole pub quietens for a moment just as Eric Clapton's 'Layla' finishes. A moment later, Freddie Mercury starts speculating about the distinction between real life and fantasy, and the moment passes.

Malory shakes her head. 'I'm bored,' she says. 'This place is a dump. Let's pick a cheap hotel at random and go to bed.'

She gets up and walks over to the door. Gratefully, Jory leaves his beer and follows her.

15. THE PRINCE

'Shafiq Rashid,' says Sir Charles Raymond, portentously. A close-up of Shafiq's face, younger and sans goatee but looking appropriately sinister, suddenly looms above them on the briefing-room wall.

'The current bearer of the Green Knight device,' Raymond elaborates, 'and leader of the Green Chapel. He's a British Muslim with radical political sympathies and a doctorate in chemistry.'

Well, if you put it like that..., thinks Jory.

'As if that weren't enough,' the Seneschal continues, 'he has a personal history with the Circle. A number of years ago, he supplicated for pagehood. Needless to say we rejected him, but we can assume he still bears a grudge.' There's an intake of breath around the room. To the other Knights, the idea that such a dangerous radical could have even known enough about the Circle to try and infiltrate it is shocking.

Less so to Jory, of course. He's too busy being shocked that the Circle have somehow worked out Shafiq's – or rather, the Green Knight's – identity. This is the first he's heard of it: he can't imagine Scar's any more likely than Bennett to have talked in prison, and he knows he hasn't.

(Now he thinks of it, though, he does recall a man-at-arms-with-techie-tendencies telling him about some recovered surveillance footage from Thankaster – not the shopping centre itself, but some premises on the main road nearby – which might turn out to be fruitful. Jory assumed at the time that Shafiq would be too canny to show up on it, but even Robin Hood gets caught occasionally.)

Aware that his reactions may be under scrutiny, Jory speaks up. 'Sir… I used to know that man. We were at university together.' He fakes outraged incredulity as he says, 'You mean *Rashid*'s been the Green Knight all this time?'

He doesn't mention Malory, although anyone who knows about his university days will know she was there too. She isn't here today – the last Jory heard she was at the Benwick Institute, supposedly to interview Willie 'the Emperor' Macari about his history with the Lucius Hiberius device. Either Sir Charles didn't think this worth recalling her for, or he has some reason to prefer her out of the way. Instead the civilian counsellor from Jory's tribunal is here, Mr Lister, sitting neatly to one side of the room clutching a folder.

Sir Charles nods. 'I'm aware of your connection, Taylor. Or should I say your rivalry? Apparently he bound himself to the Green Knight device so he could continue troubling you as Sir Gawain. We intend to make good use of your personal knowledge, don't worry.'

It's been two weeks since Alfred Noake's death at Mike Delany's hands, and Jory and Malory have made little headway in their covert investigation of their bosses. While at Benwick, Malory's supposed to be quizzing a few of the more politically inclined prisoners about whether random strangers have ever offered to give them absolute power. Meanwhile Jory's going through the everyday routines and rituals of Knighthood, in the vague hope of getting close enough to Raymond's inner coterie to sniff our something significant.

'Rashid enjoyed fifteen minutes of fame as an Olympic athlete, a few years back,' Raymond is saying. 'Since the death of the Green Knight's last bondsman, he's been involved in some of the Green Chapel's most notorious criminal acts – the Lindenvale nuclear reactor site occupation, the VisserGoossens Pharmaceuticals theft, the attempt to kidnap Henry Mainstrow MP. And, of course, he successfully abducted Taylor here from Thankaster Shopping Centre in June of this year, and held him for two weeks before trying to kill him.'

The briefing-room's less full than it was before the Saxon Shield raid. Back then a Knight's life was at stake; this time it's a matter of only ordinary urgency. Jory finds the attendance list significant, nonetheless. Aside from himself, Sir Charles and Lister, there are two sergeants-at-arms and three Knights, each with a squire. (Jory remains unsquired for now, which may be a sign that the Circle is still wary of him, or may be simple administrative sluggishness.)

One of the others is Stephen Mukherjee, whose loyalty to the Seneschal is solid, and who Jory suspects in his more paranoid moments is being used to spy on him. Another's young Theo Harte, who carries the blazoned golden sun of Sir Ector, King Arthur's foster-father and the father of Sir Kay. There's little doubt of where his loyalties will lie.

Even so, Sir Charles says: 'I'm putting you in charge of this quest, Taylor. We'll get on to strategy in a moment, but your acquaintance with Rashid, your recent experience of the Green Chapel and your device's history with the Green Knight mean you're our only man for the job.'

The fifth Knight present looks sceptical at this.

From everything Jory hears, Paul Parsons has distinguished himself as dazzlingly as one would expect in his quests since he bound himself, a scant few months ago, to the Sir Lancelot device. It was Paul who personally apprehended Willie Macari, swiping the gun from 'the Emperor''s hand with a swordstroke, then stopping his escape with a humane leg-wound. Jory guesses the Seneschal contrived the circumstances to give his blue-eyed boy a chance to shine, but he can't denigrate the achievement.

'For the duration of this quest,' Raymond is saying, 'Parsons, Harte and Mukherjee will report to you, and you'll take secular advice from Mr Lister. You'll answer directly to me, and will follow the plan Lister and I have formulated. There's no need to trouble Miss Wendiman with this. Even unofficially,' he adds significantly.

Hardly a free hand, then.

Jory's trying to weigh up the odds here. Like I say, the Circle are big on forgiveness, especially the grand, magnanimous gesture of welcoming the prodigal back into the fold. Even so, it's only a few months since Jory was colluding with the Green Chapel to hold up a truck, and forgiveness doesn't necessarily entail forgetfulness, not to the point of stupidity anyway. Sir Charles has to realise that Jory's loyalties may be conflicted here. He rather suspects that this quest may be intended as a test – under the eye of three of the Seneschal's most faithful Knights – of where his true allegiance lies.

Well, that could be worthwhile, he thinks. *It's something I really should know myself.*

Should he side with the shadowy governmental organisation which secretly backs fascists as long as it suits them, because he happens to be a member and it's simpler to assume they're the good guys? Or should he throw in his lot with a violent criminal gang who keep trying to kill him, just because he's dating one of them?

It's a question he's been actively avoiding answering for some months now.

'I'll hand over to Mr Lister for the operational details,' Sir Charles concludes, and it occurs to Jory to wonder – although he files the question away for future pondering – just who's actually running this show now.

'Thank you, Sir Charles,' coughs Mr Lister, as he takes the dais. 'Gentlemen,' he begins, 'the Green Chapel's location remains a mystery to us. This group is peripatetic, and their only campsites we've been able to locate are abandoned like the one at Kielder. Attempts to trace their recent movements have come to nothing.'

Regardless of who's tugging Raymond's strings, or indeed Jory's, the question remains: is this just about testing Jory, or are the Circle now seriously committed to wiping out the Green Chapel? Paul's presence would suggest the latter: with Stephen on the case, the Seneschal would hardly need his new rising star just to keep an eye on Jory's behaviour.

In which case… well, Malory believes the Chapel could end up being the public's best defence against whatever the Seneschal's planning for the Circle. It may be that Sir Charles has worked this out as well. Or maybe he just sees them as a wildcard, an unpredictable element that wants taking out of the equation before it's solved for good. Either way…

'Since a direct raid on the Chapel's headquarters is out of the question,' Lister continues, 'our priority must be to bring Rashid out into the open. His criminal activities are too wide-ranging and unpredictable for us to attempt to entrap him through them, so Sir Charles has suggested that an inducement to him as a *private citizen* is likely to have more success.'

Either way, with all the resources of the Circle at his disposal, Raymond can almost certainly take a single device-bearer down – even the Green Knight. Jory's done it solo, after all.

Shafiq holds a trump card, though, and if he so chooses it's one Jory can use.

The Circle believes that the Chapel's a group of followers, clustering around the Green Knight device. Nobody here knows – so nobody can blame Jory for not taking into account – that ten or so of its members are device-bearers themselves. Other than Malory and Jory, nobody in the Circle even knows there's such a thing as a Robin Hood deviceplex.

'Given what one might call the *naively idealistic* nature of Rashid's crimes,' Lister is saying, 'we felt that an invitation, sent via his parents, to attend a charity event in his capacity as an Olympic medal-winner, might be a temptation he was unable to refuse.'

The Circle think they're fighting the Green Knight, not Robin Hood. In that conceptual gap there ought to be enough leeway for Shafiq to elude the Circle…

'We felt further,' Lister continues, 'that, given his choice of Olympic sport, the best bait would very likely be an archery contest.'

…or not, of course.

* * *

There's a locksmith in Spitalfields who – or rather whose daughter, once a teenage heroin addict who ended up in the thrall of an abusive pusher-pimp, until Zara and Scar helped put him in hospital and her in a rehabilitation facility – owes the Green Chapel a substantial favour.

These days he keeps a pay-as-you-go mobile phone behind his counter, for use by Malory and anyone else she primes with the right password. She has similar arrangements in heaven knows how many other places, including with the sweet shop owner in the nearest village to the Benwick Institute.

Each Monday and Thursday during her field trip to Benwick, she's been dropping by the sweet shop at ten am to buy a bag of barley sugars, and staying for ten minutes to chat. This particular Thursday, at four minutes past ten, Jory phones her from the locksmith's back yard – a filthy corridor of concrete between the back of the shop and a wall, beyond which tube-trains growl and clatter.

He fills her in, as quickly as he can, on Raymond's plan and its uncanny similarities to those adopted by the Sheriff of Nottingham for the capture of Robin Hood.

The ground's slick with pigeon droppings, and he doesn't want to stay here longer than he has to.

'They've co-opted some big indoor archery event,' he concludes. 'Basically bought out the organisers with Circle money, then declared that all the proceeds will go to charity. Improving children's lives in the Third World through sport, or something similar. They've already announced Shafiq as guest of honour.'

'Well,' says Malory thoughtfully. 'It's clearly a response to Shaf's device, no argument there. It may not be a conscious one, though. If it is, it would mean Sir Charles knows the Green Knight is also Robin Hood, and I'm not sure he's got enough information to work that out. He's not the world's most inspired thinker. In theory he could have a spy inside the Chapel, but there was no hint of that at your hearing. A lot of what you said about the camp could have been directly contradicted by any eye-witness.'

'OK,' Jory agrees, grateful as usual for Malory's clear-sightedness in this kind of situation. 'So what does that leave us?' He goes to lean against the wall, notices the thick film of algae smothering it, and decides against it.

'Well,' says Malory briskly. She's stepped outside: Jory can hear the wind tearing off the North Sea and the occasional vocal intervention by a seagull. 'My money's on a subconscious response: Sir Charles isn't consciously aware that the Green Knight's Robin Hood, but the devices are manoeuvring him to act as if he were, so he can play his part in the story.'

'*His* part?' A tube-train trundles by, and Jory has to speak at a yell. Fortunately, only the locksmith has windows opening into this space – a window which Jory clambered out of, then asked the man to close behind him. Their privacy, at this end anyway, is as guaranteed as an anonymous mobile can make it. 'But that would mean that Sir Charles is acting as the Sheriff of Nottingham. Surely?'

'The Sheriff's one candidate,' Malory confirms. He has to strain to hear her over the train's noise. 'The other's Prince John. He was the brother of the rightful but absent King, just as the Sir Kay device is standing in for its foster-brother, the Circle's Head. It's another instance where the devices converge.'

'So the Seneschal of the Circle,' Jory says flatly, 'is turning into one of the most notorious villains in English history. Well, that's just marvellous.'

'That's my guess,' agrees Malory. 'Not that he'll be aware of it. Given that we already know you're Guy of Gisbourne, that might make Mr Lister the Sheriff.'

'God almighty, Mal,' says Jory. 'This is appalling. Raymond's one of the most powerful men in the country. Sir Kay's… well, he could be boorish, and petty and jealous sometimes, and possibly not all that bright, but he was always loyal to Arthur, always one of the good guys. Prince John – the one in the legends, anyway – is arrogant, cruel, lecherous, scheming and amoral. And pretty clever, as I recall. If I had to pick one of them to go up against, I'd have Sir Kay in a heartbeat.'

'Quite,' says Malory. 'Although *you're* not going up against him, are you? You're on his side.'

'Well.' Jory shifts uncomfortably, ends up standing in something he doesn't want to think about, and shifts smartly back again.

'We should be able to use that,' says Malory.

* * *

'Who is this?' grunts the voice. It's nearly noon, but the voice sounds like a hungover St Bernard, dragged from its kennel to be interviewed on early-morning radio. 'How the hell did you get this number?'

'Rev, it's me,' says Jory. He's using the payphone in another of the dingy pubs Malory introduced him to.

Late-afternoon light beams through grimy windows to embarrass the airborne dust. The only other people in here are two old men – one black, one white, but otherwise indistinguishable – who are speaking neither to Jory or each other. The barman's in the backroom listening to a too-loud radio. 'I'm in need of some spiritual direction.'

'Dan? That you?' Cantrell's tone is abruptly more alert. 'What… ah, what kind of "spiritual direction"?'

'The literal kind, I'm afraid,' Jory deadpans.

'Figures,' the ex-priest mutters. 'Give me one minute.'

There's a clatter of a phone being put down on an aluminium camping table, then for rather longer than a minute the unmistakeable sound of distant urination fills Jory's ears, at his expense. Calling a mobile from a payphone during the day doesn't come cheap.

'OK, big fellow,' Cantrell says, coming back online, 'what's on your mind?'

It's a big question, and one Jory feels the need to ease himself into gradually. Playing for time, he says, 'Scar told me to ask you about voodoo.' It gets him a strange look from the nearer of the two old men.

Cantrell chuckles. 'Looking to convert?'

'She implied it might be relevant to how you interact with your allies,' says Jory. 'She was talking about patron saints at the time.'

'I follow you,' Cantrell says. 'And yeah, there are analogies. I studied Haitian Vodoun at seminary. Caused some upset at the time.

'In Vodoun,' Rev says, 'there are spirits called *loa*. Go back a few hundred years and they'd be African tribal gods, but the Vodou guys dressed them up to look like Catholic saints. Like you have to, when you're kidnapped from where you grew up and sold to French plantation-owners in Haiti.'

He coughs and continues doing so for a little while. Jory nods and smiles to the old man, who tuts and shakes his head.

'Excuse me,' says Cantrell. 'Rough night. Point is, the loa can *possess* you. Not just in special rituals, this is something that happens in ordinary Sunday services. It's everyone's chance to talk with them – and you need to, because they do you favours if you ask them nicely enough. They can command respect because they're powerful, but it's not what you and I'd call worship. There's no… deference. It's like a democratic version of religion. A Vodoun priest will bargain with the loa. They broker agreements. Well, you see where I'm going with this,' Cantrell concludes.

'They treat them as allies,' Jory supposes.

'That's what my dissertation said,' Cantrell agrees equably. 'Mind you, it was a long time ago. I was a grad student and I'd just seen a double-bill of *White Zombie* and *Live and Let Die*. I might have made some of it up.'

'How did your tutors feel about all this?' Jory asks. 'How did you make it relevant to Episcopalianism?'

Cantrell chuckles in his throat. 'That's exactly what they asked me. In the end they decided I hadn't, so I had to rewrite the whole piece to make it about missionary work in Haiti.'

'So here's my question,' Jory says. 'Since this relationship is so equal… if Friar Tuck told you to do something you didn't want to do – kill somebody, say – you'd be able to resist it?'

The nearer man stares at him again, then concludes that Jory's just some loony. He turns his attention, with a sigh of palpable disappointment, back to his newspaper.

'Well,' says Cantrell. 'Fact is Friar Tuck's a tolerant soul, but I'm guessing we're not talking about him. Let me guess, you're asking on behalf of a friend, am I right?'

Jory says wryly, 'Actually, that's what I'm trying to find out.'

'Nice evasion,' Cantrell replies. 'Well, Dan, it would vary. Some allies are stronger than others, some are more… let's say *impulsive* than others. The same's true of us. A powerful ally prone to violent behaviour – Will Scarlet, say – needs to be kept in check by a headstrong host who'll fight him right back. Scar manages just fine. But take a turbulent, passionate ally from a violent time and pair them with someone who's naturally mild and gentle – well, there'll be times when that behaviour breaks through, and that won't be pretty.

'With some allies, the worse a host behaves, the better you think of them as a person. Are you sure you're asking this for someone else?' he adds.

Jory flushes. 'Rev –' he says, then breaks off in embarrassment. He's reluctant to ask the question he's about to put to Cantrell. Good Anglicans are reticent about this kind of thing. But there's a vital issue here, one which goes to the core of his identity, and he can't leave it unspoken any longer.

'Rev, how do you square what the Chapel does with your, well, your Christian… um, faith?' he asks. 'Aren't violent robbery and vandalism and kidnapping exactly the opposite of what a priest should stand for?'

Cantrell snorts. 'I guess you haven't been listening to what Jesus says, Dan. Remember how hard it is for the rich to get into heaven? Camels, needles' eyes, ring any bells? Taking wealth away from the rich – that's salvific work right there.

'See, Jesus casts down the mighty from their seat,' Cantrell continues, obviously getting into his stride, 'and he exalts the humble and meek. Remember the money changers in the Temple? Jesus took pretty direct action against them, didn't he? Our Lord was violent and vandalistic *that* day.

'Jesus said those who were persecuted would be blessed, because theirs was the Kingdom of Heaven. The Kingdom isn't something we sit around and wait till death for, Dan. Our task as Christians is to build that Kingdom right here on Earth – a world where there's no difference between Jew and Greek, slave and free, male and female, black and white, gay and straight: where everyone's as one in Christ Jesus.

'Stop me if I'm getting preachy,' Cantrell adds.

Jory laughs, surprised by the tension he's letting out. He says, rather bathetically, 'Rev, Shaf's going to get an invitation to a charity event. An archery contest. It's vital you tell him not to go.'

'Oh, that,' says Cantrell. 'I guessed that was a trap already. It's not exactly subtle, Dan.'

'It's aimed at Shafiq himself,' Jory points out. 'They don't know he's Robin Hood. '

'Sure,' says Cantrell. 'Fact is though, he's going, and he will not be talked out of it. A few of us will go along with him, obviously. But… well, you know Shaf.'

'Damn,' says Jory, though it's no more than he expected. Robin Hood is famously stubborn, and Shaf's as story-blind as any other device-bearer. While anyone else could spot at once what a terrible idea this is, it was a foregone conclusion that Shafiq wouldn't.

'Come on,' says Cantrell. 'Don't sweat it, Dan. Shaf'll be fine. Robin Hood *always* escapes from the Sheriff's men. You might as well worry about… ah I don't know, Sir Lancelot failing on a quest or something.'

'Sir Lancelot's going to be there,' Jory says.

* * *

Jory makes the third phone call two days later, from a phone booth near Oxford Circus. The incessant crowd of shoppers streaming past the glass are as anonymous as the women offering sexual services who pout from photocards plastered across the booth. Jory's anonymous, too: in shirt and jeans he bought ten minutes ago, his old clothes in a Topman bag slung from his wrist, he could be any one of them.

(The shoppers, not the pouting women. Obviously.)

The phone he's calling rings just the once before it's snatched up.

'Kinsey.' Her voice is a bark, too, but that of a chihuahua who some cruel practical joker has fed dog-food laced with coffee.

'Inspector,' Jory says. 'It's Jordan Taylor, from the Circle.'

'Taylor? You bastard, what the fuck are you doing phoning me?' From some people such a greeting might be affectionate. This sounds very much as if Jade Kinsey would like to rip Jory's throat out and run down the road with it in her teeth.

'Hello, Inspector,' Jory says. 'It's good to hear your voice. I realised I'd never thanked you for telling my bosses that you'd seen me, that day at the docks. As things turned out you ended up saving my life. So thank you.' It's a sincere sentiment, though he doesn't imagine it'll be welcome.

Confirming this, Kinsey snaps, 'I'll keep my mouth shut next time. What's this about, Taylor? Every time I run into you I end up in deeper shit than before, and I like to keep my epaulettes clean. So I repeat, what the fuck?'

'I'm guessing you're still looking for the Green Chapel,' Jory breezes. 'You remember, the criminal gang I was infiltrating that day?'

He rides out the ensuing tide of invective.

'Well,' he says, 'in that case would you like to arrest some of them?'

This whole situation is new territory for Jory. He's fine with combat tactics, even to some extent with battle strategy. Larger-scale, longer-term scheming, especially when it involves manipulating others to his own ends, is a wholly novel area for him to negotiate.

It's fun, though, and he seems to be rather good at it. He supposes his new situation's bringing out new skills. Besides, it's hardly surprising if his experiences of the past four months have changed him.

He realised days ago that some such cunning scheming is required, if he's to complete with plans drawn up by avatars of Prince John or the Sheriff of Nottingham. Even so, using Kinsey in this way makes him feel uncomfortable, even soiled.... yet also strangely elated. There's a thrill to exercising power over someone, which compares to that of losing yourself completely in a fight.

Kinsey's been silent. 'Go on,' she says eventually, as reluctantly as if he'd asked her to be a lung donor.

He tells her about the indoor archery event. 'The guest of honour's a certain Shafiq Rashid – you can look him up on the internet, though I wouldn't recommend it unless you enjoy competitive archery statistics. He's the Chapel's ringleader, and we'll be taking him in ourselves. No negotiation about that, I'm afraid. Some of his men will be there, though – probably at least one woman, too – and them you're welcome to.'

'It's not my turf,' says Kinsey, slowly. 'And my bosses are watching me, thanks to you. I'd have to call in favours, put out –'

'I don't care,' Jory says. 'Sort it out.' For a moment, the sensation of power makes him almost dizzy. 'Just be there, and in force. These people are highly trained and stronger than you think.'

'Just hold on a fucking –' Kinsey begins, but the end of the sentence is lost as Jory hangs the phone up.

He leaves the booth just as a chattering swarm of Japanese schoolgirls buzzes past, all clutching Urban Outfitters bags, and for a moment he reels dizzily. It's as if something's shifting and reforming in his brain. Still.

He rights himself and carries on down Oxford Street, a commentary running in his head. *So on the day, I do what I can to distract the other Knights, and rely on Robin Hood's natural slipperiness to keep Shaf clear of the Circle's custody. Meanwhile, if the Merry Men are arrested at all, it's by Kinsey – and she's the last person who'll hand them over to the Circle. We have the evidence against them, though, so without us, she'll have nothing to charge them with except resisting arrest. If I annoy her enough, she'll let them go just to spite me.*

All of which makes sense, he thinks, and hangs together rather gratifyingly. What makes Jory nervous is that it's a couple of steps further ahead than he has, up till now, been consciously reasoning.

And then of course there's the other thing. It's time I visited the Seneschal.

Which, before this moment, hadn't occurred to him at all.

* * *

'What is it, Taylor? I'm busy,' Sir Charles says as Jory puts his head around his office door.

'You said I was to report to you directly, sir,' Jory replies.

The Seneschal grunts. 'Come in, then.'

His office is directly above the boardroom, its rear wall a curve of bulletproof glass. From a less defensive building than the Fastness, the view of London would surely be spectacular. As it is, the window looks across to the featureless concrete of the curtain wall, and down to the courtyard beneath them.

The Seneschal's desk is black, glass-topped, its clean minimalist lines inevitably ruined by strewn and scattered paperwork. A computer screen and keyboard sit apart from these, as if embarrassed to be seen in company.

There are a number of comfy meeting-room chairs, but Jory doesn't sit. The Seneschal's a stickler for discipline.

The old man turns over the papers he's been reading, sits up stiffly in his own chair and says, 'So what have you got to report? I thought the plans for the Rashid quest were going smoothly.'

'They are, sir,' Jory replies. 'But a related matter has occurred to me. I believe that we're neglecting a potentially useful source of information, one which is also a threat we should be taking care to neutralise. Our current containment for it is… insufficient.'

'You're talking in riddles,' Raymond snaps. 'Far too much of that in this line of work. Speak plainly, man. What source? What threat?'

'Morgan le Fay,' Jory replies promptly.

It's a slight gamble. Word of the major villainous devices travels fast in the Circle, but it's still possible that Sir Charles knows of a more recent avatar of Morgan than Jory does. The last one on record was the prosaically named Clare Briggs – a freelance spy working for the Soviet security services in the mid-'80s, the targets of whose elegant honey-traps included several backbench politicians, a junior Home Office minister, an army Lieutenant-General and Sir Charles' predecessor as Seneschal of the Circle.

Briggs drowned herself in the Thames while operatives of MI5, the army and the Circle argued over which of them got to take her into custody. All told, it wasn't anybody's finest hour.

Sir Charles looks shocked, as well he might. 'Hope you have evidence to back this up, Taylor. Or rather, I sincerely hope you don't. Why do you say so?'

'It's the poem, sir,' Jory does his utmost to look good-hearted and just a little dim. '*Sir Gawain and the Green Knight*. Morgan le Fay turns out to be behind the whole thing. Everything the Green Knight does is her idea.'

'Well, so it is,' says Raymond, relaxing a little. 'If you mean the le Fay device is somehow sponsoring Rashid – well, we can't ignore the possibility. But what d'you mean, containment?'

'I hadn't realised how important she was.' Jory injects as much sincerity into his voice as he can while lying through his teeth. 'I thought she was just the Green Knight's servant. But she looked after his regalia. She brought him the axe he tried to use on me. And obviously she stuck around to see whether he succeeded – that's how we caught her. I think… I think the prisoner we took is bearing the le Fay device, sir. Marianne Millar.'

'Really?' Sir Charles seems sceptical, and with good reason. Scar and Morgan aren't exactly a match made in heaven. 'That fishwife? She'd be a bit of a contrast with the last one.'

'Well,' Jory says. 'I believe that can happen, sir.'

'The tests didn't pick up on any device,' Raymond objects.

'No, sir. But I believe there've also been a few cases of the most cunning devices cheating the tests.' This is a guess on Jory's part, but even if he's wrong he's banking on the Seneschal not knowing enough to call him a liar.

The old man harrumphs. 'Well,' he says. 'It sounds like a stretch to me. But if you have suspicions, we can't afford to take the risk. And if you're wrong, it's best we know quickly. I'll have her transferred to the Benwick Institute.'

But not, thinks Jory, *under too hefty an armed guard. Why waste the men?* 'Thank you, sir,' he says.

He's surprised he didn't think of this before, really – but somehow it never occurred to him until he talked to Alfred Noake. It's not as if he could have left Scar languishing in prison while her friends went free.

She'll make me a fine lieutenant one day, Jory thinks.

And where *that* comes from, he has no idea.

16. THE FOUNTAIN

'Let's go over the plan again, yeah?' Paul asks, affecting the enthusiastic drawl Jory remembers from their time as Knight and squire. 'Boss?' he adds lightly, as if to demonstrate how little he resents Jory's primacy.

The two of them, with Stephen and Theo, plus squires and sergeants-at-arms, are in the reception area of the leisure and conference centre's office suite, which the Circle has commandeered for their quest. It's comfy, with beige suedette sofas and a low glass coffee table, and it overlooks a long picture window. Through this the party has clear sight across the archery range that's been set up in the indoor sports pitch below, to the retractable bank of seating that's just beginning to accommodate the afternoon's first spectators.

Paul's being ironic. The plan is insultingly simple. Four Knights, three squires, twenty men-at-arms, all in plain clothes, all armed, distributed throughout the spectators, with one shared objective (normally they'd call him 'the target', but in this context that's needlessly confusing), who'll be highly visible throughout the proceedings. Shafiq Rashid is not only the guest of honour but an honorary competitor: he made it a condition of his attendance that he be allowed to take part in the shooting, although he's clarified that he'll refuse the placings and prizes that would otherwise inevitably result.

Even if Rashid brings along bodyguards, the Circle's thinking goes, the men-at-arms will easily be able to take care of them, leaving the Knights and squires to apprehend the Green Knight's bondsman. However powerful that device may be, odds of seven against one – or even four to one, if you count devices rather than people – are all but impossible to beat.

The only issue is how public to make the intervention. Raymond and Lister have left this up to Jory's discretion: public shows of force on the Circle's part are rare, but (as the good townspeople of Thankaster could tell you) not unknown. They help cement the public perception of the Circle as an unstoppable force, which in itself, the theory goes, helps to discourage wrongdoing by rival devices.

However, this appearance is deployed to best effect when the recipients of the force are as unappealing to the general public as the Saxon Shield. In Jory's view, taking a British Olympic medallist into custody at a charity match is not the kind of publicity his brother Knights would appreciate.

'We wait until afterwards,' he says. 'After the prizegiving and his speech, when everyone starts to leave. I'm not aborting the event if we can help it – we promised the proceeds to charity when we took control of the organisation. We've an honourable obligation to deliver that.'

It's also how the story goes, thinks Jory. The Sheriff's men never arrest Robin until he's had the chance to prove his skill on the range. (This is usually because he's in disguise, of course, and his skill as a bowman gives him away. Jory presumes Shafiq won't be going down that route.)

Paul, Theo and Stephen look dubious, but nobody speaks up against the general principle of honouring their promise to give alms to needy children. The Knights of the Circle are decent that way.

'He'll be armed,' Stephen points out. 'I mean to say, that's rather the point of the thing. What do we do if he starts shooting arrows at the spectators?'

'Unlikely,' Jory says, trying to imagine Shafiq doing that. Once he realises the Circle's men are there, Jory supposes he could pin a few of them to their chairs before the others reached him. He'd be extremely careful not to endanger civilians, though. 'If that happens, whoever's nearest has to take him down as quickly as possible.'

Jory doesn't mean the men-at-arms – although protecting the public from a rogue device is a pretty high priority, as far as the Circle's concerned Shafiq's device is also a Knight, and the normal rules of chivalric combat apply. The four Knights present and their squires, though out of armour, all carry swords in concealed scabbards.

'How do we know he won't skip out before the end?' asks Theo.

'We'll be watching him, naturally,' Jory replies. 'We won't risk losing him – we'll bring the timetable forward if necessary. And we have men-at-arms on the door as a last resort.' The yeomen can't shoot Shafiq without compromising the Circle's honour, but they can physically restrain him if need be. 'But if we can give these people the spectacle they've paid for, they won't ask for their money back.' He's thinking now as much of the TourneySoc charity events he organised as of the Circle's code.

Paul smirks. 'Actually, arresting the guest of honour would be *quite* a spectacle.'

'We'll do it discreetly,' Jory assures him.

* * *

I'm at the archery tournament myself, as it happens, so for once I'll be able to give an eye-witness account for a lot of what followed. I've come from one of my regular visits to the Green Chapel, who are currently encamped at Oxfordshire's picturesque Wychwood Forest. (They update me on its location using a state-of-the-art system of field communication known as 'those postcards you get in newsagent's windows'.)

I was there when Shaf's invitation to today's proceedings arrived, and I was one of the ones – along with Rev and Big Jack and anyone else who'd chime in – telling him to avoid it like the very big and obvious Circle trap it is.

He hasn't listened, of course. One day I'll think, if only we'd been able to argue with him better, if perhaps one of us had thought to send for Merry… but no. He hasn't listened to us, and he wouldn't listen to her either. He claims, in fact, to have no idea why we're so alarmed at him attending a competitive archery event. Every time we've tried to explain – and this includes Rev sitting him down and playing him the bit of the Errol Flynn movie where Robin wins the tournament, gets captured by the Sheriff's men and ends up sentenced to be hanged – he's shrugged and said he can't see the relevance.

It's a bugger, this story-blindness. I mean, you might think as a storyteller *I'd* be immune.

As I've said, when he first appears in the ballads Allan a'Dale isn't even a Merry Man – just some random travelling minstrel who comes seeking Robin's help, after his beloved gets abducted and threatened with forcible marriage to some wicked nobleman. In later treatments, yes, he's one of Robin's loyal followers, but not back then.

When I allied myself with Allan – a good while ago now – there was no Chapel. Merry hadn't yet hooked up with Shaun Hobson, so I had no Robin Hood to turn to when my new girlfriend – the daughter of a stringently conservative Pakistani family, who had previous form in terms of dating white boys – was abducted by her male relatives and forced into… well, I don't need to spell it out. The last I heard from Nazia was a postcard from Karachi, signed with a new surname and telling me – correctly – that we'd never see each other again.

I stopped dating after that.

Point is… The point is this. I didn't start seeing Naz till after my alliance with Allan. She was the first woman I did start seeing after it, in fact. Out of all the women I knew or might have met.

The allies don't control reality. It would have happened to Naz, whoever she started dating. But I'm damn sure the shape of Allan's story made it more likely to happen to *me*.

The allies adapt to fit their environment – our lives, our relationships, this modern age we walk them through. And if we let them – if we don't exert complete control, say 'no' to our allies just as often as we say 'yes' – we end up letting their stories decide the footsteps of our lives. We have to be pretty damn nippy on our toes to avoid the paths they preordain for us.

Anyway. In the end Shaf comes here today, and so do Big Jack, Rev, Zara, Squig and me. We reckon it's best just to go along with it.

It's not even a Green Chapel outing really – with Merry at the Benwick Institute and Scar in the nick, we're just the mates Shaf happens to have at hand right now.

* * *

Now, it's possible you've been looking forward to a treatise on the mechanics of modern target archery – how the traditional forms and practices have been standardised into a competitive system, how they're adapted to an indoor setting, how the ballistics work, how scores are reckoned, what the health and safety considerations are. It's more likely – and I'm only guessing here, admittedly – that you're not.

In any case, let me summarise: *Load, pull, point, twang. Repeat.*

Archery's not exactly a complex sport. To watch, it's best described as undemanding.

For me, it's local colour in any case. It's true I'm here to support Shafiq, but our priority's to stop him getting killed or arrested, rather than help him acquit himself competitively. The combat arts aren't really my bag anyway, as I've implied before.

Our bank of seats has a flimsy railing and a line of frowning stewards separating it from the range, which must normally be used as a pitch for indoor hockey, five-a-side football, that sort of deal. The floor is grey concrete covered with some kind of synthetic resin; the walls are breezeblocks painted an institutional lime-green. At one end of the range are the targets, big easel arrangements holding white-black-blue-red-yellow roundels. Along the floor – already decked out with multiple pitch markings in different-coloured paints – strips of fluorescent yellow tape show distances to the targets. The MC-cum-commentator, a man with a seriously misdirected sense of patriotic pride, makes a big thing of the fact that these are measured in good old-fashioned imperial lengths, and not these nasty European ones.

The five of us are in hoodies, though not the green ones. (We're traditionalists, not idiots.) It's broad daylight outside, but none of that reaches us here. We're lit by clinical fluorescent striplights, their ghastly whiteness making us look like unusually sun-shy vampires.

Shaf's in his British Olympic team kit, sitting in a separate bank of seats behind the judges, with the organisers and the other competitors. We obviously can't sit with him, so we distribute ourselves throughout the spectators – Zara and Rev at the end nearest the targets, Jack on his own in the middle, and Squig and me up the end nearest Shafiq. At least we can see him clearly, I think, although he'd be vulnerable to any sniper in the crowd. Not that that's the Circle's style – as far as I can judge, having attended some recent banquets in my bardic capacity. They're much mor your sword-in-your-face kind of guys, even when they abseiling from a helicopter.

Looking around the crowd, the largest group seems to consist of tolerant-looking adults with bored children, who are presumably the competitors' families. (There are children's events scheduled, I know, and being a young archer's brother or sister must bring its own very special brand of monotony.) Among the rest there's a preponderance of burly men who look uncomfortable in their street clothes. It wouldn't be terribly surprising if the sport attracted men like that, though, so at first I try not to suspect anyone in particular.

Then I start seeing faces I recognise. After a while I even spot Jory – Dan, rather – as he comes in behind us and sits up near the back of the tiered rows. Rev's told us he's been in touch, and says that for the moment we can trust him. Still, even with Merry vouching for him, I can't see him taking our side against his own people if there's a hands-on fight.

I look down and see that Shafiq's noticed Dan as well. Shaf nods coldly in his direction, and turns his attention to the proceedings.

The kids' events are first and give the MC an opportunity to patronise for England. One at a time, boys and girls aged from about eight up into their teens step up to some of the closest of the taped markers. They nock their arrows, draw their bows, let fly and generally hit the targets somewhere rather than thumping into the safety curtain. My appreciation of the shooting is confined to going 'Ooh' whenever someone hits the bullseye.

This sets the pattern for the next couple of hours. It's a repetitive sport.

(Oh, did I already say that? Well, excuse me.)

* * *

There's a break for coffee and biscuits at around three. s everybody mills around in the foyer, Squig and I do our t to look like father and son.

We avoid anything more than the most fleeting eye contact with Rev and Zara – who are hilariously pretending to be husband and wife – and Big Jack. Dan's just as conspicuously avoiding any of us. None of us dares more than glance at Shaf, who's sipping some energy drink while a local councillor treats him to a diatribe about how sending British money abroad to benefit foreigners is an offence to both God and Mammon. I just hope Shaf can get through the interval without decking him.

I'm so concerned about this that I forget one other important possibility. 'Tal!' comes a voice from behind me, and straight away I realise my mistake. If I recognise faces from my professional visits to the Circle, then so – despite the relative anonymity a storyteller enjoys – might they.

'Bollocks,' I say to Squig, but it's too late. I turn to see Bob Thackett, the Circle man-at-arms, bearing genially down on me with a cup of tea and a bourbon biscuit.

'Don't usually see you at this kind of thing, Tal,' Bob says. He's someone I've met a few times – a friendly face in a context where kindness is scarce, but not in any proper sense a friend. I don't use the name 'Dale' in my dealings with the Circle – it's more of a clue about my ally than I want to give them. Besides, it never feels as if it fits, with them. It's not as if it's *my* name, after all.

'Oh, you know,' I say. 'I was in the area. Thought I'd look in on it.'

Like I say, we bardic types have to stay impartial. We move from place to place, accepted everywhere, belonging nowhere, loyal to none except our personal friends – guests in chapel and castle, camp and croft. After all, our livelihood basically depends on it. The better we are at our job, the more compelling the stories we tell, the less anyone notices us. We blend in seamlessly with our surroundings.

Well, usually. It's a funny thing, but being a professional storyteller doesn't actually make you a good liar.

'You're into archery?' Bob asks, still surprised.

'You can't tell stories about the olden days without taking a bit of an interest in these old traditions,' I reply. I wave my hand glibly, as if to indicate the hallowed striplighting and heritage breezeblocks.

'And who's this young man?' Bob asks jovially. He doesn't offer any explanation of his presence here.

'All right.' Squig nods at him, but leaves the verbals at that.

'Ah. Yes,' I say. 'This is my son… erm, Errol. He's thinking of doing archery at school, aren't you Errol? We came along to see what it was like.'

Squig rolls his eyes, but that only reinforces the impression of a teenage son accompanying his father to a social event. Bob smiles tolerantly and says, 'My oldest will be his age soon. Nice to meet you, Errol, I'm Bob.'

We stand around awkwardly for a moment. Then Bob says, 'There's another bloke I know here, too.' He nods towards a pale young man – well, we all look pale under these lights, but I'd be willing to bet this guy would look bleached-out anywhere. He's tall, nervous and flimsy-looking. 'I'm trying to remember where I've seen him,' Bob muses.

'Why not ask him?' I suggest, trying not to sound as if I want rid of Bob.

Bob looks at me. 'Best not. We meet all sorts, my line of work. Oh hang on – I remember him, I think. He's a policeman. Jenson? Jennings? Well then, I'd better not talk to him,' he chuckles. 'They're usually not too pleased to see us.'

***

Across the other side of the lobby, Paul's nervously asking Jory, 'The objective's spotted you, hasn't he?'

As if that makes a difference, thinks Jory. He sips his tea and says, 'It was always a possibility.'

'But if he knows we're here, shouldn't we, you know, bring the timetable forward?' Paul insists.

'He knows *I'm* here,' Jory corrects him. 'For all he knows I've come alone – it's not as if I couldn't have known he was here. He's been on the most recent advertising. But he came here to compete and hand out prizes – that's what we were always banking on. He won't leave without doing that.'

'But he's, like, forewarned,' Paul persists.

Jory shrugs. 'So are we,' he says. 'We're still the superior force.'

Paul sighs. 'That little storyteller's here too,' Paul goes on. 'You know – comes to our banquets, plays the lute and stuff? Not terribly well, though.' (He's not wrong there, sad to say.) 'And some policeman, apparently. Thackett saw him.'

'I don't – good God,' says Jory, suddenly making the connection. He knows me fairly well from the Green Chapel, but this is the first time he's thought to link the Dale he met there with the anonymous figure at the Circle's feasts. 'Well, so what? There are a lot of people here.'

'Well, isn't it a bit of a coincidence?' frets Paul. 'I mean, I recognise him, too. He was there that morning you offed that Beard Collector fellow, I think.'

Jory frowns, affecting surprise. 'Do you mean PC Jenkins?' He never learned the other policeman's name, but he's not among the few black faces here today.

'Yes, him,' Paul says. 'He worked for…' and suddenly he stops, and starts casting his eyes around the room. 'And there she is,' he says, alighting on a smallish figure. 'My word – your good friend Inspector Kinsey. Now what on earth's *she* doing here, I wonder?'

* * *

The tournament continues after the break with the adult events. There are separate rounds for men and women, and for different types of bow. Shaf shoots in both the men's sections, recurve and compound, having brought along two bows from his extensive collection.

Shaf's compound bow's a bulky metal monster, needing a fiddly collection of levers just to draw it. The recurve's less elaborate, though different from the longbow he uses as Robin or the self bow of the Green Knight. The original Robin would have considered it a Saracen design, although the materials are modern, with a metal handle and laminated fibre-glass for the bendy bits (excuse me, 'limbs'). Squig, who's a bit of a closet toxophile, mutters to me that the bowstring's made of Kevlar, just like a bulletproof vest, although why that's meant to be a good thing still baffles me.

I'm expecting some striking shooting from Shaf – it's what his ally's most famous for, after all – but with the compound bow he's relatively restrained. He hits the bull's eye every time, of course, but you'd expect no less from an Olympic medallist. With the recurve he manages something a bit more special, splitting the end of one arrow in the centre of the target with a second. The MC, admiring and envious, calls this feat a 'Robin Hood', and everyone seems to accept that as the standard terminology.

Squig – always chatty once something's captured his interest – whispers to me that this isn't even all that difficult, when you're shooting with these modern carbon-fibre arrows. With the wooden ones the Chapel use for actual weaponry, it's more of a challenge. You need to split it along the grain, you see.

Even so, it's impressive enough for everyone to applaud and cheer in acknowledgement of their guest of honour's general awesomeness. There's no question that, if Shafiq was actually competing, he'd win this thing hands down.

Still, given his position here that's obviously not on, so he graciously cedes the victory in these events to those in second place. It has to be said one of them's rather less than gracious when Shaf comes to hand out the prizes.

After the prizegiving, Shaf steps forward, a bow slung casually over each shoulder, and gives the speech he really came here for. It's properly inspirational stuff – about the young archers and their ambitions, and how the money raised today will go to creating similar aspirations among the kids in deprived parts of Africa, Asia and South America.

'Let's hope, though,' Shafiq says, 'that their ambitions go beyond acquiring sporting titles, medals and trophies – not, of course, that there's anything wrong with collecting those things along the way. If there's one thing my various careers have taught me, in fields as diverse as athletics, scientific research and political activism, it's that everybody's potential is far greater than they imagine… but that potential in itself is valueless. The value lies in how it's realised.

'To use the obvious metaphor, if our potential is the bowstring – no more impressive when at rest than any length of twine, yet full of potential energy when it's drawn taut – and our attainment is the arrow, then it's the *aim* which really matters. An arrow shot with magnificent power and accuracy into a haystack is no use to anyone.

'I've been proud today,' Shafiq says, unslinging the recurve bow and twirling it against the floor, 'to see so many young people taking steps to realise their potential. Even so, sporting celebrity is a limited goal. It's a route out of poverty for some, but it does little for society as a whole. Those children overseas, who'll benefit from the money we've raised today, belong to societies which are themselves impoverished – which are kept systematically poor and disadvantaged, in fact, by the ruthless collusion of our Western governments and corporations with their own regimes.'

He whips the bow up, nocks an arrow and lets fly at one of the targets still standing at the far end of the hall. The arrow pierces the bull's eye and sticks there, quivering.

It's all done so fast that the Circle's men – and the police – don't even have time to react. Still, you can tell who they are now, by the way they just half-leaped from their seats, then warily relaxed again.

There are nervous glances amongst the organisers and dignitaries. The local councillor looks particularly dismayed.

Shaf goes on calmly, 'I don't mean that our charitable actions today are meaningless. On the contrary, they mean a great deal: that human beings are capable of selflessness and generosity, that the divides of nationality, ethnicity and faith are fundamentally meaningless, that we can all aspire to overcome the injustice of our world's distribution of wealth. But true charity isn't about handing what scraps we can spare to the poor; it's about welcoming them to our table as our equals.

'I hope that, as our equals, these young people – the young archers here today, the young sportsmen and women in those distant countries – will strive to fight injustice, poverty and oppression, not only against themselves, but wherever they are found… and perhaps even more importantly, wherever they are *caused*.'

As he's been speaking Shafiq's raised his bow again, picked another arrow from wherever he's keeping them and casually nocked it, as if it's the most natural thing in the world. Some of the Circle's men and the police are on their feet and pushing through the spectators, but they're too far away to interfere.

'To do that,' Shaf says, 'they will need to stand and face this conniving, this bullying and corruption and petty greed, in Africa and Asia and America and Europe, and tell the powermongers who perpetuate this odious status quo,' – he looks at Jory directly now – '"No more. You people have ruled over us for long enough."'

He lifts the bow and draws it: 'With enough potential energy,' – he aims in an instant – 'and the right objectives,' – he lets fly – 'one human being can set the world on fire.'

The arrow flies towards the same target as before. It slams into the back of its precursor in a perfect 'Robin Hood', impaling it along its length.

You'd have trouble catching it on film, though, since both arrows immediately burst into flames.

* * *

You can't fit much incendiary into an arrow-shaft, or even two, but it's enough to ignite the wooden target and the safety curtain behind it. With nothing but a breezeblock wall behind that there's little chance of the building burning down, but in the meantime there's going to be a lot of smoke. It billows out across the sports hall – thick, dark and tasting of that stuff your mum used to paint your nails with to stop you biting them. Only oilier.

The crowd reacts with a lot of standing and pointing and shrieking. There's no doubt now about the identities of the police, because they keep calm and start trying to usher people towards the exits, or of the Circle's men, because they're pushing through the crowd towards Shafiq, discreetly drawing swords or guns as they go.

The kids – most of them, anyway – are still gazing in awe at the fire. It's fair to say they won't be forgetting Shafiq's speech in a hurry.

Shaf, meanwhile, has flung the recurve bow aside and is sprinting for one of the closed fire exits. While he's in transit the smoke detectors kick in, filling the hall with a blaring klaxon noise and, instants later, a torrential downpour from the sprinkler system. At the same moment, the fire exit swings wide open ahead of him, and a general stampede begins.

As he shoves his way unseeing between me and Squig, Jory's focussed on reaching Shafiq before anyone else does. As for what he'll to do then – arrest him, or impede the other Knights and men-at-arms in their efforts to do likewise – well, he's hoping to remember that part of the plan before he gets there.

One other thing confuses Jory as he runs, leaping and jostling under cascading water, to make his way through the suddenly mobile rabble. There are two sets of fire doors, at opposite ends of the hall. One set leads to the sports centre's lobby, giving indirect access to the outside but also, via various internal doors, to the conference suites, squash courts and so forth. Stairs lead up from this foyer area to the office suite where the Circle held their council-of-war earlier.

The other leads directly to the car park and potentially to freedom. Shafiq is, for some reason, heading for the lobby, which means the men-at-arms stationed there have some chance of grabbing him on the way through.

Jory might imagine that this was part of some clever trickster's plan on Shaf's or Robin's part, except that, when the fire exit doors opened, the running man looked back in sudden alarm in the direction he wasn't heading in, and faltered for a moment in his headlong hurtle. It was a momentary glance, but enough to tell an attentive observer that he'd screwed up.

Whether this causes Jory hope or dismay is a question he ignores just for the moment.

As Shafiq reaches the foyer, four Circle men-at-arms converge on him. They're big blokes, especially compared with Shaf's slight frame, and they're carrying guns – albeit for show, against a Knight at least.

Shafiq's other bow sheds an arc of droplets under the waterfall of the sprinklers. In close quarters, and assuming you're not bothered about keeping it in a usable condition, a compound bow – heavy, securely grippable and with some nasty edges – makes a basic but effective impact weapon. It quickly fells two of the men-at-arms, with fast blows to the head and stomach. Meanwhile the other two manage to grab hold of Shafiq, but before they can disarm him he brings the bow's limbs down into their knees on either side of him, snapping the bow but striking the men hard enough for one of them to stagger and let go.

The fourth man's trying to bring his gun into range of Shaf's face – Jory assumes to threaten him, rather than anything more permanent – but Shafiq knocks it from his hand, skinning the man's knuckles in the process. Shaf grabs the gun as it falls, and swings the butt hard into the man's eye.

Shafiq turns, leaving two men down, two upright but in too much immediate pain to do anything about him fleeing.

As he passes, one of the fallen men, a quick recoverer, slashes at his achilles tendon with a Circle-issue commando knife. Shaf staggers but runs on. Apparently suspecting that more opposition may be lurking in the car park (it isn't), he's heading for the stairs up to the conference suites.

As Jory reaches the fallen men, a voice cries out, 'Shafiq Rashid, I am an armed police officer! Halt or I fire!' In the absence of expletives, it takes him a moment to recognise it as Jade Kinsey's. The Inspector is standing by the doorway from the sports hall, toting a police-issue Glock 17 semi-automatic pistol.

Jory turns awkwardly to take it off her, but he slips on the slick wet tiling and slides across the floor, sending up a wave of spray before he cracks his head against one of the unconscious men's. Since Shaf clearly has no intention of halting, Kinsey fires a warning shot which ricochets off the wall. Shaf lurches again, and Jory realises that Kinsey's warning was sterner than she intended.

'Rashid's ours, Kinsey!' Jory tries to shout, but his head's ringing so hard he can't tell whether he even spoke.

The rest of the spectators are piling through the doors now, streaming past Kinsey and Jory and the downed men, but at the sound of gunfire they panic even more. Some turn and run for the opposite fire exit, some dash, hands desperately covering their heads, for the main doors to the outside. Squig and I, having followed as best we could in Jory's wake, are near the front.

We rush for the foot of the stairs, which Shaf's still taking at a painful, but surprisingly swift, crouch. The flight of steps has become a cataract, and he's fighting a current as well as his injury.

Squig's got a pole he wrenched from the flimsy railing as we passed, and he's swinging it like a quarterstaff. Knowing I've got nothing, he dips into his pocket with his other hand and hands me some kind of army knife.

I stare at it as we mount the stairs like it was a week-dead squirrel, and wonder what the hell I'm supposed to do now.

***

Behind us, the Circle have remobilised. The four guys Shafiq disabled (five counting Jory, who lies dazed and soaking on the floor) are still out of the picture, but two of the other Knights are close behind us. A group of men-at-arms are remonstrating angrily with Inspector Kinsey, while a handful more, Bob Thackett included, follow the Knights, wielding their own semi-automatics with casual menace.

The two Knights start upstairs behind us, the water glinting on their swords. Ahead of us Shaf's reached the landing, but he's clutching his leg and slowing down. He won't get far without help, but if we don't buy him some time he won't get anywhere at all.

Now we've gained height, I can see back through the fire doors into the hall, where Rev, Big Jack and Zara are being held back by a row of men and a few women. One of the men is thin and pale. The short, shrill woman who I'll only later learn is Kinsey is getting angrier and angrier, and eventually decks one of the men-at-arms.

My clothes are soaked through, and I feel like I'm wearing wet tarpaulin. The smell of smoke's been washed away by the freshness of the indoor rain, but the sprinklers' din, the alarm's blare, the yelling of the crowd are all still deafening.

'Stop here, yeah?' Squig says halfway up the steps, and we do.

We turn to face the Knights. They're not nearly as frightening without their armour, but they're still strong young men in good physical shape, coming at us with large bladed implements. It's not a calming sight.

'Tal! Errol!' yells Bob Thackett from behind his bosses. 'What the bollocks are you playing at, you little arseholes? Get out the fucking way!'

I groan. I like Bob Thackett, but not nearly as much as I like the income from the Circle's lucrative storytelling gigs. All that's out of the window now – as, presumably, are my clean criminal record and my permission to set foot outside the building I sleep and eat in. Without making anything I'd call a choice, it seems I've given up being Taliesin to the Circle, and settled for being the Chapel's Allan a'Dale.

Which seems a shame right now, because frankly the legendary Taliesin was the better fighter.

Squig swings his pole and shouts, with obvious enthusiasm, 'That's far enough, Circle scum!' Unfortunately he gets a bit of water in his mouth and it comes out a bit spluttery.

I gesture feebly with the knife and add, 'Yeah…' But then I risk a glance behind us and I see Shaf, barely halfway down the corridor to the meeting rooms, curled up against a wall and holding his leg in obvious agony. The knife cut's superficial, but Kinsey's bullet's torn a big hole in the same thigh, and it's bleeding horribly.

He makes an effort to carry on, but ends up mostly rolling slightly to the side.

It's not exactly a heroic last stand.

The siren and the sprinklers finally cut out – obviously someone's got to the control panel. From outside, in the sudden quiet, I can hear the sound of fire sirens.

'Squig,' I say, and lay a hand on the boy's arm. 'I reckon it's over. Live to fight another day, eh?'

I point back at Shafiq, and Squig sees what I mean. We obviously don't have time to consider pros and cons, and Squig's not much of a thinker anyway.

'You'd best scarper,' I say. 'Place like this, there must be places you can hide, ways you can get out. Come on, you'll do no good by staying here.'

He nods, shrugs and drops the pole. It tumbles down the stairs, a soggy catherine-wheel of damp defeat.

Then he turns and runs like a bastard.

The Knights push past us towards Shafiq as I hand the knife to Bob, despising myself for the coward I am, but also thanking heaven I didn't have to use it.

'Pathetic,' the Knight who I'll later learn is called Paul Parsons mutters as he shoulders past me. Squig's already disappeared round the corner of the corridor. 'You people have no idea of loyalty, do you?'

Bob shrugs. 'Sorry about him,' he says. Then he grabs me roughly by an arm and marches me downstairs.

We're met at the bottom by the shouty policewoman. With her hair drenched and lank across her scalp, she looks like something from a horror movie. But then, I imagine, so do we all.

She's somehow prodded Jory to his feet and dragged him over with her. 'Tell him,' she orders, meaning there's something Jory needs to tell Bob.

Jory still looks faintly concussed. 'That one's for the police, Thackett,' he says, fortuitously remembering the other man's name. 'Like those others. We get Rashid.'

Kinsey looks grim, but says nothing.

'Really, sir?' Bob asks, glancing back up the stairs at the other Knight.

'Yes,' Jory replies firmly. 'On my authority.'

Bob Thackett shrugs and hands me over to the cops.

* * *

Like I say, you couldn't call what's happening here heroic. But then, we're not heroes. Not me, not Squig, not Paul or Shaf, and certainly not Jory.

What we are, we in the Chapel and the Circle and their penumbral margins, is – and this is at best – echoes. The resonances, if you want to be poetic about it, of people who were such paragons of humanity – or maybe who just happened to be doing the right things at the right times – that they became immortal: renowned not just in their own generation but by all those who came after them. They died, of course, but some reflection of their personality lived on through song and story, plays and prose, on film and video and in the microscopic 3-D patterns of organic and electronic memories.

They lived their stories, and now they perpetuate their names by persuading, bribing or cajoling us to do likewise. We are their avatars, the personae they use to interact with the world which we – naively, maybe – see as real.

Like I say, that's at best. At worst… well, you've been listening to this from the beginning. I don't need to tell you how all this sounds to normal people.

At worst we're mad.

Delusional, tripping, prone to hallucinations – however you want to put it. We reinforce each other's false beliefs, in a consensual delusion so long-lived and self-perpetuating that our national culture has accreted round it, like a priceless pearl around a dust-speck.

At this precise moment, I'm not convinced that it's a difference worth quibbling about.

III
THE WASTE LAND

17. THE ARROW

Shafiq's leg is in plaster when Jory arrives at his hospital bed this evening. Although he's more or less capable of moving around, his Circle guards aren't encouraging it, and their presence makes the single room a cramped and intimidating place.

Jory dismisses them, insisting they wait outside while he interviews the prisoner alone. Slinging his rucksack on the floor, he sits down on a stiff-backed plastic chair. The room's stark – clinical, in fact – with harsh halogen lights inset into the ceiling, a locked window looking down several storeys to some overgrown urban scrubland, and a blank TV screen on a swingable frame.

Shafiq sits on the bed, leafing through a stack of elderly back-issues of *Hello!* and *Woman's Weekly*. 'I brought you *New Scientist*,' Jory says, digging it from his bag and handing it to him.

'Thank goodness for that,' says Shaf, taking it gratefully. He seems at ease – more so than Jory feels, at any rate. Jory supposes (recalls, actually) that being locked up with no chance of escape can have a peculiarly relaxing effect on the mind. Of course it's conceivable that strong painkillers are also playing their part here.

There's a pause. Jory has a lot to tell his friend, but there's something he has to get off his chest first. He says,

'I'm sorry I called you a cheat, back in the summer. It was stupid of me.'

Shafiq gives him a baffled look. 'I'm sorry?'

'At the camp,' Jory reminds him. 'I thought your device helped you to win your Olympic medal.'

'Oh yes,' Shafiq says. 'I remember.' His mouth quirks at the edges. 'So, that's the principal thing you feel the need to apologise for, is it?'

Jory smiles. 'I saw you at the tournament,' he says. 'You shot very well, but not like Robin Hood would shoot. And your escape plan was so poor even I couldn't make sure it worked. Which I should have been able to, since it was me chasing you.'

Shafiq frowns. 'You really should have, yes. Although that cop's bullet going astray didn't help.'

'I was relying on your device to get you away,' Jory confesses. 'Robin always escapes somehow. I hadn't realised that... when you shoot competitively... he isn't there.'

Shafiq shrugs. 'He can watch. He's welcome to, like anyone else. But winning a competition's something I do alone. That's always been our agreement.'

'You... de-attune yourself, somehow, temporarily,' Jory says. 'Malory would know how that works.' And the Circle with their cherished testing of prisoners, would be dismayed to discover it's possible. 'You hadn't had time to re-establish your rapport when you tried to escape.'

'Stupid of me, really,' says Shafiq. 'I knew you'd invited me there just so you could lay hands on my device. I wanted to show you there was more to me than Robin Hood. Arrogance is a bit of a character flaw of mine.'

'I remember,' Jory says.

Shaf snorts. 'Besides,' he said, 'I was worried the bastard would make me try to kill you again.'

Jory nods. 'It's all right,' he said. 'I know how that goes.'

***

A few hours ago, Jory stood with Paul, Stephen and Theo in the boardroom at the Fastness, while the Seneschal imparted some startling news. It was early evening, some hours after the successful capture of the Green Knight and the arrest of five of his associates, and most news programmes were vaguely reporting that the Circle had contained an incident at a charity sporting event.

'I'm shocked, actually, that she'd do this,' Paul said, self-righteous as ever. 'After all the Circle's done for her.'

He glanced across the boardroom at Jory, daring him to defend Malory this time.

Jory was still slightly groggy from his fall, but bearing up well. He'd been expecting a certain amount of flack for handing me and the others over to the police without following the Circle's normal intake procedures – even if he had been mildly concussed at the time – but we'd always been small fry next to his primary quest objective. Shafiq was safely under armed guard at a civilian hospital, being treated for his bullet wound, his knife wound – worse than you'd expect, since it was made with a steel blade – and the unpleasant muscle damage he'd given himself by trying to run about the place with both.

Besides, what with the comprehensive betrayal of the Circle's security by one of its most trusted secular counsellors, Jory's superiors had been a bit preoccupied to hand out an official reprimand.

What Sir Charles had just been telling his Knights was this.

Earlier in the day, Marianne 'Scar' Millar had been transferred from prison to the Benwick Institute for a comprehensive devicial assessment. As Jory had predicted, her guard had been a minimal one – a man-at-arms and a female auxiliary with the courtesy rank of page – but still,

Millar's behaviour had been exemplary throughout. Her handover into Circle custody, their journey up the M1 and along various country B-roads, and her checking-in at the Institute had passed without incident, unless you counted her slight yet uncharacteristic smirk on being signed over into the custody of Dr Malory Wendiman, on temporary assignment at Benwick.

At around the time that Shafiq Rashid was beginning his prize-giving speech, according to the testimony both of the Institute's staff and of its CCTV systems, Millar and Wendiman had left the building together, ostensibly for a walk in the grounds. As Millar was not considered a high-risk patient, and Wendiman was a trusted affiliate of the Circle, nobody had thought very much of this until the two women were observed climbing into Wendiman's car and driving away at some speed.

The nonplussed staff had dithered for a while before informing the Institute's director, and King Pellinore's bondsman had needed considerable persuasion of the facts of the matter before realising their urgency and phoning the Seneschal.

By that time, Malory and Scar could have been halfway to Nottingham. By now, they might be on a plane to Barbados.

'This Millar can't be just a footsoldier,' Sir Charles said, following this summary. 'At the very least she's just suborned a major device-bearer.'

'She must have coerced Malory somehow,' Jory insisted.

Paul was sceptical. 'How, though?' They had the CCTV footage in front of them, and it was quite obvious that Scar had had no weapon.

'Hypnotism? Subliminal suggestion? Neurolinguistic programming? I'm not Derren Brown.' Jory was on thin ice. 'But if Millar does carry the Morgan le Fay device, she'll have skills which mimic le Fay's sorcery. I mean, the device's last bondwoman got what she wanted through sex. Not that I'm suggesting –'

'Best stop digging, old man,' Stephen said gently. 'Your friend's let us down. Probably not her fault, but even so.'

Paul frowned. 'I'm not so sure. You mentioned le Fay, Taylor. Any particular reason you think she's active at the moment?'

Jory recalled the reasons he'd given Sir Charles. 'Well, the Green Knight. He's traditionally the victim of an enchantment –'

Paul interrupted him. 'Reason I ask is this. I think there's a candidate we've been overlooking. Charmed rather more people than just Shafiq Rashid. Wormed her way into the Circle thanks to her family connections, learned about the devices from our Merlin – might even have a "special relationship" with the Knight carrying her nephew's device?'

'There's no connection between Morgan and Gawain –' Jory began, before being interrupted again.

'For God's sake leave the riddles and get to the point,' the Seneschal snapped. 'You're talking about Miss Wendiman.'

Unperturbed, Paul said, 'I think we should consider the possibility, sir, yes. She knows everything about the Circle – agenda, methods, personnel, you name it. Imagine what the le Fay device could do with that knowledge. Even a basic explanation of the devices getting out, becoming public – we'd be a laughing-stock. And that's just the media, sir, never mind our actual enemies.'

'He's right, sir,' Theo said. It was his first and only contribution to the conversation.

'That was never in doubt, Harte,' the Seneschal agreed. 'Even if Taylor's right and Miss Wendiman's somehow been brainwashed, she can't be trusted now. Don't worry, we'll put every effort into finding her.'

* * *

Now, quickly, with all the concision he can muster, Jory tells Shafiq of Merry's rescue of Scar, and of everything else he's discovered since that conversation in the boardroom. Before Shaf can quite muster a sensible response, a sharp knock assails the ward door.

An elderly white nurse enters. 'I'm sorry sir,' she tells Jory, without much sincerity. 'It's time for Mr Rashid's painkillers.' She obviously disapproves of his presence – and understandably so, Jory thinks, given that he belongs to the sinister paramilitary organisation that as far as she knows is responsible for her patient's injuries.

'I'll pop outside for a minute,' says Jory, standing up. 'Let me know when you're finished.' He grabs his rucksack, just to be on the safe side. The nurse glares at him, then busies herself preparing a hypodermic.

'Incidentally,' Shafiq says as Jory opened the door, 'did you happen to remember which country won the gold medal in archery at those Olympics?'

'I didn't. Sorry,' Jory says.

He hears Shaf humming a brief snatch of classical music as he closes the door behind him.

The men-at-arms waiting outside barely react to Jory. While the nurse injects Shafiq somewhere embarrassing, he wonders what effect Malory's still-emerging betrayal will have on his own standing within the Circle.

Would have had, rather. Given his actions so far this evening – let alone what he's about to do – all that will be academic soon enough.

The devices, as Malory told him long ago, evolve. This happens in the wild, as it were, in culture as a whole: ancient forest deities become jolly outlaws, Celtic warlords become paragons of medieval chivalry, anonymous Merry Men suddenly sprout an ethnicity and immediately become a popular fixture.

It also happens in the smaller pond of the human mind, as Malory's father and others have amply demonstrated.

One device can, under particular pressures, mutate into a closely related one: Menw to Merlin, Sir Kay to Prince John, Nimue to… well.

Much of what's been going on with his device just recently isn't particularly clear to Jory, but that doesn't mean he can't speculate. One name you've heard me mention more than once, during our forays into the Arthurian tales, is that of Queen Morgause of Orkney, mother to Gawain and his brothers. You'll have gathered her family history's a complicated one.

Morgause's father, Duke Gorlois of Cornwall, was killed in battle by the High King Uther Pendragon, who then visited and impregnated her mother, Duchess Igraine, while magically disguised as his dead enemy. The product of this union was, of course, King Arthur, but the old King's treachery – as well as the remarkable method he used to achieve it – obviously made an impression on Morgause and her sister, Morgan le Fay. Years later, Morgan learned from Merlin, King Uther's wizardly counsellor, the glamour he'd used to disguise his patron so completely that even Morgan's mother had believed he was her husband.

She then colluded with her sister so that Morgause, glammed up as the chaste Queen Guinevere, could visit their half-brother Arthur and conceive a child with him.

(Yes, I know it's complicated. I can draw you a diagram if it'll help.)

Their motives for this are predictably obscure, although revenge against the son for the father's crimes almost certainly came into it. Arthur's motives are obvious, particularly if you believe he was genuinely misled. It's not unreasonable for a man to spend the night with his wife, after all, and if he's deceived by the wiles of a conniving woman, well…

This cuts no ice with the poetic justice department, of course. Incest is incest, and the offspring of sexual sin – in legends, anyway – inevitably return to call down nemesis upon their parents.

In this case, the embodiment of fate became the traitor who brought down Camelot and eventually dealt the death-blow to his father-uncle the High King. This knight – this power-hungry, manipulative schemer – brought about the end of the Round Table, ushering in its millennia of exile as the Circle. As of now his device, bends sinister sable on an escutcheon argent, has lain unclaimed since Clifford Al-Wasati Chalmers spilled his own brains in Iraq.

He's also, I'll repeat in case you're missing that diagram, Sir Gawain's half-brother.

The nurse emerges, nodding coldly at Jory, who steps back into the room to find Shafiq tying up his pyjama cord.

'*Switzerland* won the gold?' asks Jory. 'Really?' He recognised Rossini's *William Tell* Overture.

'Let's just say not everyone allied to a famous bowman is as scrupulous as me,' Shafiq says gravely. 'You can't trust these foreigners, you know.'

Jory smiles. 'Neutrality's a treacherous habit, certainly,' he agrees. 'I'm trying to give it up.'

Gawain was Morgause's eldest son, and Mordred was her youngest. So there's a certain symmetry there.

* * *

After his conference with Paul, Stephen, Theo and the Seneschal, Jory pleaded his concussion and excused himself. Now that Malory's complicity with the Green Chapel was known, it was only a matter of time before he himself was exposed. There was something he'd been putting off following up, and it was time he got round to it.

The Circle's interim trophy room is a substantial vault in the subterranean reaches of the keep, full of sturdy metal shelves of cardboard boxes. Items from quests are stored here for three years before being shipped out to the Circle's primary trophy storage facility in the depths of Devon, which Jory always imagines looking like the secret warehouse in *Raiders of the Lost Ark*.

The interim trophy room is a more modest affair, about the size of the church hall in Thankaster. It's not an evidence room, but the Circle has come to accept in recent decades that forensic tests on captured items are sometimes necessary, and that their results can be compromised. Use of the room is monitored, therefore: Jory had to use his keycard and passcode, under the eye of a CCTV camera. So far he'd been unwilling to risk tipping Sir Charles off by visiting the trophy room without good reason, but now, on reflection, he had to consider the Seneschal's suspicions thoroughly aroused.

Somewhere in the vault, he knew, would be the grisly contents of James Ribbens' shed, the Saxon Shield's weapons and office equipment, the Green Knight's axe which Bennett dropped during the confusion at Kielder. Jory's cover story was that he was taking a sample from the Beard Collector's cloak for DNA-matching against a newly-discovered victim, but he was well aware it wouldn't stand up to a moment's checking.

The filing system isn't complicated. Jory found the box he was looking for near the end of a long row of identical boxes, with Alfred Noake's name, date of death and presumed device (they'd settled on Hengist, the survivor of the two brothers) affixed to them on a printed label.

Jory dragged it down onto the floor and pulled the lid off. He rummaged through the pockets of the raincoat Noake had discarded that afternoon a month ago, immediately after being rumbled by St Pancras's security staff. (The suicide vest had been harmlessly detonated by the sappers, although there'd been an expensive scorch mark on the concourse floor.) The mobile phone was there, the sheath-knife, a USB stick, Noake's wallet, his keys, a cigarette-lighter with the SS horse logo... It didn't take Jory long to find what he was looking for.

He went through the USB drive on his laptop during the tube ride to King's Cross station. Misspelled racist pamphlets, mostly, a few web bookmarks and a video file – Noake's last testament explaining his rationale for planning the deaths of hundreds of people. Jory listened for forty seconds before he had to turn it off.

A few minutes later, he was in the left luggage area at King's Cross, handing over the ticket he'd found in Noake's wallet, and paying an extortionate late collection charge for the dead man's holdall.

It may sound daft that nobody in the Circle had done this yet, but… well, Noake was dead. The Circle aren't detectives. Best to let sleeping dogs lie, the thinking went, although this was more a case of letting a dead rat rot.

Jory opened the holdall in a nearby laundrette, first making sure that the premises were deserted. It held a pair of trainers, a quantity of clothing which hadn't smelled good even when it was packed away, and two shabby paperbacks worn nearly to pieces. He went through the pockets of the clothes, found them all empty, and dumped them in one of the washing machines.

He turned to the books. One was a translation of *Mein Kampf*, with Hitler glaring alarmingly from the cover above a bend sinister crammed with gothic lettering. The other was the Everyman translation of *The Anglo-Saxon Chronicles*, St Edmund pincushioned with arrows and grimacing at the mock-uncial script of the title. Inside it, in barely legible ballpoint, was scrawled 'ALFIE NOAKE YEAR 5'.

For a moment, Jory wandered what that ten-year-old had been like, how he'd acquired this unlikely volume, before the Hengist device insinuated its way into his psyche and poisoned it with hate.

The book also contained ten £20 notes – which, if he'd been less honest, would have gone some way towards compensating Jory for the evening's expenses so far – a card key and the details of a self-storage warehouse in the East End.

Jory sighed. It was looking like a long night.

* * *

Shafiq's hospital wing overlooks a patch of urban waste ground, surrounded by the backs of buildings: the hospital, offices, a department store. Another building must once have stood in it, demolished perhaps with an eye to redevelopment, but economics have long since abandoned the site to the mercies of nature. The ground is covered with bush and creeper, dark hollows beneath which hint treacherously at partial excavations. The gaps between surrounding buildings are cordoned off with a corroded chain-link fence.

A tall beech tree, which must have been there longer than the hospital, stands in a far corner, nearly naked in the autumn cold. It looms like a lace-tipped pillar against the darkening autumn evening.

Like I say, it's several storeys down, the other side of a bolted window. But it holds at least a provisional offer of freedom.

'I can't run, you know,' Shaf says as Jory sets about sawing through the bolt with a string file from his rucksack. 'I can barely hobble.'

'If we're discreet, you shouldn't need to,' Jory replies.

The rucksack also holds a set of car keys, a reel of strong but lightweight plastic cable, a cloth bag with a bundle of sturdy arrows, and a flimsy folding bow. Shafiq examines these with interest as Jory works away at the window bolt. 'Hopeless bow,' he notes. 'You can't get a decent performance from a folding one. Though I appreciate they're easier to smuggle into a hospital. You're going to get into trouble for this, you know.'

'I always seem to be in trouble these days,' Jory says, as his wire finally springs free from the bifurcated bolt. 'It's about time it was for something worthwhile.' He pushes open the window. 'How bad a bow is it, exactly?'

'Not so bad I can't hit a tree at twenty paces,' Shafiq says. 'At night. Although the extra weight's going to make things tricky.'

Packing away the file, Jory picks up the remote and switches on the TV. Quickly he hops channels until a football match appears, and then he turns the volume up until the room shakes with the crowd's cheers.

Shafiq snorts. 'They're hardly going to believe we're sitting down to watch the match.'

'No,' Jory agrees. 'They'll probably assume I'm beating you up.'

Shaf grimaces. 'Consider me reassured.'

They tie the cable firmly to the arrow, then Shaf stands, aims and lets it fly towards the tree. The drum hisses on its stand as the cable unravels, then falls slack.

'It's on the ground,' says Jory. He pulls it in quickly, hoping that nobody's noticed anything on the lower floors. They re-spool the cable and try again.

This time the arrow hits the tree-trunk, but bounces clear.

'Sorry,' says Shaf. 'I'm feeling a bit groggy. It must be the painkillers.'

Jory shrugs. 'Rule of three,' he suggests as they wind the cable in once more. Folklore being what it is, device-bearers get used to failing twice before succeeding at any really challenging task on which a great deal hangs.

Of course, human beings being what they are, they sometimes fail the third time too.

Somebody on the TV scores a goal, and the crowd and commentator become terrifically excited. Shafiq's third shot propels the arrow firmly into the beech, where it sticks with a thud, its impact thrumming up and down the taut cable.

'Told you,' Jory says. 'Are you OK to abseil?' he asks, watching in concern as Shafiq reels slightly from his exertions.

‘Of course I am,’ says Shafiq. ‘It’s just falling at a funny angle. I expect I’m better at that than I would be usually.’ His consonants are beginning to slur now. ‘Have you got transport?’

‘There’s a rented car in one of the alleys,’ says Jory, looping the end of the cable several times around the fixed leg of the bedstead, and tying it in a sturdy knot. ‘I can help you over the fence. The Circle has men in the hospital, but nobody out on the streets.’

Shafiq nods. ‘Best if I go first,’ he says. ‘Wouldn’t do to collapse up here while I was waiting.’

‘Are you really feeling that bad?’ Jory asks, seriously worried now.

‘I don’t think those were painkillers, frankly,’ Shafiq says wryly. ‘I think your Circle intend to keep me here. We need to get to your car before I pass out.’

‘But the Circle wouldn’t –’ Jory stops. *They wouldn’t sedate a prisoner?* It would hardly be an honourable course of action, but who knows what the Circle’s capable of any more? ‘Never mind,’ he says.

Shaf slings the bow over one shoulder and the bag of arrows over the other, then as an afterthought rolls up the *New Scientist* and pockets it. He grasps both ends of the sheet that Jory’s twisted into a pad. ‘I think I can still keep my grip,’ he says. ‘If not, someone else gets a chance to play at being Robin Hood.’ He climbs onto the window sill, then pauses for a moment. ‘Jory –’ he says.

‘Later,’ Jory replies, not knowing whether Shafiq wants to thank him or start another fight. ‘Let’s get away from here first.’ He starts to twist a second sheet.

Shaf nods and launches himself into the twilit sky.

A shout goes up outside, and the door of the ward bursts open.

* * *

From the car rental agency near King's Cross to the storage centre in Hackney was half-an-hour's drive. Jory's usually a careful driver, observing protocol and sticking to the speed limit. Ransacking Noake's storage bay – which contained mostly worn furniture and fussy bric-a-brac, rather suggesting an unwanted bequest from some elderly relative – took around the same amount of time.

The drive back, fretfully clutching what he had eventually found tucked into the back of an old chest of drawers, went much more quickly.

Once he was back in central London, Jory used the authority vested in him as a Knight of the Circle to browbeat and threaten the security guards at the British Museum into giving him out-of-hours access to the Nestine-Gull Collection. Word of this behaviour would unquestionably get back to the Seneschal, but Jory was fast running out of time. As a curator, working late on some research project, grudgingly led him down the behind-the-scenes staircases and corridors, he fingered the ancient piece of card in his pocket.

The Collection was just as he remembered it: a gallimaufry of blades, coins, shields, bones, clothes, lutes, flutes and brooches, all arranged in order and neatly labelled by a maniac whose systems of categorisation were all his own. The larger pieces – complete sets of armour, a wooden throne that could have been a bishop's, some intact animal skeletons – had been moved around a bit since he was last here with Malory, years ago now, but all the ones he remembered were present and accounted for. There was just one thing Jory needed to check before making his way to the hospital, if he could only…

…but then he saw the Grail.

The *cup*, he reminded himself as he sank to his knees: the wooden cup which Nestine-Gull mistakenly identified as the Grail. It was no more the vessel used by Christ at his Last Supper, Jory insisted as he bowed his head reverently before it, than the mug with 'A PRESENT FROM TINTAGEL' on it which he'd bought for Malory to have coffee in when she came round.

In his mind, the Grail sang of holiness and purity and love, of chivalry and nobility and not betraying your highest principles for the sake of some floozy.

...On the whole, Sir Gawain doesn't come out of the Grail quest terribly well. Though not a bad man by most standards, for the purposes of that particular legend he's accounted as a sinful knight. His personal baggage leads him into easily-avoided errors like accidentally murdering his fellow knights, and he's always in too much of a hurry to stop and be shriven by the holy men. The Grail demands insipid saints, like flawless Galahad or pious Percival or doggedly repentant Bors, so sinners like Gawain and Lancelot find themselves shut out from the Grail castle, and possibly from God's grace altogether.

Nevertheless, after the first shared vision of the Grail which was granted to all the company of the Round Table, it was Gawain who thought they should all go off and look for the damn thing. On the mortal level at least, the whole disastrous quest – which left Camelot depleted and exhausted, ripe for Mordred's plucking – was Gawain's idea.

Come to me, Jory, sang the Grail in Jory's mind. *Turn now to God. Repent your treachery, embrace Christ and his anointed High King, and the Round Table to which you long ago swore fealty, lest you too be denied my mercy.*

'It's not the Grail,' Jory breathed, trying his hardest to remember the fact. 'It's a Romano-British goblet, lathed from elm, dug up by a farmer and flogged to a gullible aristocrat for fourpence.'

Oh, Jory, sang the Grail. *As if that mattered. Even in the legends, the Grail isn't an* object.

In Jory's head, the voice of the Grail was female. In Jory's head, it sounded more than a little like Malory.

'You're not speaking,' he replied, aware that in doing so

he was undermining his position rather. 'You're not even the cup – you're just another voice in my head. You're my guilt given a voice, that's all.'

Of course I am, the Grail sang in his brain. *The quest for the Grail is the quest for holiness. It's your guilt which shuts you off from me.*

Tearing his eyes away from the holy vessel made them hurt; standing and turning his back felt as if it was doing actual violence to his muscles. He did it anyway.

Although there was one *knight who wanted no part of my quest*, the Grail whispered behind him. *One knight who stayed behind, to serve the High King... and to betray him.*

I won't insult your intelligence by explaining who that was.

Closing his mind to the honeyed importuning in his mind, Jory forced himself to cross to the item here which he was really interested in. It was definitely in a different position from where it had been before – almost as if someone had borrowed it for a while before returning it again. Not that anyone other than the Seneschal of the Circle would have been able to authorise such a loan.

Jory knelt again, but this time for the wholly practical purpose of examining the item's exhibit card. It was modern, produced in black and white on a desktop printer. The paper was crisp, the ink new and glossy.

Jory compared it with the card in his hand, crinkly and yellow, labelled in a cursive hand in faded brown ink. The one he'd found in Alfred Noake's lockup in Hackney.

'Son of a *bitch*,' said Jory. It wasn't something he'd ever said before, but it fitted his mood.

In his mind the Grail sighed, more in sorrow than in anger.

* * *

The guards grab Jory's wrists with merciless force and hold him at the window while Shafiq wobbles to the scrubby ground. Shaf goes into a crouch, alerted by the cry, but in the dark – and with his faculties fast diminishing – it's obvious that his pursuers are invisible to him.

Jory, though, can clearly see six men-at-arms closing in through the undergrowth towards Shafiq. It's obvious that they've been lying in wait. Somebody guessed that the two of them were going to try this.

Jory cries, 'Shaf! They're –' but gets no further before a man-at-arms punches him in the solar plexus, silencing him.

Behind him, Paul Parsons' voice says quietly, 'Actually, Taylor, I don't think we can have that.'

Jory watches in horror as Shafiq turns, stumbles and tries to run before his bad leg gives way beneath him. As the men close in, he sits up desperately and props himself against the tree-trunk, fumbling with the bow.

Paul pushes past and leans out of the window. 'Don't be an idiot, Rashid!' he shouts. 'Give yourself up and you won't be harmed!'

If he doesn't… well, Shafiq's armed, and the men-at-arms down there have no Knight with them for backup. In extremis, the men are entitled to defend themselves.

'He's been drugged!' Jory manages to gasp. 'This is an assassination!'

'Not if he shoots first,' says Paul grimly. He's wearing full armour, and his face is sombre. 'Let's hope he's not that stupid though, yeah?'

The men continue to close in a ring around Shafiq, who raises shaking arms to nock an arrow and bring the bow to bear. He shudders and releases it, embedding it firmly in one man's shoulder.

The trooper swears and falls back, clutching at the shaft. The man next to him raises his semi-automatic and lets it spit one shot into the night.

Shafiq jerks and slumps. Slowly, he topples sideways, leaving a dark streak on the bark behind him. The arrow he shot from his sickroom remains buried in the trunk above him, marking the place as he dies.

'You *fuckers*,' Jory cries. He wrenches free from his captors and turns to face Paul, only to be grabbed again from behind. In the doorway stands the woman – the honorary page, presumably – who was posing as a nurse. To give her due credit, she looks disgusted and upset.

'I'm sorry,' Paul says. 'But you know, you saw what happened. Morris will be out of action for weeks with that shoulder, probably.'

'You *executed* the Green Knight,' Jory insists. 'When the Seneschal hears about this –'

'He'll what? Do the same as last time?' Paul says more sharply. 'And who was the Knight who got off scot-free then, I wonder?'

'I want to see him,' Jory snarls. 'I want to talk to Charles Raymond, right now.'

Paul sighs, says, 'Actually, Taylor, that's the plan,' and leads the way out of the empty hospital room.

18. THE CROWN

'You're a good Knight, Taylor,' Sir Charles Raymond tells Jory. 'A good Knight with a noble device. You've been led astray, but that's a common hazard in our line of work.' Perhaps he's remembering his predecessor. 'It's not surprising, though I admit I'm disappointed.'

They're standing in his office, high in the keep of the Fastness. It's just the two of them: the men guarding Jory are waiting in the outer office with Paul. On their arrival here, the younger Knight showed every sign of wanting to accompany Jory into Sir Charles' presence, but the Seneschal dismissed him at his office door.

Floodlights illuminate the courtyard below, but Raymond's office is lit dimly by a reading-light, a desk lamp and a computer screen.

'Parsons is a good man, too,' Sir Charles adds after a moment. 'Not easy to believe, I suppose, given your history together… but still, he is.'

Jory glares stubbornly at Raymond, not trusting himself to speak.

'He's overzealous,' the Seneschal continues. 'Catching you red-handed helping Rashid to escape was his idea. I wouldn't have allowed it, especially with the risk he'd actually go free. I'd already ordered him sedated to reduce his chances of escape. Perhaps I ought to have told Parsons that. He certainly should have told me what he was up to. I'm afraid Rashid ended up caught in the middle.'

Jory scowls. It's almost as if the Seneschal's apologising to him.

'There'll be a penalty for Parsons, as for you,' Raymond says. 'But there's still a place for you here. A Round Table without either Sir Lancelot or Sir Gawain would be sadly diminished.'

Jory stares at his superior in bewilderment. How far does he have to go before the Circle stops offering to forgive him?

'The quarrel between you will have to be mended, of course,' the Seneschal adds, and it clicks.

Of course the Circle deplores any fallings-out between its Knights, but those which follow the faultlines of vendettas within the original Round Table are taken especially seriously.

For most of their lives, Gawain and Lancelot were friends, but it was Gawain who, with his brothers, finally caught Lancelot in flagrante with Queen Guinevere – and Lancelot who, in his desperate escape from his accusers, killed Gawain's brother Gareth. In the legends, the blood-feud between the two families was irrevocable – though there it's Lancelot, the King's best friend, who goes renegade, while Gawain remains loyal to his cousin.

In the current scenario there's no Guinevere, Shafiq stands in for Gareth, and it's Gawain, not Lancelot, who's looking like leaving. But still, there are enough parallels with that legendary sundering of the Round Table for Raymond to feel uneasy about the breach.

'I think we're rather beyond that now, sir,' Jory replies truculently.

'I can see you're upset, Taylor,' Sir Charles continues, 'but hear me out. You talked about brainwashing before, and you were half right. Evidently the le Fay device has access to some powerful techniques in that area. I'm sorry to say you've been under her influence for quite some time.'

'Malory was never Morgan le Fay,' Jory insists. 'Marianne Millar isn't either, obviously. But Malory's device is Nimue, the Lady of the Lake. She's Arthur's ally.'

'That's what she had us all believing.' Raymond nods. 'We were all taken in by her; there's no shame in it. But Morgan le Fay had her claws into young Miss Wendiman long before you met her. It was thoughtless of Dr Wendiman, dreadfully so, to expose her to the devices at such an early age. He paid the price for that, of course.'

'Do you have *any* evidence for these slurs, sir?' asks Jory.

The Seneschal sighs. 'It's understandable you'd be sceptical. After Miss Wendiman pulled that stunt at Benwick, we went through her laptop, the university servers and the records at her private ISP. She hid her tracks well, but you can never completely erase data. Our tech men are very thorough once they've got their teeth into a problem, and privacy's no issue once we've invoked our authority.'

Jory's ire rises further still at the idea of Circle men-at-arms rummaging through Malory's private belongings, sifting her data, dogging her footsteps across the internet. He keeps his silence, though.

'You said yourself,' Sir Charles continues, 'that in the story it's le Fay who's behind the whole Green Knight debacle, and we've uncovered ample evidence of *that.* She's been conspiring with multiple renegade devices for some years now. It turns out the Green Chapel's more than just the Green Knight's entourage. It's a subversive network set up by Miss Wendiman to undermine the Circle, based on populist folklore which has nothing to do with the true Matter of Britain. Astounding irresponsibility on her part.'

'None of this proves complicity with le Fay,' Jory stubbornly maintains.

'Perhaps.' Raymond sniffs, annoyed as ever at having to concede a point. 'Bit of a moot question at this stage, though.'

It's true, of course – given the scale of Malory's treachery, why would the Circle care whether its perpetrator was Morgan or Nimue? Jory can't help feeling invested in the question, however, especially given the connection between Morgan and Mordred.

'One other thing we're sure of,' Sir Charles continues. 'Miss Wendiman was responsible for bringing on her father's… health issues. The doctors are certain now that it's his device that's been affected, and through some form of invasive psychological manipulation. Merlin's nemesis could be Morgan or Nimue, mythically speaking. Either way, such a person would be an enemy of the Circle.'

Jory is shocked, more by such a cheap attempt to play on his emotions than by his faintest suspicion that what Sir Charles says might be true. 'I'm sorry sir, but I don't believe that for a moment.'

Raymond harrumphs. 'You still think *I* was somehow responsible? You're a fool, Taylor. An easily-led fool. Whatever you may think of me, I trust you'll take my word as a Knight that neither I nor anyone in my employ had anything to do with Wendiman's illness.'

Unwillingly – despite, in fact, a strenuous effort in the opposite direction – Jory discovers that he does believe him.

'Miss Wendiman only influenced you,' Raymond says. 'Her father, she did her utmost to destroy. Ghastly woman.' The Seneschal shudders.

Jory is silent. Raymond gazes at him levelly for a few moments, then continues.

'You don't think Rashid deserved to die, do you, even after he tried to kill you? Well, your so-called Green Knight was no Knight, take it from me. His device is that of a churl.

A traitor, a terrorist, an armed robber. That's the kind of man your Mr Rashid was – the kind Miss Wendiman would turn into a hero.'

'Robin Hood *was* a hero,' Jory snaps. 'He stood up for the innocent victims of a corrupt authority. That's why there are legends about him.'

'Legends?' Sir Charles is contemptuous. 'Songs. Pantomimes. Motion picture blockbusters. Fodder to keep the common people entertained. Harmless enough in its way, till subversives start turning it into revolutionary propaganda.'

'So which parts do you disagree with, Sir Charles?' Jory asks acidly. 'Feeding the poor? Challenging injustice? Holding the rich and powerful responsible for their behaviour?'

The Seneschal's patience, never the most abundant of resources, has reached its limit. 'King Arthur did all of those things!' he thunders. 'In his reign the poor *were* fed! They were kept safe from invasion and civil war into the bargain. He toppled unjust kings by the dozen, and replaced them with men he could trust. He brought stability, and honour, and the rule of law – all things which meant very little to your hooded friend. The High King's rule was paradise for the common people, until *anarchists* like you and Miss Wendiman brought him down!'

Morgan and Mordred as 'anarchists'? It's a new interpretation for Jory.

Something's familiar, though… a piece of literary history tugging at the threads of his memory. *It's* Paradise Lost, *he thinks. Milton the Roundhead, writing about Satan's revolt against God. Whether he's on God's side or Satan's depends on whether he thought all forms of kingship are wrong – or all except one.*

Is Arthur the one true King against whom all others fail to measure up? Or is authority – even his – an unacceptable imposition on the dignity of his people?

Aloud, he says, 'That was King Arthur, sir – and even then, Britain's fate was bound up in his. If the land and the king are one, then with the king gone – or sick, or corrupt – the land's helpless. One man isn't enough of a basis for a utopia. For all the Circle's striving, have we ever, even once over the past fifteen hundred years, managed to rebuild it in his absence?'

Sir Charles looks stricken. It's clear that this strikes home… but still, he murmurs, 'Even that may change one day, Taylor.'

Jody nods. It's as he thought. 'That's what the Saxon Shield research project was about, isn't it, sir? You wanted to find out whether such a powerful device could actually be revived.'

Sir Charles doesn't bother to deny it. He holds all the cards here, except one.

'What do you know, Taylor?' the Seneschal asks quietly.

Jory reaches into his jacket for the photocopy he took at the British Museum. Pulls it out and unfolds it, smoothing it on the Seneschal's desk.

It's an A4 sheet, most of it blank – but in the centre, outlined by its shadow against the copier's lid, is the exhibit label. In this monochrome copy, the faded ink looks pale grey rather than brown.

Horſe ſkeletone, Sir Lionel Nestine-Gull opines confidently. *Antique, attr. Saxone nobility. Orig. one of a paire. 'Ye Horſe of Hengeſt' ~ Trad.*

'I saw it at the SS headquarters,' he says. 'They'd decorated it. It looked like they were making offerings to it. The Hengist and Horsa devices were gods originally.' He's been going through the bookmarks on Noake's USB stick, but he wishes Malory was here to confirm his thinking. 'Divine horse-twins like Castor and Pollux in classical myth, or the Hindu Ashvins, or the Irish Emain Macha.

'Noake and Hill wanted to get back to the root of their devices,' he goes on, '– or rather, your experimenters did.

Hill and Noake just wanted *power*, and they thought being worshipped would give them that. You gave them a holy relic so they could turn their paramilitary network a cult.

'The devices exist because people believe in them,' he says. *Just like a country, or money, or God.* 'Boost that belief, and you make them more real.' *Worshipping the devices is a bad idea, for purely pragmatic reasons.* 'Connect the Hengist and Horsa devices with the ancient Aryan horse-twins, and maybe you can turn a couple of skinhead Nazis into demigods. And it was all just a trial run to you, a test-drive for bringing back the Head himself.'

'Not *just* a trial run,' Raymond says slowly. 'Though it was that, of course.'

'You mean you thought it might succeed?' says Jory. 'But surely that's suicidally stupid? What was your containment strategy, if the SS suddenly gained that kind of power?'

Sir Charles appears to be considering something. 'I need to know something, Taylor,' he says. 'Are you with us or against us? You're one of our most promising knights, bearing one of the most auspicious devices. You're no anarchist and you're not some sorceress's dupe. If you're loyal to the Circle – *truly* loyal, which includes being loyal to its Seneschal – then I can tell you. If not… well, you know what the position is then.'

Jory knows. For him, walking away is no longer an option, assuming it ever was. Unless Sir Charles decrees otherwise, he's under arrest. If he continues to defy the Circle, he'll be brought up on a charge of treachery – for which there's ample and compelling evidence – and imprisoned in the Benwick Institute. The Institute's psychiatrists will attempt to separate him from his device, or failing that to swap it for another, so that Sir Gawain is freed to serve the Circle through some other paragon.

'There's more to tell, then?' Jory's trying to think this through. There's an urgency, and a specificity, to what Raymond's not telling Jory which suggests that he's desperate to confide in the younger man.

'My God,' he realises suddenly. 'You *wanted* it to work. But why would you want those bovver boys turned into...' *They said it would put us in charge.* 'Ah,' he realises. 'Not demigods, but demagogues.'

Jory's mind's running ahead of him now. 'You weren't going to contain them,' he continues. 'You wanted them to gain power, if they could. Was that it? You wanted to set up a fascist dictatorship, here in Britain.'

Even in Milton, Jory realises, *God created Satan.*

'You thought a homegrown Hitler taking power here would be...' He can't bring himself to complete the sentence.

Sir Charles tightens his lips, then lets out a weary sigh. 'The time of Britain's greatest need,' he confirms. 'What greater threat to the nation could there be?'

'But sir,' says Jory. There are almost too many objections here for him to list them. 'If that plan worked – if the Pendragon came back and found that you, the Circle's Seneschal, had put that dictator in place – he'd execute you.'

Raymond looks grave. 'We all have sacrifices to make, Taylor.'

Jory stares at the old man. So sad, he looks. The weight of the Circle – bearing as it does the weight of Britain – pushing down on his head. So inadequate to the task, so desperate for help, so proud he'd never dare admit it. A scared old man, longing for a reassuring figure to come along and tell him it's all right, he's done very well, now he can hand the whole thing over to the proper authorities.

And further in perhaps, far older still and weary beyond measure, a sad, tired, loyal brother who desperately misses the king he once loved.

Gently, Jory says, 'Camelot's gone, sir. It's in the past. Sherwood's a different kind of myth. It's about striving for a better future.'

It's as if the Fastness's heavy iron doors have closed across Raymond's face. He says, 'She really has brainwashed you, lad. You're telling me that you refuse to reconcile with Sir Kay and Sir Lancelot, and prefer instead to throw your lot in with Morgan le Fay?'

Jory pauses before answering, just for clarity's sake.

If he says *yes*, he'll die in prison – alone, unallied and forgotten. Admittedly Malory will have the evidence – Nestine-Gull's original exhibit label, now on its way to a Green Chapel dead-letter drop – but there's little she can achieve with it. Anyone in authority who knows enough to understand what Raymond's been attempting is likely to be on his side already.

If Jory says *no* – if he submits to Raymond, makes his peace with Paul, and goes back to the Circle – he can carry on striving for change. He'll be in a position of power and responsibility, an insider working to alter the status quo rather than an outsider railing against it. He can work to discourage insane plans like this one of the Seneschal's, or failing that to sabotage them. He can ensure, or do his best to ensure, that the Circle never aids an abomination like the Saxon Shield again.

The Circle is corrupt, he sees that, but most of the people in it, Sir Charles included, are honourable at heart. The Round Table can still be saved. Arthur's legacy can be redeemed.

…And all while they'll try to use him against Malory.

'Come *on*, Taylor,' Raymond snaps at last. 'Surely you're not going to give that loathsome woman her own way?'

And Jory can't help but smile.

* * *

The secure van is stark, a plastic-covered metal bench running the length of each side. Jory sits handcuffed between two men-at-arms, facing the stern but visibly uncomfortable figure of Stephen Mukherjee, as it rumbles and sways along the motorway towards Benwick the next morning. Around them, unseen from within the windowless metal box, the engines of cars and lorries growl and roar, advancing and receding.

Up front, Paul Parsons accompanies the driver, and two more Knights are following behind on motorcycles (horses being a little on the slow side for motorway escort duty). The Circle is taking no chances with *this* prisoner. Already rumours are flying that the Mordred device is active once again, and that this time round – its deceitfulness knowing no bounds – it has been disguised as Sir Gawain all along.

'Don't feel bad about this, Stephen,' Jory said around half an hour ago. 'I know you're only doing your duty.'

Twenty minutes ago, he said, 'They killed Shafiq Rashid, you know. Drugged him, then gunned him down in the hospital grounds. How honourable would you say that was, on a scale of one to ten?'

Ten minutes ago he said, 'However hard you try, Stephen, however hard you work to eclipse who you really are, they'll never completely accept you. They'll never believe you're one of them, not in the way they thought I was. And the saddest thing is, you agree with them.'

At no point has Stephen said anything to Jory. Nor have the men-at-arms, except for 'Get in the van.'

Jory presumes his brother Knight feels personally betrayed. It's not unreasonable: Jory has indeed betrayed him. In combat, a man's life can depend utterly on his fellow soldiers' loyalty. Jory's has been compromised for a long time now. Stephen himself is sufficiently gung-ho that he won't be too worried at his life being endangered, but Jory's certain the betrayal stings.

Each time he's spoken in the past half hour, he's been biting back an apology. To abandon a cause is one thing, but to desert one's friends…

Still, Jory has friends on both sides. He can't allow that consideration to sway him.

Jory wonders whether he'll ever see Malory again, or any of the others from the Green Chapel, or whether Stephen is the last human being he'll set eyes on for whom he has the slightest fondness. Escape from the Benwick Institute, without inside assistance and in the aftermath of Scar's audacious breakout, will be next to impossible, recapture nigh inevitable. If he's to spend the rest of his life in a secure hospital, it's best to hope that memories of Malory are all that's left to him.

He wonders whether she's heard about Shafiq. The sound of a sudden concussion comes from behind the van, followed by a grinding sound which diminishes rapidly.

Stephen looks up, alert. 'What was that, sir?' one of the men-at-arms asks.

A squeal of brakes follows, then another report – too loud to be a car backfire, or even a gunshot – and an accompanying scream, again receding speedily.

'The escort,' Stephen says, just as the driver apparently comes to the same conclusion. The van's engine noises rise in pitch, and acceleration pushes Jory up against the man to his left.

The felled Knights can take care of themselves. The quest here is to get the prisoner into secure custody.

Beyond the man to Jory's right, where the van's cab is, comes an alarming clash of breaking glass, followed by a much louder percussive thud. Their metal box swings wildly to the side, veers precariously for a moment and then starts juddering violently, slowing down slightly from its headlong hurtle. It topples rapidly, throwing Jory and his captors into a pile as it upends itself. Jory is pinned beneath a weighty human form as the metal under his face screeches with the van's momentum, then all is still.

A smell of brake fluid and burning rubber fills the air.

The man on top of him is limp and heavy, bleeding profusely from a cut in his temple. With difficulty and much undignified wiggling, Jory hefts him aside. He's still handcuffed between him and the other man, now sitting up groggily.

Stephen is already standing, sword drawn, on the van's former ceiling, facing the upside-down rear doors. He sways slightly but his face is resolute.

The engine noises from outside have receded now – their uncontrolled slew must have taken them onto the hard shoulder and off the motorway, rather than, less desirably, into the oncoming traffic. Some incoherent shouting can be heard.

'Do we just wait for them to come for us, sir?' the man-at-arms asks Stephen.

'The door's locked,' Stephen points out. 'Still, you do have a point.'

He brings his blade down once on the door-handle, cleaving the mechanism. A few blows with his hilt remove it altogether. The man-at-arms uncuffs himself from Jory – still weighed down by his bulky colleague's body – and goes to stand with Stephen.

'Count of three,' the Knight says. They count, then kick the doors open.

Stephen immediately steps back with a grunt as an arrow impacts his chest. It lodges harmlessly in his armour. He tuts and reaches up to remove it just as it explodes.

The flash blinds Jory for a moment, and the noise echoes agonisingly around the van's metallic interior. When he blinks away the afterglow, he sees Stephen lying before him, his left hand mangled, his armour ripped around his badly burned chest.

Choking on smoke, Jory checks Stephen's pulse. It's weak but regular. He grabs his fallen comrade's sword and starts hacking at the chain of his handcuffs.

Through the smoke, Jory sees the concussed guard who was standing with Stephen suddenly disappear from view. A hand reaches in past the smoke and grasps Stephen's leg. It pulls him away and tosses him out of the van.

A giant shadow leans in through the doors, grabs the man-at-arms who Jory's shackled to, and pulls. Jory has no choice but to follow, slithering on his belly across the van's bloody floor.

Outside, a huge, green-hooded man pulls him roughly to his feet, grasps his wrist and that of his unfortunate guard, and presents the length of chain to someone whose hoodie is incongruously topped by a welding-mask. Idly toting a blowtorch, the figure slices through the chain, and Jack Bennett tosses the unconscious man aside.

The cutter pushes her mask up. 'You free now,' Zara says. She adds, 'You welcome.'

They're standing on the grass verge by the motorway, separated by a bank from a long row of enormous slag heaps. The van lies on the charred grass, upended and smoking slightly from its burnt-out cab. Paul Parsons lies slumped against it, clutching his bloody stump of arm.

Jory supposes that one of the explosive arrows lodged in his armour's elbow. Paul's visor is down, for which Jory's grateful. His blackened shield lies next to him on the grass.

The traffic crawls by sluggishly, gawping at the carnage.

Around them, warily watching the unconscious men and holding back the good Samaritans who've parked on the hard shoulder, are a dozen green-cowled figures. Another, and a woman in a dark-red hoodie, are standing off to one side, holding between them a wan-looking policeman. Jory recognises the unfortunate PC Barry Jenkins.

'We couldn't wait,' I tell Jory from inside my own hood, narrator to the last. 'With you gone, the Circle and Kinsey might have sorted something out between them. The others had to come and get us out of there.'

Wordlessly, Rev hands Jory a hip flask, and he drinks from it gratefully.

'Scar's here,' Jory says, his voice scratchy from smoke. 'Does that mean –'

Our own transport draws up then, a shiny new police minibus commandeered by Squig while he and the others were rescuing us from Kinsey's premises. 'Time enough for questions later,' I say. 'We need to get going. Tell you what though, why don't you ride up front with the driver?'

We pile into the back, bundling poor Barry with us, and leaving Jory, still dazed and shellshocked, to clamber painfully up into the passenger's seat.

Paul Parsons shouts something after him, or tries to. We can't hear anything clearly over the traffic noise.

The hooded driver leans over and gives Jory a quick kiss on the cheek. 'Put on your seatbelt, sweetheart,' Merry tells him. 'It would be irritating if we lost you now.'

With relief, Jory does exactly as she says.

* * *

There's so much still to come. As we near the suburban street where we'll be abandoning the cop-carrier, we honestly – even Merry – have no idea.

Today we declared war on the Circle. True, they didn't like us much before, but this is the first time for centuries we've been in direct and open conflict. In all the years we've both existed – and the Chapel is far older than you might think – it's rarely come to this, and when it has, well…

King Arthur versus Robin Hood. Camelot versus Sherwood. The Matter and the Anti-Matter of Britain. There should be a myth.

All that's to come, though. For the moment, the priority's to ditch our ride – it's far too conspicuous. It's not only the Circle who's after us. Inspector Kinsey's wrath will be mighty and very likely lethal to somebody. Possibly her, admittedly.

We'll dump the minibus, along with PC Jenkins, and disperse. It won't take them long to find it. We'll make our way in ones and twos, hitchhiking mostly, to the new encampment in Charnwood Forest.

Merry and Jory will be sticking together, that's pretty obvious. So will Scar and Zara, I feel sure.

I expect I'll go alone. Some of us have to.

Once we're there, we'll go back to our tents. We'll change our clothes, wash off the stink of those police cells, kick off our boots, relax. Tonight there'll be a party…

…No, make that a wake.

We've got a lot to celebrate, of course. Our freedom. Happy reunions. A new recruit. It's not enough to eclipse our friend's death.

There'll be booze, obviously. We'll toast Shaf – not himself a drinker, but he wouldn't mind – get pissed and probably stoned, and sing along with various power ballads. We'll eat too much and dance like demons, talk rubbish like you can only with friends, and generally make merry.

I'll probably be called upon to tell some stories. I'll have to ask Jory how Shaf died. I'm sure if I look hard enough I can find some parallels with the death of Robin Hood.

We'll go to bed – not all of us accompanied – and sleep it off. Tomorrow our heads will feel the full weight of a world without Shafiq Rashid.

And then… the work goes on. Nothing's ever forgotten, as they say, but the Green Chapel is far more than just one man.

There are wrongs to right, injustices to avenge. There are wicked barons to vex – and wicked Knights as well. Some people are in dire need of being relieved of their wealth, while others require unconventional financial support. There's a tyrant prince to unseat, a kingdom to topple, a utopia to restore.

You think I'm exaggerating?

Don't forget, I was *there*.

To be continued in *The Locksley Exploit*

ACKNOWLEDGEMENTS

Any book takes the form it does because of the uncountable numbers of influences, huge or subtle, which have shaped its author's life up to the point of writing it. Attempting to trace all of these might be an interesting exercise, but it would be a life's work in itself.

It will be obvious, though, that this book arose largely from my childhood reading of the Arthurian legends and of the tales of Robin Hood. Arthur I remember most vividly from Rosemary Sutcliff's excellent trilogy *The Sword and the Circle*, *The Light beyond the Forest* and *The Road to Camlann*, whereas Robin I first encountered in Geoffrey Trease's *Bows against the Barons*, and so have always seen him as a revolutionary as much as an outlaw. Other influences in literary and other media would be too numerous to list (though I name many of them in the book), but I should mention – indeed recommend – three in particular: Simon Armitage's wonderful modern translation of *Sir Gawain and the Green Knight*; Richard Carpenter's seminal TV series *Robin of Sherwood*; and Chumbawamba's album *English Rebel Songs 1381-1984*, which introduced me to the traditional ballad 'The World Turned Upside-Down', a version of which Malory sings in Chapter 10.

Less distantly, the kernel of the Devices trilogy emerged from a conversation with my wife about names for our then-prospective son, during which I realised that two of my favourites could be seen as embodying entirely opposite ideals. Most of the thanks for bringing this idea to its fruition belong to my wife – partly for her wise comments on the manuscript, but mostly for frequently taking said son (now four) out of the house for days at a time so I could write it.

Other helpful notes on the book came from Helen Angove, Simon Bucher-Jones, Rachel Churcher, Finn Clark, Stuart Douglas, Lance Parkin and Dale Smith. I'm also profoundly indebted to Simon Morden, Paul Magrs and George Mann for their advice, support and practical help, and to Emma Barnes at Snowbooks for accepting *The Pendragon Protocol* and shepherding it through to publication.